ERIC JEROME DICKEY

Waking

with Enemies

D0552888

TURNAROUND

First published in Great Britain 2008 by
TURNAROUND
Unit 3, Olympia Trading Estate, Coburg Road, London N22 6TZ

www.turnaround-uk.com

First published in the US by Dutton, a member of Penguin Group (USA) Inc.

PUBLISHER'S NOTE
This is a work of fiction. Names, characters, places and incidents either are the
products of the author's imagination or are used fictitiously, and any
resemblance to actual persons, living or dead, events or locales is entirely
coincidental.

While the author has made every effort to provide accurate telephone numbers
and Internet addresses at the time of publication, neither the publisher nor the
author assumes any responsibility for errors, or for changes that occur after
publication. Further, the publisher does not have any control over and does not
assume any responsibility for author or third-party Web sites or their content.

A CIP catalogue record for this book is available from the British Library.

ISBN 13: 9781873262184

Manufactured in the U.K. by L.P.P.S.Ltd, Wellingborough Northants NN8 2PJ

for Dominique

Waking with Enemies

they made me a killer

I killed a man when I was seven years old.

Killed a man who was trying to murder my mother.

He was choking her to death.

And I shot that man with his own gun.

Without hesitation I shot him in the head with a .22.

My mother was a whore. That man was one of her customers.

We were in North Carolina then.

We left his body on the floor of our apartment and fled to the Greyhound bus station.

We left Charlotte and traveled north. Ran like we were wanted by the FBI.

I remember that day like it was this morning. I remember the smells.

We sat in the back of the bus with the rest of the poor, the scent of old people, poverty, and greasy fried chicken in the air. Everyone was eating. Everyone but us. My mother looked at me, heard my stomach growling, then humbled herself, went and asked some old people if she could have some chicken. For me. She asked them to please give her some for me.

Those old people gave her half a bucket of homemade chicken.

Biscuits. Corn on the cob. I ate that cold and greasy food like I had never had a decent meal before in my life.

Day turned into night turned into day.

We rode buses north and didn't stop running until we made it to the bilingual and bicultural land of the festivals. Jazz. Comedy. Reggae. We ran until we got to Canada.

Got off the bus in Montreal.

Montreal was a pothole-filled city that had four seasons: winter, still-winter, construction season, and almost-winter. We'd fled Charlotte and stopped running on an island that some said was shaped like a bikini, but to me it was shaped like the bottom part of a woman, from her waist to knees. Montreal was shaped like a woman on her back with her legs wide-open.

We had stopped running near the crack of that Frenchwoman's ass.

The crack of that Canadian ass was right off Autoroute 720.

We had missed still-winter and landed there during the construction season, hid out in a province that enforced Bill 101 to ensure signs were in French, and if someone dared to post a sign using both French and English, the French part had to be *twice* the size of the English.

I was scared.

Not because I had killed a man.

I'd never been away from Charlotte.

I was scared because we were in place I'd never seen before. A place I'd never heard of.

And the money was running low. We'd eaten the last of our fried chicken yesterday.

We were homeless. And hungry. Had given up everything. Because I had killed that man. Because I had killed the evil man who was trying to choke my mother to death.

Now we were strangers in a foreign country, walking the streets with the damned.

Montreal was bizarre to me. The music. The language. The people.

Not to my mother.

People spoke French to her and she talked back to them in

French. Sometimes she spoke English while they spoke French, or she spoke French while they spoke English.

But when she spoke French, her mannerisms and accent became the same as theirs.

Her accent had never fit in the South. People always said she had never sounded like the natives of Charlotte. Some made fun of her exotic tongue. She was my mother. To me she had always sounded smarter, more refined, like she was a queen who had traveled the world.

While we ate stale bread, cold meat, and wilted vegetables, we overheard the homeless people that slept in the parks and doorways on Sainte-Catherine East laughing about those *important* Bill 101 issues; issues that infuriated the rich and powerful. Rich people lived at the other end, Sainte-Catherine West, where the shops were nice and clean, and the sex shops looked more respectable. Compared to the east side, Sainte-Catherine West was heaven.

We were homeless and living in a piss-smelling hell for a few days. I was terrified, afraid of the new language, afraid to talk to people, so that left me friendless too. Despite living in the parks and resting on McGill's lawn, despite all the peep shows and sex shops that lined the area, I pretended we were camping. Camping with that .22 tucked in my belongings.

I asked, "Why did we come here?"

"I grew up here."

"Are we French? We're from Canada? So we're French?"

She pulled her lips in, lowered her voice. "My mother came here from a small town right outside of Paris when she was a child. She was from Yerres, France. Left there, went to Paris for a while, worked, saved her money, came here alone. Will tell you all about her one day."

"So we are French."

"My father died . . . and Mother . . . her new husband . . . I had to leave. She took his word over mine. I was young. And I had to leave. Had to get out in the world and make it on my own."

"He was mean to you?"

"He did things he should not have done. Same for another family member."

"What did they do?"

"Not now. One day. We'll talk about those horrible things one day. I told Margaret about all the bad things that happened to me. She was the only one I ever told. And I will tell you one day."

"Who is Margaret?"

"My best friend. My best friend in the whole wide world."

"Where is she now?"

"Heaven."

She wiped her eyes, created a smile. "You're starting to smell. Need to get you into a toilet and wash you down. Maybe we can sneak you into one in one of the malls."

"When are we going to get a house?"

"I've always wanted a house. Mama doesn't have the money. We'll get an apartment."

"When?"

"Working on a place to stay now. But I want to make sure that no one is looking for us before I get us a place. And I have to find a way to get a place to live without using my name."

My words put stress lines in her face. Saw the fear and pressure she was masking even when she smiled. What she had told me, I didn't understand all of that, but I nodded.

A man came over to her. He was monstrously large, looked like he weighed tons.

"*Suces-moi?*"

"*Oui.* For fifty."

She tucked the .22 inside my jacket, told me to wait where I was.

Nervous, I stood up. A stranger in a strange land. A child in an adult's world.

She snapped at me, said, "Don't be afraid. Be a man. Don't be afraid."

She kissed my face and smiled at me.

I sat back down. My hands shaking.

She left with that huge man. A man the size of a basking shark.

I hated the way I felt. The sensation of being powerless. The sensation of being alone.

Seemed like she was gone two years, but she came back thirty minutes later.

I ran to her.

She handed me an ice cream cone. Vanilla. Hers was praline pecan.

I asked, "What does *suces-moi* mean?"

Her shoulders weakened. She frowned and walked away.

She said, "That is not the French you need to learn."

"What French do I need to learn?"

"I will teach you. The things you just said, never repeat them. *Never.*"

We gathered our things.

I followed her, vanilla ice cream dripping down over my fingers.

We passed other people living in the streets. One man had a family of dogs with him, him and his cardboard and his mutts living in a small parklike area. We walked until we passed by a metro station, then came up on a larger park. We squatted there with the other squatters.

She said, "I hate having to do this, having to hide with the bums. But I love you and I don't want them to find out what happened. They'd ask a lot of questions. And they'd take you away from me. You are all I have. All I love. My best friend is dead. She's been dead for a long time. You are all I have. You are all I love. Would you want them to take you away from me?"

I shook my head. Part of me wanted to shed tears. But men didn't cry.

She said, "I'll find us a decent place, a room with four walls and a bathtub."

She had to have enough cash. Credit cards left an electronic trail. It wasn't the cash that slowed her down. She needed fake ID. She had to start all over with a new identity.

Another man came up. "*Suces-moi?*"

"*Oui.* For fifty."

"Forty. I'm a college student."

"Fifty."

He turned to walk away.

"Wait. College boy."

"Forty."

"*Oui.* This time. Forty for the handsome college boy."

She left with him, licking her praline pecan.

Gun hidden, our possessions at my feet, I sat down and finished my ice cream cone.

Two weeks later she found us a room.

That hostel was on the edges of downtown at Sherbrooke and Jeanne-Mance. We were about three blocks from Sainte-Catherine, on the line that divided the moneyed areas from the red-light district. We lived on the border of her dreams and her reality.

It was nice at first. It was normal.

As normal as life could be for people like us.

During the day, when the weather was nice, we walked René-Lévesque and took the side streets toward the cobblestone roads in Old Montreal, went by the waters. On weekends my mother took me to see the basilica, or we went to the observation area in Parc du Mont-Royal, watched the Rollerbladers. We blended with the crowd and watched all the street performers, one dressed like a golden Elvis, others doing henna, took all of that in while I ate ice cream and she sipped on coffee she'd bought at Second Cup.

That was August. Temperature about twenty-five Celsius. Some days we just sat on a stoop watching people get on and off the bus. I had comic books that she bought from Librairie Astro. Spider-Man. Punisher. Batman. She had a stack of paperback books that she bought from the same bookstore. Romance books. She always read romance books. She always had a cheap cigarette case in hand, smoking du Mauriers down to the filter, then flipping those filters out on the pavement. We'd been there a few weeks. Long enough to get comfortable.

As she read her book, she puffed her cigarette and said, *"Dimanche. Lundi. Mardi."*

I read my comic and repeated, *"Dimanche. Lundi. Mardi."*

"Mercredi. Jeudi. Vendredi. Samedi."

I repeated, *"Mercredi. Jeudi. Vendredi. Samedi."*

"Those are the days of the week. We'll work on the months tomorrow."

"How do you know all of these languages?"

"Been on the move most of my life. Never really had a home, I guess."

She inhaled, wiped tears from her eyes, then created a broad smile.

"We have to find you a new name."

"Jean-Claude. I like Jean-Claude."

"I like Jean-Claude too. Who should I be?"

"Catherine. Like the street we were on."

"Okay, Jean-Claude. My name is Catherine."

She smiled, leaned over, and kissed me on my lips.

An African man stopped in front of the stoop.

"Tu suces sans capote?"

"If you have a place, it can be arranged."

"How much?"

"Pour cinquantes piasses."

She left with that man, went across the street, vanished inside a worn hotel.

I sat there repeating, *"Dimanche. Lundi. Mardi. Mercredi. Jeudi. Vendredi. Samedi."*

We bounced from our hostel to renting a small room at Hotel Du Fort.

Not long after that, the money was better and we slowed down, moved into L'Appartement, a hotel-apartment in the same area of Montreal, at the crack of that Frenchwoman's ass, still walking distance to Sainte-Catherine East. She called that strip her job.

Never said what she did down there, only that every evening she had to go to work.

She'd hit the east side of Sainte-Catherine, compete with the working gay men and Frenchwomen, wearing out her high heels and chain-smoking, being one of the last to leave the *rue* before she came back to our cheap hotel room and woke me up, that weary smile on her face, dead on her feet and smelling like colognes if it had been a good night, sometimes strange perfumes if it had been a desperate night, frowning and smelling like no one but herself and her own sweat if it had been a wasted night, either way grinning and shaking me to wake me up.

"Rise and shine, Jean-Claude. Mommy will make you breakfast."

As I sat on the floor eating a hot breakfast, television on, she drank coffee and smoked.

I asked, "Why do the people up here make that funny sound all the time?"

"What funny sound?"

"*Eh*. They always say *eh*."

"You have to say it at the end of a sentence to make it work. You use it to ask a question or to affirm a position. Like, it's freaking cold outside, *eh*? You don't care, *eh*?"

"*Eh*. Bee. Cee. Dee."

She laughed. "On Saturday, want to go to the Parisien and see a movie?"

"Can we go to the underground city and ride the metro too?"

"*Eh*."

"Bee. Cee. Dee."

She laughed. "We can ride the metro from one end to the other if you like."

Days later she bought me a heavy coat. That meant we'd be there for the winter.

That coat meant stability.

We would settle into that Canadian life. I became Jean-Claude. I would go to Westmount Park Elementary. I'd get to spend more weekends up at the park learning to skate.

Jean-Claude. I'd stand in the mirror and practice my name. *Jean-Claude*.

I was going to become French-Canadian.

The man called Midnight was gone out of our lives and we were no longer on the run.

Then came the darkness.

My mother came home one night, mouth bloodied, screaming my name.

I jumped to my feet and ran to her when she came in the door.

Another man had beat her up.

I asked where this evil man was.

He was down at Avenue du Président-Kennedy and City Councillors. He'd beat her, left the hotel, and gone to Biddle's, a small jazz club sandwiched between two huge businesses, Croix Bleue and Roche-Bobois. She knew where he was because she had followed him there.

I tucked the .22 inside the right pocket of my brand-new winter coat.

I followed her out into the streets.

We hid out on Président-Kennedy, waited across the street from Biddle's.

The big man crossed the street, his inebriated stagger taking him west, toward the section of Sainte-Catherine that had the nicest strip clubs. Gun in hand, I walked behind him. Went after the evil man who had wounded my mother.

He passed Café Suprême, then paused when he saw my mother at the next corner.

He yelled, *"Putain de merde. Salope. Plote. Sale pute."*

She yelled back, "Give me my money."

"You and your tricks. Get away before I have you arrested."

"You came. You owe me for my work. And for what you did to my face."

"Your nasty pussy bloodied my loins. Consider us even."

"Last time. Pay me. Or else."

"Or else?" He laughed. "Out of my way, cunt. Out of my way or I will beat you again."

She stood there, frowning. "Just give me what you owe me. That's all. Don't rob me."

"I'll give you what you deserve. And you deserve a good beating."

He walked toward her, his fists doubled.

I caught up with him and, as I passed him, raised my gun and squeezed the trigger. The soft pop of a .22, then the bullet entered his head and rattled around his skull. He crumpled where he stood. My mother ran to him, fished his wallet of his pocket, took all of the money out, wiped the wallet down, then walked away, hurried up Union, and I followed her back home, both of us moving with speed and silence. We said nothing about what we'd just done.

She took to the edge of the worn bed, sat there pulling her hair, rocking and crying.

The cash from the dead man's wallet was spread on the tattered bedspread.

I was in the bathroom, losing a battle with nausea.

She came and stood over me, sweating, breathing hard, her face swollen.

She said, "It's okay."

Mama got in the bed, clothes on. I did the same. Neither of us slept.

The morning news talked about a man named Ian Lafreniere being gunned down.

He was from Toronto.

My mother said, "Toronto. No love lost."

Then the news said he was a police officer. Married. With three children.

Not a normal john. Not someone who would have been low priority.

My mother shivered, talked to herself, and packed as fast as she could.

I knew the routine. I rushed, packed what I wanted to take, which never was much.

Hours later we were on the run.

She said, "Give me the gun. Give it to me before we end up incarcerated at Bordeaux."

She took all the bullets out, wiped the gun down, pulled filthy trash back, pushed that gun into the bottom of the garbage can, covered it up, then put the bullets in a different garbage can.

I asked, "Where are we going?"

"We'll have to sneak through Toronto, slip into New York, find our way south from there."

That nausea rose again, made me sweat, but didn't take over.

I said, "My daddy."

"What about your daddy?"

"Tell me about my daddy again."

"Not now."

"Please?"

She took a deep breath, rocked and closed her eyes. "Your daddy . . . met him in Montego Bay . . . he was an army man. Jumped out of planes. Took sniper training, made Delta Force."

"Where is he now?"

"He's . . . he's in South America. He's down there fighting for his country."

"Can we go there?"

"No. We can't go there."

"You said my daddy was strong."

"He was strong, used to fight bulls bare-handed, beat them every time."

I wanted to be like my daddy, the mercenary who fought bulls with his bare hands.

She said, "It's time I explained to you what I do. You're old enough to know."

"I know."

"How do you know?"

"People say things."

"What do I do?"

"*Pute.*"

She struck me hard enough to split my lip. Then she struck me over and over.

Pute meant "whore."

Then she cried and reached for me. I pulled away from her. Over and over she apologized. But that first wicked blow changed everything.

On that road to perdition, I tasted my own blood.

From the hand of a woman I had killed for.

What was between us unraveled.

I had protected her. I had killed for her. And she had attacked me in return.

Love turned upside down and hate took root.

That hatred never left.

Would never leave.

Thousands of sunrises and sunsets had gone by since that last day in Montreal.

She had trained me to be a killer and in the end she had stolen from me. She had abused me, did things to me a mother should never do to her son.

The pain remained, as forever as the Appalachians.

And that hate was still there, spreading across those mountains like kudzu.

Hate had blackened the part of my heart that once burned with unconditional love for her.

Jean-Claude no longer existed.

I'd had many names since being Jean-Claude.

Now my name was Gideon.

I was a long way from Montreal.

I was on the other side of the Atlantic holed up in a hotel in central London.

And I was afraid. I'd killed a man in Tampa. Had killed a man and most of his associates. Had increased my income by over six figures honoring that contract.

And I knew that brutal death would not go unpunished.

It wasn't confirmed, but I had been followed.

That told me that there might be a contract out on me.

Revenge knew no bounds.

The hunter had now become the hunted.

I had become one of them.

The people I went to see, when I was the last face they saw.

So I was afraid. There was nothing wrong with fear.

So long as that fear was controlled.

But it was undeniable, the way it was bubbling beneath the surface.

I was on edge because I had been stalked for the last day.

Afraid because death was at my hotel room, lurking on the other side of my door.

enemies

One

trouble after midnight

Death kept moving back and forth outside my door.

But Death never showed its face.

On the other side of my pulled curtains, the skies were gray, winds were blowing hard enough to sway trees, and the rain was falling, a rain that, in this weather, felt like ice water.

London's weather was as devastating as my mood.

I was in Bloomsbury, that abhorrence from my past crimes and sins fueling me as I stood by the door, listening for sounds in the hallway, gun in my hand, loaded, angst on high.

I'd done a job in Tampa. Had killed more than a few men in the name of profit.

A gruesome hit that would stay with me the rest of my days.

That job had been a few days ago, and now that hit had turned upside down. A rapper named Sledge had paid me a king's fortune to kill his rival, another rapper known as the Big Bad Wolf. I had slaughtered Big Bad and his crew, barely made it away from that job with my life, and since then Sledge had been assassinated. And I had been followed to London by a bald man who sported a broken nose, a man who had been sent to kill me as an act of vengeance.

I eased closer to the door and listened.

So much violence and death had happened since I landed in the UK.

My mind was racing as I tried to remember it all; gun in hand, I was trying to put the pieces together. Yesterday afternoon I'd been stalked from Covent Garden to Soho, then around midnight I had realized I was being trailed as I left Soho, had flipped the script on my stalker and chased him, realized he was the same the man I'd seen on my flight from America to the UK, his broken nose making him stand out, and I had confronted him, chased him through Kensington Gardens only to have him vanish at Lancaster Gate.

Only a few hours had passed since that footrace.

And now someone was lurking outside my hotel room.

Freezing rain was falling as dark clouds strangled and smothered the sunrise.

Gun in hand, I listened to see if the messenger was outside moving around.

Behind me, in my room, I heard terrified breathing.

I looked back, saw two huge suitcases on the floor.

I'd forgotten she was here.

A naked woman was terrified, inside my hotel room, hiding in the bathroom.

Her name was Lola Mack.

She was an actress-slash-masseuse I had met on the same flight to Gatwick.

Hers was a long story, one that started with happiness in the U.S. and ended up here with her being in excruciating pain, the kind of pain that came from her flying across the Atlantic only to get rejected by the man she was in love with, that rejection coming a few hours ago.

About five hours ago she had ended up in my room, about three hours ago she had ended up in my bed. Now she was hiding in the bathroom as I tried to deal with this situation.

Bad timing. Bad fucking timing.

Now her life might be on the line.

There was another sound.

Once again trouble was shifting around outside my door.

Every time I did a job, I made enemies. I had done well so I had many enemies.

My mental Rolodex was spinning, so many enemies in my mind.

Too many to remember.

That terrified breathing echoed in the bathroom.

Even now I wondered if the woman hiding in the bathroom was part of a conspiracy.

That beautiful woman might've been sent to keep me here.

She had been waiting for me.

Right here.

In the lobby.

And she had bedded me.

Without hesitation.

She claimed she was an actress. Grifters were actors. Contract killers were actors.

I'd spent years hiding my feelings from the rest of the world. So I was an actor too.

I played it again in my mind.

A man had followed me first from America, then trailed me in Covent Garden, did the same in Soho, that confrontation coming to an abrupt end at Lancaster Gate.

Right after that Lola was waiting for me in the lobby.

She had found my hotel.

Paranoia whispered in my ear and told me she was part of the setup.

I was about to go to the bathroom, put the gun in her face, demand answers.

I'd kill Lola Mack if I had to. I'd kill her like she had killed me in my nightmares.

As soon as I made a step, there was a loud sound outside my door.

I jumped, aimed the gun at the door.

I eased back to the peephole.

Then Lola flushed the goddamn toilet. Something crashed to the bathroom floor.

I was heading toward Lola when the handle on the hotel door shook.

They were out there testing the door.

I tensed, expected the door to get kicked open right after that.

Gun aimed, I crept back toward the door.

I spied out again.

My stalker moved right in front of my door.

A bold and daring, confident stance.

I saw a face. Brown skin with long, braided hair. Same hairstyle one of the Dutch boys who had attacked me and a grifter named Arizona had sported yesterday. We'd had a battle in the heart of Chinatown during the noon hour. My stalker looked right into the peephole, looked right in my eye, that tense face becoming clearer. A beret covered those braids, French-style.

Now my problem was unhidden, still staring into the peephole.

I swallowed.

Didn't know how to deal with this.

Two

the desperate hours

I should've fired a shot right through the peephole.

That would've saved me. But it would've been hard to explain to housekeeping.

I took the silencer off the gun, put that and the gun back in the safe, but didn't lock the safe. Then I hurried and pulled on sweats and shoes, heard Lola Mack shifting around inside the bathroom, whispered for her to stay in there until I came back inside the room, went back to the peephole to make sure they were still in the hallway, and hesitated before I opened the door.

Brown skin on Jamaican heritage. Eyebrows arched thin.

We faced each other without words.

Her look was almost unrecognizable. Her untamed hair was now in braids, those braids covered with a beret; her clothes were different, scaled down to jeans and a turtleneck sweater, boots with a sensible heel, and those sensible heels made her seem shorter than I had remembered from yesterday morning, now she had on brand-new clothes, was dressed like she was a native of London, decked out in gloves and a high-end trench coat, head to toe all of her gear was still shades of black, all of her clothing still the various hues of sadness and mourning.

It was the other woman I had met on the plane this morning.

The woman I had bedded as soon as I made it to London.

Her name was Mrs. Jones.

She had been sitting in the same section with me and Lola.

For eight hours we had been crammed in three seats on the back of a British Airways Airbus. She had cried from America to the UK, heartbroken by her husband, a husband she was divorcing. She left like we were done, now she had come back at sunrise.

The woman I had just bedded, Lola Mack, was naked and hiding in the bathroom.

The woman I had bedded yesterday morning, Mrs. Jones, was outside my door at the start of a new day, her expensive perfume lighting up the hallway.

Nowhere to run, nowhere to hide.

This was so fucking awkward.

She wasn't the man I had chased in the thick of the night.

Wasn't that drama at my door.

But still.

I should've shot her so I didn't have to deal with this new breed of drama.

I said, "Mrs. Jones."

"Gideon."

"You came back."

"Surprised?"

"Yeah."

"Shouldn't be. You're a good swimmer."

Mrs. Jones stood in front of me, prim and proper, that sophistication that had first caught my attention on the flight from Atlanta to London enveloping her. She looked like a superwoman. Rich. Powerful. She began smiling, expensive wine perfuming her every exhale.

Yesterday her hair had been big and wild, in neo-soul Afro, now it was braided and tame.

I said, "I liked your hair better the other way. Liked it looking wild."

"Good morning to you too."

"Good morning, Mrs. Jones."

"Bad time?"

"I have company."

"Is she French? Russian? Swedish?"

"She's Polish."

"Where did you meet this Polish woman?"

"Met her in the lobby."

"Just when I thought I was irreplaceable."

"I offered you first right of refusal. You chose to leave my bed and walk in the rain."

"You met someone in the lobby." She smiled. "Maybe I shouldn't have left so abruptly."

Mrs. Jones gave me a more chilled overlook that was 100 percent professional.

She lowered her voice. "I smell her on you."

I expected anger. Was ready for some level of rage.

She said, "I was . . . I came back . . . part of the reason . . . I wanted to talk business."

"What kind?"

"What we spoke on earlier."

Hours ago we had talked about killing her husband. Letting her have revenge on the man who had betrayed her with another woman, who had left her marriage "irretrievably" broken.

She left that at that.

In her eyes I saw parts of who she used to be, saw the damaged remains of Henrietta Kellogg, the woman who had, in the middle of the night, fled Jamaica in the arms of her father to escape his crimes. And I saw the trouble that was stirring deep inside who she was now.

I recognized her need for revenge. I nodded.

"We can talk. Tomorrow."

"Regarding your husband."

"Not my husband."

"Change of heart."

"Some boys hurt my daughter. Them . . . I would like to talk about . . . finding them."

"We can do that."

"Have a hypothetical conversation. Along with a hypothetical price."

"Of course."

The door to my room opened. Hair wild, Lola stuck her head out.

At first Lola looked scared, then that fear changed to surprise, the kind that left her mouth wide-open. Me and Mrs. Jones, outside my hotel room, whispering and plotting.

Awkwardness invaded the hall, marched in Gestapo boots.

Hours ago Mrs. Jones was inside that room, on that bed, doing the same things I had done with Lola no more than two hours ago, had Mrs. Jones on her back, had her kissing me while she spread her legs and allowed me to put something wonderful deep inside her.

Lola blinked a few times, said, "That you, Mrs. Jones?"

"Lola Mack?" Mrs. Jones was just as surprised. "Is that you, Lola Mack?"

"Didn't think I'd see you again."

"Sorry . . . sorry . . . sorry if I interrupted . . . if I disturbed you and Gideon."

"What's going on?"

There was a pregnant pause.

Mrs. Jones said, "Was trying to get a room."

"This hotel is booked solid."

"Will be hard to get a room anywhere this time of night. I mean morning. Whatever it is."

"I know. What are my options?"

"You're all wet, Mrs. Jones."

"It's storming out there."

"Compared to Los Angeles weather this is Siberia. Feels like sleet is coming down."

"You can't go out in that weather. You'll end up getting pneumonia."

"I don't have a choice."

Lola came out into the hallway, leaning forward, curiosity leading her nose, her hand reaching back, holding the heavy door open. Her hair down, unkempt, sex perfuming her flesh. Her terry-cloth robe came undone, that wardrobe malfunction causing her housecoat to slip away, show off her graceful neck before plummeting and being caught right below her nipples, the eyes on those dark twins admiring me and Mrs. Jones. The fullness of Lola's breasts. The taut peaks of her nipples. The flesh at the top of her thighs. All seen. Lola reached for her robe, but the door to the room started to close.

She gave up fighting with the robe, raced for the door, that robe falling away, revealing her frame, showing the warm and hairless place between her legs. Her breasts, her flat stomach, her hairless pussy, all of that was revealed for a moment.

Lola moved in increments, didn't rush, not ashamed of her body, not at all.

Her girl-next-door look. Small breasts. Shapely buttocks.

Mrs. Jones sighed.

I looked at Lola, became aware of the heart in my chest, the dryness of my throat. She wasn't as beautiful as Arizona, but she could hold her own, especially with that breathtaking body.

Arizona was exotic, a Filipina with skin the hue of sunrise in an exotic land. Arizona was slender, streamlined, body made for being the centerfold in *Playboy*. Lola had curves and healthy breasts, the kind of body that would be on the cover of *King, Maxim,* or *FHM*.

Lola bumbled, turned the dead bolt on the door to keep it from locking, then pulled her housecoat back together; still, her legs and bare feet told the rest of the story.

Another awkward moment was born. Lola looked embarrassed. I don't know who chuckled first, me or Mrs. Jones, might've been Lola, but that chuckle broke the tension.

Lola blushed.

Mrs. Jones asked, "What happened with your boyfriend, Lola?"

"Son of a bitch."

"What happened to *Rent*?"

"Long story. But I ended up humiliated and homeless. Stranded. Broke as a joke."

"Are you serious?"

"I needed help, came here looking for you, and ran into Gideon. Guess I got lucky."

"Guess you did."

"Want to hear about it? I have to tell you what that cheating son of a bitch did."

"Lola . . . I . . . you and Gideon . . . I can check with another hotel."

"You already said you don't have anywhere to go. I know what that feels like, being stranded in another country. And you said you'd never been to London, so I know you don't know your way around, and you don't know anybody over here, so come on in, get dry and warm."

They paused; eyes came to me for permission.

This was getting out of control, but still I nodded.

Mrs. Jones weighed her options, realized that, like Lola, she had none, and she nodded as well. "I have a few things downstairs. I went to Oxford Circus. Sort of got carried away."

"Go get your things and come on up. Show me what you bought. I'll make some coffee. You can get dry. Get warm. At least get some sleep. I don't want you homeless."

They hugged again.

Lola said, "And I can tell you all about Sonofabitch. That no good son of a bitch."

That electricity that lived inside Lola, I saw it spark, saw it move through Mrs. Jones.

Lola said, "Smells like you've been getting your drink on too."

"Château Chasse-Spleen. Nineteen fifty-nine."

"Dag. That sounds very expensive too."

"Only the best."

"Well, I really don't want you walking around a strange country all tipsy and shit."

"Smells like you've had some spirits as well."

"Sake. Sipped me some sake. Still buzzing now. Got some left if you want some."

Lola laughed and let her go.

Again, that small sigh escaped Mrs. Jones. She sighed and shivered the way she did when I was over her, entering her, breaking her skin and moving across her fleshy folds.

Lola vanished back inside the room, disengaged the dead bolt, then the door closed and locked behind her.

That left me and Mrs. Jones.

For a moment nothing was said.

I waited for her to bring up her need for revenge.

She asked, "Did you enjoy Lola?"

That surprised me. I said, "Sure you want me to answer that?"

"The look on her face . . . she enjoyed you."

"You okay?"

"I'm good." She paused. "Life should be about pursuing pleasure. I've had enough pain. Had enough tears. I only want to feel what makes me feel good for as long as it feels good."

"You left so soon."

"With regret. With much regret." Then she whispered, "Lola Mack?"

"You're mad because she wasn't Polish."

"You seduced me *and* slept with Lola Mack?"

"Lola gave *you* an orgasm first . . . then you came to my room and took advantage of me."

"Oh. Yeah." She took a deep breath, shook her head. "Oh, God."

"Guess you forgot about that."

"I'll never forget about that. *Never.* She touched some nerve . . . made me come on the goddamn plane. Whatever she did . . . they way she touched me . . . she made me come."

"You came pretty good, from what I remember."

Mrs. Jones looked back toward the hotel door. Her gaze said she hadn't forgotten how she was on the back of the plane, writhing toward an unexpected orgasm.

I said, "You held my hand when she made you come. Held my hand so tight I thought you were going to rip off one of my fingers."

"That was . . . unreal." She shook her head. "On a damn plane."

"Maybe you should break out the oils and rub Lola down, return the favor."

Mrs. Jones looked at me, unsmiling, not blinking.

I asked, "What's wrong?"

She swallowed. "So, how was it with Lola?"

"What she lacks in experience she makes up for in enthusiasm."

"Who was better?"

"You." With a wink I told her what she needed to hear. "You were. Much."

She shifted, her lips curving up at the edges.

She whispered, "Wish I could've . . . seen her . . . and you . . . wish I could've watched."

The smell of coffee came from my room, wafted into the hallway.

Again Mrs. Jones smiled.

We didn't go toward the elevator; I opened the door to the emergency exit and we took the stairs. We had descended to the second floor when Mrs. Jones stopped walking.

She whispered, "Can't believe I want to ask you this."

"About the price for going after the two boys?"

"No, about Lola."

"What about Lola?"

She swallowed. "Did you go down on Lola?"

"Where did that come from?"

"When she came into the hallway . . . when her robe fell . . . did you taste her?"

"Why don't you taste me and see."

Mrs. Jones faced me, kissed me, savored my tongue like she was trying to suck every morsel of Lola away from my flesh. Mrs. Jones pushed me back on the stairs until I sat down.

"Did Lola suck her pussy off this sweet dick, Gideon?"

"She didn't get down like that."

"Damn shame. That's a damn shame."

I tried to get up. She stopped me.

She whispered, "Don't get up. Not yet."

I looked in her eyes; saw that erotic vampire that lived inside her.

She whispered, "I've been thinking about this all day as well."

"Lola is waiting."

"Lola will be fine." She licked the corners of her lips. "Lola will be just fine."

She got on her knees, slid between my legs, took me in her mouth, again stealing what Lola had left behind. I didn't have the heart to tell her that I had used a condom. I didn't get an erection, but what she was doing to me, what she was doing in search of Lola, it felt good.

The weighty metal door above us opened.

I looked up, expected to see Lola in shock, staring at us, her mouth fixed to scream.

I saw his suit before I saw his face.

It all came back. Everything I was trying to ignore came back in a flash.

I jerked, tried to get up.

But Mrs. Jones wouldn't let me go.

I looked up, searching for the bandages on a broken nose.

It was a middle-aged man. Benny Hill in a dark suit. Golden tie. Raincoat over one arm. His umbrella and briefcase over the other. He stood in silence. His breathing not audible.

I had grabbed Mrs. Jones's head, her beret slipped, but she refused to yield, she kept feeding. The man didn't leave. He stayed where he was. In shock. Eyes wide. Mouth tight.

His cellular phone rang.

I jerked.

Mrs. Jones's rhythm didn't break, she didn't stop making her braids sway.

The man fumbled with his phone, answered, his accent crisp and cockney, told the caller he was on the way downstairs. Said that like he was irritated by the disturbance. He hung up.

The man came down the narrow staircase, slow steps, had to turn sideways to get by, brushed against me, brushed against Mrs. Jones, stumbled by us without saying good morning.

The man looked back up, shuddered, took slow steps, watched Mrs. Jones work.

Mrs. Jones made wet sounds, her head rising and falling in a slow, deliberate rhythm.

The man licked his lips and moaned.

Mrs. Jones was massaging and sucking, sucking and stroking, performing for a crowd of one, doing that like she was in Atlanta, at the place called Trapeze, the center of attention.

The man readjusted his briefcase, did the same with his coat and umbrella.

Then he was gone down the stairs, first tiptoeing, then moving at a normal pace.

London remained overcast, gray skies turned black, rain fell sideways, winds howled.

Inside this hollow stairwell, muffled moans and the sounds of wetness echoed.

Eyes blurry, the world now opaque, my hands went to the top of Mrs. Jones's beret.

The sound of her mouth was wet, her determination was loud.

Little moans escaped me, echoed in the stairwell.

"Was just thinking . . . all day was thinking . . . been with one man most of my life . . . hadn't had fun when it came to sex . . . not the kind of fun that other people . . . Lola . . . and you . . . wow . . . guess I should be jealous that you enjoyed Lola . . . but I'm not . . . I'm not. I'm intrigued. It excites me."

I moved her beret, held her braids like reins, shifted so I could watch her work her magic.

Mrs. Jones smiled. "I'm going to ask Lola Mack to let me watch you make love to her."

I moaned. "I dare you."

She licked her lips. "Never fucking dare me."

Three

bad girls

Moments later we were hand in hand, heading down the stairs.

Uneasiness crawled across my skin.

Distrust slowed my pace.

But I kept going.

Kept holding Mrs. Jones's hand and going down to the ground floor.

When I made it to the lobby, once again I was vulnerable. She had left me both excited and dizzy. Distrust never evaporated. I wondered if Mrs. Jones had lured me down here. I kept her in front of me, left her standing between me and a bullet, and spied out on Bayley Street.

Dark skies and rain. Black cabs and small cars.

Saw coats, suits, and umbrellas passing by.

So many men in suits. Any one of them could've been the man I had chased from Knightsbridge. That was where the man with the broken nose had followed me, that was where I had turned it all around, ended up chasing him in the bowels of Lancaster Gate.

He'd run for miles. And he'd run fast without breaking a sweat.

The thought of that chase seemed surreal. The soreness in my legs told it was real.

Whoever he was, he was strong.

Mrs. Jones went to the counter, gave them a ticket, and asked the concierge to collect her luggage. My eyes took in everyone in the area. I went to the dining area, looked around, looked up and saw the television near the bar was on CNN. Images of the Big Bad Wolf were on a special report. The man I had killed was staring at me, still following me, reminding me that this wasn't over. Images of Sledge came up next, footage from sunny Trinidad showing the carnage from a rental van that had been blown up, killing him and all of his family. Weeks ago we were face-to-face in Atlanta in a meeting, discussing how to kill his rival. That footage of his exploded van was juxtaposed against peaceful waters. It reminded me of footage from wars in Baghdad.

Like it was part of a much larger war.

Big Bad Wolf's image came back, glared right in my eyes.

I scowled back at his glare. Despite the mild chatter in the lobby and restaurant, that buzz remained, I still heard voices from a bloody alley in Tampa whispering my name.

Fear and anger swirled inside me.

Because I knew.

Even though I had done it over and over since that foot chase through Kensington Gardens, I retraced my steps, this time going backward, from Lancaster Gate back to Soho, to being on the train with Arizona. The man with the broken nose always showed up after I'd been with Arizona.

I had left Arizona in anger and found my mother, tried to give her that anger.

It took years, but I had found the source of my pain again.

I'd found the woman who had birthed me and made me a killer.

My mother was hiding in London, selling her pussy in the red-light district.

Violence.

Sex.

My life had been filled with nothing but violence and sex.

I grew up in a home perfumed by the musk of many thirty-minute lovers.

Sheets stained by lust.

It was always like that. Wherever we went.

After we fled Montreal, we lived in so many ghettos, were always hiding in a different ghetto. I'd pass by my mother's bedroom, see her on her back. Some strange man on top of her, his pants at his ankles, the headboard hitting the wall like a steady drum, his belt loose, clanking and singing along with the loose change in his pockets, his own percussions of pleasure. My mother's body was flat, motionless, uninspired, as the man huffed and puffed and impaled her.

Things were damn horrific between us by then.

My mother turned toward the door, saw me watching, and simply said, "Close the door."

I did as she said.

A moment later there was a knock at the front door. I thought it was her next customer; sometimes they showed up early. It wasn't a customer, was one of my mother's coworkers.

Despite her aroma she was a beautiful Filipina lady. Golden skin. Long black hair.

The Filipina smiled at me. Her thirtysomething smile meeting my teenage grin. She'd traveled from city to city with my mother off and on, both of them outrunning the law.

"Where's your mother?"

I nodded toward the hard drumbeats and jingles.

She smelled like cigarettes, hard liquor, and cheap perfume, just like my mother.

"Sounds like that motherfucker is trying to kill your mother in there."

I glanced at my watch. "She'll be done in five minutes. Unless he's paying extra."

"How've you been?"

"Fine."

"Haven't seen you in a week or two."

Without her asking, I got her a tall glass of ice water, that headboard still banging.

She gazed at me like she always did. When I handed her the water, she held my hand.

She sipped, made a satisfied sound, then asked me, "Ready to get some pussy today?"

I nodded, not knowing how to say no to her. Knowing I didn't want to say no to her. And still never knew what to say to her. I just smiled a little and nodded. That was my answer.

She laughed a little, then, holding my damp hand, followed me to my bedroom.

Then there was the sound of two headboards banging.

After my mother had finished her job and that man had paid and left, thirty minutes passed before she stuck her head inside my bedroom door, nightgown on, her wig red and crooked. She saw me naked, her Filipina friend naked and asleep. She stood in the door-frame, smoking, shaking her head.

I snapped, "Close the goddamn door."

She closed my door hard.

I was too young to understand that anger and jealousy were first cousins.

My Filipina lover rolled over and kissed me.

Then she sat up and opened her purse. She took out cocaine, powdered her nose.

She asked, "Want some blow?"

I shook my head.

"Good answer. Don't ever start doing this shit."

When she was done, she lit up a cigarette, pulled the covers up to her breasts.

Down the hallway the front door squeaked opened and closed hard. I heard footsteps heading toward the other bedroom. Then the headboard began slapping the wall again.

My bed companion was high, eyes glazed over like her world was surreal.

She sighed hard, frowned.

I asked her what she was upset about.

She said, "Be glad when this shit is over."

"What shit?"

"I fuck you three more times and my debt is paid."

"What debt?"

"Your mother bailed me out of county. This is how she wants me to work down my tab."

"Thought you came to see me because you liked me."

"You're cute. But I'm older than your mother. Sweetie, I have three kids your age."

I jumped up.

Naked, I left the room, stormed toward my mother's bedroom door.

Without knocking I pushed her door open. Pushed it hard.

The short-haired woman who was in bed with my mother, she saw me and froze. Seeing a naked boy holding a .22 had that effect. That fat woman was on her hands and knees. My mother was in her birthday suit, on her knees, behind that pale woman, that fat woman naked in high heels, my mother wearing a strap-on doing to that fat and flabby woman what a man had been doing to her moments before. My mother didn't discriminate. Money was money.

I snapped, "You're making her fuck me to pay off a goddamn debt?"

"Are you crazy? Put that gun down. Close the goddamn door."

I rushed in the room and pushed her away from her customer. My mother's client tried to move, but couldn't. She was handcuffed to the bedpost. The gag in her mouth muffling her screams. Mother sold fantasy to anyone who had enough green to make it worth her while.

She slapped me hard enough to split my lip. "Have you lost your mind?"

Since Montreal she had taken to drinking more and striking me in anger.

Nose to nose, mouth bloodied, I yelled, "Are you making her fuck me?"

"I'm doing you a favor."

"Are you forcing her to have sex with me?"

"Don't you see me working? Get out of my office. Go to your room."

I left, that taste of blood flooding my senses.

She yelled, "Close the damn door. Come back and close the damn door."

I went back and slammed the door so hard the apartment building shook, birds left their nests, and the roaches ran out of their cracks and crevices in unadulterated fear.

I went to the bathroom, washed blood from my mouth.

In the background my mother was trying to calm down her angry customer.

But what was done was done.

My mother's overweight customer ran out of the bedroom, bolted through the front door.

The front door squealed and closed hard.

Back in my bedroom, the Filipina was relaxed, doing more coke.

She said, "We done or do I have to work off some more of my debt today?"

I told her to get out.

The Filipina wiped her nose, cigarette in hand, smoke pluming from her head.

My mother screamed, called the Filipina a cocksucking bitch.

That Filipina laughed and told my mother to go fuck herself.

Again our front door squealed and closed hard.

Then I went to my mother.

She was sitting on the edge of her bed, head down, tools of her trade at her side.

In an uneven voice she asked, "You hate me?"

The way I stared at my .22 and grimaced at her, that made her question rhetorical.

She whispered, "You hate me."

I nodded at the woman who was pimping everyone she touched.

I hated her.

Hated her enough to kill her.

I had promised myself I would visit her, as I had visited so many others.

The hate inside me was a reminder that my mother and I had unfinished business.

Maybe this was her doing. My being followed. I had killed for her over and over.

And in return she had abused me. She had stolen from me.

Her putting a hit out on me wouldn't surprise me.

I gritted my teeth. Thought about it and shook my head. The woman who had birthed me and taught me to kill, her having a contract out on me wouldn't surprise me at all.

Again I looked around the lobby. The scent of beans and toast coming from the dining area, the sound of Big Bad Wolf on the television, eyed many men in suits.

Mrs. Jones came and stood next to me. "My luggage is ready."

I turned and faced her, my smile so warm, the coldness hidden deep inside me.

I asked her to wait a second, told her I needed to check with the front desk.

I faced a petite young woman, her smile thin, her accent Russian.

I told her I was here on business. She nodded. Then I told her I had met with an American, described his height, his build, told her that he was bald, that his skin was fair, maybe untanned, told her that I couldn't remember the bloke's name, but I needed to contact him regarding some ventures back in America. Again she nodded. I told her that I had lost his business card, didn't have an e-mail address, told her my company would be upset if I failed to locate the gentleman. The intensity behind my smile had her attention. Again I described the man I was looking for. Again I told her that the man I was looking for had a broken nose.

She told me she hadn't seen anyone who fit that description. I asked her to ask her coworkers. The lobby was small, had only one elevator next to the front desk, only one way in for customers, and no more than three were working the desk. It only took her a few seconds to ask her coworkers; neither of them had seen the man who was stalking me.

I asked her if she and her crew would work the front desk all morning.

She told me she and her coworkers would be here until late evening.

After-hours the only entrance to the hotel was locked, the front of the hotel manned with an overnight concierge, guests who had keys being the only ones let inside.

I thanked her, then asked her to ring my room if my friend showed up.

She nodded.

I went to the elevator, where Mrs. Jones waited with her baggage.

Four

while the city sleeps

Mrs. Jones had bought herself a collection of top-shelf Tumi luggage.

She had gone out and spent more than a few thousand American dollars on two big, red-and-black suitcases, gear that made Gucci luggage look like it came from the swap meet.

She had been feeding another addiction. Again in the pursuit of pleasure.

We loaded up the small elevator, and as soon as the doors closed, Mrs. Jones kissed me. She put her body on mine and gave me her tongue.

She said, "I'm going to ask her, you know that."

"I dare you."

"You'd love that, wouldn't you?"

I smiled. "You're incorrigible."

"Glad you noticed."

Then she kissed me again, eased her wine-tasting tongue inside my mouth, moved slow at first, then became so intense, almost got out of control. She pulled away, smiled as she wiped my lips, removed all traces of her lipstick, did that as if she were hiding evidence of her crimes.

When we went back in the room, Lola was getting out of the

shower. The bed was made. Lola came out wearing the terry housecoat over 24 Hour Fitness shorts and a T-shirt.

"Dag, Mrs. Jones." Lola laughed. "You bought everything but London Bridge."

"I found places to shop. Piccadilly Circus. Oxford Circus. Self-ridges."

"You did the damn thing."

"Just warming up. I heard about Harrods. I want to find that place."

"I heard Harrods has everything from top designer clothes to caviar."

"Yeah. It's like a five-star Wal-Mart."

"What do you know about Wal-Mart, Mrs. Jones?"

They laughed again. I put Mrs. Jones's suitcases in front of them, opened them then. Mind ablaze, I moved around the room while they chatted and looked at Mrs. Jones's new gear.

Both of her sturdy suitcases were on wheels, one filled with shoes, the other filled with new clothes, incidentals, unmentionables from Ann Summers, the UK's answer to Victoria's Secret.

"Your perfume smells nice, Mrs. Jones. What is it?"

"Chantecaille's Frangipane."

"Smells sexy and expensive."

Then Mrs. Jones asked Lola about the row between her and her boyfriend.

Lola said, "Well, I got to the hotel lobby, kept calling his room. He answered, pissed off. Not a morning person, you know? Then he heard it was me, adjusted his attitude. I told him I missed him. He kept whispering, told me the same. I asked him how bad he wanted to make love to me. He said real bad, then asked me if I wanted to have phone sex. I said why don't you let me come up to your room and we can do the damn thing for real. He freaked out."

"What happened after that? Did you go up to his room?"

The room was closing in on me, was crowded, like a mind with too many thoughts.

Like Lola, Mrs. Jones had at least two hundred pounds of cloth-ing, all brand-new.

"He came downstairs. As soon as he got down there, I could tell something was wrong. He was pissed. Then the elevator . . . they call it a lift . . . the lift opened again and this bitch got off looking tore up from the floor up, weave every which-a-way. Bitch was angry as hell. She knew who I was. But I didn't know she was his bitch until the bitch started telling me off, telling me they had been a couple for months, said that he had said I was a stalker, bitch was calling me all kinds of names, had security throw me out of the hotel. I mean . . . damn . . . it got ugly. I went Naomi Campbell and threw my cellular phone at that bitch. Hit her in the middle of her face."

"What did your . . . the guy you came to see . . . what did he do?"

"He was freaking out. Kept asking me what I was doing in London. Kept asking me why I didn't tell him I was coming. Trying to calm that ugly bitch down, trying to keep me away from that bitch. It was twenty kinds of loud and fifty kinds of ugly going on in that lobby. The police came, or bobbies, whatever they call Five-O over here. They came. They don't play over here."

"Uh-huh."

"So I dragged my luggage out of there before I ended up on lockdown."

"Your boyfriend?"

Every word made the room smaller. Four suitcases, none mine. Three backpacks, the lightest one mine. Lola had things over the dresser. Same for the bathroom. Bags and clothes were everywhere. I moved some of their baggage to the side, left a walking path, then I went to the bathroom, showered again, ran water over my thoughts, put the same sweats back on.

I had my cellular with me. Tried Arizona's number. No response.

Felt like two huge hands were on either side of my head, pushing in hard.

When I came out, Mrs. Jones and Lola were on the small sofa, the heavy red curtains partially open, grayness from Bayley Street leaking inside. Lola had her feet pulled up under her. Mrs. Jones had her shoes off, one foot on the sofa, one on the floor, a masculine and controlling position for a woman so feminine. Both had cups of coffee, the little porcelain cups that came in the room. Lola was doing most of the talking, as usual, most of the conversation repetitive, still telling Mrs. Jones about how she went to the hotel her boyfriend was staying at, describing the surprise on his face, telling her how he didn't want her to come up to his room, then finally admitting that he was living in the hotel with someone else. Lola's tears came back.

"Lola, did he at least have the decency to talk to you at all?"

"He ran out and talked to me . . . followed me while I struggled with all this damn luggage . . . then I was going down to the Embankment station and one of the bags got away from me, rolled by the T-shirt vendors and knocked down a Chinese family . . . my ass should've done the carry-on thing . . . was out in the damn cold . . . got tired and stopped trying to get away from him. He tried to help me with my bags. Cursed him out on the streets. Shit happens, all he said. He said he had fallen in love with that ugly bitch. I asked him when did he fall in love because forty-eight hours ago he was talking about how much he loved me. Was talking about having babies."

Lola Mack cried again.

"Knew something was wrong. Had been having bad dreams about us breaking up, not being able to sleep because of the stupid dreams, but he told me I was just being paranoid, just being a silly girl. I did my best, you know? I'm not surprised. I am, but I shouldn't be. Two years . . . when your man is gone that long . . . things get kind of off, you know? Things get weird."

Mrs. Jones looked at my discomfort. She nodded. I bounced my leg, nodded back at her. She had misread my anxiety, thought I was on edge because I was trapped in a room filled with women emoting. Being the shoulder to lean on and letting my ear be the one they vented to wasn't my specialty, and any other day their emotional chatter might've worn me down.

Any other day.

Mrs. Jones asked Lola, "You didn't have any idea?"

"He was hard to get in touch with. He used to call, and then the calls died down. When he did call, it was different. Nothing flirty anymore. A woman needs that fire, you know?"

"I know. Believe me, I know."

"He was always snippy, said it was because he was tired, you know? I understood. He said he was doing shows every day, two on Saturdays and two on Sundays."

"Uh-huh."

"I mean, I understood. But it got to the point that I'd ask him questions, simple questions, you know, just trying to get a conversation going, and everything I asked became stupid. Believe that? Said I asked stupid questions. I told him not to call me stupid."

"Disrespect is the beginning of the end."

"He said he didn't call me stupid. I mean, who in the fuck asks stupid questions? Stupid people. So he called me stupid without calling me stupid and thought I'd be too stupid to notice. Not like we connected that much. He was always out after the show but never had time to talk to me. Never called me from his room. Was always out walking around when he called me. He had a bitch living in his damn room. Now I see why. Now I see the fuck why."

"Lola."

"Sorry. Rambling. I'll let you get some rest."

"No, was just wondering . . . if it was like that . . . why did you come here?"

"Love made me. Wanted to make things right. Thought it was me, you know? Thought I wasn't trying hard enough. Figured if I walked the walk and came here, showed him how I felt and not just talk about it . . . you know . . . guess I watch too many movies with happy endings."

"I understand. I've struggled to hold on to what I needed to let go of as well."

"Hard to believe it ended like this," Lola went on. "Because the first year we were together was re-mark-able. We were shacking in West Hollywood, splitting the rent. Whatever. Guess he thinks he's all that since he's been on the road with *Rent* for two years. I'll get me a show. Or a movie. I'll blow up and his ass will be calling me for favors. Son of a bitch."

Mrs. Jones: "Sounds like it's time to move on. Time to leave the pain behind."

"Yeah. It's time to move on."

"Now I think you're the one who should be getting pampered and massaged."

Mrs. Jones held Lola and looked at me, comforted her and sent me a smile.

Lola broke away from her tears, shook her head. "Enough about me, that son of a bitch and *Rent*. How was your first day in London? Better and less traumatic than mine I hope."

Mrs. Jones told Lola that after shopping she had eaten a wonderful Italian dinner at Il Siciliano, then caught a cab over to St. Martin's Lane, pulled her luggage through the theater district looking for *Rent*, heard it wasn't playing, and dragged her bags into another production.

Lola let her anger die, stopped crying, asked Mrs. Jones what production she had seen.

Mrs. Jones sipped her coffee, moved her braids from her face. "*Blackbird*. The play was called *Blackbird*. Picked it at random. Write-up was interesting. Went to the evening show."

"Never heard of *Blackbird*."

"It was interesting. About a pedophile. But more importantly, in my eyes, it was about a woman who wouldn't let go. And I found that interesting. The way it spoke to me. Interesting."

"Good interesting or bad interesting?"

"The play opens twelve years after a man had fallen in love with a twelve-year-old girl."

"Like *Lolita*."

"Nothing like *Lolita*. Still, it was both disturbing and awesome. The man, the actor, he actually pulled his pants down, and the woman was undressing, showed her breasts, in a very passionate scene where they were about to get it on."

That interested me. A play about a woman holding a grudge for over a decade. There was a lot of that going around. Me and my mother. Arizona and her sister. Mrs. Jones and her husband. Part of my anger was rooted in the same theme the play owned.

Lola said, "That's London theater."

"I swear, they were damn near naked. Tits and ass and balls everywhere."

Lola grinned. "Oh, they will get naked."

"I thought they were about to start having sex onstage."

"Please. You should see some of the foreign films. They actually have sex in the films."

"Do they?" Mrs. Jones leaned toward Lola. "You mean . . . real sex? Like porn?"

"*Puh-lease*. They show oral sex, the man's penis, which is only fair because they always show the woman's vagina. They show penetration, they show real oral sex, the whole nine. And these are real actors in stories that have real plots. America gets the edited versions."

"Too bad Blair Underwood and Denzel aren't in any foreign films."

"Or Gary Dourdan. Or Boris Kodjoe. Or Larenz Tate."

"Or Vin Diesel."

"Oh, hell yeah. I'd sign up to play the part of the woman who gives the blow job."

"That line would be like the cattle calls for *American Idol*."

They laughed. I smiled.

Mrs. Jones asked, "You like those European films? Which would you recommend?"

"I saw *Intimacy. 9 Songs. Devil in the Flesh*."

"Are they erotic?"

"Very. In *9 Songs* they show the man coming."

"Like special effects?"

"No. The real deal. He has a happy ending, it squirts out. And it was a *hella* lotta come. The sex scenes they have in those movies make what Halle Berry did in *Monster's Ball*—the uncut version—seem like a Disney film. I mean, the men have come squirting all over the place."

Mrs. Jones chuckled. Sounded tipsy. "Those movies . . ."

"Yeah?"

"*Intimacy. 9 Songs*. Are they worth renting? I mean are they . . . do they excite you?"

Lola blushed. "What's the point of watching them if they don't?"

Mrs. Jones moved her braids, rubbed her neck. "Books excite me more than movies. Lately I've been reading a lot of erotica. Novel after novel. What we can't get, we read."

"Good books?"

"Especially books edited by Maxim Jakubowski. The book I was reading on the plane. I met him today. He has a bookshop up the road. Murder One. I shook his hand and got my book signed. Love erotic short stories. Amazes me what words can do. Words are powerful. Woman in one short story was talking about how she liked to be tied up. Her hands up over her head."

Lola asked, "She liked her boyfriend to do that?"

"She was with another woman."

"Really?"

Mrs. Jones sipped again, erotic fantasies in her eyes. She glanced at me, then at Lola.

My gaze dared her.

Mrs. Jones smiled at me.

Mrs. Jones said, "Lola. You're both an actress and a professional masseuse."

"Uh-huh. Been acting since I was three years old."

"How long have you been a professional masseuse?"

"God. Years. Started in high school. Why?"

"You have . . . this energy. When you touched me . . . on the plane . . . did you know you . . ."

"Do I know what?"

"Did you know that you gave me a happy ending on the plane?"

Lola smiled. She knew.

"On purpose . . . did you make me . . . have an orgasm . . . did you do that on purpose?"

"You were tense."

"Did you do it on purpose?"

"Crying like a baby."

"Did you, Lola? On purpose."

"Well. Sometimes that, you know, helps."

"So you did."

"You mad?"

Mrs. Jones said, "Hardly seems fair."

"What?"

"That you gave me pleasure without . . . reciprocity."

"What do you mean? 'Without reciprocity'?"

The door had been opened and the warm breeze of curiosity was blowing in the room.

Mrs. Jones halted right there, let her words hang, let her words test the waters. Lola didn't withdraw. An inebriated smile bloomed on Mrs. Jones's beautiful, full lips.

A small victory.

In a matter of minutes she had manipulated the conversation to this point.

Like she was in escrow.

All she had to do was figure out how to close the deal.

"Would you be offended if I asked you something, Lola?"

"You have to ask to find out."

Mrs. Jones smiled at Lola Mack, but the smile was unsure.

Mrs. Jones whispered, "In private, Lola. Let me ask you in private."

"Okay." Lola sounded a little nervous. "Sure."

Mrs. Jones put her cup of coffee down, stood up, and extended her hands.

Mrs. Jones said, "Step into the ladies' room with me."

Lola stood up.

I watched them cross the room, maneuver around two hundred pounds of new clothing, then around Lola's two hundred pounds of luggage and clothes, stepping over new shoes and coats, watched them go inside the small toilet hand in hand.

Once inside the toilet, Mrs. Jones left the door ajar.

I listened.

"But first, can I ask you this?" Mrs. Jones asked.

"Okay."

"Lola, would you classify yourself as a voyeur or exhibitionist?"

"What do you mean?"

"When it comes to sex, if you had to be one, voyeur or exhibitionist?"

"Exhibitionist, I guess. Love being onstage. What about you?"

"I guess I'm a voyeur. An observer of life. But I wanted to be an exhibitionist with my husband. Used to want the world to watch us make love. Wanted to make that statement. Wanted to be in the middle of a room inspiring others, making others green with envy."

"Sounds wonderful. And you never did that with your husband?"

"Never."

"Is that why you and he split? Because of sex?"

"We stopped having sex years ago."

"Dag. Always hear that married people stop having sex. I mean, how was sex with your husband when you were having sex, if you remember, if you don't mind my asking?"

"Our marital problems ran deeper than sex."

"But how was it? When you're married . . . does it not stay good? Does it get that bad?"

"It was good. At first. Always good at first. New is good. New is unknown. When you love somebody, you take what they give and let it be as good as it gets, because when you're monogamous, that is as good as it gets because that's all you're going to get. Get it?"

"Got it."

Mrs. Jones said, "But having one sex partner, being monogamous, has its limitations."

"True. You don't get better if you play the same team all the time."

"Nice sports analogy."

"Anytime." Lola smiled. "So you were saying monogamy has its limitations."

"You're bound to their desires . . . bound to their sexual . . . limitations. And if you're not on the same page, then it limits, stymies the fulfillment of your own desires. Restrictions create frustrations. Guess I've been aggravated for a long time. Being monogamous is for the shits, you can only have sex if they want to, when they want to, how they are willing to. You're limited. Or you compromise and engage in sex when you're not in the mood. Would you agree?"

"I guess so. Yeah. I agree. Guess you can only get as freaky as your man."

Another brief pause.

Lola asked, "What did you want from your husband . . . sexually . . . that was so challenging?'

"Just wanted a few fantasies to come true."

Lola made a naughty sound. "What kind of fantasies?"

There was another brief pause.

Mrs. Jones asked Lola, "Have you ever been watched?"

"Having sex?"

"Yes. Have you ever been watched?"

"I'd have to get my nerves up to be watched. Have you?"

"No. I've wanted to be watched. Once I watched other people engage in pleasure."

"In Los Angeles?"

"Not in Los Angeles. I was in Atlanta. At this club in Atlanta."

"Seems like everyone ends up in the ATL."

"Some friends encouraged me to go to Trapeze. Christian friends who were on the brink of divorce, but had been honest with each other and spiced up their sex lives. Told me I could go watch people have sex . . . or participate . . . would be up to me . . . to do whatever . . . my friend . . . she's a judge . . . her husband flew her to Atlanta . . . to Trapeze . . . let her get with men . . . and women . . . she said the women were the best lovers . . . her husband let her . . . gave her fantasy after fantasy."

"And you went?"

"Of course. Once and only once. Very upscale place in a very indiscreet location. Professional people. I sipped wine and watched one black woman; she had several experiences during the night. Great conversation, beautiful breasts. She asked me to join her. She tried to kiss me. I didn't let her kiss me, but I let her touch me. I touched her too. She had the most beautiful experience imaginable. She did it all with her man whispering in her ear."

"Sounds explosive."

Another pause filled with a strange silence.

Mrs. Jones asked, "I have a fantasy, Lola."

"What is it?"

"Well, with this in mind."

"What?"

"Yesterday . . . on the plane . . . you watched me have an orgasm."

"Yeah."

"You *made* me come."

Lola's voice softened. "Guess I did."

Another curt pause.

Mrs. Jones whispered, "You and Gideon."

Lola paused. "What about me and Gideon?"

"Both of you watched me come. On the plane, both of you saw

me come. You were touching me and I was holding Gideon. Both of you felt me having a happy ending. Both of you."

My heart moved up to my throat.

Mrs. Jones chuckled, spoke playfully. "And reciprocity is fair play, don't you think?"

"What do you mean?"

"Now I'd love to watch you and Gideon please each other."

Another pause, that one long and heavy.

I rubbed my palms on my legs.

Lola said, "Excuse me?"

"I want to sip wine and watch you and Gideon exchange happy endings."

The world stopped rotating.

Five

someone to watch over me

"I would love to watch you and Gideon exchange happy endings."

Lola said, "You're joking, right?"

"Not joking."

"You want me have sex in front of you?"

"Yes."

Lola sounded angry.

I waited to hear Lola scream, fight, maybe curse, and run away from Mrs. Jones.

The bathroom door closed all the way.

Then I heard nothing. Nothing at all.

No words. No battle. It was as silent as outer space.

I picked up the remote, hit the green button, the television came on, and I left the sound on mute, the closed caption turned on. I found CNN. Once again I saw Big Bad Wolf. I kept looking at that news, reading the closed caption like I was looking for clues. Then the man who'd put the hit on Big Bad Wolf came up, Sledgehammer Jackson, his name in bold letters, his birth and recent death dates under his image, an image that had been immortalized the moment his van exploded. They had images of Big Bad Wolf and Sledge when they were younger, in the same rap group, showed old interviews with both of them at a rap concert, back when both of those men were still friends, before fame and money had driven a wedge between them.

Arizona had put me in contact with Sledge, had made that transaction possible.

Again I took out my mobile, tried to call her.

Her calls were still being diverted. Now she was unreachable.

I thought about what went down in Chinatown.

Arizona had been followed and attacked yesterday afternoon.

People were after her and she could be dead.

I swallowed, shook that imagery out of my head.

Across the room, in the safe, was a package that Arizona had delivered here last night. She had dropped off a package on Sierra, her younger sister. She wanted her younger sister dead. And her younger sister probably had the same feelings. Sierra had already sponsored one attack, an attack that ended in Arizona's favor. That sibling war was just beginning.

I stood up. Thought about leaving.

I had no idea where Arizona was. Doubted if she could help me if I found her. Right now, until I figured out what was going on, this hotel room seemed like the safest place to be.

I sat back down, eyes on the gray skies peeping through the deep red curtains.

Curtains the color of blood.

All of a sudden, I couldn't breathe. The room felt like a coffin.

A sliver of time passed before that sensation of suffocating passed.

The bathroom door opened, not all at once, a little at a time.

A different kind of tension flooded the room.

I was ready for a different kind of argument, for a brand-new fight.

When they came out, Lola was blushing.

Mrs. Jones was smiling like a lawyer who had just won a big case.

They were holding hands.

Lola whispered, "I've never done anything like that before."

"If it's okay, I'd love to watch you. Would love to watch you and Gideon make love."

Something floated between us. Something I couldn't describe.

An energy that despite our all being jet-lagged and living on an eight-hour time change made me feel alert. The brokenhearted wife. The hopeless romantic whose ideal view of love had been turned upside down. And me. The man who killed people, the man who wanted a woman who was out of his reach.

They looked at me.

Lola said, "She told me she already asked you and you said it was cool."

Surprised, I nodded.

Lola smiled. "If you're down, then I can be down."

Then everyone was smiling. Gentle smiles between lovers and strangers.

Any problem I had was on the other side of that door.

And those problems would have to wait.

Mrs. Jones said, "Gideon, give Lola pleasure. Give her another happy ending."

Lola giggled. "Don't believe I'm going to do this. I mean, in front of you."

"If you don't want to . . ."

"If Gideon wants to, if he's cool with it, if he's down, I want to."

Mrs. Jones asked, "You sure? It's up to you, Lola. Only if you're sure."

"This will be different. Never had anybody watch me."

"You're a single woman."

"I am. As hell. Single as hell."

"You can do whatever you want to do."

"I can. I sure can."

"You can ignore the pain and get pleasure. You can get revenge in your own way."

"I sure the fuck can."

"And we're in London. Whatever we do here, nobody has to know. We're safe in this room. No judgments. And no pain. Inside this room there shouldn't be any pain. Just pleasure."

Lola looked at me, bit the corner of her bottom lip, waiting for me to say something.

I nodded, that nod saying what we did here stayed here.

As if I'd ever see them again.

Lola said, "You're a man of few words."

"When I need to talk, I talk."

"Well, right now . . . guess we can stop talking for a while."

"Guess so."

I went to her. Gave her little kisses, tender kisses, tested her sexual barometer.

That energy she had rolled through me, her touch more stimulating than a little blue pill.

Just like that I forgot I might be a wanted man.

I asked, "You sure?"

Lola kissed me, soft and easy, at first awkward, as if being watched made her uneasy, then she loosened up, focused on me, forgot about the other passenger on this ride.

"I've never done anything like this, Gideon. Never did anything . . . wild."

We kissed some more.

I said, "This is your chance to let go."

"Always wanted to . . . to . . . let go. Try something new. And different."

"Yeah."

"So hurry up before I come to my senses and change my mind."

We smiled and I undressed her. Had her naked in a matter of seconds. She had a nice body, a frame she wasn't ashamed of. I touched her skin and she shivered with ecstasy. Now my touch had become electric. Or maybe Mrs. Jones's eyes were the source of her stimulation. Lola was wide-awake. Nipples hard. Her kiss intense. This excited her more than what we had done before. Mrs. Jones moved to the other side of the room. I didn't watch her, just felt her trying to find a good place to stand, the right place to fulfill the fantasy she had in her mind.

Mrs. Jones wanted to experience the joys of Lola through me.

My hand went between Lola's legs. Infinite wetness soaked my fingers. She was ready.

Maybe this excited her more than it did Mrs. Jones.

Lola got on the bed. Again she was nervous. I went to Lola, kissed her. Mrs. Jones closed the curtains, moved to the radio. Corinne Bailey Rae whispered the sweetest song.

While I gave Lola my tongue, Mrs. Jones sat on the side of the room, legs crossed, hands on her knees, back straight, watching without shame, squirming, licking her own lips.

"Taste her, Gideon."

Lola trembled. "This is crazy."

My eyes went to Mrs. Jones's sensual smile.

Mrs. Jones smirked. "I dare you."

I went to my knees, my tongue gliding between Lola's legs. I was sucking, nibbling, making figure eights, tasting Lola. She was as sweet as blackberry jam. I held her ass so I could move my tongue deeper, then backed away, became a tiger lapping at the sweetest milk.

Mrs. Jones whispered, "You are so good at that Gideon. That's it. Find the center of her unhappiness, lick it away, take her to that wonderful place, let me see you give her joy."

Lola moaned, she moaned deep, her body shaking, her hands holding my face, pulling me deeper into her vagina, getting turned on by the slurping that came from between her legs.

Lola cursed and cursed and cursed.

Mrs. Jones moaned, "My God, my God, my God."

I moved Lola to the red chair, her back to me, her knees sinking into the cushion, offering me ecstasy with hesitation. Eyes closed, she moved her ass side to side, subtle movements of anticipation. I stared at Mrs. Jones. She smiled. I moved toward Lola, eased toward her paradise. Rain was falling pretty hard, had a steady rhythm, those skies dark and gray.

The man with the broken nose marched back into my mind.

Had to shake him out of my thoughts.

Lola said, "You're right, Mrs. Jones."

"About what?"

"What you said in the bathroom. You're right."

"It's true. We're supposed to be together. All of us."

"You're supposed to be here, Mrs. Jones."

"I don't think it was by chance I ended up sitting with both of you on the plane. This is by design. After what you've gone through . . . after what I've gone through . . . this is supposed to be."

"Yeah. This is supposed to be."

"I feel the same way, Lola."

"We're supposed to help each other. We're supposed to comfort and heal each other. We're supposed to help each other move from despair to ecstasy. Let's have pleasure."

"We're supposed to give each other happy endings."

I was behind Lola, my fingers tracing her skin. Wanted her to know I was there. She kept moving, biting her lip, moving her head to one side. I touched her butt, spread her cheeks, and let my finger play with her. She moaned, closed her eyes tight, wiggled. I put my hardness up against her, moved it up and down, felt how wet she was. She moaned again. The heat from her fleshy folds, so nice. I stretched her open a little at a time, felt her body change, heard her breathing change from smooth to desperate and choppy, felt her turn into a raging fire.

Then I was sliding inside her bliss, massaging her insides with my hardness.

My breathing went choppy and I forgot about the world outside this room.

Lola's breathing was rugged inhales followed by choppy exhales.

Mrs. Jones's breathing owned the same sensual and staccato rhythm.

My eyes went to Mrs. Jones.

She licked her lips and moaned like she was in ecstasy.

Her moans danced with our moans, those moans connecting us all.

We were all in those places. Wounded. Pain. Despair. Ecstasy.

My damp skin was slapping against Lola, my balls hitting her clit. Hitting it steady. Then slowing down when it started feeling too good. Squeezing her ass, a round ass that was soft the way a woman's ass should be. Moving my hands to her waist, I eased her back into me over and over. Measuring. Stroking. Going deep. Hitting her skin so hard the chair moved. She held the arms of the chair with a tight grip. Then my hands were on her shoulders. Riding hard.

Lola released a moan that was made of pure gold.

I gave her the sweetest torture. Then I slowed down, tried to control the fire.

I changed positions, stood up, picked Lola up, surprised her with my strength when I flipped her upside down, stood and held her vagina to my face, her hair falling, lying on my feet.

"Oh, God . . . don't drop me . . . don't drop . . . don't . . . don't stop . . . that feels so damn good."

She relaxed, gave me her trust, her golden moans now the softest song.

Mrs. Jones made an orgasmic sound. Sounded like Mrs. Jones was about to explode.

I ate Lola out that way, ate her good and slapped her ass. First Lola's hand found my penis, then she stroked me. Lola took me in her mouth. I wasn't ready for that good feeling. Wasn't prepared for that blessed light she created while she sucked the tip of my erection. I held her firm, all of that sweet body upside down, bouncing her up and down, sucking her button, sucking her good. She kept me in her mouth, moaned, and we worked that vertical sixty-nine.

Her legs tightened around my neck.

Lola jerked. "Oh, God . . . gonna come."

I moved Lola to the bed.

Again I looked toward Mrs. Jones. Her mouth was wide-open. Her nipples erect.

Her breathing had caught in her throat like she was intimidated and impressed.

I smiled at Mrs. Jones. "Take your clothes off."

She blinked out of her amazement. "No . . . no . . . I'm . . . I'm just going to watch."

"I'm daring you."

"Don't dare me."

"I dare you. Take your clothes off."

Mrs. Jones started undressing, nervousness and excitement in her eyes.

Corinne sang, her voice like a butterfly in flight, graceful, innocent, and sensuous.

I was on top of Lola, moving slow, doing it the way people did it in real life, her legs wrapped around my back, her mouth on my neck, gasping and sucking my skin, her hands in the small of my back, then her choppy breath resting between my neck and collarbone.

Lola whispered, "Never in my life. Never did anything . . . like this."

I don't know who looked across the room first, me or Lola, but my sex-blurred vision focused on the red curtains, then came down to the beautiful woman sitting on the sofa, the naked woman who was watching us in silence, her wedding ring sparking in the vague light.

Lola moaned, her arms outstretched, her voice floating. "Swear to God. I've never done anything like this before."

I turned Lola on her stomach, kept her legs closed, straddled her, crawled inside that hot and wet slice of heaven, my eyes on Mrs. Jones as I gave Lola steady, even strokes.

Mrs. Jones squeezed her thighs tight, did that over and over.

Lola cursed me. Growled. "My spot . . . you hitting my spot . . . you're all on my spot."

She bit her lips, stopped fighting what she was feeling, let her back arch, and she came, a long, drawn-out orgasm, her moans never-ending.

Mrs. Jones whispered, "Oh, that is so beautiful."

My strokes remained steady.

Lola was crying, tears rolling down her face, moaning in short spurts, each moan louder than before, as if being watched took her to a new level.

I looked toward Mrs. Jones.

I told her, "Come here."

She shook her head.

I said, "Come try something different."

"I just want to watch."

Mrs. Jones swallowed, looked nervous.

Lola was moaning, on the edges of another orgasm.

I said, "Come here, Mrs. Jones. Come touch Lola."

Mrs. Jones didn't move. Her breathing shut down. Her mouth partially open.

I whispered, "I dare you."

"Don't ever dare me."

"Come get some of this. I dare you."

"Don't dare me, Gideon."

"I fucking dare you."

Six

better than chocolate

I was riding Lola like I was on I-285 going north.

Lola cringed like she wanted to cry. Lost it. Grabbed sheets. Grabbed pillows. Threw pillows out the way. Grabbed at me. Quivered. Kept struggling to breathe.

I repeated, "I fucking dare you, Mrs. Jones."

Mrs. Jones came to us, got on the bed, the mattress sinking under her weight.

I whispered, "Kiss me."

Mrs. Jones's breath caught in her chest, then she leaned in, brought her tongue to mine.

We unified, became the unholy trinity.

Mrs. Jones moved from me, rested on her back, legs together, but moving like they wanted to open. I left Lola, kissed Mrs. Jones on her lips, her hands coaxing my mouth to her breasts, then her hands asking me to go lower. I went down on her, tasted her flavors, Lola off to the side, singing, becoming the voyeur, doing the same thing Mrs. Jones had been doing before.

Mrs. Jones whispered, "Lola . . . is this okay?"

Lola moaned, glowed like she was being baptized under a truer light.

"Lola . . . are you okay with this?"

Lola arched her back, struggled to breathe.

While I tongue-praised Mrs. Jones, she let out soft sounds and brushed her face against Lola's skin, her long braids falling across Lola's full breasts, across her taut nipples. She petted Lola. Held her, and two lovers became three. Mrs. Jones soothed Lola as she was being soothed. Again Lola was releasing golden moans and crying. Swimming in pleasure.

Mrs. Jones softened her tone. "Lola . . . let me . . . do something different . . . let me taste you."

Lola panted, struggled to move, crawled toward Mrs. Jones's face, a slow crawl filled with uncertainty and curiosity, moved as fast as an iceberg, then paused at Mrs. Jones's breasts.

Lola straddled Mrs. Jones right above her belly.

I watched.

Lola took in deep, strong breaths as she touched Mrs. Jones's breasts.

Lola whispered, "I'm not a Joanne."

"What you mean?"

"I'm not lesbian or nothing like that."

"Neither am I." Mrs. Jones rode out a long moan, cooed as the good feeling carried her away, then managed to find enough wind to whisper, "I'm just curious. I'm not a Joanne."

"I love dick."

"Me too. Can't live without it."

"I love dick more than I love my mama's hot-water corn bread."

They laughed.

Lola played with Mrs. Jones's braids, eased closer to her face.

Lola whispered, "So we're just trying something new."

"Consenting adults having fun."

"I ain't . . . ain't . . . never . . . never done this before."

"It's up to you, Lola." Mrs. Jones moved with my tongue, made generous sounds as her fingers grazed Lola's legs. "Up to you. Would you like to be bold and try something different?"

"Maybe." Lola sang like a bird in flight. "Depends."

Mrs. Jones rode her own moan. "I'm listening."

"As long as what happens in Europe . . ."

"Stays in Europe."

I stopped licking Mrs. Jones, my fingers now taking the place of my tongue. I watched them. I'd fallen away from their conversation, let it progress without my involvement.

I remained quiet, knew when to talk and when to shut the fuck up.

"You're beautiful, Mrs. Jones."

"You are too."

"Love your breasts."

"Had them done."

"They're awesome."

"Squeeze them for me. Pinch my nipples."

Lola's hands covered Mrs. Jones's breasts; Mrs. Jones touched Lola's backside. Curiosity was in Lola's eyes. The same curiosity that lived in Mrs. Jones's eyes. Mrs. Jones touched Lola again, rubbed Lola in a gentle way, did that in a way that said now was the time to try new things.

Lola bit her lip, gave me half a smile, then looked at Mrs. Jones, massaged those perfect breasts, swallowed, and closed her eyes. I moved away and Lola straddled Mrs. Jones, sat across her stomach, then Lola eased her warmth and wetness toward Mrs. Jones's tongue.

I became the voyeur.

It was a slow, erotic journey, the ultimate foreplay, watching Lola move her fleshy folds toward the tongue of a woman who was starved for the touch of a beautiful woman. Lola sat there, caught her breath, spoke to God, closed her eyes, and set free a shudder of amazement that spoke in volumes, a shudder that said she had crossed the line, releasing short, flat moans, soft yelps that went on and on like it was stream of consciousness, as she moved up and down.

Lola opened her eyes, her breathing tight, her eyes glossed over. She whispered, "Gideon."

"I'm right here."

"Come here . . . touch me . . . I need to . . . feel . . . your hands . . . on me . . . please . . . touch me."

I did.

She gazed at me as if she were imagining that she was on top of me.

Melodies and countermelodies flooded the room. Lola was

moving toward orgasm and avoiding bliss at the same time. She was so deep in pleasure she was drowning.

Lola looked me in my eyes and repeated, "Gideon."

"Lola, you okay?"

"Oh . . . my . . . God."

Lola moved against Mrs. Jones while she sucked my tongue. Lola had risen to the edges of nirvana. When she slowed down, when the hurricane ended, I moved away from Lola.

I spread Mrs. Jones's legs, entered her that way, with Lola riding the waves of her storm, staring at me, crying one long tear. Lola twitched like hot wax was being dropped on her flesh. My spine tingled. Then Lola turned around, faced me. She was still riding Mrs. Jones's face as she stared in my eyes. Like she was imagining I was the one giving her oral pleasure. I imagined I was inside Lola. I imagined I was living inside Lola. I strained, set free my own coarse moans that sounded as attractive as a car door scraping against a curb.

Mrs. Jones was multitasking, moving with me, pleasing Lola.

Lola said my name, reached for me, gave an erotic glare that almost took me over the edge, made my legs tense. Mrs. Jones bucked, moved against me, did that like she wanted me to come. Blood rushed between my legs, added girth and strength to that rigid part of me.

My breathing shortened. That good feeling almost got out of control, but I stopped, pulled out of Mrs. Jones, backed away, saved it, didn't want to blow my load and get sidelined.

I changed position.

Mrs. Jones stopped.

Lola shifted away, more like fell away, panting, still on fire.

I went to Lola, was on my back with her straddling my face, looking down on me, watching me pick up where Mrs. Jones had left off. Lola was so turned on, so weak, would do anything at that point. Mrs. Jones watched us, then crawled to me, and while I savored Lola, Mrs. Jones mounted me, rode me, her hands coming around, squeezing Lola's breasts.

We moaned and set free rugged sounds like were we in the same out-of-tune choir.

We were no longer in control.

What we were doing had taken on a life of its own.

Lola's moans became vicious. She came long, came hard.

Then Lola fell away from me, collapsed on the bed, straining like she was suffocating.

Mrs. Jones kept riding me. Her rise and fall became devastating. She fucked me and she came, sucking my tongue, moaning, her body trembling, legs tensing, toes curling, keen and short howls in her throat, her nails in my back, bucking like a wild stallion.

Lola was groaning, wiping sweat from her face.

I rode Mrs. Jones until she told me she was coming again.

Lola moaned, "I want to watch."

"*I'm coming*," Mrs. Jones sang and moaned. "*God, I'm coming.*"

"I want to watch, Mrs. Jones."

"*Coming . . . hard . . . shit.*"

Mrs. Jones tensed her face, raised her head, and looked at Lola.

Mrs. Jones's orgasm took her to the mattress, made her lie next to us, trembling, cursing.

Lola crawled over and took me in her mouth, sucked me for a moment, then she eased on top of me. She moved in ways that should be illegal, each stroke so damn smooth.

Mrs. Jones ran her fingers over my skin, over Lola's flesh, then got behind Lola.

While Lola rode me, Mrs. Jones's hands were touching her, rubbing her skin slow and easy. Lola's breathing grew short, those soft moans growing coarse. Again her legs stiffened.

I was almost there, fighting with my pleasure, losing that battle. Then.

Mrs. Jones told Lola to lift up off me.

Mrs. Jones took me out of Lola's vagina . . . eased me inside her mouth . . . put me back inside Lola . . . Lola couldn't stand the teasing anymore . . . hiked her ass up toward my face.

I tasted heaven.

Mrs. Jones mounted me, moved like she wanted victory, wanted to make me come.

I came grunting, that river rushing out of me as I held on to

Lola, pleasing her with my tongue. Then, as I came, Lola twitched, tensed, wailed, rode the final waves of her own orgasm.

Lola fell away from me, struggling to breathe. I held on to Mrs. Jones's hips, my chest rising and falling as I searched for air. Mrs. Jones brought her mouth to mine, sucked the flavor away from my tongue. Then we disconnected, and she moved her mouth to my fading erection, cleansed me with her tongue. I held the sheets, jerked and moaned, my blurry vision struggling to focus on Lola. Lola was panting, watching Mrs. Jones, studying the master, learning.

Lola wiped sweat from her face, touched her breasts. So damn beautiful.

My blurry eyes searched for Mrs. Jones. She was sprawled out, legs twitching.

She crawled to the edge of the bed, lay on her side, eyes toward the red curtains.

Nobody moved. Nobody talked.

Nothing shared now but rough breathing.

Then deep breathing.

Then sleep.

Something banged in the hallway. Right outside the door to the hotel room.

That violent noise caused me to wake with a start.

The door opened faster than I could move.

I was on my feet, everything out of focus, hands in fists. Had to get to my gun.

I expected to see him, the man with the broken nose.

Two European women came inside, mops and towels in their hands.

They saw me standing up butt naked, manhood swinging, two naked women in my bed, all of us looking like naked warriors at the end of an orgy. The housekeepers yelped and rushed out of the room; what sounded like apologies followed, those apologies followed by giggles.

Heart was beating strong and fast. Hands had become clammy just like that.

Glad I didn't make it to my gun before I had my senses.

That could've been ugly.

I crawled back in the bed.

I stayed in the middle, on my stomach. Lola was on the side nearest the bathroom. Mrs. Jones was still on her left side, her back to me, facing the heavy red curtains.

I stared at the ceiling.

Legs moving like I had restless-leg syndrome.

Like I was running. I was chasing.

My brain was on fire. Electrical synapses firing up my cerebral cortex, mental images coming at me so fast. In my mind I was running hard, chasing him toward Lancaster Gate.

My mind kept replaying that film starring me and the man with the broken nose.

Seven

naked souls

Lola was the first to move.

She crawled out of the bed. Stretched. Then she staggered inside
the toilet, came back with warm towels, wiped me down. Mrs. Jones
rolled over, struggled to get to her feet, staggered to the dresser, and
brought me and Lola cups of water. It took all of my energy to raise
my head.

I sipped, thanked her, and closed my eyes.

Lola put the DO NOT DISTURB sign on the door and crawled back
in the bed.

Angie Le Mar was on the radio, introducing another song. Mrs.
Jones turned off the music and yawned her way back to bed.

Lola eased out of the bed, went to the toilet, used it, washed her
hands, came back, eased under the covers, shifted around a bit,
rubbed up against me awhile, then stopped.

In a dreamy whisper, Lola asked Mrs. Jones, "You sleep or
what?"

Mrs. Jones shifted, turned around. "Or what. Not sleeping."

Outside the rain was coming down like my thoughts, not as hard
as before, now a drizzle.

Their warm bodies touching mine, my thoughts remained in a
cold, dark place.

Lola said, "Skin sticky. Need to shower."

"Yeah. Me too."

Lola sang my name.

I didn't move. Mrs. Jones ran her hand across my face.

Mrs. Jones whispered, "Wake up and give me an upside-down orgasm."

"You didn't get enough, Mrs. Jones?"

"I don't think I ever get enough."

"Me either."

They laughed.

Lola said, "His ass is knocked out."

"Typical."

"Can you wake the magic stick up?"

Mrs. Jones put her mouth on me, sucked me, stroked me, sucked me.

"Sorry, Lola. Mr. Happy is knocked out too."

"Knocked out like Tyson."

Their hands rubbed my skin, played with my lips, same with my limp penis.

More girlish chuckles.

My eyes looked closed, but were cracked enough for me to spy on them.

Mrs. Jones got up again, staggered toward the bathroom door. Soft giggles from Lola. The bathroom door opened. Lola made it to her feet, followed Mrs. Jones's path. Both moved around the bathroom like they were team leaders of a naturist community, as if being naked was the norm and clothing what God had given them was an abomination, strolling around that small space like they were Eves in search of Adam. Lola's pubic triangle as bare as it was when she was born. Mrs. Jones had a thin line of hair, like a landing strip, a guide to the grotto of pleasure.

Lola asked, "Mrs. Jones . . . will you ever get married?"

"I am married. Legally. Not emotionally. Not spiritually. Just bound by man's law."

"I mean after your divorce is over. Think you'll ever get married again?"

"Let me get out of this fire before you offer me another match."

Lola laughed. "I hear you."

"Why you ask?"

"After this breakup, not sure if I want to ever have a boyfriend again, you know?"

"So you flew all the way to London and found out your man was—"

"Ain't that some shit, Mrs. Jones. Ain't that some shit."

They fell into a pool of silence.

Lola coughed, moved around, said, "You said you have a daughter."

"Yes." Mrs. Jones stretched. "She's incarcerated."

"*Get out.*"

"She . . . she refuses to see me. Blames me for everything wrong in her life. A wall of hate exists between us. I had to leave her. Had to or I would've gone insane. So much had happened. Hanging on to bad things, trying to change people, it's toxic. Maybe I'm already insane, that's how I feel some days, after enduring so much. Feels like I'm already insane."

"What happened?"

"I don't want to talk about it, Lola."

"I'm sorry, Mrs. Jones."

"I haven't cried for a few hours. Don't want to cry, not right now."

"Me either. Let's just chill out and let the skies do all the crying for a little while."

There was noise outside the door again.

I jumped. Listened. It was the housekeepers, chatting and walking down the hallway.

The shower came on.

I jumped again.

It was a struggle, but I opened my eyes and saw the frosted door had been closed behind them. My backpack was on the floor. I made it to my feet, went over to my gear. Took out a BC Powder. Downed the fine particles dry, let my saliva wash that analgesic down my throat.

The nine I had, I took it out of the safe, put in the backpack, put the backpack under the desk, left it hidden in plain sight. I went to the front door and looked out the peephole, saw an empty hallway. I needed to go, but I didn't have anyplace to go hole up, didn't have a safe house.

I was awake but I was tired. Mind on fire while I was dead on my feet.

Leaving this exhausted, leaving with my nuts drained, leaving when I was weak and my mind wasn't sharp, could cost me my life. And the jet lag, the long day I'd had, that didn't help.

I went back to the bed, got underneath the covers, fetal position, a child back inside the womb. A while later I turned on my side, pulled a pillow between my legs, and tried to sleep.

The bathroom door opened. Steam, soft words, and girlish laughter came out. And the smells came to me. The scent of peaches and strawberries, maybe ocean breeze.

Just like that the room smelled damn sensual.

I looked at those women. Mrs. Jones was at the counter cleaning her face. Lola was getting out of the shower, her hair pulled back, reaching for a towel. Then she stood next to Mrs. Jones drying off. Damp, naked asses and bare breasts, long, flowing hair.

Lola bumped Mrs. Jones and laughed. "I did a three-way. I actually did a three-way."

"Always wondered what that experience would be like."

"That . . . is this . . . was that your first time?"

"Yes. And. That. Was. Awesome. You sure that was your first time?"

Lola let her hair down, picked up a comb. "Hell yeah."

Lola hummed, sang some nice song about lighting candles.

When Lola stopped singing, she chuckled. "I had an upside-down orgasm."

"That looked wicked."

"You have no idea. That shit was wicked."

"Upside down." Mrs. Jones was hand-combing her braids. "Would love to try that."

"Upside down. You believe that shit? Never in my life . . . came upside down."

"That looked intense." Mrs. Jones chuckled. "Gideon is a friggin' animal."

"Hell, you were pretty wild yourself. Scared me for a minute. I'm serious. You rock big-time. When you were giving Gideon the oral sex, your technique . . . damn . . . off the hook."

"Fellatio is my specialty. I *love* doing that. Just comes naturally for me."

"Comes naturally. You got jokes."

Mrs. Jones laughed.

Once again I heard noises in the hallway. Again I jumped and looked at the door.

Lola came out into the bedroom, tiptoed around four hundred pounds of luggage, grabbed a bottle of something, then tiptoed back inside the bathroom.

Mrs. Jones whispered, "Is that Aveeno? I love Aveeno. I forgot to buy lotion."

"Help yourself. Aveeno. Nivea. I have plenty of lotion."

"Thanks, Lola."

"What was I saying? Oh, yeah. For real. You should teach a master's blow-job class."

"Oh, please. The way you move that backside of yours, good Lord."

"Not like you. I was following your lead, like a freshman and you were like a Ph.D."

"What I just did . . . that surprised me as well."

"Maybe if I could've let go like that I wouldn't be breaking up with . . . that son of a bitch."

"Baby, I'm that good, willing to think outside the box, and I'm still getting a divorce."

"Good point."

They laughed as they put on lotion, their laughter now sounding lethargic, weighty.

Lola said, "You worked me too, Mrs. Jones. You gave me head . . . like . . . like . . . damn."

"That was my first time doing that."

"You lie. No way."

"Something about you, Lola. I felt safe. Safe enough to . . . to . . . do something different."

"Something about you too. Wanted to try . . . see what it was like . . . you made it feel and look and sound so damn good . . . I wanted to . . . wanted to reciprocate and give you head too."

Mrs. Jones yawned again. "Why didn't you?"

"It was feeling so good. You and Gideon. You guys are like a damn tag team."

"Would you have been more comfortable if we were alone?"

"Maybe. But . . . nah . . . not sure about that . . . liked a man being here."

"Me too. Kept it from feeling, what did you call it? *Joanne?*"

"I love the way a man feels. His skin. His hair. How he opens me up. Nothing compares to the way a man feels inside me. Love the way a man stretches me open."

"Me too, Lola. Me too. If only my husband had appreciated what I have to offer."

"Guess since I'm in London . . . since that son of a bitch is laid up with some other bitch . . . I mean . . . shit . . . I'm single now . . . I can do what the fuck I want . . . so why not try something different?"

"Same here."

"Having a man in the room . . . kept it from feeling . . . too . . . too . . . too *rainbow flagish.*"

Lola Mack claimed she was an actress. And a masseuse.

Mrs. Jones claimed that she was an attorney. Her marriage broken beyond repair.

The only thing I knew for sure was that I was a contract killer.

My occupation had a short life expectancy.

Or the expectancy of long jail time with no chance of parole.

I should've packed up and left before they finished showering.

I could've been on the tube before they realized I was gone.

Mrs. Jones leaned out, a towel wrapped around her body. Her braids hung down over her skin, stopped right above the darkness on her nipples. She'd had work done on her breasts. Expensive work that looked both natural and wonderful. Her breasts were nice, full, I'd even say powerful, and the way her legs flowed into her hips and ass, how every part of her body went together, that arrangement was priceless. She was beautiful. So fucking beautiful.

I sat up, inhaled the erotic scents, and stared at her.

The woman who had been dressed in black.

The woman whose marriage was irretrievably broken.

A woman who wanted pleasure to soothe her broken heart.

Mrs. Jones grinned at me. "You're awake."

I nodded.

She winked at me, then whispered, "See what happens when you dare me?"

I stared her down.

I needed to leave her. Needed to leave Lola.

I needed to get the fuck out of here right now.

Needed to go find a man who may have been sent to kill me.

But when I left this room, all of this would become a fading memory.

The warm room. The soft bed. The taming smells. The beautiful women.

I didn't want to leave this castle in the sky.

Wasn't ready to deal with Violence and Death.

Nothing but hell was waiting for me outside of this room.

The hotel room was small, it was crowded, but this hotel room was Paradise.

I wasn't ready to leave Paradise.

Mrs. Jones asked, "What's wrong?"

I stood up.

Her voice trembled. "Why are you frowning at me like that?"

I motioned toward Mrs. Jones, whispered, told her to come to me.

She shook her head, her long braids moving side to side.

In a soft and deadly voice I whispered, "I dare you."

Mrs. Jones was dying.

She was dying a thousand little deaths, each death accompanied by its own moan.

I had her in my arms, upside down, her braids swinging and tickling my legs as I put my tongue deep inside her well of goodness.

She was moaning and coming, talking to God like it was first service on Easter Sunday.

Lola sat on the edge of the bed and watched. "Now that's what I'm talking about."

Blood rushing to her head as she came, Mrs. Jones held on,

tightened her legs around my face, shuddered and wailed and sang like she was taking the short route to heaven; Lola stood up and clapped her hands like thunder, her breasts bouncing as she jumped and applauded.

I eased Mrs. Jones down, her braided hair hanging wild and free, laid her on the bed, left her trembling, the aftershocks from her orgasm trembling up and down her skin.

Lola was staring at me, licking her lips. My breath caught in my throat.

I whispered, "Lola."

"What? Why do I feel like I'm in trouble? Why are you looking at me like that?"

"Open your legs."

She swallowed, moved closer to the headboard, those toned legs easing apart.

She shuddered as I headed toward that sliver of pinkness.

I paused.

Paused and remembered how I had made love to Arizona in New York, about how I had tried to please her when we were in North Carolina at Chapel Hill.

I imagined Arizona.

I licked Lola a few times, got her moaning, then pulled away, took her foot in my hand, sucked her toes, licked her legs, eased my tongue up her sweet-smelling skin, licked away the peaches and strawberries, then licked around her vagina, let my tongue pass back and forth, then stopped, left her squirming. I breathed on her pussy for a while, let her know I was there, let her feel pleasure lapping at her door. I gave her the tip of my tongue. Then gave her more. I eased a finger inside her, kept that shallow, and my anxious tongue followed. Lola was squeezing her breasts, pulling at her breasts, long pulls that ended with her pinching her own nipples.

While I ate Lola out, Mrs. Jones shifted around, did her best to recover, still moaning, her skin on fire as she touched me and maneuvered her mouth across my skin, her tongue moving up my back, across my ass, over my thighs. She took the heat inside her mouth toward my groin, did that to me as I licked figure eights on Lola's fleshy folds.

Mrs. Jones took me in her mouth, sucked me slow and easy.

Then Mrs. Jones kissed her way down my leg, did the same to me as I had done to Lola, and sucked my toes . . . that aroused me more . . . got me harder . . . she licked my toes like she was sucking ten little penises . . . licking and suckling each toe while I twitched and licked and sucked on Lola. Mrs. Jones was . . . swallowing my toes whole . . . her tongue going up the sides . . . then in between each toe . . . the fire Mrs. Jones stirred inside me was given to Lola in return.

Lola moaned. I had hit her spot, a spot that I refused to leave. She closed her eyes tight, held her breasts, and made pre-orgasmic faces. One of Lola's hands came to me, started rubbing my head; her other hand came to my face, pulled me deeper between her legs, and I gave her more tongue, then her hands moved to my shoulders, her touch setting me on fire.

I ate her like she was better than chocolate.

Mrs. Jones took my erection in her mouth again, sucked smooth and easy. We were like that, slow and easy, moaning and moving around each other, touching each other, three cats lapping milk under a gray sunrise. Every lick took us closer to nirvana, but we kept it steady, no rush to reach our final destination, just ride that road of pleasure until, once again, the heat became too much to bear, nerves were ablaze, moans became deep and spiritual.

Then it became too much to bear.

We grabbed and licked and sucked all we could grab and lick and suck. We fucked until the covers fell off the bed, until the pillows were on the floor. We fucked until fucking took on its own life, fucked until everything spun out of control, fucked until what was slow and easy had given in to its own urgency, until lovemaking was long behind and hard fucking was all we could do, and that fucking was brutal, that brutality shared between us all, shared in the way Mrs. Jones sucked me and stroked me, shared in the way Lola's nails dug into my flesh and scarred me.

Lola came and pushed me away, pushed me like she couldn't take any more.

I let Lola get away and grabbed Mrs. Jones, made her get on her knees, ass up high, facedown in the mattress, and I slapped her backside, made her spread her cheeks, and I fucked her without mercy, fucked her and looked Lola in her eyes, fucked Mrs. Jones and panted like I was fucking Lola, closed my eyes and held her hips, yanked her back into me, fucked Mrs. Jones with force, that force throwing Mrs. Jones into the flames of another wicked orgasm.

Lola moaned, "Oh, my God."

I slowed down, opened my eyes.

Lola was squeezing her breast with one hand, touching herself with the other, first squeezing her pussy real tight on her forefinger, then stroking her clit hard and fast.

Lola closed her eyes, bit her bottom lip, cringed like she was close to coming.

Mrs. Jones was coming.

Mrs. Jones's moans echoed, made her sound like a one-woman choir, her orgasm loud and long. Her orgasm took her to the mattress, took away all of her energy, left her powerless.

It was too much for her.

She needed a moment to recover.

My eyes went to Lola. To the pre-orgasmic frown on her face. She was watching, still touching her breasts with one hand, the other hand between her legs, her finger moving up and down, pinching the pinkness as she shifted side to side, her long hair wild, shadowing her face.

Lola whispered, "Come here."

"You want me to fuck you like that?"

She nodded.

I went to her, sucked the juices off her fingers, then turned Lola over, put her body across Mrs. Jones's leg. Lola's back arched, her ass rose in the air.

Lola was wet. So damn wet. I slipped deep inside her, went deep.

Lola moaned, grabbed the sheets, moved against me, and I almost lost control. Mrs. Jones crawled out of the way, moved like an injured solider leaving the battlefield. Lola put her hands against the headboard, pushed back, and bucked into me, swerved her ass in a wicked rhythm that stirred me and amazed me all at once. She pushed back into me hard.

I had to adjust my position and focus to keep up with her.

My orgasm was rising, that pleasure building each time Lola pushed back into me, tingles creeping across my skin each time her skin slapped into mine, and I fucked her back the same way she fucked me, fucked her hard and fast, then I let go, sped up, double-timed, and stroked like I wanted to get that feeling out of me.

Lola came. I was going deep, tried to come with her. But I couldn't get there.

Dammit, I couldn't get there with her. I wanted to come on her orgasm so bad.

She moved like she was out of control, whined, growled, and pushed back into me.

I growled and fucked her.

I sweated, closed my eyes, gritted my teeth, and did my best to come.

My orgasm was stubborn. It was at the door but refused to leave my body. My orgasm teased me and drove me mad. But I refused to let it go back the other way. I stroked hard.

"Come for me, baby," Lola sang. "That's it, get your nut. Get it, baby. Get that nut. Fuck this pussy however you need to fuck me to come. Fuck me so you can come. Fuck me like that."

Her wild tone and vulgar words excited me. Her words pulled me closer to the edge.

I was getting harder with each stroke. But I didn't come.

Body on fire. Every muscle excited and spent. Penis throbbing for relief.

This road to pleasure was filled with agony.

I slowed down for a moment, slowed down so I could catch my breath.

Lola asked, "You come?"

I shook my head.

I held myself deep inside Lola and she squeezed her vaginal walls tight on me . . . she kept squeezing . . . then letting go . . . squeezing . . . holding me tighter than a business handshake . . . then letting go . . . did that over and over . . . showed me she was in control of her vaginal muscles.

Lola's energy moved through me.

She moaned, "Don't move, baby. Don't move. Keep it right there."

She began to quiver, a shock wave tore through her body. I felt it. Felt her coming. Felt the orgasm that almost took Lola to her belly. I held her up. Her orgasm vibrating through me.

Mrs. Jones came over, massaged my balls, did that nice and easy.

While Lola came in magnificent ripples, Mrs. Jones stirred my juices.

I was so excited, too excited.

Lola caught her breath, began moving against me once again.

She asked, "You come?"

"Not yet."

Lola squeezed her vagina again. Released the heat that surrounded my member.

Mrs. Jones massaged me, while Lola did her thing.

I concentrated. Focused on coming. Ached to come. But I still couldn't come.

Mrs. Jones stopped massaging my balls, moved away, never took her eyes off us.

I sped up.

Lola stopped squeezing and releasing, moved with me, gave it to me like I gave it to her.

Then Lola was in overdrive, trying to make me get my nut.

Or trying to come again.

I couldn't tell which.

Either way I was angry, on fire, determined to keep up with Lola's pace.

I couldn't, not the way she was bumping back into me.

"Come for me, baby, come for me, get that nut, come on and come for me."

I reached across the bed, grabbed the towel that had been wrapped around Mrs. Jones's body, then reached around Lola's stomach, put that towel under her, adjusted it until it was around her waist like it was a horse's rein, held both ends of that towel tight, and I rode her, yanking on the towel, pulling her back into me over and over, our skin colliding hard.

Lola bucked against each of my thrusts, growled, made noises like I was killing her.

If she had died, I wouldn't have stopped, not until I was done.

I gritted my teeth, closed my eyes, rode Lola like I was a cowboy chasing my orgasm. Then it was in sight, just on the horizon. I sped up, got so close to coming, tensed and felt it at the tip of my penis, and grunted loud. My orgasm would be an explosion that rose from deep inside me. But that explosion refused to come. I was close. So damn close to getting this violence out of my body. I strained to get every drop out of me, strained and stroked and pounded Lola as my dick went so deep my testicles slapped her skin over and over.

I came holding the towel to keep her from getting away, yanking her back into me, I came stroking her as deep and hard as I could, then, when the orgasm was at its peak, I grunted and dropped the towel, grabbed her by the waist, slapped her ass, squeezed her ass, held on to her ass like it was a life preserver, grunted and pounded her with all I had from shaft to balls.

The orgasm hit me with force, rose from someplace deep inside me, a place filled with hurt. Felt like every part of my body was shaking, trembling violently. I stroked Lola hard. She looked back at me, fear in her eyes, but her words telling me not to stop. The fear I had grabbed me, held me, reminded me of when I was a boy in Montreal, when I had been left alone, when I was terrified. My orgasm overwhelmed me, consumed me, and I made sounds like a wounded animal. I held Lola like I was afraid to let go, held her and struggled to get this out of my body.

I came groaning things in French, a language I hadn't used in a long time.

I came grabbing and moaning and grunting and thrusting.

I came pushing fear and bad memories out of my mind. I gritted my teeth, closed my eyes, released liquid stress, spewed out dark secrets, ejaculated pain, discharged my trepidation.

Lola kept telling me not to stop, kept demanding me not to slow down.

She was growling, pushing back into me hard, did that like she wanted every drop.

I gave her every memory.

Gave her every emotion I couldn't stand.

Then it was all gone.

When I slowed down, she kept rocking into me, did that until she realized the dance between us had changed from hip-hop to jazz, and she breathed heavily and slowed down, but didn't stop, moved into me and panted, caught her breath, pulled her hair from her damp face.

We didn't disconnect.

She moved like she wasn't done.

I kept moving slow, but I was moving steady.

Insanity had passed. We were back to being gentle.

I was still hard enough to make her moan. I kept moving in and out of her, our connection wet and slippery, kept moving until I was too soft, kept moving in and out.

"Oh . . . my God . . . baby, don't move . . . Gideon . . . right there . . . don't move."

Lola started shuddering and moaning as she came again, her orgasm not violent, just soft and beautiful. She kept wiggling against me, did that like she was determined to please me.

In that husky voice Lola asked, "You come?"

I caught my breath. "Yeah. You feel it?"

"Felt you . . . you . . . damn." She struggled to get her breath. "You were pulsating."

"So were you."

"I've never come that many times. Never in my life."

We looked at Mrs. Jones, Lola and I still breathing hard.

It was as if Lola and I were alone and Mrs. Jones magically appeared.

Naked, braids hanging down across her swollen breasts, Mrs. Jones was smiling.

I was so far gone I didn't know she was right there, right next to us, an arm's reach away.

Mrs. Jones clapped five times, like at the end of a play, and she closed her eyes.

I moved against Lola until I was so soft and spongy I slipped out of her.

Lola purred, "Are you through?"

"I need some rest."

"Me too. I need a hella lotta rest. I'm so satisfied right now."

I asked Mrs. Jones, "You okay?"

"I'm so damn good." She hummed. "I'm good for about a month."

Lola shook her head. "Shit, if I go another round, I'll be too tender to walk."

Mrs. Jones chuckled. "They'll have to take me out of here in a scooter."

Lola grunted, moved her hair from her face, said, "You and me both."

I collapsed between Lola and Mrs. Jones.

My manhood was aching, felt that part of me throb with every breath.

Mrs. Jones came to me, her mouth went to my penis, tasting, cleaning.

Shivers ran through my body as she licked me up and down.

My eyes went to Lola, her beauty blurred by what Mrs. Jones was doing to me right now.

Lola blushed, shook her head a little bit, her body language saying she was amazed.

My breathing choppy, I struggled to ask Lola, "You okay?"

She smiled. "Light-headed."

I felt a little embarrassed. The way I had come. How violent and out of control I had been with her. I moaned, glanced down toward Mrs. Jones, put my hand in her braids.

As I touched Mrs. Jones, I looked at Lola and asked, "Was that too rough?"

"Not at all. Not at all."

"You have a lot of energy."

"Gideon. Be honest. Did I do okay?"

"What do you mean?"

"You know . . . did I do okay . . . did I please you just then. Was I okay?"

I was surprised by her insecurities, but didn't let it show. Her man had taken another lover. Maybe part of her performance was more than revenge. Maybe she needed to prove to herself that she was a good lover, better than her rival. She had fucked like she needed to get rid of a pain that was deep inside her. Maybe that's why her orgasm was so hard, it was the unanchoring of her angst. I didn't know, could only guess what she was feeling deep inside.

I smiled, told her what she needed to hear, said, "You did great."

"You sure?"

"You were off the chains."

Lola grinned.

Another abrupt moan escaped me. I twitched. All of that being reaction to the licking and caressing that came from a warm mouth down below, Mrs. Jones working me like she was turned on by all she had seen, dealing with her needs, dealing with her marital rejection in her own way.

In a flash I thought about Arizona, how she rejected me, how she toyed with me.

She'd let me know that she didn't want me.

Didn't need me.

Lola gazed at me, that gaze tender, like she wanted and needed me right now.

I pulled Lola to me, sucked her breasts. And while I sucked Lola's breasts, Mrs. Jones remained between my legs, working me . . . swallowing me whole . . . holding me in her mouth.

Lola whispered, "Awesome. Man, this is awesome."

She was experiencing postsex emotions, the ones that made a woman tremble and cry.

I nodded, stopped sucking Lola's breasts, touched her nipples, kissed her on her neck.

Mrs. Jones was . . . deep-throating me . . . and stopping . . . deep-throating . . . stopping . . . sucking hard . . . making my penis pop when it left her mouth . . . did that over and over . . . kept me twitching.

I kept licking Lola's breasts . . . my hips moving against Mrs. Jones's motions . . . bumping the back of her throat. Mrs. Jones . . . she . . . she . . . she had me jerking, tiny spasms running through me.

Lola had tears in her eyes.

I was about to come again. Mrs. Jones felt my energy, she sped up, slowed down and worked me, sped up again, slowed again, her mouth tight, damn tight, so tight that orifice felt better than the way Lola had worked me when she squeezed and released her vaginal walls.

Lola put her hand up to my face. I kissed her fingers, then sucked each finger the same way Mrs. Jones was savoring me. Lola was still quivering, her breathing uneven and patchy.

Tears fell from her eyes.

Had to close my eyes. I was coming.

As I came, we kissed. It was an energetic and passionate kiss that went on until it became a spent kiss, until the storm passed and it turned into a lethargic kiss filled with exhaustion.

Mrs. Jones finished feeding on my energy, ran her hand over my skin as I shared tongue with Lola. At the same time Lola's hand went beyond me, touched Mrs. Jones where she could.

When our kiss was over, Lola whispered, "You are so awesome, Mrs. Jones."

Lola wiped her eyes, the dampness from her hand leaving a moist streak on her skin.

I couldn't talk. The place I was in refused to allow me to give the moment any words.

Mrs. Jones moved in closer, sucked my neck for a while, her hand rubbing Lola's flesh.

I kissed Mrs. Jones, tasted hints of my liquid energy in her mouth.

Lola rubbed me, her magical touch again creating sparks.

Kissing. Rubbing. Touching.

For a moment it felt like we were going to start up again.

Maybe they were trying to kill me. Maybe they were trying to kill me with passion.

But we cooled down, stopped kissing and touching, but stayed next to each other.

I was drained. My erection had subsided. The tingling had faded as well.

Lola reached across the bed, found the towel that had been wrapped around her waist a few minutes ago, dragged the towel between her legs, let it absorb my come as it drained out of her. Mrs. Jones grabbed the sheets from the floor, staggered as she spread them across us, then got back in bed, collapsed on the side nearest the window. I crawled over Lola, went to the door, made sure it was chained, made sure the dead bolt was on, then barely had enough energy to crawl back in the bed and pull a pillow over my head, my body feeling like it weighed ten tons.

In a flash my next thought was on the man with the broken nose.

The memory of being trailed through Soho, the memory of that foot chase didn't stick.

Not with me being sandwiched between two beautiful women.

Not with me being drained like this. Had never been this drained in my life.

We all moved around until we were comfortable, kept cooling skin against cooling skin in some way. Lola was behind me, spooning, her face against my back. Mrs. Jones's hand came to me, eased between my legs, held my penis in a gentle way. She didn't stroke it or massage it, just held it. Her touch felt nice. Lola felt nice. All of this felt nice. Felt damn nice. Exhaustion shackled me, closed my eyes, held me down as sleep eased across my drying skin.

"What's your goddamn name?"

I heard his heated voice in my dreams, a preacher whose wife had paid me to visit him in the middle of the night, heard the desperate tone from one of the many I had killed years ago.

"The wrong you're doing . . . stop doing evil while you can. Stop because one day somebody will come for you. One day what you do to other people, that will be done to you."

He screamed at me as bullets from a .38 whizzed by my head and hit the wall.

I felt everything I felt that night, felt pain in my kneecaps as I scampered across the frozen marble, my own screams echoing in my ears, felt the sting from the sweat in my eyes, even felt the throbbing in my lower back as I struggled to pull my .22 from its holster.

In my dream it was the same as it was on that cold night near Oakland University.

I was trapped against the wall, broken television behind me, Death in front of me.

Death was a preacher man the size of John Coffey, maybe larger.

Once again it was his .38 against my .22.

His anger and fear faced my fear and anger.

I was ready to shoot it out like we were at the O.K. Corral.

Only my .22 wouldn't fire this time, as I lay wounded from our battle, broken televisions and expensive artifacts all over the frozen marble floor, he had his .38 aimed at my head.

"*Satan will not defeat me. Not in my home. Not in the Lord's house.*"

Near me was his Bible. I stared at the cover and saw my name in golden letters.

Gideon.

I scowled up at the reverend, saw no mercy, no forgiveness in his eyes.

"*Our Father, which art in heaven, Hallowed be thy name . . .*"

He prayed and aimed at the center of my head.

"*Thy kingdom come.*"

Aimed at me the way I had aimed at a man named Midnight when I was seven years old.

"*Thy will be done, on earth, as it is in heaven.*"

In the midst of supplication, the reverend frowned and pulled the trigger.

I jerked awake, cold sweat dampening my naked skin.

I felt as cold as a Siberian wasteland. The same way I had felt that night.

The same way I had felt in North Carolina when I killed Midnight.

The same way I had felt in Montreal when I killed that man for my mother.

The same way I had felt many nights.

A silhouette lurked near the window, heavy red curtains still drawn, the room dark.

The shape of her body. The long hair. It was Arizona.

I said, "What the fuck are you doing here?"

The silhouette remained motionless. She wasn't hiding, but she wasn't moving.

I pulled the rumpled covers back, looked next to me. Lola was still in the bed, same position, her breathing deep. The other side of the bed was empty.

As my panic lessened, the shape remained, but her long braids came into focus.

It was Mrs. Jones. Not Arizona.

I wiped the chilled sweat from my brow and asked, "You okay?"

She was naked, arms folded across her breasts.

"The police are out there." Her voice was strained. *"So many police cars are out there."*

Half-awake, I rushed to my feet, went to the window, looked out at Bayley Street.

Mrs. Jones's small hands became big fists and she snapped, *"Make them go away."*

Outside of people walking in the rain, outside of black cabs and Mini Coopers, I saw nothing. I opened the curtains a little wider, looked past the flats toward Centre Pointe.

It was late afternoon, but the gray skies had the same hue as a cloud-covered sunset.

Mrs. Jones snapped, *"Stop them. Don't let them take her."*

"Where did the police go? Did they come in the building?"

"Don't let them take her. Do something."

Curtains open, the room awash with grayness, I faced Mrs. Jones. Sweat covered her skin too, more sweat than was on mine. She looked like she was living inside a sauna.

She snapped, *"Don't let them take our daughter."*

Her eyes were out of focus. She wasn't here. Not at all. She was a long way from here.

"Do something, dammit. Do not let them take my daughter away from me."

Mrs. Jones was nightmare-walking.

"This isn't right. Make them go away. Please. Make them go away."

When she stopped battling her demons and calmed down, I led her back to the bed.

She lay down, mumbled something that sounded like a prayer.

"The good that I wish I do not do, but the bad that I do not wish is what I practice."

I stared at the woman who had run away from all of her problems. Those problems were here with her, inside this room, invading her dreams, giving her walking nightmares.

Then her breathing thickened. She shifted until she was in the fetal position, sleeping like nothing had happened. Now I was wide-awake, watching over her like I wanted to protect her.

Nobody could run from themselves. Nobody could run from the things they'd done.

Cars were passing by the hotel. The people in the room above us kept taking hard steps across the wooden floors. Noises had me on edge. I was jumping every time the wind blew.

Lola stirred, then raised up on her elbows, scratched her backside, yawned.

She got up, moved like she was on autopilot, made another trip to the toilet, emptied sake from her bladder, washed her hands, got back in the bed. Just like that she was asleep again.

I couldn't stay here. Couldn't keep doing this over and over. I needed to keep moving.

I moved like a cat, went to the toilet, wiped sweat from my face and neck, wiped the dampness away from my back, splashed water on my face, went out and gathered my clothes, tiptoed over four hundred pounds of clothing, and was dressed in less than ten minutes.

I was at the door, troubles packed, hand on the knob, when I turned around.

Lola had my mind.

Her tears, the way she had cried, that moment stuck with me.

Lola was stranded. Had spent yesterday evening eating leftovers at Pizza Hut.

She'd spent her last dime to come to London to be with her lover, that love thrown back in her face. She'd ended up in this room, exorcising the demons from her by means of passion.

She was a good woman. Too good for the likes of me.

I took out some cash. At least two thousand British pounds. Didn't count it out. That money was put in an envelope and left near the television. That was for Lola. I put her name on the envelope. Then I looked at her. I had made her a promise. She was stranded.

Needed to get back home. That was more than enough. I kept my promises. Mrs. Jones had bought half of London, so I knew her pockets were fat and her credit was good. Lola had a different situation. She didn't have a dime to her name. Like I had been when a child, living on the streets of Montreal. My intentions were good, but when Lola opened that envelope she might be offended.

It didn't matter. Not in the long run.

I was the bastard son of a man who killed bulls with his bare hands.

My mother was a woman who traded pleasure for money.

I shouldn't have bedded Mrs. Jones.

Same for Lola.

Both deserved a better man than the kind I had become.

Then.

It hit me. A wave of conflicting emotions hit me like a tsunami.

This was how Arizona had felt.

When she vanished from my hotel room in New York. When she left me sleeping at the hotel in Chapel Hill. She had felt like she had to leave. Staying wasn't an option.

Like I was a distraction. And distractions were dangerous.

I didn't need any distractions, not at this point in the game.

But still.

What was in this room was nicer than the coldness on the other side of that door.

Lola Mack. The actress who had her heart shattered a few hours ago.

Mrs. Jones. The woman who's marriage was irretrievably broken.

They had been my hiding place. My warm place to hide. I had given them solace as well. Couldn't hide forever. I'd stop hiding, go out into the cold, leave these wounded women.

Big Bad Wolf. My mother. The friend I had killed yesterday evening near Lakenheath.

The list of people who would love to see me sleeping under dirt was long.

That wretched list was damn near a million dollars long.

It didn't matter who had sent the man with the broken nose.

All that mattered was that the dead had a representative.

And the motherfucker was in London looking for me.

I had to leave this room the same way Mrs. Jones's family had fled Jamaica.

It was time to leave without a good-bye.

It was time to load up my gun.

It was time to find Death before Death found me.

*the man with
the broken nose*

Eight

brute force

**The man with the broken nose stood in front of thousands of
T-shirts.**

None made him angrier than the one that read DA NOBODY FUCKS
WITH JESUS!

He couldn't believe that was what one of the T-shirts said. In
plain view. Like it was no big deal. Seeing the F-word and Jesus'
name in the same sentence bothered the man with the broken nose,
stole his mind away from killing Gideon, if only for the moment.

The T-shirt next to that sacrilegious message had a picture of
Adolf Hitler on one side and President Bush on the other: SAME
SHIT DIFFERENT ASSHOLE. Other T-shirts for *Scarface*, Muhammad
Ali, *Clockwork Orange*, Elvis Presley, and Che Guevara dominated
that area of the flea market. He scowled at the ones with Jesus and
Bush.

He shook his head and muttered, "British sons of bitches."

Fifteen pounds for an offensive T-shirt. Thirty dollars. Insult to
motherfucking injury.

He was at a low-end flea market, its sign proclaiming this was
the WORLD FAMOUS SOUVENIR CENTRE. The *U* in the worn-out sign
was hanging upside down like it was drunk, and the *O* was MIA,
maybe it had run off to be on a better sign.

He was waiting on Sam, his UK contact, the man who was arranging the hit on Gideon.

It was early evening, less than twenty-four hours since he had followed Gideon through Soho. For a moment he thought about Gideon's whore, the prostitute Gideon had gone to see last night. The man with the broken nose had gone to see her in the middle of the night. To question her about Gideon. To beat and torture her if needed. To kill her if it came to that.

That was late last night. Now he was in Camden Town, standing in the crowd at the open market, in need of sleep, waiting on Sam. He had been waiting for ten minutes.

Sam was late with the merchandise. The man with the broken nose was pissed.

Sam couldn't seem to broker this deal in a timely manner.

The man with the broken nose walked to a vendor, a young man who wore a belt decorated with spent gun casings. One pant leg was red, the other black. Hair in a three-foot-tall flaming Mohawk. Doc Martens. Short leather jacket decorated with zippers, spokes, and studs. His clothes were weapons. RANCID and DEAD KENNEDYS patches on his jacket.

That vendor fit in. The man with the broken nose knew he didn't.

It was a Goth area. Where Herman Munster would shop for his wife and kids. Where they slapped the word *vintage* on tattered Salvation Army clothes and quadrupled the price.

The man with the broken nose asked the Goth vendor, "When is Sam going to get here?"

"Sam will get here when Sam gets here, broken nose motherfucker."

The vendor sporting the flaming Mohawk pointed at his bandaged nose and laughed.

The man with the broken nose said, "So you think my broken nose is funny?"

"Your nose is funny. You are a funny motherfucker. So motherfucking funny."

He touched the bandages on his injured nose, a reminder of a job that had almost gone bad. A reminder that couldn't be ignored. A reminder that was being made a goddamn joke.

The man with the broken nose paused, then asked the vendor, "Where are you from?"

"Istanbul."

Reggae and rock music collided while incense perfumed the damp air.

He sat on his aggravation. "Your English is good. To be from Istanbul."

"I watch *Baywatch*."

"Sounds like you learned your English watching Samuel Jackson movies."

"I'm tired of motherfucking snakes on the motherfucking planes, motherfucker."

The man with the broken nose wasn't amused.

"Well, I'm from Texas. You heard of Texas? Same place our president is from."

"You come from a country ruled by a warmonger. A country filled with warmongers."

"I think you should apologize." He confronted the man from Turkey with a smile. "You disrespected me. I really think you should apologize. I'm man enough to accept your apology."

"You're a funny motherfucker. Broken nose motherfucker."

"You sure you want to ride this road with me?"

"Look, motherfucker. Sam is not here. Sam will be here soon. You can wait or you can come back. Standing in my face disrupting my business will not make Sam arrive sooner."

He rubbed his broken nose. Felt like dynamite wrapped in nitroglycerin.

The Goth man laughed again.

The man with the broken nose took a breath. "Thanks for being so goddamn helpful."

Thirty aggravating minutes passed.

Sam showed up. Slender man. Fifty years old or more. Dressed in all black. Scarf around his neck. Tongue pierced. Lip pierced. Ears pierced a dozen times. Eyebrow pierced.

The man with the broken nose nodded, checked his watch.

"Sam, where I'm from, a man says to meet him at a certain time, the man shows up at a certain time, if not fifteen minutes earlier. If he can't make it at a certain time, he makes a phone call before the certain time they are supposed to meet, so the other party's time isn't wasted."

"I apologize. Somebody took ill on the Northern Line. Signal failures. Got stuck on the tube. Part of the Central Line shut was down. Battery in mobile phone died. Bad travel day."

"Man-to-man, I'm just saying, in the future respect my time."

"What, you think Sam's motherfucking time is free?" That was the Goth Turk from Istanbul. "Motherfucking American, you think your time is more special than our time?"

The man with the broken nose smiled. "I'm talking to Sam. Not you."

The Goth man from Turkey held his ground. "Be gone, broken-nose warmonger."

The man with the broken nose smiled, was about to say something, but let it go.

He followed Sam away from the vendors, back toward the main drag, into Gothville.

As he walked, his jaw remained tight.

He said, "Don't disrespect my time, Sam. Never again. Understand?"

"Understood."

They slowed at a Goth-black building, the Dragonfly, and headed toward apartments on Hawley Road. Postal code NW1 posted on the corner units and Camden Interiors, a purple building across the street. The apartments were light-colored brick. The only normal thing the man with the broken nose had seen since he'd gotten off the tube. A seed from the ghetto had flourished here. Huge satellite dishes were outside front windows, windows that were small and narrow, about the size of a four-year-old.

He told Sam, "Didn't know you were from Turkey."

"Not from Turkey."

"Guy at the booth is a Turk. Where are you from?"

"Morocco."

"Guy at the booth was talking a lot of Istan-bullshit."

The flat Sam took him to was decorated like a college dorm. Posters of *Pulp Fiction*. Samuel L. Jackson and Travolta with guns. A thousand posters of *Scarface*. Pacino with a machine gun. *Butch Cassidy and the Sundance Kid*. Newman and Redford with guns drawn, that final scene, where they charged the Mexicans, both going out in a blaze of glory.

He asked Sam, "You live here?"

"My flat is in Hackney. You've been there. This is a safe house."

Sam left the small room, went into another small room. In those seconds the man with the broken nose thought about the whore he had visited. Gideon's whore. Those thoughts went away when Sam returned, black briefcase in hand. Sam put it on the coffee table. Opened it up.

Inside were six new barrels for his Desert Eagle. More than he would need.

Sam closed the briefcase and slid it to him.

The man with the broken nose said, "The other guy at the flea market. The Turk."

"What about him?"

"Is he your friend?"

"Not really. I'm fucking his sister. She's ugly as a goat, but she fucks good. Why?"

He touched his broken nose, the insults still fresh in his mind, but didn't answer.

He looked at his watch. He needed to leave. Another urgent appointment.

But first. The other business. The main reason he had waited that long.

"Gideon. I need to know if he's still in London. I need a location."

"On it."

"Wanted to tell you face-to-face, don't screw me around."

"I'm doing my best."

"You need to do better. Because right now I'm pissed the fuck off. And you don't want me pissed the fuck off, Sam. You really don't. And I'm close to showing you how pissed I am."

"Relax, my friend. Relax."

"Don't you ever fucking tell me to relax."

He stood up, hovered over Sam.

Sam looked terrified.

The man with the broken nose repeated, "Find Gideon."

Sam nodded.

The man with the broken nose left the apartment, briefcase in hand.

He remembered her eyes. The eyes of the whore he had gone to torture.

He crossed the street, went through the Stables Market, looked back toward the Esso petrol station and Silks and Spice restaurant. All was clear. He continued walking across the uneven bricked walkway. He came out on the high street, walked beyond the tube station until he saw Waterstone's bookshop. He crossed at Delancey Street. Went inside Waterstone's.

Beautiful music met him. Not the kind that was creating noise pollution at the flea market, not the kind that insulted and assaulted his senses. The music was beautiful and angelic.

Like a theme song of hope.

He looked straight ahead and saw her.

Tebby was there. Like she said she would be. Twenty minutes early. A woman who respected time. She was easy to find. Six feet tall and bald. She wore flat shoes. Walking shoes. He'd told himself that he wouldn't call her. Last night, after their date had abruptly ended, after he had dumped her at Leicester Square and gone after Gideon, after everything had gone wrong, he had told himself to let Tebby go, had reminded himself not to get distracted.

Mixing business with pleasure was always bad.

But he couldn't forget about her.

He'd had a long night and woken up at the crack of dawn, called her early this morning. Called her before she started her morning. Had already called her three times today.

He told her that he wanted to see her again.

And now she was here.

She had on tight jeans. A black sweater. A short jacket. A purse. A small overnight suitcase on wheels was at her side. He smiled. He knew how this evening was going to end.

A CD display was up front, said the store was spotlighting pop music by Syren, a singer from Wales. Her music was what he heard. It was so beautiful it caused him to pause. Made him look at

Tebby as it played. As if that wonderful music was her theme song. He picked up a CD, put his glasses on, read the cover. Said Syren was born in the late seventies, in Caerphilly, South Wales. Syren had started her piano lessons and ballet classes at the age of three.

Just like his little girl.

Maybe he'd get Melanie to study at the Royal School of Music London too.

If he could keep her focused.

Syren sounded like an angel.

With Syren's music playing, it became the sound track as he watched Tebby.

Watched her stand in the aisle and read. She looked so intellectual. So sexy.

He took three of the CDs. Would send one to his little girl. Hope it inspired her.

Then he crept up behind Tebby and hugged her. She smiled and laughed.

He kissed her on her lips. "Find anything good?"

She held up a book by a black American. A plot-free novel laced with sex.

He asked, "You like those smut books?"

"I was reading some of it. A lot I don't understand. What does *heifer* mean?"

"It's a small cow. Why you ask?"

"A calf is small cow."

"So is a heifer."

"The women in the book call each other that all the time."

"Oh, that kind of heifer. They're insulting each other."

"All of these negative things Americans say to each other. I don't understand that. How do Americans take normal words and make them so derogatory? Like a bitch is a female dog. The word has been taken and made into something vulgar. And *mofo*. What does that mean?"

"Means 'motherfucker.'"

"Really? I can see *mother* coming from *mo* . . . but the *fo* part . . . I don't get."

"You're thinking about it a little too hard. Some things can't be intellectualized."

"I like black-American books. Terry McMillan floors me. Read *A Day Late and a Dollar Short*. Beautiful book. Love her books. It is hard to get *good* black-American books here."

She followed him to another part of the bookshop. He picked up Harry Potter books.

Tebby raised a brow.

He said, "For my daughter. Need to send these back home."

"What kind of books does your son read?"

That simple question almost broke his heart.

Skeeter. His son. His only son. The one who would make sure the family name never died. The man with the broken nose took a breath. Started to tell her. But decided against it.

He said, "Skeeter . . . he's not much on reading novels. He loves comic books though."

"Just like a boy."

"Yeah. Just like. Give him Captain America and he's your best friend."

Tebby walked toward the romance section.

That was the section women went to to lie to themselves. Shit covered with flowery prose.

He went to the other part of Waterstone's. Found Dostoyevsky.

He picked up *Crime and Punishment*. He'd read that book more times than he could count. Then he picked up *The Brothers Karamazov*. He picked that one up and smiled.

His favorite quote came from that book.

"Above all do not lie to yourself," he mumbled. "A man who lies to himself . . . falls into disrespect towards himself and others."

Whenever he recited that quote, he felt like Tony Soprano.

He saw Tebby browsing books over in the romance section. In Fantasyland. He hated those books. Even though he'd never read one. His soon-to-be-ex-wife sat in bed and read those books, then looked at him with all that disappointment in her eyes.

Mad because her life hadn't mirrored some fake-ass book.

"I need to feel alive." She had told him that. "I need attention. I need to feel special."

Nice home. New car. Two kids. Great job. And she needed to feel special.

He read between the lines. All the new clothes his soon-to-be-ex had bought at the Galleria. The new perfume. The new swank hairstyle. The extra time she had to spend at work.

He had cut to the chase and asked, "You fucking somebody?"

"Yes."

"Who?"

"A Frenchman who is teaching at the University of Houston."

"The Frenchman you hired."

"Yes. The Frenchman I hired."

She told him. Just like that.

He'd already known she was fucking the poetry-quoting Frenchman at the U of H. She was the head of the English department, fucking an immigrant coworker, and he didn't give a shit. But still, he didn't expect her to tell him, not like that, not in their bed.

He asked, "Why?"

"Gravity."

"What about gravity?"

"Gravity is the natural force of attraction exerted by a celestial body upon objects at or near its surface. I feel gravity when I'm with him. With you I'm floating away. I've floated away."

The only reason he didn't go O.J. on her was because he would've been the first suspect.

Besides, they had kids. He wouldn't kill the mother of his children.

Skeeter had come to the door. Skeeter looked at them, then walked away.

Then his soon-to-be-ex had shaken her head at him, not a tear in her eyes. "It's over."

"Yeah. It's over."

And that was that. Somebody had to say it. And she had said it.

His wife left the bedroom, never to return.

Skeeter passed by again, looked at him. He smiled at Skeeter. Skeeter smiled back.

Skeeter was his son's nickname. His real name was Fyodor.

Named after Fyodor Dostoyevsky. But Skeeter was what he was called. His wife had named their daughter.

Skeeter moved on.

The man with the broken nose listened.

All he heard was the kids arguing, the dogs barking, and the parakeets chirping.

His soon-to-be-ex cranked up the stereo. Bobby Womack. "If You Think You're Lonely Now." Same song that was playing when he met her in Houston. The original. Not the fucked-up version that the skinny-ass guy from Jodeci did, not the version with the incoherent, mangled lyrics.

She played the one by The Poet. Now that theme song had become their farewell song.

He never wanted to marry her anyway.

His first wife had just died. Breast cancer.

His second wife, before she was his second wife, had just ended a five-year relationship.

Two unhappy people met at a bar, ended up laughing and shooting pool at Jillian's.

They had bonded in misery.

You had to have happiness to miss happiness.

Happiness had never been the foundation on which their house was built.

He lay there staring at the ceiling.

Kids screaming. Dogs barking. Parakeets chirping. Bobby Womack singing.

A hand touched his shoulder. Made him aware.

Tebby. Smiling. She said, "Ready to get on queue?"

He nodded. "Ready whenever you are."

He followed Tebby, briefcase loaded with barrels for his Desert Eagle in one hand, CDs by Syren, Harry Potter novels, and Dostoyevsky in the other.

He kissed her again. "Where's the cinema?"

"Odeon's one block up. Almost across the street from the tube."

"How many Odeons are there in London?"

"Almost as many as there are Angus Steak Houses."

He was still thinking about his first wife.

The love of his life.

Before her cancer.

Before the chemo. They were still happy. Healthy.

They still owned the world. They still had plans to have a family.

She was a Trini. From Trinidad, Colorado. Home of the Trinidaddio Blues Fest. Population less than twelve thousand. Less than fifteen miles from New Mexico. Not a small-island girl, but a small-town girl who had become a contract killer. Almost as good as him.

It was a fantasy. Like in those books, true happiness was always a fantasy.

But still.

He felt something when he was around Tebby.

Something he never felt with his soon-to-be-ex-wife.

Something he'd felt with his first wife.

Gravity.

He felt gravity.

London Famous Jazz venue was across the street from the Odeon.

That reminded him. He handed her the Bob Marley CD. Bootleg. *The Best of Marley.*

And he gave her one of the CDs by Syren.

Her smile broadened. "You paid for my books. You don't have to go and do all that."

He smiled. "What movie are we seeing?"

"Children of Men."

He thought about his own children. About his daughter. About his son.

Tickets were almost nine pounds each. That was forty dollars, almost. He handed the man the American Express. He didn't care. Wasn't his money. Same at the concession stand.

The movie was in theater four. Upstairs. They passed the toilets on the way.

The seats were small and old. The kind with fixed armrests that didn't allow for cuddling. Ten rows, five seats on each side of the aisle, hundred seats total. His brother, the dentist, had a place larger than this in his home in Maryland. His brother in the outskirts of Memphis had the largest home. Four-car garage on two acres. Four cars, two for him, two for his wife.

Tebby leaned closer, ran her hand across his bald head.

He kissed her. His tongue on hers. Their second real kiss. Both in public.

Ads and commercials came on. One had Native Americans—faces painted and dressed in war gear—chasing an Amtrak in the name of comedy. Images like that would never air in the US of A. The next one was for potato chips, had white people dancing while a black woman held a tray and played the part of the maid.

He was bothered. He was still pissed the fuck off.

Not just because of the disrespect on the screen. Nobody respected the US of A.

He told Tebby, "Be right back. Going to the toilet."

She ate her sweet popcorn as he stood up. He looked at her. Deciding. Smiling at the way she enjoyed her sweet popcorn. Popcorn in the UK came in sweet or salted. Not drenched in butter like back home. Tebby liked her popcorn sweet. As he passed, she sipped her soda.

Briefcase in hand, he took to the stairs, went out the front door of the theater, jogged by the 168 bus, passed by men dressed in black leather and matching black lipstick, a thousand T-shirts for sale, and less than a minute later he had crossed the small bridge, was hurrying through the narrow corridor that led into the flea market, the one with the vowel problems.

Leather whips and chains. Goth T-shirts praising porn. Sacrilegious messages.

The Goth man from Turkey was smoking a cigarette and talking to a customer.

The man with the broken nose gritted his teeth, went right at the Goth man from Turkey.

Without saying a word he gave the Goth man a hard punch to the nose.

The Goth man's nose was destroyed. Blood spewed from where his nose had been.

"You think a broken nose is funny, do you? Laugh, *motherfucker.*"

The man with the broken nose stood over the bleeding man.

"Say something, *motherfucker*. Talk to me like I'm a *motherfucking* cockroach."

Face bloodied, the Turk struggled to his feet, ran through the market.

The man with the broken nose headed out of the flea market.

On the way he yanked down the Hitler/Bush T-shirt, stomped it into the ground.

Briefcase in hand, he adjusted his suit and went back to the movie theater.

He sat next to Tebby. The racist ads were done. The previews were just ending.

He held Tebby's hand as they watched the movie.

Halfway through, she leaned to him like she wanted to tell him something.

Tebby whispered, "You need to stop and buy something before we go to your hotel."

It took him a moment to understand. He chuckled. "Okay."

A proactive woman. He loved that. His soon-to-be-ex-wife never initiated anything.

Except for the divorce.

Nine

breakfast, lunch, and dinner

The man with the broken nose held Tebby's breasts, pinched her nipples.

Tebby moaned. "Don't start something you can't finish."

They were back at Tower Hills.

Naked.

In his bed with the covers pulled back.

Bob Marley was playing. Soft and low enough to encourage but not disturb his mood.

He kept sucking her breasts. His soon-to-be-ex didn't have breasts that nice. Two kids had left her breasts looking like flat tires. He put his fingers between Tebby's legs. Felt like her vagina had a fever. So hot between her legs. Like Fourth of July in downtown Houston.

She jumped. "Wait. Wait . . . hold on, baby."

"What's wrong?"

Tebby got up and went to her purse. Took out nail clippers.

She said, "You have fingernails as sharp as a surgeon."

He gave her his hand and she trimmed his fingernails. Then filed them down smooth.

"Me no want female circumcision."

When she finished his manicure, she eased his hand back between her legs.

He felt her global warming. First he teased and played with the edges, then the lips.

Then he moved his fingers in and out of her vagina.

"Much better . . . much . . . much better."

He put his hand on her chin, pulled her face to his, kissed her.

She moaned and moved against his hand.

He kissed her while his finger probed her dampness.

He whispered, "Think I might want some breakfast."

"You are wicked, Bruno. Wicked."

His tongue moved from her mouth, to her breasts, moved south and replaced his fingers. Then his tongue worked with his fingers. Moved soft and slow.

Tebby moaned. "Get your breakfast."

"You like this?"

"Good Lord, yes, please get your breakfast. Get your lunch. Get your dinner."

He tongued her until she begged him to get on top of her.

He reached for a condom. Opened it. Rolled the latex on.

He mounted her, moved inside at a snail's pace, kissed her, sucked her neck.

Tebby moaned like she had third-degree burns all over her skin.

He stroked her. She asked him to slap her ass. So he slapped her ass, squeezed her ass, touched between her legs, rubbed her clit while he stroked her, asked her to touch herself while he stroked her. He slapped her ass so hard she cringed. He smiled when she cringed. Then he put her on her belly, held her down, and found his way back inside her wetness, held the small of her waist and straddled her. Rode her from the back, made her a prisoner.

A prisoner.

In the dim light he looked at her from the back. Her butt. Her small waist. Her strong back. Her shoulders were toned. He looked at her head. At her bald head.

The way her head gave way to her neck and back. Without hair, from his position, her head, her back, for a moment it looked too . . . *masculine*.

A woman with no hair. From behind. Looked like a man. With no hair. From behind.

He lost his rhythm. Felt his erection waning.

For a moment it looked like he was behind Michael Jordan.

"Don't stop." Tebby was moaning. "Don't tease me like that."

He closed his eyes. Had to close his eyes to maintain his erection.

He imagined actresses. Singers. Britney Spears. Janet. Madonna.

Still, he was losing his erection.

He closed his eyes tight. Imagined a harem of women with long hair.

He felt Tebby's soft ass. Her breasts. Felt everything that made her feminine.

Gideon's whore.

He thought about Gideon's whore.

He clenched his teeth and thought about the prostitute he went to torture.

The woman he wanted to beat until she told him what she knew about Gideon.

His blood rushed. His erection came back. Everything tingled. Toes curled.

He strained. Slowed down. Got his breathing right.

But the tingles expanded. He felt a watermelon-size nut brewing on the horizon.

He sped up. Stroked her hard. Almost out of control. Barbaric and unmerciful.

Tebby reciprocated the barbaric behavior. She fucked like a warrior.

His soon-to-be-ex-wife never fucked like that. Never. Not even on their honeymoon.

Tebby made sounds like she was dying a slow death, like she was being murdered one stroke at a time, one stab at a time, and she cursed, said things in her native language, said sexy and vulgar things in English. She wasn't a dead fuck. Not like his soon-to-be-ex.

He'd had two kids with a dead fuck.

Good Lord . . . you're putting a hurting on me, Bruno . . . you're trying to ruin me.

He stopped . . . wrestled with his orgasm . . . shuddered . . . grunted . . . Tebby laughed at him . . . laughed like she knew he wanted to come . . . like she knew she had him at the brink of madness . . . and she laughed like she was in control . . . that angered him . . . excited him . . .

He grabbed at her hair . . . was going to pull her hair . . . but there was no hair to pull.

He grabbed her hips . . . her ass . . . held her rough . . . turned her over . . . more like flipped her over . . . sucked her breasts . . . bit her nipples . . . rushed to get on her . . . rushed to fuck her strong.

She told him his loving was good. Told him that his loving was damn good.

He kept giving her measured strokes. He kept plunging. He kept stabbing with his dick.

His body was on fire, he wanted to come, wanted his seeds to spill inside Tebby's body, inside her mouth, on her ass, on her breasts, on her buttocks, wanted his seeds to cover her skin from head to toe, wanted her covered in his jism, wanted her to drown in his come.

Again his hand went to her hair. Pulled nothing but a damp, bald head.

Fucking a woman with no hair was like riding a horse with no reins.

He held her head. Pulled her neck. Pulled her ears.

He felt her nails going deep in his back, into his ass, and he fucked her harder, made her scream, made her scoot away from him, shuddering, and he chased and fucked her harder.

She moaned, *"OH MY GOD. Oh my God . . . oh my God . . . oh . . . my God . . . my God . . ."*

He loved her screams. Made him want to beat his chest and yell back at her.

His soon-to-be-ex-wife had been a silent, expressionless, motionless fuck.

Tebby was his dream fuck. His ego fuck.

He had forgotten that it could be this good.

Tebby came so damn loud.

He fucked her until he began to drown in his own orgasm.

He backed off. Paced himself.

When he slowed down, Tebby didn't slow down. She sped up.

She was coming again.

"Please don't stop, Bruno. I'm not done, I'm not done . . . don't stop please . . ."

Tebby grabbed his sweaty neck.

"Dammit don't stop don't stop don't you dare stop."

She flipped him over. Got on top. Squatted over him. Used the headboard for support.

Her backside was going up and down hard and fast, driving him into the mattress.

Her eyes were tight. Her teeth biting her bottom lip. She was coming.

Her skin slapping against his sounded like the ultimate battle.

All he could do was let go. He surrendered. Gave in to the orgasm.

His orgasm rose from deep inside him. Crawled across his skin. Consumed him.

He jerked, shuddered, groaned, wailed, tensed, grunted, moaned, panted, pumped.

He came hard, a roaring dragon spewing liquid fire inside latex.

He held Tebby, moaned, and came like it was his first orgasm ever.

Ten

Marylebone

Late in the evening I exited the Hammersmith and City Line at Baker Street.

Darkness was covering a busy and upscale area where everything was a tribute to Sherlock Holmes. I was in the shadows of Marylebone, an area of central London in the City of Westminster, bounded by Oxford Street to the south, Regent's Park to the north, Edgware Road to the west and Great Portland Street to the east. There were lots of businesses, but the area was lined with flats and mostly residential with a generous Arab population on its far-western border around Edgware Road. That area had its tube station and red buses blown up by terrorists when the shit hit the fan on 7/7, their equivalent of America's 9/11.

The second I stepped out into the city's lights, I made a call.

I said, "I'm here."

She said, "Step to the intersection."

"Toward Madame Tussaud's?"

"The other way. Toward the Sherlock Holmes Museum."

As soon as I headed through the crowd, a Mini Cooper that was dressed up like St. George's Cross pulled up. Behind the wheel was a Filipina woman with skin the hue of sunrise over Le Blond Beach in Brazil. The driver was Arizona. The woman known as Queen Scamz.

I hurried through the crowd, tourists who were taking nighttime photos in front of a statue dedicated to the world's greatest detective. I looked down at the plate on the front of the car she was driving, memorized that information, not intentionally, out of habit, then hurried and got in the left side of that red-and-white symbol on wheels.

As Arizona pulled away and mixed with traffic, I said, "Long time no see."

We'd seen each other yesterday morning and evening.

Our last meeting ending in hostility.

Traces of that hostility still showed in her face.

I was in London because of her. She'd brought me here to do a few jobs. And she had referred me to the rapper known as Sledgehammer, the man who had paid me to slaughter Big Bad Wolf in Tampa. Me and Arizona, we had history, both personal and professional. We'd been intimate in New York; we'd been intimate in North Carolina; both encounters weeks ago on the heels of a job. Both times she'd had sex with me and vanished while I slept. And she denied both encounters. She was the woman I wanted and couldn't get.

I'd been hustling to earn a million dollars, wanted to have enough to please her.

But that had been rejected.

So we had our own tension. She whipped through the part of London where fictional characters like Sherlock Holmes, James Bond, DangerMouse, Sexton Blake, and Basil the Great Mouse Detective have all resided. I enjoyed the ride, decided to let her talk first.

She asked, "Did you get my package?"

"Called you a few times last night."

"Did you get my package?"

I told her, "I got your package."

"So you know what I want you to do."

"You're putting a hit out on Sierra."

"Yes."

"She's your sister."

"She's a traitor. She's always been a traitor. And traitors need to be taken care of."

A little more than twenty-four hours ago Sierra had sent some boys from Holland to do damage to Arizona. I'd come to London and landed in the middle of a sibling battle, my own problems be damned. That anger and fear showed in Arizona's face, in her words.

Her cellular rang. She looked at the number, then hesitated before she answered.

She snapped, "Yeah?"

Arizona and her sister's rivalry went back at least a decade; that hate went back to a con man named Scamz, a man who had been Arizona's lover and mentor, a man who had betrayed Arizona and bedded Sierra as well. Rumor was he was sleeping with them both and both of them knew about it, both of them competing for Scamz's love until he was gunned down. Even then, both of them were at his side when he died inside a pool hall out in North Hollywood.

"Yeah." Arizona said that in her business tone. "I've still got your car."

Maybe she pictured her sister as the one who had betrayed, not Scamz.

"Heading to a meeting. Will get back to you on that."

I had finally gotten in contact with her. Told her about my evening, about being stalked.

She hung up the phone, said nothing, but looked uncomfortable.

I asked, "Who was that?"

"Local hookup. I'm borrowing one of my client's vehicles."

"This car hot?"

"It's clean."

I left that at that.

Yesterday she asked for my help.

Today I needed hers. I'd made calls all day, came up with nothing.

I said, "You said you had some information for me."

"I do."

"Well, when do I get this information?"

"Be patient."

I asked, "Where are we going?"

"DB Wine Bar."

We headed deeper into postal code W1U and parked on Blandford. She took me to a place where they had poetry slams, an event called Respect the Mic. The wine bar was located downstairs, a place that was well hidden. There was one entrance, making it impossible to creep into this place unseen. This spot was discreet and underground, a gem of a restaurant once we came down the metal stairs, sexily stylish, had numerous nooks and crannies with private eating areas, lots of curved white walls, the place jazzed up with colorful artwork, most of it bold, all of it fit to be in a museum.

I asked, "What's this?"

"It's called a restaurant."

"You know what I mean. You have a meeting down here?"

"It's called eating dinner."

"I don't have time to eat dinner."

"Then you don't have time to get this information."

"Don't fuck with me, Arizona."

"You like Caribbean food?"

"Yeah. Whose spot is this?"

"Guy named Ike runs it. It's safe."

We passed the wine bar, several alcoves with tables, then went down another level, passing at least fifty people who were laughing and talking and having intimate meals.

We were led to a private section. Obviously Arizona had a hookup.

I took my gun out of my bag, left it at my side.

She looked at me.

I said, "Just in case."

She nodded.

Arizona took out a small computer, one barely the size of a paperback novel. She fired it up and got online, typed in a few commands. She showed me the screen.

I said, "That's the outside of the restaurant."

She nodded.

I said, "You've tapped into the CCTV."

She nodded.

I said, "You're good."

She nodded.

That meant nobody could sneak inside without being seen.

I relaxed a bit, not much.

A beautiful woman with easy brown skin and long brown hair came and took our order. Beautiful black woman with an American accent. Might have been Southern. I didn't ask.

Seconds later drinks were on the table, as were peppered *crevettes*, basted and seasoned with Jamaica's Scotch bonnet pepper, then tucked into an authentic jerk chicken.

Arizona said, "I'm famished. I'm going to order a lot of food."

"Suit yourself."

"When I get upset, I eat. When I'm stressed, I eat. Before I do anything, I'm going to eat."

"Your sister has you on edge."

"She's not the only one."

"What else is going on?"

She didn't answer.

She ordered jerk chicken and honey wings served with cinnamon fries, callaloo and tomato bruschette served on West Indian sweet bread, Red Stripe, king prawns basted in smoked barbecue sauce and garnished with a wedge of lemon, sea salt, and cracked black pepper with a garlic-mayo dip.

She ordered like she was coming off a three-week hunger strike.

As we ate, she sent for more food, had them bring out a steamed whole sea bass, served with okra in white wine and coconut rundown. A side order of fried plantain showed up after that.

For a finale she ordered homemade Caribbean rum cake.

We ate and drank like we were the royal family.

Not until then did we talk.

Arizona was working on a dirty martini. I was babysitting a Jack and Coke.

The first order of business, as far as she was concerned, was handling Sierra. All I knew was that in the middle of my problems, on her side of the fence, a sibling war was going on.

Arizona paused. "Is there a problem accepting the contract?"

"She's your goddamn sister, that's the fucking problem."

"She sent men to rape me. You heard them."

I nodded.

"She wanted them to rape me. Cripple me. That is *worse* than death. I'd rather be dead than raped and crippled. She wanted me to live as an invalid and suffer the rest of my days."

I nodded.

Arizona finished her drink. Another was ordered. I was still sipping my Jack and Coke, and not sipping much. This wasn't the time for me to numb my senses.

Arizona went on, "That's what that bitch wanted. Her big sister beaten and raped."

"But it didn't happen."

"Well, I'm being kind. No torture. No rape. I want her dead."

I closed my eyes. "You. Sierra. Sergeant. What's really going on?"

"Told you. FEMA."

I wanted to know more about their FEMA scam, wanted to know how she and Sergeant—a man she had me kill yesterday evening—had ended up in business together, wanted to know how her sister came into play on that deal, wanted to know what went wrong, but I wasn't much on details, not those kinds of details, not when all that was someone else's business.

But still I couldn't help asking a question or two.

I said, "Yesterday morning your sister sent the Dutch boys to . . . assault you."

"And I owe you for being there. You saved me. I can pay you if you like."

I shook my head. "Whatever is between you and her . . . sounds like more than FEMA."

"It's bigger than money."

"What is it about?"

"Let's talk about that later."

"Answer this. Have you seen her?"

"I went to Amsterdam not too long ago. Met with her."

"What happened?"

"Later. If I get into that, later. If then. That's not what I want to talk about right now."

"My information. You said you had some info for me."

"Sure. Let's talk about what's important to you." Arizona ran her hand over her hair. "Contacts finally came through. Got some information on the guy who's been tracking you."

I said, "I'm listening."

"My contacts told me a hired gun did a contract in Jacksonville, took out an executive at the Modis Building. It got out of control. They think the assassin was hit in the nose with a lead paperweight during the melee."

"That will break a nose."

"He stayed at the Omni, called one of the local docs who makes house calls and works for major cash and got patched up off the books. My contact told me that. The hit wasn't as clean as your work. Jacksonville saw Angela Spears delivering the report on the noon news."

"You sure about that?"

"I'm sure. My contact works at WTLV, has a hookup at the police department, so he had information that didn't air. Some people said the hit man was black. Others said he was white."

"Sounds like the guy."

Having those details helped, but didn't do much for me. I needed more information.

I asked, "Who you think ordered the package on Sledge?"

"Let me make some calls, see if I can reverse-engineer that hit."

The check came. I tried to pay for the meal, but she wouldn't let me.

She motioned at her laptop, said, "I'm keeping an eye out."

"What do you mean?"

"I'll make sure you're safe."

"Calling in reinforcements?"

"If I have to. Always have people on standby. But I have a few tricks up my sleeve."

"In the meantime?"

"I have work to do. And you still have work to do."

"That guy's out there. I can't do shit until I handle that."

"You're Gideon. He'd be stupid to show up again. Focus on your work for now."

"I have promises to keep."

"Take care of the local package. When it's done, be ready to travel and visit my sister."

She turned off her computer and I tucked my gun back in my backpack.

Then we headed through the restaurant, passed the alcoves, and took to the street again.

Arizona asked, "How's the hotel? The one where you're letting a room, how is it?"

"It's fine. Why you ask?"

"Everything's okay there, I take it."

"Why did you drop the package off and leave? Why didn't you wait?"

"Did you want me to wait?"

"A million dollars, Arizona. What do you think?"

She stared at me like she wanted to say something, but she didn't.

I asked, "What's wrong?"

"I want to apologize for the things I said yesterday evening. That was mean."

"Same here."

She nodded, paused.

She asked, "How was your night?"

"Long. Didn't get much sleep."

"It shows."

"You look worn yourself."

"Was in front of the computer most of the night."

"Working."

"Getting connected to cameras around the city. Looking at things."

"These things have to do with me?"

"You could say that. Guess I was being your cyber-wingman."

"Then you were awake when I called you."

"I was."

"Needed you last night. Why didn't you answer?"

"Because I didn't want to."

She stared at me as if the true answer was deep inside her eyes. Hostility returned, painted her skin. Looked like she was struggling to get free from a tangled knot of strain.

She said, "I'll keep looking out for you. Keep your mobile on. Answer if I call you. I'll try to fix this. I put you in contact with Sledge, so I feel responsible. I will see this thing through, no matter how it ends, I will see this through. That is my promise to you."

She finished her speech and stood in front of me, her eyes fixed on mine, as motionless as one of the figures inside Madame Tussaud's famous wax museum.

I asked, "Are we okay?"

She paused like she wanted to say something harsh, something vulgar.

Instead she gave me a fake smile and said, "Why wouldn't we be?"

With that she headed toward her car, left in a hurry.

As she walked, she adjusted her purse and laptop, took out a pack of cigarettes. I didn't have to see the brand to know they were Djarums. She lit one and smoke blew back in my direction, that smell of cloves washing over me as she hurried in her car and pulled away.

I took the narrow side streets back toward Baker Street and the tube.

Near the tube I looked back, saw a teenage girl walking not too far behind me. She'd come from the direction of the Giraffe Restaurant, maybe from Oxford and Bond streets.

Arizona was gone.

I'd taken the side streets and that girl remained behind me. I caught her reflection in a shop window. She was rail-thin, barely five feet tall. She had on dark parachute pants, the trendy kind that had silver zippers all over. A black hoodie was pulled up over her head, hiding her face, black backpack, can of Red Bull in one of her gloved hands, a mobile in the other.

She hung up her mobile when we went down inside the Baker Street station. No signal underground. I headed for the Jubilee Line, and she ended up going in the same direction, then hurrying onto the same car I rode. I exited at Bond Street exit, slowed down, let the impatient crowd rush by me. The girl passed with the crowd. When I made it up top, I blended with the madness, headed toward Tottenham Court Road. A couple of blocks later I looked back; the girl was there, pretending to browse windows. I made a U-turn, headed toward her, and she walked inside a shop. I stood in the window while she browsed funky T-shirts with raunchy slogans.

Store security went over to her, motioned in a way that told her to take her hood off.

She resisted taking her hoodie off, but security didn't back down.

She pulled her hoodie back and I saw her face. She wasn't any more than fifteen, either Middle Eastern or East Indian, the black Gothic makeup she wore around her eyes and lips made it hard to tell. Everything was the color of midnight, from her fingerless gloves to her fingernails.

I walked by people, looked back to see if she was going to trail me again.

The young girl wasn't there. I looked around, tried to determine if anyone else was on my ass. I couldn't tell. And didn't know how long I'd been followed. I needed to get off the streets.

"One day what you do to other people, that will be done to you."

I hopped in a black cab.

As the cab pulled away, I saw the young girl standing on the curb, watching me vanish.

I had the driver go in the opposite direction I needed to go, take to the side streets, then double back to Tottenham Court Road and drop me off in front of the British Museum. From there I headed back toward MyHotel.

I looked up at the CCTV cameras. Saw those eyes everywhere.

Outside of those mechanical eyes, nobody was watching me.

I headed back inside MyHotel. I stopped by the lobby long enough to ask the same workers I'd talked to this morning if they had seen a man with a broken nose on the premises.

They hadn't. But that didn't mean much. I could slide by them unseen and unheard.

I took to the stairs, took my gun out of my backpack, put it under my jacket, and hurried to the third floor. I was worried. Being followed by that girl had me afraid for Mrs. Jones and Lola.

Gun in hand I opened the door, expecting to see chaos, bloodshed, and dead bodies.

I found two women on my bed.

The door opened and closed. I made noises and neither stirred. They were not moving. Still. Like they were dead. I moved around four hundred pounds of luggage and stood over Mrs. Jones. Not until then could I tell she was breathing slow and easy, relaxed, at peace.

I put my gun away, went to Lola. She still had the towel between her legs. I sat on the edge of the bed, moved her hair from her face. She was walking the peaceful *rues* of dreamland.

Both were sweating. Not a lot. Just enough to leave them dehydrated. With the wine and sake they had, they'd wake up with headaches. The room was too warm. I turned the heater off. Then I put my backpack down and went to the window, pulled back the heavy red curtains. The hotel had double windows. I figured out how to open them to let some cold air inside.

The money I had left for Lola was still on the dresser, untouched, just as I had left it.

I'd been gone all day. They hadn't gotten out of bed, didn't notice my absence.

I put the money back inside my backpack.

The information Arizona had given was good, but useless.

Her information didn't get me any closer to the gun-for-hire.

I stared out at the capital city, knowing a man like me was out there somewhere.

And he was looking for a man like him.
We'd meet again.
Behind me two women began to stir.
They were waking up.
So was I.

Eleven

sweet smell of death

In the middle of the night the man with the broken nose was awakened with a start.

His broken nose ached, it was hard to breathe.

Tebby was curled up next to him, holding him, sleeping on his chest.

The condom was still on. The fruits of his labor stuck to his inner thigh.

He sat up, got comfortable, corrected his breathing, inhaled.

His nose ached. Not as bad as it had ached two days ago. But it ached.

On the other side of that pain he smelled flowers.

He looked around the room. Not a flower in sight.

Still the flowery aroma permeated the room.

He shifted, moved away from six feet of beauty and warmth.

Tebby shifted a little, moved away from his chest.

He took another deep breath.

The scent of flowers was obnoxious, getting stronger by the minute.

He stood, turned the music off, and went to the window.

There were no flower shops out there. Only pubs, castles, tubes, trains, and churches.

Right outside his window was 1 Pepys Street. The flat the WAG he had killed had let was directly across from his rented hotel room. Her window was right across from his. He didn't ask for the room facing the crime scene. It just worked out that way.

He looked down. And was both amazed and amused.

Down below, in front of the dead WAG's residence, a street that, with cars parked on both sides, was barely big enough for a Smart car to drive down, that pathway was filled with flowers.

Hundreds of cards and flowers had been left outside the building's front door.

Cards and flowers were spilling into the street, reminding him of the respectful yet fanatical way people had mourned Princess Diana.

Poster-size pictures of the WAG were all over the front of her place of death. Dozens of teddy bears had been left. Pictures of the WAG were all over the narrow boulevard.

A lane filled with flowers. Hundreds of flowers.

Like she was Elvis. She wasn't Elvis. She was just a WAG.

That mystery solved, he headed back toward the bed.

Tebby was sitting up. She asked, "Everything okay?"

"Guess you wore me out. Fell asleep with my raincoat on."

"Your raincoat?"

He pointed at his penis, the condom dangling from his limp member. "Need to throw this baby juice in the garbage can."

"Garbage can? What's that?"

"Trash. Refuse. Garbage can. Thing you put rubbish inside."

"You mean the rubbish bin. In America you say *garbage can.* Gotcha."

"Yeah."

"Just flush it. Don't leave it for the hotel people to see your business, you know."

He yawned. Loved her accent. Wondered, "What language do you speak at home?"

"My native language is Setswana."

"Is that what you were speaking when we were doing the do?"

"When we were . . . oh. When I was coming." She laughed. "Oh, God no."

"What language was that?"

"It was gibberish. I don't know what I was saying. You had me speaking in tongues."

"Sounded raunchy. Sure that wasn't Setswana?"

"Setswana isn't raunchy."

"Your English is good. Better than mine."

"Back home educated people speak more English than they do Setswana."

"You don't talk dirty during those special moments?"

"In English. Your language has all the vulgarities the world needs."

He headed inside the bathroom. Pulled the latex off his member. Dropped it in the toilet. As he flushed the condom, his phone rang. The hotline. He left the toilet, hurried to the dresser. Saw Sam's number on caller ID. Tebby was getting out of the bed, heading into the bathroom.

She took her cellular with her, had flipped it open before she made it to the bathroom. She closed the bathroom door. He put on the Syren CD, had it loud enough to veil his chat.

He answered his mobile with a snap. "Talk to me."

"Gideon was spotted in Marylebone. He went from there to Piccadilly Circus."

"Is he still there?"

"From there he took a black cab. My worker lost him when he took the cab."

"Who is this worker of yours that's feeding you this information?"

"I put Zankhana on it."

"Who is Zankhana?"

"Girl who brought you the Desert Eagle on the DLR."

"Yeah. Right. The teenage, Goth alcoholic crack- and gun-selling freak from the train."

"Yes. She's good at tracking people as well."

"So Gideon was in Marylebone, from there he was back near Soho."

"Yes."

He looked toward his clothes, his Desert Eagle hidden right across the room.

He asked Sam, "Can you tell me if he's still down in that area?"

"Not sure at this point. She was unable to follow the black cab."

"But he hasn't left London."

"He's here. A Sig-Sauer and some other hardware were sent his way. Those items would not be taken on an aeroplane or a train leaving the country. Too much security."

"So he's hanging around because he's working."

"They think he did a job up near Lakenheath. Not sure. He's a hard one to track."

"What else you have for me, Sam? Who the fuck is this Gideon?"

"They say he killed a minister in Detroit a while ago. Unconfirmed."

"Hold on. That job sounds familiar."

"Should. You turned it down."

He swallowed, that anger as intense as his last orgasm. "Guess it's a good thing I did."

"You hear about Tampa? He did a marvelous job in Tampa."

"Are you praising him, Sam?"

"No. Of course not."

"You said *marvelous*. Sounds like praise. You don't think I'm *marvelous*?"

"Was just offering to tell you what others said about what he did in Tampa."

"I don't give a damn about Tampa."

"Look . . . this is hot . . . this information didn't come from me."

"Of course not."

Sam told him some of what he knew. It wasn't much. But it helped.

He asked Sam, "How many men you have I can put on a temporary payroll?"

"Gideon's in good with Queen Scamz. Nobody wants to touch him. Everybody is scared of her. He does a lot of work for her. That's why you got the contract. Part of the reason."

"Queen Scamz? Who the fuck is that?"

"You don't know Queen Scamz?"

"Sounds like a fag name." He touched his nose. "Or a rock group made of felons."

"She's getting to be pretty ruthless. Worse than Scamz. You haven't heard of her?"

"Been out of the loop for a few years. Was busy doing the husband-and-family thing."

"You knew Scamz?"

"Worked for him once. That was over a decade ago. Where is he now?"

"Dead."

"Not surprised. Most of the guys I worked for back then are dead."

"Look . . . man . . . had no idea this was that deep . . . I don't want to be involved."

"Well, it's too late for that. How many heads can you get me?"

"Don't do this to me."

"You see the smart-ass Turk who worked the T-shirt booth? He got off easy."

"You threatening me, Bruno?"

"I'm threatening you, Sam. Don't give me a reason to come to Hackney."

"Bruno . . . look . . . okay . . . okay . . . I know some of Brixton's Bad Boys. Couple of cats down on Saltoun Road. They hang out in front of Ritzy, so they're easy to find. And I might be able to get you some muscle from Lewisham. Blokes owe me a favor. I can get you a few."

"Have them on standby. At least six. I'll need six to be sure."

"Keep my name out of this."

"Be professional and do what I tell you to do and we won't have a problem."

"Gideon is still here. I'll do my best to locate him."

"Do better than your best on this one, Sam."

"What happened when you followed him last night?"

"What?"

"Last night. Before midnight. You called and said you had found him in Soho. You said he was with a whore. You said you were following him, that you would find where he was hiding."

"All that matters is Gideon got away."

"How did he get away? If you told me more, that might help us all."

"He saw me on his trail and ran like a coward."

"Where did he run?"

"He ran to Lancaster Gate."

"So he was in that area?"

"No. He made it on a train before I could catch him."

The man with the broken nose clenched his teeth. Held on to that lie. A lie that if he kept repeating would become his truth. A lie that, after he had caught and killed Gideon, would be told over and over until it became legend. Sam wanted to know more, but he left it at that.

Sam asked, "What happened after that?"

"I went to have a little conversation with the whore he visited."

"What did she tell you?"

"Sam, *enough* with the questions. Do your job. Find the son of a bitch."

"I will do my best."

"Do better than your best. He's seen me. He knows I'm after him. So right now I need you to get off your ass and do better than your best. Your family would appreciate it."

Tebby came out of the bathroom, put her cellular in her purse, crawled in bed.

He whispered to her, told her he was wrapping up a real estate transaction.

He said, "Hopefully we can locate the property, get out of escrow, and close this deal in the next day or so. So, Sam, when you locate the property give me a ring. Talk soon."

Sam understood.

He hung up on Sam, kissed Tebby, then went to the bathroom. There was mild pain along the edge of his nose. Looked at his injury. He took out bandages, changed the dressing.

Tebby called out, "That music is lovely."

"You like?"

"Brilliant choice. I'll have to see if she is on the Internet. Maybe on MySpace."

He finished dressing his nose, went back to Tebby.

Six feet of woman took up most of the bed. All of her assets waiting for him.

He wondered how his nose looked to her. If it was as grotesque as the Turk's.

He wondered if the Turk still thought a broken nose was hilarious. He doubted it.

The swelling wasn't as bad. His eyes were dark and black. Looked menacing. He liked the look. For now. He was breathing better. He'd get a new nose as soon as the swelling was gone. He went back to the bedroom. Back to the six-foot Botswana beauty in his big bed.

Tebby smiled, extended another condom his way.

He nodded. He'd never gone twice with his wife, not the same night.

She said, "Last night you had me worried."

"How so?"

"Last night, I wanted to come to your hotel with you and do you proper."

"I didn't know."

"I really wanted to put one on you, but you wouldn't let me."

"Was trying to be the perfect gentleman."

"You put me in a cab like my shift was over and somebody else was coming to finish."

"You should've told me."

"I wanted you to ask. Been single for a while and hadn't been laid in a minute. I badly wanted—no, scrap that—needed some. I thought it was for a man to ask . . . to ask . . . *oooo . . . Bruno.*"

Condom on, he was easing inside her. She was so wet. So damn wet for him.

Tebby had velvety skin, perfect shape, deep brown eyes that could melt a man's heart.

Tonight was better than last night. When he had visited the whore in Soho.

While he fucked Tebby, he thought about the whore on Berwick Street.

The working woman he had gone to visit last night.

The prostitute Gideon had visited before their run through the park.

He thought about her. She'd been moving in and out of his mind most of the day.

Gideon's whore. He couldn't stop thinking about Gideon's whore.

Last night.

The man with the broken nose had gone to Berwick Street in Soho, went in the stench of the red-light district to question the whore, beat her, kill her if he had to.

When he climbed the concrete stairs in that narrow hallway and stood in front of that prostitute, as he stood under the scent of piss and sweat that mixed with the faint smell that came from her sweet perfume, in the kindest voice she had asked him, "Full service or blow job?"

The combined aromas were toxic.

Then he looked into her eyes.

Exotic eyes. Hypnotic.

Unlike the other meat-rack girls of Soho, she looked so young and innocent.

She said, "I was about to stop working. I have to get dressed. I'm leaving."

He swallowed. Her voice was melodic. Soothing.

She was so beautiful. So damn beautiful he had been totally distracted. Derailed.

She added, "But I have time. You can be my last, if you like."

She saw his nervousness and smiled.

She said, "It's okay. I won't hurt you. I don't hurt people. Not intentionally."

He nodded.

He took her hand.

She led him inside her small living room. A room with too many movie-star posters, shoes, and wigs, a room that had too much junk. There was a St. George's Cross in the grimy window, that symbol being lit up by red lights. The room was airless, smelled stale and like perfumes and smoke. The sofa was old, red, worn, stained.

Several small suitcases were lined up on the sofa. Looked like she was leaving this filth. He glanced at the clutter as she led him three steps away, took him from that cluttered room into a small bedroom. The bedroom was the size of a walk-in closet and wasn't any better. A small bed that was worn-out, barely twin-size, pushed up against the wall. Dull, psychedelic wallpaper was peeling off the dull blue walls. A small shower was in a small bathroom. The room was less than a prison cell.

She undressed him.

With her eyes and smile she thought she had seduced him into becoming her john.

But something else had seduced him.

Something that numbed him to the smells. Something that blinded him to the rubbish.

She reminded him of his first wife. Before the cancer.

Hair long like his first wife's hair, before chemotherapy robbed her of her beautiful mane.

He asked, "How much?"

"I will give you a good price."

"American Express?"

"I really need cash. Sven will need cash."

"Sven. Your pimp?"

"If you can pay in cash, I will give you a better price."

"I don't have cash."

She bit her lip. She looked disappointed. Or afraid. Maybe both.

He said, "Sorry."

"Wait. Credit okay. But I'll have to charge a little more. They have a surcharge."

"How much for an hour?"

"Sixty pounds for half hour. One hundred for hour."

"That's kind of pricey."

"First off, I'm better than the Russians. Or the Asians. Better than anything you'll find on Tisbury or Peter Street. They give you awful blow jobs and the worst sex you ever had."

"Is that right?"

"With me, you get a wicked time."

"I'd like to spend an hour with you."

She smiled.

Her soft smile disarmed him.

He could live in the past for an hour.

He decided that he was going to ask questions about Gideon after he finished. After he had dumped his manhood inside her. After he had proven himself. But she did a little dance for him. Undressed him. Massaged him. Put the condom on him. She sat next to him, spread her legs, and put lubrication between her legs. He'd hoped his touch had created natural lubrication.

He'd hoped she was as turned on by him as he was by her eyes and smile.

He said, "I want you on top of me."

"Positions cost more."

"No problem."

With a smile, she got on top of him. She rode him. Blood rushed and his erection filled the condom. She moved with him. Yielded an occasional moan. A sweet moan that ran through him and made his toes curl. She stood up, turned around, touched her toes, took it like a woman. He wanted to make her come, but he knew she wouldn't. She wasn't in it for the pleasure, only the pay, he knew that. Still, he had enjoyed her so much he had paid her for a second hour.

It was cold out. The weather and the streets nasty. Air damp with the promise of rain, the same rain that was a half mile away over Bloomsbury would be here soon.

It was a slow night for her. And he was in no hurry.

Someone came in the front door.

The man with the broken nose pushed her off him, reached for his gun.

Then the bedroom door flew open. Light green eyes and long blond hair looked inside the candlelit room, saw the whore on her knees, saw the gun pointed their way, then apologized and closed the door quick and hard. Then the front door opened and closed again.

Footsteps hurried down the stairs, light and quick.

He asked, "Who was that guy?"

"Sven."

He put the Eagle back in its nest.

She spread her legs, reached for her lubrication, and smeared a dollop between her legs.

He said, "Getting dry?"

She nodded.

When she was done, she pulled him toward her. He eased between her legs. It was different now. The lube felt cool. She no longer was hot and wet. She was dry and cool. Her rhythm had changed. The interruption had messed up the night. The whore had stopped pleasing him like before. He rolled away from her, grabbed her, put her back on her knees. He kept his eyes on the door. Now he was Tony fucking Soprano. He wasn't done. She had stirred him up and she had to finish. She wasn't done giving him the relief he was paying for.

He came. It wasn't a good nut. Nonemotional nuts were never that good. But he came.

He felt as if she had rushed him toward the end. Rushed him because of that Sven guy.

He wondered what she and Gideon had done last night.

A clock beeped.

She pulled her long hair from her face, gave him a small smile, whispered, "Time's up."

He nodded.

She said, "I'll need your charge card."

"I need to ask you about a customer."

"I don't discuss my customers."

He could've grabbed her by her hair. Thrown her against the wall. Put the barrel of the Eagle down her throat, make her suck that metal the way she had sucked him.

But her eyes.

Her eyes created that old memory and disarmed him.

He gave her a flirty smile, whispered, "I'll pay you extra."

"Why are you so interested in one of my customers?"

"I'll pay you an extra three hundred pounds."

That paused her. He knew it would. Working women were all about money.

She shrugged. "I don't know my customers anyway. They give fake names. They do what they have to do and leave. Some come back, some go to other girls. Men like variety."

Still he had to be certain.

He asked, "Did you have a regular yesterday evening?"

"No regulars. Most were tourists. Like you. Most I don't re-member anyway."

His mind replayed all he had seen Gideon do last night.

Gideon had searched the area, gone door-to-door, from model to model, before he picked this whore. Before he asked how much she charged for a blow job.

He had asked her the price.

That meant Gideon wasn't a regular.

It was random. Gideon stopping to see her had been random.

Maybe Gideon had heard that this whore was one of the best in Soho. He'd seen several men lining up to get serviced by this working woman. He nodded, convinced himself that it had been a random selection. She was beautiful, but she was no one special. Just another bottom-feeder. A beautiful bottom-feeder, a hypnotic bottom-feeder, but still a bottom-feeder.

In the softest voice she said, "The charge card? I need it now, if you don't mind."

He nodded.

He handed her his American Express card. She ran it through a reader.

He wiped his penis with a cheap paper towel, grabbed his tailor-made suit, got dressed.

She asked, "The extra three hundred pounds?"

"Sure."

"I could give you more time, if you like. More positions."

"You got pretty dry at the end."

"I have lube."

"That won't be necessary. Consider it a tip."

"Sven will be pleased."

He didn't care. It wasn't his money.

He stood in the living room. Looked at the suitcases.

He saw the clothes that were folded and ready to be packed.

When she came back with his card, her eyes were puffy and wet.

That caught him off guard.

He said, "You're crying?"

"Personal stuff. Have to sort . . . sorry." She wiped her eyes. "Sign here."

He signed the receipt. The whore thanked him for his business.

She thanked him like he had bought a dozen doughnuts at Krispy Kreme.

He stared at her, amazed at how much she reminded him of his first wife.

He said, "When will you be back? Was hoping I could buy you a drink."

"I don't drink. Stopped years ago." She took a breath. "Did unforgivable things."

The whore went to a small dresser and picked up a Bible, held it to her chest. She was afraid and crying. He didn't say good-bye, just left in a hurry, the Desert Eagle tight in its holster.

Downstairs men were moving up and down the shit-smelling street. Groups of foreign boys and men were going in and out of every door that advertised models. Whores were working tonight. Kids were still playing football in the dim streetlights. On shit-smelling concrete.

Men were walking in and out of narrow doors advertising tender, international models.

He looked for Sven. Sven was across the street at Somerfield, holding up the wall while men went into the gay porn stores in the alley. They made eye contact. He nodded at Sven. He was done. Sven headed for the door, staring at him with the coldest glare he'd ever seen.

Umbrellas up high, customers were still going in and out of shit-smelling brothels.

Children were still playing football on the streets as if they were immune to the rain.

It didn't seem fair.

The man with the broken nose hunched his shoulders and moved through the crowd.

He hurried through Leicester Square, his suit smelling like a whore, his soles like shit.

While he waited on the tube at Embankment, the smell from the beautiful whore rising from his loins, he wiped water away from his head and face, and he thought about Skeeter.

He wished he could fix everything that was wrong in his son's world.

As he boarded the train, he knew that was a wasted wish.

As he lay in bed with Tebby, sleep didn't come his way, not immediately.

Two in the morning became three in the morning.

The scent of those flowers smothering him.

He walked the room, the lie he had told Sam becoming heavy on his mind.

He had rewritten history. He had run from Gideon last night, but tonight, in words, he had rewritten that engagement. But he was determined to rewrite that history in the real world.

He did the runner's stretch. Did yoga stretches. Did two hundred sit-ups.

Then, with a sheen of sweat on his skin, got down on the floor, on his back, meditated.

He focused on each part of his body, concentrated on each muscle.

Tensed the muscle. Held for five seconds. Released. Tensed. Released.

He did that until his body relaxed and sleep arrived.

He dragged wicked thoughts into his sweet-smelling dreams.

In his dream, Gideon was beaten and terrified.

In his dream, he caught Gideon in front of the entrance to the Seven Sisters tube.

In his dream, he took out his Eagle and put hot lead in Gideon's back.

In his dream, he lifted Gideon over his head as a red double-decker bus zoomed his way.

In his dream, he was better than Gideon.

In his dream, he was *marvelous*.

Twelve

murder, my sweet

The next evening I was still near the capital city of England.

I had journeyed the Northern Line from Tottenham Court Road, changed to District Line at Embankment, and ridden that train straight into Wimbledon. Had camped out and waited for my target to return to his flat. When he walked in his front door and tried to turn on the lights, he found out his power had temporarily been disrupted. Ten seconds after he closed the door, he found out that I was the power disrupter. He froze when he saw me standing in the darkness.

Streetlight came though the open curtains. Illuminated their faces.

He wasn't alone. I had expected him to be alone. I didn't want collateral damage.

He said, "Who are you? Why are you here in me flat?"

I whispered a name to him, the name my employer had told me to whisper, the name of the daughter of a man and wife who lived in Louisville, Kentucky, and he knew why I was there.

Sig-Sauer in hand, in a soft voice, I told him, "The girl you molested, bad move."

He swallowed. "She said she was twenty-one."

"She was thirteen. That's statutory rape."

"She looked twenty-one. Don't you think she looked like she was twenty-one?"

That fat bastard clocked in at close to four hundred pounds. Three hundred of those pounds were above his waist, one hundred of those pounds in his breasts.

His companion was a young girl. She had come in with him, that look of abuse in her dark brown eyes. A thin, pale, black-haired child who wasn't older than thirteen. Deep brown skin. Small mouth with thin lips. Keen nose. Long black hair. East Indian. I spoke to her and she looked terrified. She shied away, responded in French, then tried to talk in English, a language that was foreign to her. I almost smiled at her. A young and naïve French-born Indian girl who spoke broken English. I spoke to her in French, told her to leave, that the bad man would not touch her anymore. She asked me who I was. I told her I was her friend. She swallowed. I motioned toward her and she hurried by me, left the flat, and took to the stairs.

That left me and the fat man alone to deal with this matter.

I said, "She's young. Very young."

He shivered. "She's . . . she's . . . a runaway."

"I hate pedophiles. You have no idea how much I hate pedophiles."

"No. I was . . . was . . . helping her. Was going to help her get back to her parents."

I moved from the shadows and stood close to that man. A brand-new black suit. I wore a black suit. A black suit and a black shirt. All Italian. Black shoes. A Sig-Sauer was in my gloved hand. He looked at the weapon. I stood in front of him, unmoving.

The Sig I had in my hand, I tossed it, made it land at his feet.

I told him, "Pick up my gun."

"Are you bloody serious?"

I moved to a bistro table, picked up a match, lit five of the seven candles on a menorah.

When I finished illuminating the room, I smoothed out my suit jacket, faced him again.

"I'm serious. Take the gun. Take it. It's the only weapon I have."

"Is this some sort of a trick?"

He picked up the gun, looked at it, then his mouth dropped open.

He said, "It's loaded. The bloody thing is loaded."

"Of course."

The pedophile aimed the death maker at me, its barrel pointed at the center of my chest.

He asked, "Who are you?"

I whispered, "Gideon."

He gasped. His legs wobbled. A wet spot appeared in his crotch. The reverend had been right. Every killer had to have a name. Then people would know who to fear.

"You're Gideon . . . *the* Gideon that massacred . . . the Big Bad Wolf . . . his bodyguards . . ."

I nodded.

He said, "I saw the pictures . . . online . . . I saw those . . . horrible . . . those bloody pictures."

He lowered the gun like it suddenly weigh a thousand pounds. Terror invaded his eyes.

I remained calm.

I said, "You have three choices."

"If you're Gideon, if they sent you here, *I don't have any bloody choices.*"

"Stop interrupting me."

"I apologize. You said I have three choices?"

"Yes. You have three choices. Shoot me. Or shoot yourself."

"The third?"

"Guess you only have two choices, really."

"And if I shoot you?"

"You'd best kill me."

"If I don't kill you?"

"I'll kill you a thousand times."

"Then . . . then . . . then . . ." He pointed the gun at my face. "*I'll bloody kill you.*"

"Don't talk about it. Be about it."

"What?"

"Bloody kill me."

I held both hands out at my side.

He took a harsh step toward me, my candlelit face showing him no fear.

I smiled.

"Gideon . . . you are him . . . you are indeed Gideon."

He backed away from me, slipped in his own piss, regained his balance.

He said, "You're *the demon*."

"The what?"

"*The demon*. One of the supernatural spirits from Arabic mythology."

"They call me a demon?"

"They do. On the Internet. You're a legend. They say you can find anyone. Anywhere. You're made of fire or air . . . maybe both . . . you can assume human or animal form."

"What else have you heard?"

"That . . . you . . . you are the cause of many accidents and diseases."

I took a step toward him. "Then let's have a little accident."

He trembled.

Then with his flabby arm, he raised the gun again, but not at me, this time he pointed the barrel underneath his chin. He closed his eyes, tight, as if someone else was holding the gun.

He cried, "I'm sick . . . let me get some help . . . please . . . I need counseling . . . I'm sick."

"I don't take too kindly to child abuse. I find abusing a child . . . unforgivable."

"*Please*. I'll come back to bloody America. Back to Louisville fucking Kentucky. I'll stand trial."

"I'm not a bounty hunter."

"You are a beast. The agent of death himself."

"Die once or a thousand times. Your choice."

He said, "What if I miss?"

"Tampa."

"My God, and what you did to those men in Tampa. Pictures are circulating on the Internet, you know. Of what was left of their faces. It was . . . horrible."

I turned around and walked away. "Count to ten. I'll be counting too."

The pedophile's voice followed me. "Ten. And you say I have to count to ten."

"Don't let me get to eleven."

"I'm sorry . . . tell them I'm sorry . . . that I was . . . I was sick. Out of control."

I said, "Wait."

"Yes?"

"Lock the door behind me. Put the dead bolt on."

"May I be proper and leave a note?"

"That's been taken care of."

"Taken care of? How . . . ?"

"I was on your computer. I e-mailed everyone on your mailing list the details."

"You hacked into my computer?"

"Posted your confession out on the university Web site and on your page at MySpace."

"You told the MySpace community? I have a lot of friends on MySpace."

"I sent images of you with children. You piece of shit. Time to be honorable."

"You e-mailed everyone. No. No. Everyone will know."

"By morning. Everyone will know you're a disgusting pedophile."

"Fucking Internet. Never should've signed up for the bloody Internet. It's the devil's tool."

I paused, checked my watch. "I just want you to do the right thing, that's all."

Piss running down his pant leg, that blubber of a man cried like a child.

I said, "Don't let me get to ten. Don't make me come back."

I left the flat, pulled the door up behind me.

Ten . . . nine . . . eight . . .

Then came the sound of the dead bolt being engaged.

Seven . . . six . . . five . . .

I headed down the stairs, each step swift and unheard.

Four . . . three . . . two . . .

I was almost on the streets when I heard the explosion, the report from that Sig. There was a bang followed by the sound of his overweight body crashing into the hardwood floor.

I was on the corner of Compton Road and Worcester Road, outside a two-level duplex, the one on the other side of the former pedophile vacant, I'd verified that when I got here.

I started walking.

She stepped out of the shadows and startled me.

The French girl, she looked at me, emptiness in her abused eyes.

She reminded me of my days in Montreal. When I wanted to be French-speaking.

I called out in French, offered to help her get home. She gave me her middle finger.

I wondered if my French was that bad.

But her French was of Paris. Mine was of Quebec.

Still I understood her version of French better than I spoke the language.

And what I didn't comprehend, her aggravated body language interpreted for me.

The kid went off on me, cursed me like she was fifty years old.

She was terrified but she was pissed off. I had destroyed her meal ticket, now she had to find another bed. I caught up with her, again struggling in French, this whole experience feeling like it should have been in black and white with subtitles. She was a child, but her eyes and coarse body language told me that she had had a rough life, each year like a dog year, so her fourteen was really ninety-eight years of strife.

I said, "You are from Paris?"

"*Oui.*"

I offered her a chance to go back home. Told her I would get her back to her parents. She cursed me, told me I had messed up her chance to eat this evening, her chance to have a place to sleep for the night, each French word sounding corrosive. I gave her fifty pounds. She snatched the money and sprinted so fast she looked like a streak of lightning fleeing the scene.

When she was a safe distance from me, she stopped and lit a cigarette.

Behind me I heard neighbors banging on the door of the home I'd just left.

In English accents they were calling for the professor, asking if he was okay.

My eyes went to the young girl. She was hurrying away. As she turned a corner, smoke pluming around her tiny head, she told me good-bye, once again with her middle finger.

I gazed around me, at all the European architecture, the gray skies, and started walking away, not rushing, each step moving me deeper and deeper into what felt like a surreal foreign film. Speaking French had taken me back to Canada. Had taken me back to Quebec.

In that moment I was seven years old, walking René-Lévesque, was on the cobblestone roads in Old Montreal, then I was staring out at the waters. Basilica. Parc du Mont-Royal. L'Appartement. Inside that moment, I missed Montreal. I never had a chance to become Jean-Claude. Wished we had never fled that place. Wondered who I would be if I hadn't left the apartment on that night and killed for my mother, wondered who I would be if we had stayed.

I mumbled, *"Dimanche. Lundi. Mardi."*

In the distance I heard the wail of police sirens. Those wails, my alarm clock.

I divorced myself from those memories of Quebec, started moving, again on the run.

Thirteen

night and the city

Sirens wailing, I looked back every few seconds.

I hurried in the opposite direction from the young French girl, walked by Willington Boys Prep School, made a right at Worcester House Hotel, and kept to the shadows on Alwyne Road, passed by small properties that were labeled mansions. Sirens were getting louder. I stopped and checked my watch. Lights on a parked car that was parallel parked flashed twice. The lights from police cars were behind me, around the corner. A Mini Cooper started its engine. The red-and-white car looked like a rolling version of St. George's Cross. I looked down at the license plate on the front of the car and eased up. It was the same plate that I had memorized before.

It was the same car that had picked me up on Baker Street.

I went to the passenger side, got in. As soon as I closed the door, the car sped away.

I put my seat belt on.

The ride was smooth. The music enchanting. Miles Davis was ending a song. Couldn't remember the name of that one to save my life. Miles retired and Coltrane came on. "Equinox."

Arizona said, "I think I know who ordered the package."

"Who?"

Five police on BMW motorcycles whipped around the corner and sped toward us.

Then they were on us.

Arizona didn't move.

Those policemen sped by, their wails adding to the sirens a block way.

Arizona made a left at the light, then was caught by another red light. Across the street, in front of Halfhide jewelry store, the French girl was at the bus stop, all alone as people passed by, smoking, waiting on the 93 to take her away. I stared at the French girl. She was about the same age my mother had been when I was born. Living the same life. Love and hate jumbled up inside me. I took a final look back at that girl. She saw me, flipped me off again, turned away.

I'd wanted to save her. No one had come to save me when I was a child. And it felt like I had to save somebody for my own redemption. She had rejected me. Felt like I had failed.

To free a whore you had to first convince a whore that she was a whore.

Arizona shifted gears, zipped by WHSmith and all the high-end shops at Centre Court.

I asked, "Who do you think ordered the package?"

"Big Bad Wolf's little brother. His grieving little brother ordered the package."

"Didn't know he had a brother."

"Pit Bull. They call him Bull for short. Sometimes he goes by The Bull."

"These fucking comic-book names are killing me. Another freaking rapper?"

"Raps some. Better producer than rapper. More of a P. Diddy type. Can't really rap, but raps anyway. Can't really dance, but dances anyway. Makes a grip being mediocre."

"Where is he?"

"Still in Tampa. In the hospital."

"What happened to him?"

"*You* happened to him. He was with his brother the night you killed Big Bad."

"A lot of guys were piled in the stretch SUV with Big Bad."

"The word I got was Big Bad's brother was the one that didn't die."

"Thought the one that didn't die was in a coma."

"*Was*. But they didn't tell the media he was awake."

"Is that confirmed?"

"Just passing on what I just found out. Tampa left them scared. You scared them shitless. My guess is that as soon as he came out of his coma, he ordered the package."

"He came back into the world, his brother slaughtered, revenge in his heart."

"You left one of them alive. The wrong one."

"He wasn't the primary. Wasn't paid to kill him. Big Bad was the one."

"You should've killed them all. You have to kill all of your enemies. If you don't, they will come after you. No matter who they are, you have to put your enemies in the ground."

She said that with enough venom to kill an elephant.

I didn't think she was talking about the Tampa crew.

Arizona was talking about her little sister.

Her sister was her one true enemy.

The Cain to her Abel.

The Abel to her Cain.

Arizona offered to drive me back to Central London.

I told her to drop me off at the nearest tube.

We rode awhile, neither of us speaking, both of us checking the rearview often.

"Gideon?"

"Yeah. Whassup?"

She paused. "You have time to go to the Globe Theatre tomorrow evening?"

"Don't tell me you're offering me another contract?"

"I know you are a Baconian. But *Antony and Cleopatra* is playing tomorrow. *Coriolanus* the next day. I haven't seen Shakespeare in eons. Thought that maybe we could go together."

"Last Shakespeare I saw was *Titus Andronicus*."

"Saw that one. It was so damn bloody."

"*Antony and Cleopatra* is an excellent play."

"It's wonderful love story." She laughed a little. "You want to escort me?"

"Sierra . . . your sister sent the Dutch boys to fuck you up. You're not scared?"

"I'm not going to let fear keep Queen Scamz locked up in a room."

"I asked you a question."

"Thought that maybe we could have some fun, lose some of the tension between us."

"Is this another professional thing, is what I'm asking?"

"No contract."

"What is it then?"

"A date. We could make a night of it. Hang out in Leicester Square after that. I know a few good pubs and a spot that has cool dancing."

"One minute you're July, the next December."

"Maybe we could pick up where we left off in New York and Chapel Hill."

"Never been to New York or Chapel Hill."

She took a breath. "Okay. I deserve that."

"Thanks for the offer." I shook my head. "But let's keep this all business."

She absorbed the rejection. Now I knew how I looked when she shot me down.

Silence consumed her. I didn't talk either. London had a million sleeping policemen, what they called their speed bumps, stationed a few yards apart throughout the residential areas. Arizona hit those speed bumps every few seconds, those sleeping policemen stationed up and down every anorexic avenue. When cars came toward us, the streets were so thin drivers had to decide who was going to pull over, who was going to be polite and let the other go by.

She pulled over at the station. She had taken the long way. I could tell. A lot was on her mind, there was a lot she wanted to say, but she didn't know how to talk to me. Coltrane had finished his masterpiece and Wes was on now, his music seductive and mesmerizing.

I was thinking about a family that had been blown to pieces on a beautiful island.

Arizona said, "She was pretty."

"Who was pretty?"

"The girl that was in the lobby at your hotel. Long hair. Smooth skin. The one who was crying her eyes out until you came. The one you took upstairs to your suite. She was pretty."

Now I understood the attitude she had the day we met at Baker Street. The night she had dropped off the package on her sister, Lola Mack had been in the lobby. That was after midnight, when the tubes had shut down. Arizona had passed by Lola Mack when she went to the desk and dropped off the package. And she knew Lola had gone upstairs to my room.

I didn't question how she knew what she knew, or how much she knew.

Her knowing did piss me off. Her knowing more about me that I did about her kept me off-balance, and that was how she wanted me. Even now, she wanted me off-balance.

I said, "Keep it professional. Don't start acting like a square."

"I'm just saying she was attractive. Anything wrong with me saying that?"

I moved around, didn't feed into her conversation.

She asked, "Where you off to dressed up in a suit?"

"Text when you're ready to handle Amsterdam."

"You sound angry."

"I'm not trying to stay in London too long."

She looked in the other direction. But I saw her reflection in the window.

Saw a combination of anger and sadness in her face.

Once upon a time she had told me that if I had a million dollars in the bank she would be mine. Now that I was at that milestone, she told me that a million dollars wasn't enough.

And now I had hurt her feelings.

Good.

Let her swim in rejection for a while.

Let the tides of wounded hearts rise and cause her to drown in rejection.

I wanted her to feel what I felt.

Wanted her to feel that a million times over.

I said, "And make sure my fee for tonight's work is transferred in the next hour."

"No problem."

"One more thing. For Amsterdam, I want my fee up front."

"That's not how it works. Half and half."

"If you want it done, that's how it will be. I want you to be sure you want it done."

She hesitated, knew what I meant. "Sure."

"But I don't think you want it done."

"Why would you think that?"

"I have the package, but I haven't seen any money get transferred."

She didn't respond to that.

I said, "And thanks for the info on the broken-nose guy."

"Watch your back."

"What you mean?"

"Revenge knows no boundaries."

"You do the same. Watch your back."

She reached under her seat, took out a Glock, sat that death maker in her lap.

Arizona said, "We work well together, you know. In Chinatown, we kicked ass. I've always liked dealing with you on that level. We've always been like Nightwing and Batgirl."

Her purse was in the backseat. I saw the handles of at least two long-bladed knives sticking out her handbag. She had all bases covered, was rolling military-style.

I said, "We could've been good together."

"Past tense."

"Yeah. Past tense."

"You caught feelings for me."

"Now I'm cutting bait and throwing them back."

"I held on to my ghost too long."

"You still haven't let that irreplaceable ghost go. But I have let you go."

"One of the squares you met?"

"I'm out."

"I take that as a yes."

"Text me if you need anything."

"You're not a square, Gideon."

"I know what I am."

"You'd be better off with me, you know."

"Sure about that?"

"Just like I could be better off with you."

"Love talk is for squares, you know that."

"Stab me with my own words."

"Like you said, I caught you at a good time, you had needs, I had needs, and we fucked."

"We made love because I was attracted to you. And I couldn't handle it. Common sense is the enemy of romance. It's been a battle with me. I enjoyed the time I spent with you."

"Always July and December."

"It was nice in New York. Better in Chapel Hill."

"I don't remember New York or Chapel Hill."

"Don't be mean to me. I'm letting my guard down right now. I'm being vulnerable."

"I let my guard down with you a long time ago, Arizona."

"Face it, we have a lot in common."

"I let my guard down with you ten years ago."

"Fuck, Gideon. Give me a damn break. I'm trying to make it right between us."

"The shit we have in common is the shit I need to forget."

She twitched like a thousand wasps had stung her heart.

I got out at the tube station, left without a good-bye, heard her speeding away as I slapped down my Oyster card and breezed through the electronic gate. I zigzagged through the crowd, stayed to the left, and ran down the escalator, checking my watch, did the same at the stairs, made it on the train. Checked my watch again. Didn't want to be late for the next appointment.

Tears had been gliding down Arizona's golden cheeks as she pulled away.

I knew how it went.

Knew how she was.

If I had taken her to my bed tonight, again, I would've woken up alone.

Like at the Parker Meridien in New York.

Like she had done in Chapel Hill.

We'd make love.

Then she'd vanish.

Then we'd pretend it never happened.

That was our cycle.

And I wasn't sure if I could handle that.

I didn't want any more pain.

Not tonight.

I wanted pleasure.

Fourteen

squares and heat

An hour later I was drinking a Cobra Indian lager.

I had devoured most of my jerk chicken. Ackee salt fish. Spoon bread. Plantains.

Lola asked, "What's up with the suit?"

"Told you." I smiled. "Had a business meeting."

"Gideon ran out and got GQ for a late-night meeting." Lola laughed. "He had a hot date."

"Looking good. Smelling nice." That was Mrs. Jones. "You're right. He's cheating on us already."

"He's just another Sonofabitch."

We laughed.

Lola was next to me, done eating, margarita in hand, her leg touching mine. Mrs. Jones faced me, her foot occasionally rubbing my leg, or reaching for my crotch. A bottle of red wine was on the table, almost empty, a second bottle already ordered.

We were at Banners on Park Road. Trendy restaurant with first-class service and a variety of food. Down in Crouch End, an area that had more restaurants than should be allowed. They were here waiting for me. Mrs. Jones dressed in black, her dress short and tight, her boots thigh high with black leggings, the same style that many of the London women sported. Lola had on sinful jeans and a dark blue blouse, a silky number that curved around her breasts.

Lola got excited, said, "Guess what I found out today? I was down in the gym running, and somebody had left one of the African newspapers behind, a *New Nation*, and guess what I found out?"

Mrs. Jones and I both asked what at the same moment.

"They have this pro-black movement over here. A Just African Movement for Unity. AJAMU for short. That's their NAACP, I guess. They hold meetings for Africans and Jamaicans and black people and want everyone to hook up and share their experiences in this racist bitch. That way there will be some unity. Unity in the hope of making their lives better on a global level. Check it out. Liverpool used to manufacture slave ships. They had slaves here, and they made ships and shipped slaves from Africa, did that shit right here in England."

I said, "Is that right?"

"They have a Slavery Remembrance Day. Something America won't do. Still Liverpool acknowledges its role in the slave trade, which, again is better than America, but at the same time the UK refuses to acknowledge the effect that this has had on the racial dynamics of the city today. They got rich off selling black people. They remain rich by keeping black people as second-class citizens. America got rich off black slaves. England did the same thing."

No matter what was going on in my world, I'd found it impossible to leave them.

I was clinging to them like they were life preservers in the sea of normalcy.

Lola. Tipsy. Rambling. "Check it out. On the Town Hall building, they have the bullshit they did chiseled in stone. They have sculptures of slaves in chains, like they are still celebrating slavery, show them trading Africans as goods, still have the slaving ships carved in stone."

Mrs. Jones. Tipsy. Methodical. "What are they doing about that part?"

"Check it out again." Lola sipped her spirits. "They have sculptures of Neptune with his hands on the heads of two little black boys. Arms, legs shackled. *Shackled.* Motherfuckers refuse to remove it because they claim it's a part of history that we shouldn't forget."

"Are you serious?"

"I read it in the paper. They apologized for slavery but black people still can't get a job or a decent place to stay in the city. I read that Liverpool was the most racist city in the country."

"Amazing. Sounds like the South."

"Hence, over here they call it Liver-Alabama-Pool." Lola sipped again. "It's all connected. Global disrespect. No respect for the black man. They should go ahead and have an international Disrespect the Black Man and Woman Day."

Mrs. Jones said, "They already have that."

"They do?"

"It's called Monday, Tuesday, Wednesday, Thursday, Friday, Saturday, and Sunday."

They laughed.

"Impressive." Mrs. Jones smiled at me. "You look good in a suit, Gideon."

"He doesn't notice it, Mrs. Jones." Lola was shaking her head. "Not at all."

I said, "Notice what? Wait . . . your silver cross is on Lola's neck."

Lola shook her head. "Not that. I'm wearing Mrs. Jones's cross, but not that."

I asked Mrs. Jones, "You okay?"

"Look at my left hand."

I did. It took me a moment to realize what was different. "Where's your wedding ring?"

"Packed away. I think I'll save the diamonds, have them made into earrings."

"And wear them. Cool."

"No. Give them to my daughter as a present. That ring means nothing to me anymore."

Lola said, "He didn't notice what else you did. Gideon is as blind as Stevie Wonder."

I asked, "Besides giving Lola your cross, what else did you do, Mrs. Jones?"

"You are so right, Lola." Mrs. Jones smiled. "Stevie Wonder can see better than Gideon."

"Much better."

I didn't get it.

They shook their heads and laughed.

I asked, "How was your day?"

Lola. "We went to see Buckingham Palace."

Mrs. Jones. "Westminster Abbey. Big Ben. London Wheel."

Lola. "They call it the Eye."

Mrs. Jones. "What?"

"The London Wheel. They call it The Eye. Nothing but a big Ferris wheel."

"Then we thought about going to the London Aquarium."

"I wanted to see the sideways-walking crabs. But we caught a play instead."

"*Stomp!*"

I smiled. "You women have too much energy for me."

Lola said, "I want to see all the locations from the movies *Notting Hill* and *Closer* too."

Mrs. Jones sipped her wine. "We should do Paris. It's only two hours away."

Lola rolled her eyes. "I heard they love Jerry Lewis and hate black people over there."

Like the Village in New York, this area was populated by musicians and journalists who didn't care to live thirty minutes away in the city. Bar up front. Wood-paneled walls and light-colored wooden floors. Waitresses dressed in black. A stoplight was wedged in a corner, a section that featured a wall-size photo of Bob Dylan. An Isle of Man Festival poster was on the wall over our wooden table, along with posters depicting singers mixed with Japanese art on sale for two thousand pounds.

Our waitress came over. Scottish accent. Warm smile. "Everybody finished here?"

I answered, "Yes."

"Did you enjoy it?"

Mrs. Jones smiled. "Loved it."

Big smile from the waitress as she deferred to me. "Dessert menu?"

Soon coffees were on our wooden table. Our decadent desserts were almost gone. The man at the table across from us took out a filter and rolled a cigarette. Europeans who weren't afraid of black lungs and slow, painful deaths crossed their legs, rolled their own cancer before and after dinner. This was the world I wanted to be a part of. I wanted this to be my home.

On the television the news was on. Special report. First were images of a crime scene, then the pictures of the man I had just visited. SUSPECTED PEDOPHILE COMMITS SUICIDE IN WIMBLEDON. My cellular beeped. A text message: FUNDS TRANSFERRED.

I had killed a pedophile then come here for fish and beer.

As if it was no big deal.

A gentle wave of nausea passed though me.

Lola asked me, "You ever fall in love, Gideon?"

"Once. Fell for a girl I met in a pool hall. Didn't work out in my favor."

Mrs. Jones said, "I've only been in love once too."

"That's tragic." Lola said that. "Damn tragic."

"It is tragic. To only love one man. Not cool at all. The part of me that knows how to unlove is broken. I need to find a way to fix the part of me that knows how to unlove."

"New dick, Mrs. Jones. All it takes is new dick."

We all laughed, laughed hard and loud, like Americans.

In the middle of that laughter was when I noticed two things. Not both at once.

The first thing was Mrs. Jones.

The first thing I noticed was pleasant.

I said, "Your hair. Wait a minute. Mrs. Jones, you took your braids down."

Mrs. Jones frowned. "You really didn't notice, did you?"

"I like your hair like that. It's looks great . . . damn sexy when it's wild like that."

"I did it because you said that you liked it this way."

I put my hand in Mrs. Jones's wild mane. Her big Afro was pure neo-soul.

I apologized for being so distracted.

She leaned over and kissed me, accepted my apology.

Mrs. Jones was forever stunning. She wore a black dress, tight, with plunging neckline that showed off her top-shelf jewelry. Her hair framed her beautiful face. Her diamond necklace so classy. So much had been on my mind that I hadn't noticed a lot about her.

Lola looked like a different woman. She had on heels and jeans with colorful embroidery down the sides. No wrinkled Old Navy gear tonight. But even if she had chosen to go Old Navy, it would look priceless on her. She had just enough makeup, her hair was down, hung below her shoulders and framed her face. Her cleavage was respectable yet undeniable.

Lola sipped her wine and asked, "You see the African sister who had bleached her face? She was two tables over. Her neck was as dark as licorice and her face was ten shades lighter."

Mrs. Jones tsked. "Saw her when I came in. Horrible."

I looked toward the front door. Didn't see the woman they were talking about.

That was when I noticed the second thing.

This one deadly.

The second thing readjusted my mental landscape and fucked me up in a major way.

The man with the broken nose was here.

He was watching me.

My laughter ended with abruptness.

The man with the broken nose was only a few feet away from me.

Hidden in plain sight.

Didn't know how long he had been staring at me.

I became sharp and lucid, became angry and defensive, all of those emotions hidden behind a mask of nonchalance. The only thing that would've given me away was an abrupt swallowing of nothing. I looked at the man who had been stalking me.

The women unaware, still laughing and talking about irrelevant shit.

Lola asked, "Why do they do that to themselves? Why would anybody bleach their skin?"

Mrs. Jones answered, "Ask Michael Jackson."

"That's cold. Leave Michael and his white *chirren* alone."

Lola's and Mrs. Jones's words became muffled. The only sound I could hear with any clarity was the sound of my beating heart, and my heart was beating fast and strong.

Lola shook her head, sipped her wine, her intoxicated words soft and easy. *"I read in* The Voice *that a lot of Africans have been doing that mess a long time."*

"Bleach is only skin-deep, but fucked-up psyche goes to the soul. Poor blacks with huge self-image problems are funding a multibillion-pound industry."

"Tell Michael Jackson."

"You are so drunk."

Lola pumped her fist; in my mind she was moving in slow motion. Everything was moving in slow motion. *"Well, I'm black and I'm proud. Do I need to say it loud?"*

Laughter echoed like laughter in a house of horrors.

I had no laughter to give.

I looked around the room at the people. Tried to see how deep he was rolling.

Lola said, *"Seems like the only man who loves a dark-skinned sister is the white man."*

Mrs. Jones chuckled. *"All they care about over here is* Big Brother *and* EastEnders."

He was up front, sitting at the counter, sipping spring water, his face still in bandages.

"Europe ain't no different than America. Dark skin is still associated with failure and light skin with success. That's the disease Jerry Lewis needs to have a telethon for. Some of these African and Caribbean women have been brainwashed into thinking beauty equals whiteness."

Mrs. Jones shook her head and sipped her wine. *"Same all over the world, I imagine."*

"Especially since the U.S. started exporting Baywatch."

"Oh, God. Those skinny white women with huge breasts messed the world up."

I stared. He didn't move his eyes away, held that poker-faced glare.

Lola: *"Bleaching skin like Michael Jackson? They need mad therapy* over here. *And some better beauticians. Sisters over here have some jacked-up basket weaves. Weaves in the States didn't look that damned bad back in the eighties. They must be sewing in the hair the sisters in the States is throwing away. I could make a grip if I turned them on to the laced-front wigs like Beyoncé, Janet, and Tyra are pimping. But that's another story. The bleaching kills me."*

The man with the broken nose was only a few feet away from me.

On this rugged road we traveled, I was damn near within point-blank range.

While Lola and Mrs. Jones rambled, I kept my eyes and attention on him.

"You are tipsy and on a roll, Lola."

"Shit, I'm just getting warmed up. Hand me another drink and a microphone."

He nodded at me. He did that like he was real cool.

I returned the subtle gesture, mailed it back to him the same way.

What was going on between me and the man across the room was unmistakable.

Mrs. Jones's laughter overlapped my heartbeat. *"Lola, you are killing me over here."*

"Okay, I'll stop dissing the sisters. But you know they talk about us. Shit, ain't like any of them ran to America to bring us back home any damn way. Their fault we were damn slaves."

"You have me laughing so hard I need to go to the bathroom."

"Toilet. Or they call it the loo. Or the water closet. They laugh and mock us when we say bathroom. *Why? I have no idea. These British people are weird, I kid you not."*

Then the bloodied-nose bastard did something I didn't expect.

He smiled and motioned at the empty chair next to him.

He wasn't going to run away this time.

I looked around the room, tried to see if he was alone, if he had brought backup.

Mrs. Jones grabbed her coat and purse, headed toward the toilet. Lola went with her.

They left unaware that I was in a death stare with a man across the room.

I took my time, pulled out my wallet; left enough British money for the bill on the table, sipped my drink, then stood and stared at my friend. He glanced at me, not surprised that my face was intense, exuding anger, now the prince of darkness, ready to do battle.

My hand eased down, picked up a steak knife from my table.

Blade in hand, a smile on my face, I marched toward him.

every killer must die

Fifteen

where the sidewalk ends

He remained smooth, waited like he was in no hurry.

My heart was slamming against my ribs, muscles burning, hot breath searing my throat and nostrils. I felt like an animal that was being hunted and tortured, prey before the big kill.

I didn't hide my blade.

He pulled back his jacket, showed me he had a friend sitting in his lap. Desert Eagle. Titanium finish that made the gun look like a striped tiger. A tiger that spat out .50 slugs.

He said, "No need for that."

"Is that right?"

"Unless you're holding aces and eights."

I put the blade on the counter, left it within reach, kept my eyes on the Desert Eagle. I'd bet that was the same Israeli cannon Sergeant told me someone had tried to buy.

He said, "Beautiful women you're with. Each could dethrone Miss Black Britain."

"You ran away from me down in Covent Garden."

"I didn't see you at Covent Garden."

"Just when I thought we were getting somewhere."

"No reason to lie."

"Same at Knightsbridge. You ran."

"I'm not running now."

I asked, "Who are you working for?"

He reached into his Waterstone's bag. I was about to stab him in his neck. He took out a book. Hardback. The man slid the book to me. A James Patterson novel. *The Big Bad Wolf.*

All doubts evaporated. Everything that was opaque became clear.

The steak knife I had left on the counter, I gritted my teeth, put my hand over the handle.

He moved his hand to his Desert Eagle, the barrel of that cannon trained on my gut.

He said, "Unless you're interested in your guts becoming some pretty fancy artwork on that back wall, I'd suggest you take it down a notch. If I wanted you dead, you'd be dead."

I nodded, moved the weapon again, this time slid the steak knife away from both of us.

He moved his hand from his gun. But not too far away.

He shook his head. "Enjoy the beautiful ladies you're with. Enjoy the rest of the night."

I nodded. "Make sure I don't see you first."

"Good. I love a challenge. Especially from a man with your reputation. It'll be an honor. In the meantime, get your houses in order. Seattle. Palmdale. Georgia. Very nice homes."

That got me. He knew where I lived. He was telling me he could find me anywhere.

He was telling me that someone had put together a package on me.

He said, "If you run, you'd better keep running."

I wished I had put that knife deep in his throat as soon as I had crossed the room.

He said, "And one last thing before we part. A word of advice."

"Which is?"

"The tubes. Jubilee has better platform doors, so I'd stick to that tube as much as I could. Otherwise you'd better mind the gap. People slip and fall in front of trains all the time."

"I'll keep that in mind."

"Have your lady friends do the same. Make sure they mind the gap."

"Is that a threat?"

He smiled.

I said, "You have a name?"

"I don't need a name."

"Good or evil, everyone must have a name."

"Only men who are about to earn a tombstone need names, you know that, Gideon."

He got up and walked away.

Arrogant fuck.

I waited to see if anyone else got up and left with him.

Nobody in the small restaurant moved. Nobody stopped eating or laughing.

Then I went to the door and tried to see how he was traveling.

He had vanished.

I went back to the counter, picked up *Big Bad Wolf*, dropped that message into the trash.

I sat down and rubbed my head, angry at myself for taking that job in Tampa.

Then I panicked. I didn't know if he had been alone. I had been looking for men to be with him, but a woman could be on his team, like Arizona had been on my team earlier. That Goth girl who had followed me from Baker Street, she could be here. She could be a killer.

Lola. Mrs. Jones.

He had threatened them.

They could be in trouble right now.

I grabbed a knife and rushed back toward the toilet area.

Mrs. Jones was coming my way, Lola in tow, both laughing and smiling.

Both of them were so happy and tipsy they wouldn't notice an earthquake right now.

I put the knife inside my coat pocket. Then I grabbed another steak knife to keep the first one from being lonely. Wanted to grab more, but the inebriated women had taken my arms.

I hurried them toward the door.

There was a full moon, and the werewolf inside me was fighting to get out. I opened and closed my hands. Wanted to become the hunter, didn't like being the goddamn prey.

I told Lola, "Let's get a cab and get out of this area."

"This is a nice area. Let's look at some of the architecture."

Mrs. Jones said, "Let's walk off some of that food."

"Yeah," Lola said. "It's kinda nice tonight. Let's walk."

The drunken women took off arm in arm, laughing like they were going down the Yellow Brick Road. Lola and Mrs. Jones stopped a few businesses down, stopped in front of a shop called Mirror, Mirror and began looking at wedding dresses. I kept walking, kept my eyes on the road, noticing cars, people, anything that was moving. Strolled by parked cars, looked to see if anybody was hiding, if anybody was waiting. There were business and homes on this two-lane road. Plenty of bushes. Plenty of places to hide. I crossed the street, came back. Mrs. Jones was still in front of the shop that had wedding dresses on display. Lola had stopped at a store and was looking at erotic sculptures.

I called out to both of them, "Let's get a cab. Get out of here before it rains again."

I called them several times, only to get waved off. I walked toward the high road, stopped across from a bar called Monkey Nuts. I spied toward the clock in the center of town. I stopped right before Middle Lane. From here it was almost two miles to the nearest tube. I didn't want to chance a bus from here to Finsbury Park or Wood Green. Buses were too easy to follow.

Anxiety and trepidation were becoming anger and frustration.

Mrs. Jones stayed in that window. Frozen. Her eyes on those wedding dresses.

Lola caught up with me, left Mrs. Jones alone with her thoughts.

Lola kissed me. Kissed me with the softest lips, kissed me and pressed her body against mine. A woman's kiss could be the sweetest thing a man ever tasted.

Just like some poisons.

I said, "Not now, Lola."

She kissed me again. Kissed me until I had to pry her away.

She held on to my arm, smiled like she had just been crowned Miss America.

She whispered, "Thanks, Gideon. You are so wonderful. This has been the best week of my life. I mean it went from being a tragedy to a fairy tale. A damn freaky fairy tale."

The werewolf inside me stopped growling so loudly.

Lola kissed me again.

The beast inside me stopped clawing and snarling. The beast wasn't gone, just chained.

I told Lola, "We need to talk about getting your ticket back to Los Angeles."

"When?"

"I can put you on a flight tomorrow afternoon."

"Tomorrow? Can I kick it with you a little longer?"

"Look . . . tomorrow . . . you should . . . might be better if . . ."

"Is it another woman? Am I talking too much? Does my breath stink?"

"Not at all. I have some business to take care of, that's all."

"What kind of business?"

I paused. "I do evil things, Lola."

"How evil?"

"Evil enough for evil people to want to find me."

"What did you do?"

"You don't want to know." My voice stressed. "So don't ask me, okay?"

She chuckled. "We all do evil things, Gideon."

"Not everybody. Not like me."

She saw how serious I'd become. There was a short pause, and evaluation.

She kissed me again.

Lola said, "I want to stay here with you, Gideon."

"Didn't you hear what I just said? I do evil things, Lola."

"You do good things too. That's all I see. The good things you do."

My eyes went back to the cars as they passed. Everything was peaceful.

But at any second I expected to hear the report of a Desert Eagle.

I needed to get away from here and get in contact with Arizona.

I barked at Mrs. Jones, my tone now stiff and impatient.

Mrs. Jones broke away from old memories and the new wedding dresses, her heels clicking as she caught up with us, her lips pushed up into a brokenhearted smile.

Tears in her eyes, Mrs. Jones took our hands and we moved down Middle Lane toward Crouch End Broadway.

My mind was on that Desert Eagle.

With two women at my side, I'd become a speedboat weighed down by two anchors.

Like I was trying to swim while carrying over two hundred pounds of baggage.

No cabs were in sight. I got them to keep moving, my mind ablaze, no longer talking. I tried to hurry them along, but it was impossible to get women in heels to walk too fast.

Then something happened just as we passed the brick clock tower.

Mrs. Jones's stroll slowed.

She stopped, face became tense with pain, looked like she was dying.

"What's wrong?" I freaked out. "Answer me. What's wrong?"

"I . . . can't . . . breathe."

Lola was calling her name.

My heartbeat sped up.

Mrs. Jones was suffocating, the same as Sergeant had done.

She'd been poisoned.

Sixteen

the man who never was

I held Mrs. Jones, tried to keep her breathing.

When I first arrived in London, I had killed a man with poison.

Now it looked like the man with the broken nose had done the same.

Somehow he had slipped some sort of venom in Mrs. Jones's food.

Maybe paid the cook at Banners to season her food with death.

Lola was freaking out, but her breathing was okay.

I was too tense to tell if poison was in my system as well.

I looked at Mrs. Jones, my tone urgent, said, "Need to get you an ambulance."

Mrs. Jones shook her head, then struggled to get something out of her purse.

I asked, "What is that?"

"Need my albuterol. Need my inhaler."

I didn't understand, not right away.

Again I cursed under my breath.

Mrs. Jones put her inhaler to her mouth, took a hit.

We waited.

One minute.

Two minutes.

Three.

It was that long before Mrs. Jones took a decent breath.

I asked Mrs. Jones, "What happened?"

"I feel so silly. Asthma attack."

"What triggered it? Was it something in the food . . . what made that happen all of a sudden? You sure it's asthma? Look at me. Can you breathe? Are you sure you're okay?"

"Just . . . stress. Saw something in the window."

"What window?"

"Wedding dresses. Saw the wedding dresses. And . . . and . . . guess I got upset."

"Wedding dresses made you have an asthma attack?"

"A memory. That's all. Saw a fantasy unfulfilled."

She stood there, put the inhaler back up to her face, sweat covering her brow.

I backed down, tried to think, my own stress level deep enough to drown in.

Lola touched my arm. "What happened to you back there, Gideon?"

"What you mean?"

"You were acting like you were about to weird out. What did you see?"

"Not now, Lola. Look, I need to get us away from here."

"Bite my damn head off. Geesh. Was just trying to help."

She was too tipsy to comprehend my urgency.

She went to Mrs. Jones. Made sure she was doing okay.

I imagined the man with the broken nose was here, in the shadows, amused.

Mrs. Jones started walking at a better pace. Her breathing was better, some, not much. The sexiness easing back into her stride with each step. She put up a painful smile, tried to act like she was doing better than she was, ran her hand over her wild Afro, adjusted her clothes.

Mrs. Jones said, "Lola, what you asked me earlier, about getting married again."

"Uh-huh."

"No more wedding dresses."

"Really?"

"I'll never . . . *never* . . . put another one on. Never should have worn one the first time."

"Wow."

We walked some more. Mrs. Jones's breathing was much better.

Lola said to Mrs. Jones, "Never? Don't you want to get married again?"

"Marriage serves no purpose in my world. It does not benefit me. Marriage is for people who can't afford to buy a house on their own so they are forced to partner up. It's for people who dream of having children but know they can't afford to take off work so they need a partner to pull the weight. I don't need any of that. Not anymore. Never will travel that road again."

"Geesh. Thanks a lot." Lola let her sarcasm flow. "Makes my broke ass feel hopeful."

"I stayed too long, I know that now. Guess I tried to, as they say here, top up my marriage. Tried to add time. I guess my relationship, if not most, had a sell-by date. So I guess there is no need topping up something that has already spoiled. No need to top up rubbish."

Lola asked, "What are you saying, Mrs. Jones?"

"From now on I date. I date and walk away when dating no longer suits me."

"Or until it no longer suits him."

Lola was speaking from her own pain. Her man that had dumped her.

Mrs. Jones said, "From here on out, I'll always be the first to leave."

"At least be nice enough to let people know when you're breaking up with them."

"I'll date and remain true to my desires. To my unquenched needs."

"Don't let them get all the way to the UK and find out . . . that was some fucked-up shit."

"I want to be with someone, not love them, be happy with them without loving them."

"Without loving them?"

"Love is the cruelest trick of life."

"Nothing feels better than being in love."

"And nothing hurts worse than unrequited love."

"Unrequited?"

"Unreturned. Unanswered."

"You kill me with the big words."

"Not until you've been in love do you feel true pain. Not until the source is eradicated do you feel better. Love's bond is broken only by death."

"All I know is, if you can't be with the one you love, love the one you with."

That tipsy girl-talk conversation didn't interest me so I fell behind them, no more than a few feet, played sentry. Kept looking back every time headlights came my way. Looked for a .50 to be aimed out of the window of a Smart car or a Mini Cooper, my head in its crosshairs.

He was right. If he wanted me dead, then dead I'd be.

He knew who I was. He knew where I lived.

A thousand questions ran though my head, none of them answered.

"Gideon?"

Mrs. Jones glanced back at me. Her bottom lip was trembling.

She took her inhaler out again.

I caught up with them.

Lola asked Mrs. Jones, "You okay?"

"I'm fine. Not to worry. Just give me a moment."

She stood still for a good two minutes.

Out in the open. Might as well paint a bull's-eye on my back and chest.

I couldn't leave them. Wouldn't leave them.

Would rather die here than let them get hurt because of my occupation.

We were moving like snails through a busy area with lots of pubs.

I flagged down a black cab, this one painted with a picture of a black man sporting a fur coat, gold jewelry, huge diamond earrings, and a monster Afro. The image showed the black man holding a red die between two fingers, two more red dice off to the side of his head.

Lola protested, "Why does the pimp-looking black man have to promote gambling? They're worse than America on the damn stereotypes. Why can't they have Prince Charles or Sir Elton John doing that shit? I swear. I need to get to Brixton and find the NAACP over here."

They fell into the hackney laughing like idiots, Lola's drunken protests cracking them up.

For the hundredth time I looked back.

My heart had damn near broken out of my chest.

I took a deep breath and struggled to refocus on Lola and Mrs. Jones.

I was paranoid.

And they were redoing makeup and laughing. Having the time of their lives.

Mrs. Jones said, "I want to go dancing."

Lola was beyond excited. "Me too. I want to go dancing."

They were tipsy. Neither one of them wanted the night on the town to end.

Lola dug inside the back pocket of her tight, low-rise jeans, then handed me a couple of flyers. Mynite Productions was hosting a GORGEOUS event on Mincing Lane.

I said, "You just had an asthma attack, Mrs. Jones."

Mrs. Jones frowned. "Fuck asthma. Not going to let a little asthma ruin my night."

"You heard Mrs. Jones, Gideon. Fuck asthma."

They laughed like it was the best joke in the world.

These drunk and party-hungry women were pissing me off.

I gritted my teeth.

Mrs. Jones shook her head. "This date's not over until we say it's over."

Lola cosigned. "Not over until we say it's over."

"And it's not over."

"It ain't over. Party's not over." Lola danced and sang. *"Groove me, baby, tonight."*

Seventeen

sudden fear

Postal code EC3R.

We were in the southeastern corner of the City, on the north bank of the river Thames, between London Bridge and Tower Bridge. Across from Minster Court, near Davy's Wine Bar.

If that bastard had followed me here, there would be a lot of bloodshed.

Lola asked the driver, "What tubes are near here?"

He answered, "Monument. London Bridge."

Lola said, "Dude, London Bridge fell down. Didn't you hear the song?"

Then she laughed at her corny joke all by herself.

Mrs. Jones paid the driver. We got out, the Erotic Gherkin high behind us.

Mincing Lane of London was the top spice-trading center of the world when the British East India Company successfully took over all trading ports from Dutch East India Company.

Tonight it was party central. Minster Court. Subway sandwich shops. Sainsbury's. Next. Boots. Woolrich. A lot of tall, cold buildings on slender one-way streets.

North Londoners. South Londoners. East Enders. West Enders.

Jamaicans. Blacks from Trinidad and Tobago. Ethiopians. The children of Somalia. South Africans.

DJ on stage spinning. Beats like thunder. Lights flashing like lightning.

Women in stylish jeans. Men dressed hip-hop or Beckham style.

Vodka. Beer. Whiskey.

My senses were overwhelmed. Impossible to think. Impossible to get focused.

Lola said, "Now this is how the world is supposed to look, dammit. Look at this. The Ethiopians and Somalis have put their differences to the side and are getting their groove on. Look at them jamming to the misogynistic lyrics and the hard-core beats. Just like Americans."

"Dance with us, Gideon."

"Yeah, dance with us."

We got to the club, mingled in a packed house, danced up on each other, stayed on the floor, and sweated with R&B, hip-hop, soul classics from the seventies and eighties. Hips shaking and asses popping as the bass line roared like a lion in heat. Mrs. Jones started whining like she was a dance-hall queen, her moves so smooth it damn near shut the room down. Had no idea that aristocratic woman could move like that. Lola was so sexy, shaking her ass, crunk dancing, moving like a hip-hop queen who was bound to be centerfold in *King* magazine.

Mrs. Jones's breathing seemed okay.

I tipped away from them.

Figured they were safe in this crowd.

No one was after them.

I sent Arizona a text. Told her who I'd seen. Told her I needed her assistance. Told her that he had brandished a Desert Eagle with a titanium finish. Asked her to see if she could find out if anybody in her circle of hoodlums and rascals had unloaded that Israeli-made cannon in the last few days. I sent text after text. Waited ten minutes. She didn't hit me back. I called. All of her calls were being diverted. Straight to a voiceless voice mail.

I cursed.

Tried not to be, but I was worried for her as well.

As far as I knew, Arizona could be dead. It was that kind of business, that kind of life.

On this side of the street lives ended abruptly.

More died from a bullet or a knife than from old age.

With a new fear clutching my heart, I kept trying to reach Arizona.

Music was bumping inside that dimly lit club. International bodies all over each other, dancing and drinking. I saw a wild Afro coming my way. I'd been gone too long. And now she was moving through the packed house looking for me. Mrs. Jones hurried through the crowd.

There was panic in her dank face.

She called my name with much distress. "Gideon."

I took my cellular away from my ear, asked, "What's wrong?"

Over the thumping music, yelled one word: "Lola. She's drunk and in a goddamn fight."

She grabbed my hand and dragged me back toward the crowd.

I closed my cellular and ran with her, her heels clacking, us moving through the heat, through dim lights and a hard bass line, wondering if I had been stalked here, if Lola had been attacked, expecting to see her laid out on the floor like Robert Kennedy at a hotel in Los Angeles.

The crowd thickened and we were forced to stop.

But I could see what was going on.

Drink in hand, Lola was out on the floor, body language hostile, screaming at a guy.

Six-four. Two hundred pounds. Jeans. Trainers. Leather coat. Hair in cornrows.

I recognized his face from the program Lola had inside her luggage.

The actor from *Rent*. The guy who played the straight landlord. The one Lola had come to London to ride the Eye and live on *Love Island* with. Of all people it was Sonofabitch.

London. Not that big. Ethnic London was smaller. People who

partied were bound to run into people they wanted to see. Bound to run into people they *didn't* want to see too.

Sonofabitch was here. But he wasn't alone.

A mixed-race woman was at his side, screaming at Lola as well.

Thin woman. Long hair. Tight jeans. Black *Rent* T-shirt with red letters.

Was easy to tell who she was. Lola had told me and Mrs. Jones that as soon as she made it to London, she had gone to see her boyfriend and damn near come to blows with his new lover. That was him, and that had to be her, the girl who had replaced Lola as the leading lady in his life. From the look in both of the women's eyes, this was the sequel to the original battle.

Alcohol. Club. Anger. Jealousy. Women. Men.

Scorned lovers.

Sharp objects.

Recipe for disaster. This one just as deadly as the danger I'd been running from.

Lola was yelling. "*Sonofabitch, you better tell your bitch to get her finger out my goddamn face.*"

The other woman yelled back, "Who are you calling a bloody bitch?"

British accent. She had the home-court advantage.

Lola snapped, "Move that finger before I bite it off."

"You slag slut whore piece of shit cunt arsehole pussy."

Fingers in faces, name-calling, necks rotating, Lola and the girl were going at it like they were New York and Deelishis going toe-to-toe on the grand finale of *Flavor of Love*.

"I don't know what you done heard. *But I'm Lola Mack, bitch.*"

"Well, Lola Mack. He tell you that I'm Mimi? Did he tell you that he arranged for me to audition for Mimi and I got the part? Did he forget to tell you he loved me so much he did that?"

Lola froze.

Her ex finally got a word in, said, "Back down, Lola."

"You got this ugly bitch the audition?"

"Back down, Lola."

"Back down? Your cheating, no-singing ass wouldn't even be in *Rent* if it wasn't for me."

"I'm Mimi. So you can pack up and go back to America."

"Bitch, that's the last time I'm going to tell you to get your damn finger out of my face."

The other woman went off. "Bitch, I'll whup your bloody ass back to America."

Lola slammed her drink in the woman's face. Glass and all. Threw it hard enough to draw blood. The woman grabbed her vodka-soaked face and screamed like she was on fire.

Lola went after the woman.

Before Lola could get to her rival, Lola's ex had grabbed her hair.

He touched her and my insides exploded. Rage was unleashed.

I cursed, pushed through the crowd, knocked men to the side and pushed women off-balance, moved like a linebacker and opened a hole, Mrs. Jones running right behind me.

I pushed that motherfucker off Lola.

He turned and looked at me like he was going to rip me a new asshole.

The girls were screaming. Cursing.

Goddamn club fight.

A man with a gun was already fucking with my head.

This was the last thing I needed.

Last fucking thing I needed.

We were turning to walk away.

Lola's ex sucker punched me in the back of my fucking head.

Not hard enough to hurt, just hard enough to stagger me.

Just enough to wake up the Hulk inside me.

That other side of me sprang to life.

The part that had done damage in Amsterdam and Tampa.

That darkness opened the doors, took me along as a passenger.

The fight was on.

Lola was already back in the ring swinging.

Her ex was trying to hold her, trying to control her rage.

His woman coming at Lola at the same time.

Women. Goddamn women.

Without a thought I grabbed an empty Foster's beer bottle that had been set to the side.

It was either the bottle or one of the knives I had stashed in my suit pocket.

And Lord knows he didn't want me to come at him with a blade.

I went right at that motherfucker.

That bottle broke across his left eye so fast he didn't know what was going on.

He was blinded.

My fist followed and introduced him to some more pain.

A few good blows and pretty boy wasn't so pretty anymore.

My feet meet his ribs, had to make sure he didn't get up anytime soon.

Music had stopped.

The crowd was going crazy.

I turned to Lola.

That fight was outrageous.

Mrs. Jones had grabbed the other girl's hair, had become Lola's wingman.

She had come alive, dropped her aristocratic demeanor, and had Lola's back.

Mrs. Jones set the Jamaican in her free and yanked out handfuls of the Brit's weave.

Lola was hitting and scratching the shit out the woman's face.

Behind me, face bloodied, Lola's ex had almost made it to his feet.

I gave him another blow that encouraged him to hug the floor.

But he insisted on getting up.

Wiping blood from his eyes, he rose and was greeted by a head butt.

That took him right back down, nose bloodied and crushed.

I stood over him, faced him.

My expression asked him if he wanted to keep going toe-to-toe.

Blood from his first wound ran down his face, blinded his left eye.

He had to make a decision before I made my own.

He made it to one knee, then my foot went to his face.

He went down hard.

His new woman called out for help. Her British accent was strong as she screamed like she was trapped in a burning building.

Lola was all over the girl.

Hitting.

Kicking.

The girl's pretty face was now bloodied.

Even when the other woman had surrendered, I had to pull Lola off her.

The girl collapsed to the floor, ass kicked, crying, crawling, but still talking shit.

Trying to save face in front of the crowd from the motherland and the islands.

Gobs of store-bought hair littered the floor.

They never stopped calling each other bitches.

Lola yelled, "My boyfriend just kicked your punk-ass boyfriend's ass, beeee-yatch!"

I dragged Lola, took Mrs. Jones's hand, and we headed for the emergency exit.

Eighteen

the fugitives

We ran through postal code EC3R, took Mincing Lane, passed a Boots drugstore, headed to Fenchurch Street, and slowed in front of Hoffi barber shop.

I looked up, saw tall buildings with plenty of alcoves to hide us. I moved as fast as I could with two drunk women in high heels. Moved them by Next clothing store and Ernest Jones jewelry shop, made them turn down Rood Lane, a narrow strip that led toward the high street. We had to get to the high street and get a damn cab.

We made it to the Guild Church of Saint Margaret Pattens before we slowed down.

Then trouble yelled, its footsteps sounding like a cavalry of rage.

Two men. One had a short Afro. The other had braids. They must've run out behind us, sprinted to catch up with us, heard them huffing up on us as we rounded a corner.

Short Afro. "Yo, son. We need to have a word with you."

New York accent. Bad news.

Lola said, "They're in *Rent* too. His homies from New York."

Fuck. East Coast madness was jumping off in the middle of London.

This was déjà vu a thousand times over.

They had missed the matinee and were showing up for the second show.

Short Afro motioned toward Lola and Mrs. Jones. "Need to have a word with your bitches too. Yo, son, don't think you can just run up in here and throw down on my crew."

I didn't say anything, not right away.

The one with the short Afro was doing all the talking, five foot eleven, the shorter of the two. The one with the braided hair was taller, larger, and owned a mean face. Obviously the enforcer.

I said, "It's over."

"Oh, hell naw. It ain't over. It ain't fucking over."

I told Lola and Mrs. Jones to keep running toward the high street.

Never turn your back on the enemy.

The big one came up to me, fists doubled. I charged him, delivered strong blows from my right hand to his face. A good one to his jaw and he went down in pain, his jaw now broken. His eyes would be swollen so bad he'd be blind for a week.

Those blows had left agony in my hands.

No way could I hit again.

The one with the short Afro came at me hard.

But still he couldn't help his crippled friend. Seconds later he was crumpling in the darkness, dealing with his own agony. He was down on the cold and damp concrete bleeding, blood running from his thigh. He'd come at me and I'd gone low, steak knives I had stolen from Banners in each hand, and cut his leg as deep as I could, then swiped at his face.

That last swipe opened a gash on his chin, that was my last warning.

Seeing his own blood leaving his face, that was more than enough to scare him down.

His partner couldn't get up off the ground.

And Short Afro was bleeding, struggling to keep his balance.

I walked over to them. "We done?"

One answered in agony, the other in pain.

I threatened, "Police come after me or the girl, I come looking for you motherfuckers."

Again agony and pain replied.

Then I turned around to run away.

I thought they were gone. Hoped they had run on and found a black cab.

Lola was right there, eyes wide, her mouth wide-open.

Mrs. Jones was behind her, the same expression plastered on her face.

They'd seen the whole thing.

They'd witnessed my darkness.

They'd seen the darkness inside me that people feared.

They looked like they wanted to scream.

They looked horrified by what they had seen.

We paused.

Lola said, "We better raise up out of here real quick."

Mrs. Jones nodded.

I took the women by their hands, made them run in high heels.

We ran down Rood Lane, made a right at the Royal Bank of Scotland, saw no taxis on the road, kept moving, took another left down a narrow strip between HSBC and Citibank, the women running downhill, stumbling across that bricked road until we made it to Monument Street.

They stopped, needed to catch their breath.

Lola bent over and cringed. "I gotta pee."

I snapped, "Hold it, Lola."

"Can't. Gotta pee real bad. And my feet hurt. My feet hurt and I have to pee."

She staggered toward the historical monument. A freestanding pay toilet was there.

She yelled, "It costs twenty pence to pee. Damn. Twenty p to pee."

While we waited, Mrs. Jones took out her inhaler, took another hit.

I asked, "You have to go pee too?"

She shook her head.

"How's your breathing?"

She nodded. "Okay. But my boots . . . my feet are killing me. Can't run anymore."

I looked up the bricked road. Didn't sound like anybody was running after us.

But that didn't mean they weren't coming.

I'd guess we were five to six miles from the hotel. No way they could run that far.

A minute went by before Lola staggered out of the toilet.

Lola's face was alive with anger and sweat.

Lola said, "Damn . . . you whooped the whole fucking cast. Well, the straight men anyway."

"Rest of the cast? Were they there?"

"The rest of the cast is either female or gay. If they're in London, they're at a gay bar."

We still had to get out of that area. No time to wait for Mrs. Jones to get her breathing right. I picked Mrs. Jones up like she was a child. Carried her, hurried down the high street.

Lola said, "I'm sorry . . . I'm sorry . . . Sonofabitch . . . he just . . . I saw them and . . . I lost it."

Not a word came from me as anger seeped from my pores.

"Gideon. Gideon." That was Mrs. Jones. "The sign says Monument tube is right there."

"We're not going in that direction. They'd expect us to go there."

Lola called out: "We need to get to a tube."

I took a hard breath. "Too late for a goddamn tube anyway. After midnight."

Wild hair against my face, Mrs. Jones asked me to put her down.

Off to the side, we hid out for a moment.

I was aching, tired from carrying her like luggage. Tired from running in a suit.

I asked Lola, "You tell him where you were staying?"

"I didn't tell Sonofabitch nothing."

"You sure?"

"Sonofabitch was surprised I was still here."

"Do you tell him, yes or no?"

"No. I didn't tell him."

"Have you called him since you got here?"

"No." She took a hard breath. "Once. To curse him out. Had to curse him out."

"Did you use the hotel phone?"

"No. From an Internet café."

"When did you call him?"

"When we were out today. I didn't talk to him. She answered."

"You called from a café. Caller ID. Even if he calls the police, they can't find you."

"Sonofabitch grabbed my hair. That was a bitch-ass faggot move."

I left Lola to her anger, paid attention to Mrs. Jones.

I'd beat down three men, all three in need of a trip to Royal London Hospital. If I'd beat the last one any worse than I did, the Lady in Grey would've paid him a visit before sunrise.

I looked up. CCTV cameras were everywhere.

It was dark enough to make us all shadows.

I said, "Keep your heads down. Don't look up."

Lola asked, "Why? Scared Jesus might recognize us or something?"

"Just do what he says, Lola. Sometimes it's best to not question a man."

We took Lower Thames Street. Victorian buildings and businesses surrounded us.

Mrs. Jones said, "We kicked ass up in the club."

Mrs. Jones raised her hand, Lola gave her a high five.

Lola: "Gideon, damn. You came and rescued a damsel in distress."

Mrs. Jones: "He was vicious. A moment ago . . . he was vicious."

"You too, Mrs. Jones."

"Jamaican, baby. You were buck wild out there, Lola."

"Got it from my mama."

"Be quiet." That was me. "Both of you. Be quiet. Just shut the fuck up."

They did.

I wiped the sweat from my brow only to have twice as much take its place.

We stopped underneath London Bridge, the dividing point for Upper and Lower Thames.

I said, "Take the stairs. We need to get to another high street."

We hurried up the winding stairway that led to the bridge. Mrs. Jones was moving slow. I picked her up again, my hand under her ass as I carried her up at least fifty stairs.

We came out into a crowd of people heading toward the tube. Thousands of people dressed in dark colors most moving in the same direction. There were four lanes of traffic. Red buses and cars and motorcycles in numbers that would make Times Square envious.

It would be impossible to find us now.

"This is London Bridge? *This is it?*" Lola looked around, saw lanes of traffic, but nothing fancy on the bridge, not like most of the others. "I thought London Bridge fell down."

"Shut up, Lola."

"They had me singing that song all those years, and the bridge didn't fall down."

"*Shut the fuck up, will you?* You too, Mrs. Jones."

"I didn't say—"

"And don't say shit. I'm not trying to end up in jail over here playing Scrabble and bullshit board games and looking at tropical fish so I can get a one-pound-ten-pence credit on the books."

They looked afraid of me. Neither said a word.

I walked. They followed. Four heels clicking and clacking across hard concrete.

We were close to Borough High Street before we stopped in the middle of the madness. Looked like this was where all the red buses congregated. Small businesses and a million signs that said there was office space to let. A thousand black cabs passed by. And every black cab had its light off, already taken. The tubes had closed and everybody was competing for a cab. A good five minutes passed before I saw a taxi that was available. It had stopped right by us, was letting people out. I jogged to the taxi and claimed it before anyone else could.

I claimed it with a rudeness that identified me as American.

I didn't give a shit.

Right now, if I had to, I'd jack a cabdriver to get away.

I looked back the way we had come.

For a moment I thought I saw the man with the broken nose on London Bridge.

But a thousand men in dark suits were heading my way.

And just as many men dressed in urban gear like Lola's unfriendly associates.

The world was after me.

We loaded up as fast as we could.

Moved like were in fugitive mode. Dead on our feet, we wiped away the sweat from our battle, instructed the driver to head toward section W1 and Bayley Street, back to our hotel room.

Before we made it off the bridge, police sirens came from nowhere and everywhere.

We were assaulted by flashing lights.

Police officers on BMW motorcycles whizzed by us, those sirens fading in the distance.

A few blocks later Mrs. Jones started breathing.

Lola did the same, shaking her head.

I sighed. Looked at my hands, wished I had BC Powders in my pockets to kill the pain.

Fingers aching, I loosened my shirt. It was cold out but my skin was on fire.

Lola kicked her shoes off. Mrs. Jones took off her boots. Everybody looked back.

Lola took a deep, nervous breath, looked at me, and asked, "You mad at me?"

Mrs. Jones raised a finger to her lips, asking Lola to shut up.

Lola sighed. "Damn. Guess I'm in time-out."

My mind wasn't on the club fight, it was back on that gun with the titanium finish.

Lola said, "Don't be mad at me, okay? Please?"

I touched Lola's hand. That let her know we were cool.

She asked, "Can I talk? Or am I still in time-out?"

"You can talk. What's on your mind?"

"Liverpool has never had a black mayor or a black judge."

I smiled a little. Not much. "Let's skip resurrecting Liver-Alabama-Pool."

She said, "I just read that black Britons' numbers were dwindling because of all the interracial relationships. Heard the Caribbean race was almost gone and the African race was a minority compared to mixed race. What the fuck is going on over here in the UK?"

"And you brought that up because . . . ?"

"Because Sonofabitch was with a mixed-race bitch."

"Let it go."

"Black Brits going extinct."

"Let it go."

"Weave-rella won't be laughing when she hears my name, not anymore."

Lola leaned her exhaustion against me. Again Mrs. Jones sat facing me, eyes closed, her well-bred posture made sluggish by alcohol and being comfortable around us.

Lola asked, "What you thinking about, Mrs. Jones? What's that look on your face?"

"God, having a man stand up for a woman like that. My husband never stood up for me, not like that. Sad, huh? He stood up for the bitch he was seeing. Abandoned our family for her. Didn't stand up for me. Or for his own child. Not like Gideon just stood up for you. Gideon became so . . . so primal. He handled that without fear. Looked like he was going to kill for you."

For a moment it looked like Mrs. Jones was about to start crying again. Then, without warning, Mrs. Jones eased forward, kissed me, gave me her emotional and intoxicated tongue.

I wanted to push her away, but violence was an aphrodisiac to be reckoned with.

I relaxed into her aggressive rhythm. Her tongue pulled me into a better life.

Lola sang while we made out. The sleeping policeman didn't stop our flow.

Mrs. Jones was out of control.

"Sonofabitch . . . his ugly bitch . . . had the nerve . . . ," Lola vented. "He got her the audition. That's some bullshit. I'll still play Mimi. Watch. Fuck both of those losers. Coming at me like I'm a punk. Don't take my kindness for weakness. We whooped ass. That was better than being in *Rent*. Bet that ugly bitch gets cut from the play. We kicked some ass. We showed 'em."

Mrs. Jones: "Lola . . . the brawl . . . how Gideon handled it . . . that get you hot and bothered?"

"The way Gideon took control of the situation . . . I mean, damn. Her came up in there like Batman. *Wham! Kapow!* Onomatopoeias flying all over the place. Then he made me shut up."

"I'm not talking about sweating hot and irritated bothered."

"Oh, God. When he told me to shut the fuck up. That shit got me *so damn aroused*."

"Was beginning to think something was wrong with me."

"What you mean?"

"Gideon . . . he's . . . damn. I mean, damn. I have *never* behaved this badly."

"Me either. Gideon reactivated that nympho gene inside me. Hadn't wanted sex in so long. Wasn't getting any. Now I'm a fucking fiend. Doing all kinds of Sodom and Gomorrah shit."

Mrs. Jones got on her knees, unzipped my pants, reached inside, pulled out my erection. She licked the corners of her mouth first, dampened her hand, made it real wet.

I whispered, "What are you doing?"

"Thanking you."

I put my hand inside her thick mane, held her by her hair, her Afro became my reins.

From tip to root, over and over, in smooth strokes, my erection vanished inside her face.

Lola whispered, "I want to learn to give a blow job like that."

Mrs. Jones's face in my lap, caressing and licking me, I gazed Lola in her eyes.

She licked her lips, winked at me.

Lola whispered, "I'm horny too. Drunk and so damn horny."

The fight had excited her too.

Lola rubbed Mrs. Jones's back, closed her eyes, sang the nicest song. "Without You."

Little moans escaped me.

Lola sat next to me, kissed my neck.

I surrendered, swallowed a thick and heavy grumble.

Mrs. Jones's mouth was making wet, greedy sounds, her Afro bobbing up and down.

She was sucking the rage out of my body.

Lola was kissing me while Mrs. Jones worked the hell out of me.

Again I swallowed a groan the size of London herself.

Lola watched Mrs. Jones for a while. Then Lola moaned, pulled my face back to hers. She kissed my neck again. Sucked my ear. I was so damn gone. Like I was IV'd to a sedative.

Mrs. Jones had me on fire. Tingles ran up my legs as sweat dripped from my brow.

Lola whispered, "Save some of that honey for me, okay?"

Mrs. Jones tilted her head, moved her bushy hair away, smiled at Lola. "Lola?"

"Yes?"

"Are you ready to learn how to give a proper blow job?"

Nineteen

last night in paradise

The hedonism that started inside the hackney continued back at MyHotel.

Nobody had followed me. Nobody was here waiting.

Mrs. Jones popped in a CD and said, "Gideon, sweetie, go lie on the bed."

Lola: "Well, teacher. Break it down for a student."

I lay back while Mrs. Jones came to me, put her mouth on me, her slow licking and sucking resurrecting what I thought was dead. She worked me and talked to Lola, slapping my skin when I wiggled too much, told me that I better behave, not come and mess up her lesson.

Mrs. Jones demonstrated. "Use your tongue. Don't be afraid to use your tongue, Lola."

"Okay."

"Brush your face against his penis. Like this."

"Okay."

"See what I'm doing? Be gentle. Sexy. Brush your face against his testicles too."

"Okay."

"Oral intimacy is not just about giving him pleasure."

"Okay."

"It has to be a wonderful experience. More wonderful for you than for him."

Lola touched Mrs. Jones's hair. "You go, girl. Damn you go."

Mrs. Jones said, "Basically giving a good BJ is about wanting to do it. You *have* to love everything about it. You have to love to see, taste, touch, everything about it. You have to want it in your mouth. I love the smell of it. Actually I love giving head, more than sex."

"Do you?"

"I like the slow agony and anticipation of having my mouth on a man's penis. You know what's about to happen and you control what's about to happen. Nothing like having a man on his back, his legs open, watching him and waiting. I like to take my time . . . and it's on from there."

Mrs. Jones rolled her face over my penis, her wild hair brushing against my skin.

She said, "Look at his tool. So hard. So swollen. So beautiful."

Each time her face passed by my penis, her tongue teased me. She started kissing what she was admiring, licking it up and down, biting. My hands touched her skin, went from her back to her breasts. She showed Lola how to treat a penis with love and care, how not to be afraid because the dick was her friend, showed her how to lick the sides, hold the base if she didn't want to take too much all at once, how to control that part of a man.

I moaned, I moaned, I moaned.

Mrs. Jones told Lola what to do. Then Lola went through it step by step, stroking me, getting me close to orgasm, keeping me from coming, had me writhing and pulling sheets.

Mrs. Jones said, "It's all about communication. You have to listen your lover's body."

"Uh-huh."

"His every moan, his every breath, the way his body tenses, it's telling you something."

"Uh-huh."

"Now let me show you the art of tea-bagging."

Mrs. Jones took control again, moved on with her lesson plan, and moved from tea-bagging to showing her anxious pupil the art of the deep throat. Showed Lola how to give head with no hands, with no teeth, how to make her mouth feel better than a vagina, showed her how to relax as she took it all inside her mouth, her gag reflex a force to be reckoned with.

I lay back and enjoyed what could be the final moments of my life.

"Lola, do what I just did. Use both hands, kneading, up and down, be gentle."

"I can't do that."

"Try. Just try. Make him moan, Lola. Take away all of his problems. Make him moan."

Her tongue traced the length of me, slow licks, warm circles around the head, then Lola eased me inside her mouth. She glided up and down.

"Show me how to do that again."

"Okay, Lola."

Mrs. Jones demonstrated.

I moaned.

Lola said, "Okay. Let me try again."

"Take him in your mouth, Lola. Deeper. Slower. Don't be afraid. Relax. Deeper."

Lola couldn't deep-throat all of me, kept trying her best to imitate Mrs. Jones, still ambitious, so damn determined to get it right, gagging, almost threw up, but she didn't stop trying.

Mrs. Jones coached her. "That's it. You're working it. That's it. He's about to come. Don't stop. Take it all, Lola. Take that sweet nectar and swallow it. Love what he's giving you."

My hips rose toward Lola's face, my hand on the back of her head. My testicles tightened. I hardened. Grew inside her mouth. Moaned like I was at the door of heaven.

Mrs. Jones put her mouth next to my ear. "Are you about to orgasm, Gideon?"

"Almost."

"Don't you dare. Hold it as long as you can. Lola, don't stop. You're in control now. Make him suffer. Enjoy his pain, make his pain be your pleasure. Enjoy his misery."

My legs were trembling, hands gripping Lola's face, trying to give her this explosion.

If she wanted to pull away, it would have been impossible.

My body twisted, turned, my orgasm feeling so huge, so magnificent.

Mrs. Jones was applauding. "It's not about making a man come. It's about feeling good."

"Uh-huh."

"It's about making him want to come, then allowing him to come when you're ready for him to come. You take him to the edge, then back away, only let him come when you're ready."

Lola stroked me, sucked me, didn't let me get away from her, took my orgasm in her mouth, sucked the pleasure out of me while I shuddered and shook and grabbed sheets.

Then she hurried to her feet, staggered to the bathroom, and spat out my seeds.

Mrs. Jones took my penis in her mouth, sucked the last of what Lola had left behind.

She said, "Liquid cocaine. This is liquid cocaine. And cocaine is a helluva drug."

She hopped up, stretched like she had been rejuvenated, and followed Lola, laughing.

Sounded like they gave each other a high five.

Lola asked, "Any notes for a sister?"

"Notes?"

"Yeah, notes. Told you, I want to learn to give head like you do."

"Sure. Just remember, the dick is your friend."

Lola laughed.

Mrs. Jones said, "Control the dick. Don't let the dick control you."

"Okay."

"Enjoy. You have to enjoy it."

"What's the secret?"

"Breathing through your nose."

"Now you tell me."

"Can't give good head if you're breathing through the mouth."

"And how you use your hands. Like you're playing an instrument."

"It is like playing an instrument."

"Well, you're using two hands and playing the dick like you're in the marching band. The way you do it . . . massaging and sucking . . . that's hot. That shit is hot."

They laughed.

Lola said, "You'll have to show me again."

"Overall you're doing fine."

Lola chuckled. "Am I?"

"Men hate a dry, fast BJ. Right, Gideon?"

I sat up, made a rugged sound, it echoed like I was being stabbed.

Lola asked, "What did that crazy noise he just made mean?"

"He agreed with me."

Lola said, "Maybe that's the problem with mine. I do it, but I don't enjoy it."

"You have to enjoy it. It's about you, not about the man. It's empowering."

"You do it like you were born to do it. I do it and want to get it over with."

"And swallow the nectar. Spitting is so unladylike."

"You've been brainwashed."

"You've been lied to. Try it. You'll like it. Especially since Gideon has a good diet."

"Did my best. Was scared I'd choke."

"Gag reflex can be mastered."

"I can't take it all, not like you did."

I made it to the door, spied out the peephole, saw an empty hall.

Mrs. Jones went on, "I was watching a horrible very low budget porno where this lady clearly did not want to give head . . . it was so bad. I got pissed just looking at her. You really, really have to *want* to do it, and actually like doing it."

"Does it matter?"

I went to the safe. Opened it up. I straightened my clothes. Was about to leave. Didn't. Didn't take the weapons out either, left the safe unlocked. Just in case I needed quick access.

"If a man was eating you out, and you could tell he didn't want to eat you out . . ."

Lola said, "I'll do better next time."

I stopped in front of Lola's open suitcase.

"On the real. Be brutally honest. Outside of spitting, how did I do?"

"You were magnificent."

"That deep-throat thing . . . did my best."

Mrs. Jones laughed. "Relax, Lola. That's the main thing. All you have to do is relax."

"Breathe and relax."

"You got it."

"I'm serious. When can I get another lesson?"

"Hell, I need to get a few lessons from you too."

"On what?"

"If I could move my *bloody* backside the way you do. Good Lord."

They laughed. Then they were brushing their teeth.

Lola. "Gideon defended me."

"He sure did."

"Not just me, Mrs. Jones. He carried you when you were having your asthma attack."

"I know. That surprised me. He swooped me up. Like I was a princess."

"So Sonofabitch got that ugly British bitch the audition. And she's playing Mimi."

"That's messed up."

"Well, he got what he deserved tonight."

"You're going to be okay?"

"Oh, hell yeah. I'll get the part. I'll audition back in the States. I'd rather be on Broadway anyway. Hell, might just say forget *Rent* and hustle up an audition for *The Color Purple*."

The humming caught their attention.

The humming made both of them jump.

The humming made four breasts bounce.

What they saw scared them.

I was standing there, my suit wrinkled and sweaty, a weapon aimed at each of them. I had gone inside Lola's suitcase. I had taken out Lola's vibrators, had one in each hand.

Enough of this madness.

It was time to get even.

Twenty

revenge, so sweet

Two naked women were in my king-size bed.

Coltrane on sax playing "Crepuscule with Nellie." Curtains open, the city's illumination keeping the room from being dark. The two naked women were next to each other, shadowy legs touching. Both were blindfolded. Both were moaning. Lola was comfortable. She had moved from being fuck-shy to superambitious.

"That's right . . . that's right."

Almost as determined and uninhibited as Mrs. Jones.

"Oh, yeah . . . yeah . . . . oh, yeah . . ."

They were intoxicated with vintage wine and new pleasures.

Mrs. Jones ran her fingers across Lola's skin, Lola reached over and did the same, touched Mrs. Jones's sweaty flesh, then Mrs. Jones cupped her hand around Lola's breasts.

Mrs. Jones shifted, took her mouth to Lola's breasts. Her blindfold never moved. Soft licks, intense nibbles, as if Mrs. Jones were savoring her own tits.

They held each other, moaned like sexual spirits living in perfect harmony, Lola being the lead moaner. It was like listening to R&B and gospel. Billie Holiday and Sarah Vaughan in concert, or Badu and Jill Scott doing a duet, all the riffs, all the runs, all the blissful and earthy sounds made me want to sing, made me want to dance.

Mrs. Jones arched her back as she held back her orgasm, her face so intense, and she held her orgasm back like it was a monster, then she lost that battle, sang and let that orgasm go as if she were letting go of all the bad things inside her, releasing tension from deep inside her body. Lola was right there, moving from her R&B groove to hard rock, each breath a breezy alto.

They cooed and came almost at the same time. Mrs. Jones's orgasm arrived first, then as she surrendered to nirvana, Lola arched her back and joined her, Lola's orgasm being as sharp and brief as it was powerful, providing background music to Mrs. Jones's continuous chorus.

"Gideon."

"I'm right here, Lola."

"You're brilliant," Lola sang. "London is lovely. But can you take me to Greece?"

"I can take you anywhere you want to go."

"Greece. Take me to Greece . . . so I can see heaven."

I rushed to get my belt undone, couldn't yank my suit coat off fast enough, threw it across the room and struggled to drop my pants, only got them below my knees before they bunched up.

I turned Lola over, rubbed her sweet backside, got behind her warm and rotund blessing, left her blindfolded, silver cross hanging from her neck, swaying between two glorious mountains.

Coltrane changed songs, played "Sweet and Lovely."

Mrs. Jones was blindfolded, humming, back arching, still on fire.

I held Lola's wrists, went inside her slow, pulled her arms back behind her, over and over, easing her back into me, her face charting a course between Mrs. Jones's open legs. Mrs. Jones was holding Lola's head, raising her hips, making Lola eat her pussy like it was key lime pie.

Inside the shower. Lola was on her knees. Her hands on my butt. Practicing, determined, taking me down her throat. Smooth movements made her silver cross sway.

Mrs. Jones was at the counter washing her face.

She said, "Relax. Lola, relax."

Hot water was steaming up the bathroom, hitting my back, that same water spraying across Lola's skin, drops of water raining from her soft flesh like tears.

Mrs. Jones stood to the side. "Much better, Lola. Much better."

Skin wet, towel around her body, Mrs. Jones left the steamy bathroom.

Left us alone.

Lola had me moaning like an old man, each moan and groan echoing in this tight space.

Not long after that she stood up, more like tried to stand up, and I had to help her get her balance. Her face came up, grinning, then her smile came to me. Our tongues danced. She was kissing me while she kept stroking me, her tongue tasting like the part of me she held on to.

She said, "Bathtub hurts my knees."

I struggled. "Okay."

Lola stepped out, grabbed a towel, headed toward the bed, water dripping from her body.

I flexed my muscles, caught my breath, let the water rinse me a few seconds.

If I died tomorrow, God knows I'd never forget tonight.

I took her to the bed. Put her on her back, her legs up on my shoulder.

I said, "Tell me . . . what you want me to do . . . tell me . . . how to . . ."

"Stroke it . . . stroke it deep . . . deep and fast. I like it deep and fast."

I did what she asked.

Lola gave it to me like I gave it to her. We moved slowly and she moaned deep.

Mrs. Jones sat to the side, glass of wine in hand. She said, "This is amazing. Simply amazing. Lola, the way you can isolate your lower region, it's just plain remarkable."

Lola moaned. "You have your Jamaican thing going on, Mrs. Jones."

"Not like that. Maybe I need to take Pilates or yoga."

I was riding Lola hard, electricity running down my spine, so close to the edge.

She scooted away and I chased her.

Mrs. Jones laughed. "Get her good, Gideon. Get her good."

Lola slid off the bed and I followed, took her trembling and quivering and moaning to the floor, my hardness invading her orgasm, giving her another orgasm before that one could finish. I made her get on her knees, spread her legs, and I took her that way, my strokes short and circular, stirring the coffee, my hands on her waist, pulling her back into me, refusing to let her run away, but she fought with me, finally got free. Then she laughed. She panted, sweated, and laughed as she grabbed her damp skin like her heart was trying to break out of her chest.

Lola groaned. "This is insane. Oh, shit, I'm coming, baby. God-damn, I'm coming."

"Look at me look at me, Lola. *Look at me.*"

I laughed a little, then I moaned a lot.

She laughed too. "Dammit . . . will you come already? Please. Come for me."

"I will."

"Come before I . . . God . . . don't make me come again . . . damn . . . you're killing me."

Moans came from across the room. Mrs. Jones was watching us, in a trance.

Lola asked, "You coming?"

I strained. "About to."

She hurried and took me in her mouth, sucked me hard, sucked me as I held the back of her head. She struggled to breathe through her nose, held me, gave me all of her heat.

Mrs. Jones applauded. She stood up and applauded like it was the end of a Shakespearean play. My eyes went to our audience. She was blurry. So damn blurry.

Lola waved like she was at curtain call. "Next show eight P.M. My understudy will be filling in. Jaws are hurting and the coochie needs a break."

We laughed the best we could.

Lola said, "I've had more sex in two days than I've had in the last three years."

As soon as the good feeling began to fade, the image of a Desert Eagle came to mind.

The fangs of fear began to claw at my warmth.

Mrs. Jones staggered to the bathroom, her hands in her wild hair.

Lola licked her lips, wiped her face, rubbed my skin, smiled.

She whispered, "I swallowed."

"I know. I was there."

"I've *never* swallowed before."

"That was damn good, Lola."

"Anything for you. I'll do anything for you."

"That was incredible."

"You sure? I mean, did I do okay?"

"Shit. I mean that was damn good."

"You're the best." She kissed me. "I'll do anything for you, you know that?"

"Where have you been all my damn life?"

She chuckled. "I was asking myself the same thing. Love you. For real. I do. I'm yours. What you did for me tonight, I'm yours. No matter how you need me. However. Whenever. Wherever. I love you. I love you. I so love you. Mean it. I'm yours. All this is yours."

Coming from her, those warm words scared me. Like my three words had terrified Arizona. Lola didn't know me, but she loved me. There was no justice in the world. None at all.

I smiled at her.

She was in heaven.

"Anything for you. Wash your car. Build you a house. Have sex with you in a cathedral on Easter. You just tell me what you want. I'll do anything for you. Well. Maybe not the cathedral. Would hate to get on bad terms with Jesus. Have to draw the line somewhere."

I leaned to her and kissed her.

Mrs. Jones came back with two warm towels, cleaned us both.

I got the vibe that she was a nurturer. She needed someone to take care of.

Life didn't get any better than this.

But I needed to get them away. Away from me. Away from London.

Hiding my worry and fear, I said, "How would you ladies like to go to Paris?"

"Paris?" Lola looked like a kid on Christmas morning. "Are you shitting me?"

"My treat. Both of you."

"You don't have to ask me twice." Mrs. Jones smiled. "When do we leave?"

Mrs. Jones had read *The Da Vinci Code* and wanted to see all of the locations from the book, take *The Da Vinci Code* tour that was being offered, seeing the pyramid at the Louvre being at the top of her list, then abuse her American Express card and shop on the Champs-Élysées.

"Just you and Lola." I held my smile. "I have to go to Amsterdam on business."

Mrs. Jones looked concerned.

She asked, "If we go to Paris, will you be meeting us there?"

I shook my head.

Hurt underscored her disquiet.

"Can we roll with you, then go to Paris?" Lola asked. "After everything that went down tonight, hell, I need to hit a coffee shop or two or three before rolling to Jerry Lewis country."

"Sorry." I shook my head. "Serious. Maybe you should get away from here. In case he called the police. In case they're looking for two beautiful women and a man. Let this cool down. Get to Paris. Leave early as you can. Paris will be my treat. One hundred percent."

Lola said, "You hear that, Mrs. Jones?"

"Hear what?"

"The Eiffel Tower is calling your name."

Laughter.

I said, "I'll put you two up in Hotel Brighton."

Mrs. Jones didn't look thrilled. "Nice hotel?"

"Overlooks the Tuileries Gardens."

Lola asked, "Far from everything?"

Far enough away from me, I thought. Far enough away from danger.

Out of range for a Desert Eagle.

I said, "In the heart of Paris, close to the Louvre, the Opera house."

They pouted, Lola pouting the most.

They wanted to come to Amsterdam with me.

I said, "Champs-Élysées makes Rodeo Drive look like the swap meet."

Lola said, "And you said the shopping is your treat?"

"My treat."

No woman could resist shopping in Paris.

I told them I would take them to the Waterloo Station in the morning and buy them two first-class tickets on the Eurostar. Told Lola that I would give her some spending money.

Mrs. Jones smiled. "Okay, have I died and gone to heaven and don't know it?"

Lola asked, "How long will you be working in Amsterdam?"

"Two days. Forty-eight hours."

Mrs. Jones smiled, but suspicion remained in her body language. That Henrietta part of her that would never go away, I saw it there. She knew trouble and its smell. She didn't ask, but I saw a thousand questions in her eyes. A thousand questions that I knew she'd never ask.

Lola thanked me and told me how wonderful I was.

She whispered that she loved me.

Those three words unnerved me.

Those three words made me want to run.

The same three words I had whispered to Arizona while we were at the Parker Meridien.

Those three words could pull people together.

Or push them apart.

Evoke warmth.

Or cause fear.

Love.

That one word never meant the same thing to two people.

That word had no decent definition.

A woman would tell a man she loved him.

But women loved shoes too.

Some loved shoes more than men.

Women kept shoes.

And changed men.

So maybe *love* was a useless word.

No definition that was absolute.

I didn't know what love meant to anybody else.

Just knew what it meant to me.

It meant I wanted to be normal.

Lola fell asleep first.

Mrs. Jones whispered, "Amsterdam. That was abrupt."

I nodded. "Something happened tonight."

"What happened?"

"I'm being followed."

"Since when?"

"Since I got here. Maybe before I came here."

"This has been going on a few days?"

"Think so. Not sure. Just know he found me at Banners."

"By whom?"

"He was on the plane. Think he came here after me."

"Who?"

"He had on a suit. Bandages on his nose."

She didn't remember him. "Gideon, does this have to do with . . . what you do?"

"With something I did." I nodded. "Have to sort this out. Need you to not be around me."

"I suppose I shouldn't ask any questions."

"You shouldn't. Already said too much."

"Anything I can do to help?"

"Yeah."

"What?"

"Come here. Put your head right here."

Mrs. Jones rested in my arms, her hand on my chest. "Lola told you she loved you."

"Yeah."

"I am totally besotted with you as well."

"Is besotted a good thing?'"

"Besotted is a great thing."

"I am totally besotted with you too."

"Lola told me that she loved you, but she was afraid to confess that to you."

"How do you feel about that? Both of you feeling that way?"

"It's beautiful. If you feel the same way for us, then it's a masterpiece."

We smiled. A man had threatened me tonight, but right now I was happy. My life was on the line and I didn't care, not at this moment. Had to enjoy this calm before the storm arrived.

Mrs. Jones was crying, wiping her eyes.

She asked, "Amsterdam . . . are you coming back? Or will you vanish from my life?"

"Shhh. No questions, remember?"

"When you're besotted, it's hard to not ask questions."

"No questions."

"Are you going to be okay? Just tell me that. Are you going to be okay?"

"Don't know."

"If something happens, how I will I find out?"

"You won't."

"Gideon . . ."

I shushed Mrs. Jones again. She held on to me.

Some time went by before I whispered, "Tell me your favorite television shows."

"Not big on television. But when it's on, I love watching the Discovery Channel."

"Do you? You seem more like a CNN and *Headline News* kinda woman."

"The Disney Channel too. I could stay in bed and watch the Disney Channel all day long. *That's So Raven*, *Kim Possible*, I am so hooked on those television shows. And *Girlfriends*."

I told her, "I like *Lost*. I'm into watching BBC America."

"*Grey's Anatomy*?"

"Like that one too. *Law and Order*. *Sopranos*. Cop shows. Hate reality television."

"I like *American Idol.*" She yawned. "But, most of all, I love *Grey's Anatomy.*"

That whispering about nothing went on for a few minutes.

There was no husband in her past.

There was no man with a broken nose in my future.

It was all about this moment.

I was safe.

They were safe.

For a moment I was a normal man. Having a nice conversation with a normal woman.

She said, "I have a daughter who hates me. A husband who will no longer be my husband. I have a life that I don't want to return to. What I have is this, what I have is now."

I hugged her. Didn't know what else to do. I lost my vocabulary.

I wondered if she had given Lola her silver cross because she had lost her faith.

I asked her what I was thinking.

She said, "I don't know. Feels as if I've lost the connection to my soul. I'm so disconnected from . . . from . . . from everything. I'm trying to get beyond my suffering. Trying to embark on a journey and find my own healing. Trying to find out who I am, you know?"

She cried and tried to pull away. I didn't let her go. I held her.

She fell asleep, holding the son of a whore, tears raining from her eyes to my chest.

Twenty-one

the big sleep

While the women slept, I stood in the window staring out at Centre Pointe.

I was wide-awake and naked, my gun at my side. Still lucid and alert. On fire. Annoyance and rage were coming back alive, pecking at the back of my brain.

Coltrane continued to play, low and easy, the rain now falling on Bloomsbury.

I looked toward Soho, imagined I could see the red lights glowing on Berwick Street, wondered what the foot traffic was like over in the neon-lit section with the postal code W1.

The television was on in the background, sound muted. BBC1 had replayed the news about the tube killing and the death of the WAG. This time I paid attention to both.

The James Patterson novel he had left on the counter. *Big Bad Wolf.*

He'd thrown it in my face. Then sat with me at point-blank range.

For the hundredth time, I replayed the little sit-down in my head.

Coulda. Woulda. Shoulda.

Even if I had killed him, I would still need to know who sent him. He was only the messenger.

Killing the mailman wouldn't stop the IRS from sending another bill.

He was a fool. All I could think was that either he was crazy, or a goddamn fool.

He was taunting me. Taunting had to be his shortcoming. He was a man who lived to play cat and mouse. Maybe not. My guess was that he was waiting on something.

Money.

Had to be waiting on money.

Mrs. Jones sat up for a second, saw me naked, lit up by the city, gun in hand.

She paused. *"Why are the police in front of our home?"*

She looked right through me. Her focus in another country, in another time.

"Don't let them take my daughter. Don't let them take my child."

Tears ran down her eyes. I said her name. No answer. I said her name again.

She stood up, her hair wild, her hands in fists, her angst making her look one hundred years old, and continued talking in her sleep, continued begging, the words indecipherable.

Her tears still falling. In an instant she cried more than she did on the plane.

"I'll kill you, Keith. I'll fucking kill you. If it's the last thing I do before I die, I'll kill you."

I saw the Henrietta Kellogg part of her that lived right below the surface.

I saw the depth of her anger. The depth of her pain. Saw her viciousness.

Then she lay back down.

In the frailest voice she whispered, "For what I am working out I do not know. For what I wish, this I do not practice, but what I hate is what I do . . . but now the one working it out is no longer I, but sin that resides in me. For I know that in me, that is, in my flesh, there dwells nothing good. For ability to wish is present with me, but ability to work what is fine is not present."

She quieted, but she was in the fetal position, rocking herself. Her voice dwindled. "For the good that I wish I do not do, but the bad that I do not wish is what I practice. I find, then, this law in my case: that when I wish to do what is right, what is bad is present with me . . ."

Then her breathing turned heavy. She stopped rocking. She was asleep.

I wondered how many nights she'd done the same thing, walked and talked in her sleep, battled her demons. Wondered if all of her battles ended in the same Bible verse.

Her mantra damn near took me to my knees.

I stepped over luggage, panties, bras, my discarded suit, shoes, moved through the dimly lit room and stood over her. Her sleep was deep and soundless. Her face once again peaceful.

Revenge only needed to make sense to the person who wanted it done.

Lola stirred. Her heartbroken face was just as peaceful.

Rage lived inside her as well. Saw her rage on the dance floor tonight.

Saw her other insecurities as she took lessons from the pro of fellatio.

I rubbed Lola's shoulders, massaged her, but she didn't wake.

I wanted her to wake up and stand behind me, her breasts on my skin, arms around me.

Wanted to tell her I'd do anything for her too.

I went to Mrs. Jones, rubbed her wild hair, kissed her heated face.

Her nightmares had faded.

Her face relaxed.

I watched her until I turned cold. I'd turned the heater off. The room had chilled.

I pulled the sheets and covers up over them.

Gun resting at my side, I went back to the window.

The truth was the truth.

I had made a major mistake. Two major mistakes. Lola and Mrs. Jones.

Being with the women had made me lose my rhythm.

I understood Arizona. Understood her frustration with me.

Understood why she was always so distant.

People like us should never get close, especially this close to squares.

It was safer that way. Safer for them. Safer for us.

I looked down at my hand. It was trembling. My soul felt like it had been wrapped in ice. Then unbearable heat overwhelmed me. Sweat dripped from my brow. That sick feeling rose.

I went into the bathroom, closed the door, and in the dark I vomited.

Heaved up everything I had had to eat or drink.

Then I heaved up nothing.

Spasm after spasm came.

That violence lasted forever, took me beyond suffering.

I collapsed on the floor, sweat coming from every pore.

Not long after that I grunted, struggled, pulled myself up to my knees.

I sat there and listened, didn't hear anybody calling my name, no one at the door.

The women didn't wake up. I cleaned myself up.

Then I cleaned the bathroom, tossed those dirty towels out into the hallway.

I showered. I baptized myself. Tried to wash away all of my old sins.

I whispered, "What I wish, this I do not practice, but what I hate is what I do."

Twenty-two

nightmare alley

The time had come.

I opened the safe, took out my money. Counted it out in silence. Found envelopes in the desk drawer. I put enough money in an envelope for Lola to stay in Europe for another week. Enough for her to have a good time in Paris. In another I left enough American money for her to buy a one-way ticket back to the States. I loaded my weapons in my backpack. Put on jeans, trainers, dark sweater, leather coat. My aches spoke to me, whispered they were still with me.

Tampa was still with me, the ghosts of the dead hovering over me.

I downed another BC Powder, washed it down with tap water.

Then I headed for the door.

"Gideon."

Startled, I turned around. Mrs. Jones was sitting up.

Nothing was said for a moment.

She said, "I saw you packing your gun."

Her voice was thicker. Thickened with worry.

I said, "Make sure you leave this hotel. Make sure you take Lola Mack to Paris."

She nodded. She understood.

"Promise me that you and Lola will get to Paris. And you will have fun in Paris."

"When Lola wakes and you're gone . . . what do I tell her? She adores you, Gideon. You told her that you were going to take us to Waterloo. You know she wants to say good-bye to you."

"Tell her . . . tell her . . ." I shrugged. "Improvise. Tell her that she is the best actress in the world. Not to give up. To get that Mimi part in *Rent*. Tell her I'll come to all of her shows."

We smiled. Stared at each other like we were trying to memorize each other.

She said, "Stay."

This was why people left in the thick of the night. Long good-byes were excruciating.

I said, "Lay back down. Close your eyes. Count backward from one hundred."

She did what I said. She closed her eyes, tears draining and dampening her pillow.

In the softest voice she whispered, "One hundred . . . ninety-nine . . . ninety-eight . . ."

I left.

I wasn't a square. I had square moments, but I didn't belong in their world.

And I didn't need to drag them over on this side of the fence.

I left the hotel, made it down to Bayley Street, looked up at the hotel window.

Mrs. Jones was in the window, watching me as I had watched her days ago.

Now it was my turn to leave.

I moved on, took my eyes off her pain and moved away as fast as I could.

It was time for me to stop procrastinating, time to do what I had to do.

It had to be done.

Like the pedophile I had visited last night, this too had to be handled.

For the things he had done, he had paid with his life.

He had deserved to die.

Tracking a man who carried a Desert Eagle would have to wait.

I knew I should track him now.

But something else was churning deep inside me.

Its flames consuming me.

I had to deal with this fire that was inside me.

My first stop was going to be in the heart of postal code W1.

It was time for Thelma to pay what she owed.

It was time for Frankenstein's monster to destroy his creator.

Twenty-three

need for revenge

Berwick Street reeked.

A damp soccer ball was inside the narrow door the led to the flat Thelma let.

Thelma.

My mother.

The whore who taught me to kill.

The whore I had promised to kill in return.

I took to the concrete stairs, the stink of piss damn near suffocating me, rain dripping from both me and my backpack. Her door was open. Stickers covered the ragged door and the chipped walls at the top. Hadn't noticed that before. Stickers for Arsenal, Charlton, Chelsea, Fulham, Tottenham, Watford, pretty much every football team was represented.

Perfume, cigarettes, drying sweat, and the funk of a thousand men met me at her door.

Inside her small living room, she sat in a wooden chair. Long skirt. High-heeled shoes.

A red light was in her window and a Bible was in her hands. New Testament.

The red light was off. The Bible was open.

She was amazing, always had been. The room brought back memories. Now, like she had then, she had the same pictures of Dorothy Dandridge, Sophia Loren, Audrey Hepburn, Tina Turner, Marilyn Monroe, Lauren Bacall, Lana Turner, and Eartha Kitt Scotch-taped all over her small flat. The memory chilled me. She was still a slob. Wigs and shoes were spilling out of a small closet. A St. George's Cross covered one of the dirty windows. A small fan rested at the edge of the stained sofa; it was on low, circulating the stale air that rose from the wall heater. I looked at the pictures, at Lana and Sophia, glanced at all the women she admired. Thelma was none of those women. She could've been better than all of them. But she never would be.

Two packed suitcases were near the front door.

I motioned toward the luggage. "Leaving?"

"Waiting on you."

"You're dressed like that waiting on me?"

"I've been waiting on you. I've been waiting all day. I knew you'd come for me."

"Sure you're not running away again?"

"I can't run from you all my life."

"Is that right?"

"That's right."

"Liar. You're all packed. Your luggage is in front of me and you're still lying."

She looked at the luggage, rubbed the Bible, then raised her teary eyes to mine.

I said, "Guess you didn't leave fast enough. You should've left."

"Please. Last request. Please. You have to do something for me."

"I don't have to do a damn thing for you."

"After . . . when you're done with me . . . I need you to . . ."

"Are you deaf? I don't have to do shit for you."

"I'm here. Waiting for you. I've been running from you for years. I'm not running from you, from who I am, from what I've done, I'm not running anymore. I'm tired. So fucking tired."

"You're afraid to die like the thieving whore you are?"

"Wanted to see Death wearing respectable clothes."

"What difference would that make?"

"People say what you die in is what you spend eternity wearing."

I said, "Put the Bible down. Stand up."

She put the Bible on the table. Her body trembled. She took short steps toward me.

She said, "I'm sorry. For everything I did to wrong you, for every offense, I'm so sorry."

I slapped her to the ground. She fell hard, landed on the edge of a tattered sofa, bounced to the ragged carpet. Her sofa was water-stained. At least I think that was water.

She cried. "You're like your father."

"So I've heard."

"He was a mean son of a bitch."

"Get up."

"If that mean son of a bitch . . . that evil and mean son of a bitch was your father."

"If?"

"I have to tell you something. I have to tell you this."

One shoe off, she was down on one knee, looking up at me, tears in her swollen eyes.

"I'm not your mother."

"Don't fuck with me."

"I'm not your mother."

"I'm tired of your lies."

"She'd dead. Your mother, her name was Margaret. She died when you were a baby. She was killed. Murdered in an alley. By a john. You were a toddler. Barely a year old."

"How many lies can you tell?"

"Look in my purse."

"How many damn lies can you tell?"

"I'm old enough to be your big sister, not old enough to be your goddamn mother."

"Are you telling me that you're my goddamn sister?"

"No. I was your mother's best friend, dammit."

She made it to her feet, shaking, fear consuming her body.

I tried to slap the lie out of her mouth. Again she fell on the sofa.

She held her mouth. "She was my friend. Your mother was my best friend."

I put my foot on her lies, held her down, took the gun out of my backpack.

"If I had left you, the system . . . you would've been put in the system."

I pressed my foot down harder. "So you're telling me you kidnapped me?"

"I saved you. I did for Margaret what she would've done for me."

My foot tried to press her through the floor. *"You fucking kidnapped me?"*

"I saved you. Nobody kidnapped you. Margaret was like family. She was like my sister."

"You're making this shit up."

Liquid fear ran from between her legs, added to the piss stink in the building.

"Your father. That mean and evil son of a bitch."

"What you know about him?"

"I'll tell you . . . what I know . . . about your father."

"Talk."

"I can't . . . you're choking me . . . stop . . . please."

I moved my foot, she cried, rolled away, struggling to breathe.

"My father was a mercenary. He fought bulls and killed them with his bare hands."

"He was an army man. The rest, about the mercenary, about the bulls, I made that up."

I clenched my teeth. "He was a mercenary and killed bulls with his bare hands."

She shook her head, slid away from me, went to a stack of papers on the table.

She handed me an old, weathered newspaper clipping, its edges torn and frayed. A prostitute from Opelika, Alabama, had been found killed, her body left in a Dumpster. Prostitute. That's all it said. No name. Just another prostitute found dead. Not even a real person. Just another dead sinner left in an alley Dumpster. Like that was where all whores belonged.

I asked, "What's this crap?"

"It's Margaret. Your mother. That's your mother. My best friend. That's her."

She said that with tears and passion, with honesty and depth.

I snapped, "I don't believe you."

She sat on the floor, shivering, getting smaller, like she was sinking in quicksand.

Death was in the corner, wearing his Sunday best, waiting for his cue.

My voice lowered, cracked as I asked, "Why did you do what you did to me?"

"*I was drunk.*" She caught her breath. "I'm sorry for what I did. I was drunk."

"Why would you do some bullshit like that to me?"

She shook her head awhile, crying, breaking down. "I loved you."

"Are you fucking sick?"

"You've been the only boy . . . the only man . . . the only male who has been in my life . . . the only one who didn't come and go. And you were starting to hate me. I saw that. I panicked."

"Why would you do some shit like that to me?"

She huffed and growled. "Don't. Pretend. Don't pretend."

"Don't pretend? Don't pretend what?"

"Don't pretend you didn't have feelings for me."

"You're my mother. I'm supposed to . . ."

"Sexual feelings. You had sexual feelings for me."

"You're *sick*. You're so fucking *sick*."

"I'm sick? I saw you watching me work. Saw how you used to stand in the door and look at me. Saw your pants, saw how it excited you. I saw the way you used to look at me."

I read the words on the tattered paper. A streetwalker found dead in Alabama.

I looked down at Thelma. "I will make you suffer slowly and deeply for this lie."

She was crying. "I have been suffering. Look around you. Look at my life."

Death took three soft steps toward her.

I asked, "How much money did you steal from me?"

"How much did I *steal*? How much money did I *spend* on you? For years. I took you with me. I did what I *felt* was right. I became your mother. I am the only mother you know."

"Nobody asked you to fucking kidnap me."

"Kidnap? I worked, sold my pussy and fed you. I put a goddamn roof over your head."

"You kidnapped me and fucking molested me."

She cried. "I worked with Margaret in Alabama. We hustled. The hustle is all we knew. It's all I know how to do. Gideon, she went out one night. Didn't come back. A john killed her and nobody gave a shit. She was just another dead whore. And you. Her baby. She had left you with a sitter. I went and got you. The sitter called the next morning and I went and got you."

"I don't remember that . . . I don't remember any of that."

"You were a toddler."

"You're my mother. *You're my goddamn mother."*

"Your mother is dead."

I pointed the gun at her head. My eyes wide. I wanted to burn the flesh off her bones.

"If you're not my . . . if my mother is . . . if this Margaret was . . . where is she buried?"

"Wherever the State of Alabama buries dead whores."

She had become a trapped animal, eyes going everywhere, looking for a way out of a snare. I could kill her right now. But death was no less certain for being postponed a little while.

I said, "You sent me out to kill people."

"I sent you to kill men like the man who killed your mother."

"You sent me out for your own revenge."

"Yes. *Because one of those bastards killed my best friend."*

That halted me. She'd said that like she was a righteous vigilante.

She snapped, "I sent you to kill people who deserved to die."

"My father's words."

"My words. Some people deserve to die. They do."

Again I swallowed. She'd justified using me to exact her revenge. And profit.

She said, "Margaret . . . was my best friend . . . *your mother* . . . she was murdered . . . killed by a john the same way Mr. Midnight tried to kill me. I did the right thing. I took you like you were my own. Kill me for the bad things I've done, but I will tell you the right things I've done. I could've left you . . . I could have . . . but I took you with me . . . took you with me before the police came . . . before social services came . . . I did that to keep you from being sent to the system."

"Why would you do that? Why kidnap me?"

"Because I was orphaned and grew up in the goddamn system."

"You said your mother remarried . . . that her new husband . . ."

"I grew up in the system. No matter how I got there, I grew up in the system. I sold this pussy to eat. I sold this pussy to take care of you. I did what I thought was right."

"What you did was wrong. *Why did you take me?*"

"Because nobody gives a shit about a trick baby."

An earthquake erupted inside my head. *"Where is my family?"*

She cried hard, shook her head emphatically. "I went through Margaret's things and tried to find your people. But your mother had been a teenage runaway, kept no ties with her life. We were outcasts. Most of us are outcasts. Bottom-feeders. We had nobody but each other."

Eyes burning like the devil's headlights, I put my finger on the trigger. Hand shaking.

I swallowed, my saliva now liquid flames. My voice cracked. "My daddy?"

"He was married. Had his own life. And he wasn't happy a whore had a trick baby and claimed that baby to be his. He didn't want anything to do with you. Or a whore."

"Where is he?"

"Dead. Been dead a long time." She sobbed. *"Your father is dead, Gideon.* Your mother was murdered and your father is dead. I had to take you with me. I *had* to."

"How many different lies can you tell in one breath?"

"I'm telling you the truth. Before I die, I'm telling you the whole goddamn truth."

"What do you know about my father?"

"I knew him."

"You've never mentioned him, not once."

"Your father was one of my customers too, dammit."

"If that john was my father . . . if he . . . ," I fumed. "How would you know? *How?*"

"He was one of our regulars. If Margaret wasn't available . . . then . . . he'd . . . with me."

"Where is he? Wait. You . . . he was married? With kids?" I paused, head aching so bad. "One of your regulars. You talking about Sergeant? You telling me Sergeant was my father?"

"Oh, God, no." Tears falling like rain, she shook her head. "Not Sergeant."

She shivered. Suffocated. Heaved. Gagged like she wanted to throw up.

Hand shaking, teeth clenched, I watched her bawl and wallow in her own piss.

I struggled with myself. "Why are you lying to me? Why all the damn lies?"

"Gideon, your father died when you were seven."

I shook my head.

She said, "You killed your father when you saved my life."

Twenty-four

where the truth lies

Hand steady, my finger was tight on the trigger.

Saliva rivered from my mouth.

My teeth remained clenched.

Head shaking away her lies, I kept the gun aimed at her head. Kept my finger tight on the trigger. In this world, as long as there were people, as long as there was hate and envy, as long as there were insecurity and greed, I'd never stand in the soup line with the unemployed.

The things people needed in order to live without pain.

Lola wanted justice for being rejected. Mrs. Jones needed justice for her daughter.

Big Bad Wolf's brother wanted my head.

So many people had sought after justice, checkbooks in hand.

I had joined that group of restless souls that needed vindication to survive.

I wanted justice.

I growled, "I have to. No matter who you are . . . this is who I am . . . this you deserve."

The door at the bottom of the stairs opened hard, slammed the wall down at the narrow streets, that urgency echoing in the piss-smelling hallway. Someone rushed inside.

German. Someone rushed up, screaming in German.

I moved the gun away from Thelma's head, trained the weapon on the door.

Thelma struggled to get to her knees, waved her hand, yelled, "No . . . please no . . . no . . . he . . . don't let him see . . . I beg you . . . do what you want . . . just not in front of . . . no . . ."

My eyes went to the luggage.

That was when I saw the stickers on the luggage. Just like the ones on the front door. All football. Arsenal. Chelsea. Tottenham. Three soft taps and the warped door creaked opened. It was one of the kids I'd seen playing football down on the narrow streets.

It was the dark-skinned boy who played like he was a little Pelé.

He came in the flat like he lived there.

He said, "Sven? Are you here, Sven?"

The dark-skinned kid that was no more than seven or eight years old.

He saw Thelma on the floor, her mouth bloodied, piss under her backside.

He saw me with tears in my eyes, one hand in a fist, the other with a gun at my side.

I heard his mind *click*, photographing this moment. He dropped the soccer ball and ran.

Thelma called after him. The boy stumbled down the stairs, screaming for help.

I ran to the door, only to see him vanish, then turned to Thelma and asked, "Who is he?"

"His mother works . . . she's a provider . . . they are from Van-rhynsdorp."

"Who is he?" I motioned at the luggage. "Is he . . . who in the fuck was he?"

"He plays with my son. He teaches my son football."

"Your son. What son?"

"I have a son. I have a five-year-old son."

"The other kid . . . blond hair . . ."

"Sven."

"Where is he?"

"He's safe. All that matters is that he's safe."

"Where?"

"I knew you were coming . . . I sent him away."

"When . . . when . . . were you . . . when . . . pregnant?"

"Amsterdam. I was pregnant when you saw me."

"You weren't pregnant. You didn't look pregnant."

"Yes, I was pregnant. Was just pregnant. I ran to protect my unborn."

"When did you send him away?"

The two suitcases. She had packed his things. Next to the luggage were papers.

I went to those papers. There was money inside. Almost five thousand British pounds. The note said the money was for a boy named Andrew-Sven. And instructions for his care.

She didn't want the boy to know what happened to her, only to be sent away.

I snapped, "Don't do this to me. Don't you fucking do this to me."

"Don't do what to you?"

"This. This shit. Don't drop this on me and rob me of my revenge."

"I am not robbing you. I did not run. I am right here."

"Why are you doing this to me?"

"Get it over with. Just get it over with."

My words ended and I stared at the death maker in my hand. I wiped my eyes, shook my head, stuffed my weapons back into my backpack as fast as I could, then glowered at her.

I snapped, "You touch him?"

"Is that all you see when you look at me?"

"Answer me. *Do. You. Touch. Him?*"

"I'm his mother."

"Do you touch him like you touched me?"

"That was over eight . . . almost near ten years ago. What I did . . . that was ten years ago."

"Answer me."

"And I was drunk. *I touched you once.* Every day I regret what I did back then."

"Do you touch him?"

"No. Never. I'm not the animal you think I am. *I am not a bad person.*"

"Why did you do that to me?"

She cried, shivered. "Because . . . because . . ."

"Because what?"

"Because that is all I know. That is all I know. Before I went to the . . . before I was put in the system . . . things happened to me . . . my stepfather . . . he . . . my uncle . . . they . . . they . . ."

"Don't do this to me. *Do not. Do this. To me.*"

"I just didn't want you to hate me."

"Do not do this to me." I choked. "Don't fucking do this to me."

Down below the door opened hard. A woman ran up the stairs, no doubt the mother of the boy who had just fled, yelling for Thelma, the concerned woman's accent more British than African, but it was rooted in Africa nevertheless, each word, even the simplest words, even as she screamed, panic rolled off her tongue like cerebral instructions from a professor at Yale.

She met me at the door. Jeans and plain white T-shirt. A long knife was in her hand.

We made eye contact. She was so young she could've passed for a child herself. She was beautiful, in a worn and cruel way. Skin so black it looked like the most beautiful of purples.

And she was breathing hard, terrified, but her fury and intellect overshadowed her fear.

She would kill me to protect her friend if she had to.

Several women appeared behind her. African. Chinese. European.

The International Sisterhood of Mary Magdalene had been called to arms.

Face flushed, I demanded, "Get out of my way."

The beautiful woman from Vanrhynsdorp refused. "You're American."

I tried to get by her. She blocked my way with her blade.

I snapped, "Move."

"American. You are American."

"Move out of my way."

She held her knife like a skilled warrior, that blade extended at me.

Thelma called out, "Nusaybah . . . no . . . get away. Go away."

The woman refused to move. "He has beaten you. We will call nine nine nine."

"No, Nusaybah. No. Leave us alone. Please. Leave us."

She looked down at Thelma as she called her friend, her eyes on me, her words for the woman who had been my mother all my life, the only mother I remembered. She saw her bruises, and with words both deep and promising, threatened to kill me where I stood, threatened to kill me and throw me to the dogs.

I eased by Nusaybah, my eyes on that blade. She moved, rotated her deadly position with slow steps, our dance of caution putting her inside the room while it left me near the door.

I hurried down the stairs, women stepping to the side, their fear giving me an opening. I passed the dark-skinned boy who stood at the bottom the stairs, a child with a short knife in his hand, held tight, as if he were going to protect his mother. The boy looked at me like I was a goddamned monster. I hurried away from his eyes as if they were my own.

People were rushing by. None were concerned with the secret lives of prostitutes.

Out on Berwick Street, the neon lights advertising sin and bisexual satisfaction had dimmed. I headed that way, bolted into the narrow passageway between strip clubs and porn shops, then made a hard left and took the path that led toward Chinatown and Leicester Square.

Underneath a dull sky, anger and confusion fueling my flight, I left running.

Rain dampened me as I ran by workers and johns in search of early-morning satisfaction.

In Leicester Square I ran by herds of men and women in suits and jeans, all heading to their day jobs. I ran by the young and the old at Charing Cross, ran until I got to Embankment.

Big Ben and the Westminster station were dead ahead, as were Parliament and Westminster Abbey. The London Eye and Waterloo tube were down Bridge Street, across the overpass. I took to the overpass so I could see. I climbed concrete stairs that led to a bridge crossing the Thames River, slowed down, and spied around, trains whizzing by me as I adjusted my backpack and tried to look normal. My eyes moved from all the umbrellas and went to the buildings. I saw them staring at me. CCTV cameras were all over Central London. Big Brother was always spying. I sped up. My fast walk became a trot. Again I ran, no destination in mind.

Buildings and landmarks older than anything in America went by me in a blur.

Thelma. I couldn't outrun the psychological damage she had done.

She had corrupted me, disowned me, rattled my brain, claimed my mother was dead.

She told me that my mother was left rotting in a Dumpster.

That I had killed my own father.

That she was not my mother.

That she had birthed a son.

In a few words she had shattered me once again.

I had run away from the red lights that illuminated the women of the night.

I ran beyond the Aquarium and London Eye, went inside Waterloo tube station, sweat pouring from my flesh, mind spinning, wondering if I had killed my own father.

Twenty-five

slave of pleasure

The man with the broken nose woke to a peaceful morning.

Cold. Raining. And peaceful.

The kind of weather that made a man want to call in sick and stay home all day.

The man with the broken nose was in his hotel room. He had just looked at his nose again, the swelling was getting to be a bit much. He couldn't wait to get back across the pond.

Sam was on the phone. The money still wasn't in place.

He could've ended it last night.

But the money wasn't in place.

The man with the broken nose was pissed.

Right there in Banners. He could've put a bullet in Gideon's heart.

And walked away.

He was talking to Sam, trying to understand why this contract was so damn difficult.

"The Gideon contract came from a politician. Years was spent putting that package together. Investigations had to come and go. So the politician would not be connected with any fallout from a previous hit, no longer be a suspect in another contact. And now the time is right."

"Especially with Gideon out of the U.S."

"Especially. So I need you to bear with me. The client is legit. I swear."

"I need more than that if you want me to stick around."

"You have to trust me."

"So it's political."

"Didn't say that. Just saying it's for a politician."

"Don't mess with me, Sam."

"Not messing with you."

"It's from a politician. Which state?"

"One where it gets cold."

"Cold is relative. People from Brazil think Dallas is cold."

"More like Canada."

"A Canadian thing."

"Something like that. That's all I'm saying."

The man with the broken nose was naked, except for his reading glasses. He had a box on his bed. Was filling out papers for the post office. He had gone to Forbidden Planet, bought comic books for his son. A Marvel number with Union Jack on the cover. A red, white, and blue Union Flag T-shirt that read MY DAD WENT TO LONDON AND ALL I GOT WAS THIS LOUSY T-SHIRT.

Nothing for his soon-to-be-ex-wife.

He was filling out the mailing info as he talked to Sam.

"Stop bullshitting me, Sam. Which job?"

"It was something you turned down a while ago."

Sounded like Sam was smiling.

The man with the broken nose smiled in return. He was beyond impatient.

Sam said, "Do me a favor and I'll tell you."

"The favor?"

"François. My competitor. I'm taking most of his business."

"And you want it all."

"Deal?"

"Give me the information first. If it's worth it, deal."

Sam told him. "A candidate for mayor in a major U.S. city."

"First it's Canada and now it's U.S."

"We have a deal?"

The man with the broken nose stood up and said, "You're shitting me, Sam."

"Honest to God."

"You are fucking full of shit."

"Serious as a heart attack."

"And the politician is having problems moving money, Sam."

"Take the AMG. Just found out it was reported stolen three weeks ago. The client was setting this up. Has been setting this contract up for a long time. Has been as patient as Job."

"Not feeling the AMG. I need money. American money. Not this British shit either."

"Back in the States, on a nice day, you'll look good in that convertible."

"Give me the rest of the intel. Who the fuck is ordering this bullshit? New York mayor? Do they have mayors in Canada? Vancouver? Toronto? Give me longitude and latitude."

"Not saying. I've already said too much."

"Who is this incompetent fuck? Give me initials. Or a word that rhymes with the name."

"Not saying. Just consider the trade. I would. It's worth a hundred large."

"And the AMG is in Canada."

"It's in Canada."

"What side is the steering wheel on?"

"Left. Are we in business?"

"I'll be stuck with it. If I try to sell it, and they trace the serial back to me . . . no way."

"Look, the car will be clean. If you're not comfortable, you could chop-shop it."

"Do I look like a damn car salesman? Why in the hell would I risk going to a chop shop?"

"Was just saying."

"Why doesn't the damn politician chop-shop it and pay me and stop jerking me around?"

"Who wants to cut up an AMG? That would be heartless."

"The pieces are worth more than the car."

"I just know what the initial offer was. And the AMG, well, that's a nicer payday."

"Tell the son of a bitch to get the damn money I was promised."

"Consider it. And more work will follow. This Gideon contract will elevate your status."

He rubbed the back of his neck. "You think so?"

"I know so. Your next few jobs, you can double your fee. Well? What do you think?"

"And this politician will get me more work?"

"Guaranteed."

"It's Hillary Clinton, isn't it?"

Sam laughed.

"Obama?"

Sam laughed harder.

There was a knock at his door.

He spied through the peephole.

He worked with Sam but didn't trust him. He'd bet that the car didn't belong to any politician. Rappers bought shit like that. His money was on the AMG belonging to a bling-bling rapper who had bad money management and wanted to move the car to pay for the hit. Report the car stolen, let his insurance cover the loss, pay a deductible, damn near getting a big hit for free. He looked at the picture of the AMG, saw something he hadn't noticed before.

He was no fool.

He told Sam, "Get my goddamn money."

"Sorry about this delay. I truly am. This was unforeseeable."

"Tell your client that the goddamn IRS doesn't take AMGs as payment."

"I understand."

"How in the fuck would I explain a brand-new AMG to Uncle fucking Sam?"

"It could be worked out."

"How in the fuck would that get worked out? I register that shit, red flags everywhere."

"It'll get sold to you as salvage."

"As a goddamn salvage? You want me to work for salvage?"

"The car is new. The paperwork will claim water damage from Katrina. Worth nothing on paper. Even if you resold it, you'd make more than your money back. It's no-lose, Bruno."

"You got it all worked out, huh? Think you got it all worked out."

"Think about the AMG. And the prestige from taking out Gideon."

"Hold up, hold up. This delay. You entertaining someone else to pick up this contract?"

"Not at the moment. Feel free to complete the transaction."

"Not before I'm paid. I do the work first, bad business, and I'll never get paid."

He went back into the room, hid the box he was mailing to his two kids in the closet.

More taps came at the door.

Sam said, "Understood."

"And the politician will get me more work, guaranteed? Real work, not bullshit."

"Fuck yeah."

"Let me think about it."

"Okay."

"In the meantime, find Gideon. He's seen me. So I can't go out looking for him."

"Already in motion."

They hung up. He opened the door. Tebby was drenched in sweat, had on her workout clothes. She'd been gone an hour, had gone to the hotel gym and trained. She came in the room with a bucket of ice. She put ice in a plastic laundry bag, then put the plastic laundry bag in a towel and held it to his skin, sat with him, made sure he iced his nose for twenty minutes.

She said, "You should rest with your head on pillows. Sleep like that too. Keep your injury higher than the level of your heart. That will keep the pain and swelling down."

"How are we going to make love if I can only rest like this?"

"Guess I'll have to get on top."

"You're a regular Florence Nightingale."

She laughed. "You taking anything?"

"Not really."

"I'll get you something to take."

"Thanks, Tebby."

"I think you should have a splint for your nose."

"You think?"

"Has it been bleeding?"

"Not much."

"Hold your head back. Let me see inside your nose."

"I'm not letting you look up this booger shooter."

"Move your hand."

"What are you looking for?"

"Let me make sure you don't have blood collected up in there."

"How do you know so much about broken noses?"

"I don't. I looked it up on the Internet. Wanted to make sure you were properly taken care of. I like you, Bruno. Can't have your nose getting infected and falling off in your lap."

He smiled.

This woman was a keeper.

While Tebby inspected his nose, he ran his hands over her body.

Tebby laughed. "You're pussy-whipped already."

"Takes more than pussy to whip me. But, yeah, I'm whipped. Already."

"Let me take a shower. Don't want to be late for work."

"Wish you didn't have to go."

"Keep this on your nose. Ten more minutes. Not a second less."

He held the ice package and smiled. Nobody had cared about him in a long while.

He loved his soon-to-be-ex-wife half as much as she loved him.

And she didn't love him at all.

Tebby undressed where she stood.

Six feet tall.

She asked, "Are we doing anything later?"

"Let's see another play."

"What did you think of the one I picked last evening?"

"Outside of not being able to understand a word they said, from what I picked up and put together, the plot was incoherent. All that booty-shaking and singing didn't really add up to a decent theatrical production. They charged twenty pounds to see something that should have been on a high school stage. That was a fifty-pence production if ever I've seen one."

"Okay. Anything else?"

"No, that's about it. I've said enough. *Township Stories* was much better."

"If you have more to say, then say it, Bruno."

"When the play started the house was only twenty percent full, and the play started on time. Forty minutes into the play the house was packed. And the guy in the black suit, the one who had his hair slicked back and had on blue-lenses glasses, didn't you think it was wrong for him to stick his head in during the performance and yell to see if his friends were there?"

"Anything else?"

"I mean, people were walking in like they had no idea what time the play started. These were local people. And the ushers let people come in anytime they wanted. Babies were crying, Tebby, we were on row J and the crying baby was three seats away on row M. That baby cried for thirty minutes and she never took the baby out of the theater. It was ridiculous. And the play had sexual stuff and curse words and people were sitting up in there with kids like it was nothing."

"Anything else, Bruno?"

"Not just that. People were talking, chatting, and having conversations the whole time. And one girl next to me sang at the top of her lungs, sang every song like she was up onstage."

Tebby laughed. "First time at a Jamaican play?"

"And the last. It's West End from here on out. So we need to see *Guys and Dolls* or *Wicked* or *Avenue Q*. Anything. As long as it's on the West End."

"*Stoosh*. You are so *stoosh*."

"I'll take that as a compliment."

"You're stoosh and I love it, Bruno."

Tebby laughed hard.

He smiled at her as she headed for the shower.

She said, "I love your American accent. I am desperate to get back to America. I will one day. It's all I dream about, you know? Being in America, having my own restaurant."

He laughed at her. "Now who's acting all stoosh. Or chav. Or whatever."

Tebby enjoyed everything they did. He liked that. Actually he loved that. He felt like he had a lot to offer Tebby. And he felt like he could learn from Tebby at the same time.

Tebby was nothing like his soon-to-be-ex-wife. The French-fucking woman who was disappointed because her life hadn't turned out the way she felt it should've turned out.

Nobody's life turned out perfect. Not even Princess Diana's fairy-tale wedding had a happy ending. Reality had a way of fucking shit up. Hell, he bet if he had a chance to sit down and chat with Prince Charles, the prince would say he hadn't planned all this drama in his life.

The man with the broken nose nodded.

If Tebby wasn't here, he would've left two days ago.

He had stayed to be with Tebby. Not for the contract. He wanted the contract. He needed the money. But if not for the warm nights with Tebby, he'd be back in Katy.

Gravity had kept him in London.

He looked at the picture of the AMG again. Put his glasses on and looked closer.

Part of the plates showed. Four of the numbers. And he figured out the state.

He smiled. He could find out what he wanted to know.

Sam and his bullshitting. Now saying this hit was political. That was rapper country. He'd know which rapper ordered this hit. Not that it mattered. He just wanted to know.

He put the picture of the AMG back in his suit coat.

Ice to his nose, he followed Tebby.

He watched her soap herself, clean herself. God bless chance encounters.

He said, "You said you wanted to move to America. That restaurant thing."

"That's my dream, yes."

He watched her. Thinking. Wanting.

He asked, "Would you want to go back to America soon? I mean real soon."

"Are you offering . . . what are you offering?"

"I want to take you back with me."

"To visit?"

"You can visit. Or you can stay. You said you wanted to live in America. Your call."

"Are you joking? I mean . . . where would I live once I got there?"

"If you want, I can find you a place to stay. Get you an apartment in Houston."

"We will live together?"

"No. You will have your own place."

"Really? I have never had a place of my own. Always have had flatmates."

"Houston is less expensive than here. Could set you up in River Oaks, maybe downtown, the heights, galleria area. Depends on if you like it and where you want to be."

She didn't say anything for a moment. "Will I be able to find a job there?"

"We can get your visa in order. I know people who know people."

"I have to send money home for my boys. So I will need a job."

"We could work it out. My divorce won't take long. I'll take care of your bills." He imagined taking the AMG as payment, riding toward Galveston, top down, Tebby at his side. "We could see how it works out between us. No promises, just saying we could try. You could meet my kids at some point. I could meet yours. If it worked, great. If not, at least we tried."

Tebby fell silent. He watched her. She had no expression. None that was readable.

He said, "And I'll make sure your boys are taken care of too."

He felt like he had said too much. Tebby had nurtured him, put ice on his nose, eased his pains, and like a lion with a thorn removed from his foot, he had fallen into fantasy.

Like the characters in that Nicholas guy's books.

When they met a girl. The right girl at the right time.

And said all the right things. Like Prince fucking Charming.

That was how he felt. Like Prince fucking Charming.

He would love to walk through Katy, Texas; parade Tebby in front of his wife's friends.

Tebby said, "I'm more than what's between my legs."

"Well, so am I."

"Just letting you know."

"Well, so am I."

He backed down. Didn't want to make another bad decision. Like Sir Paul.

No fool like an old fool.

He wished he could get in contact with Sir Paul. Save the man a king's fortune.

He told Tebby, "We sort of got off to a fast start."

"Want you to know, this is not normal for me."

"Well, all I usually get at Starbucks is coffee."

"I'm serious. This is not normal for me. Meeting a man one day . . . and then . . . in his bed the next . . . I mean . . . all of this . . . this is unlike me."

"We can slow it down. Whatever works for you."

"Slow it down? You're leaving me soon."

"Unless you come with me."

"I can't just hop on a bloody aeroplane and leave."

"Whenever you're ready. Come whenever it's convenient for you."

Tebby finished rinsing off, eased out of the shower, and took his hand.

Then the hotline started ringing. Started ringing and wouldn't stop.

That meant Sam had some important information.

He got dressed, grabbed his mobile, made no eye contact with Tebby.

Without looking at her, he told Tebby he'd be back in a minute.

She asked, "Are you angry?"

He shook his head.

And walked out the door.

Disappointed.

He felt disappointed.

He had put it out there.

Had offered to make her his Cinderella. His princess Tebby.

But his offer had been slapped down.

Like he had read one book too many.

And looked at his life wishing it turned out like that.

Tebby was just a fantasy.

He'd get over her.

He'd go back home and get over her.

He wouldn't go out like Paul McCartney.

Twenty-six

where sleeping dogs lie

The man with the broken nose took the elevator to the lobby.
He stood in the front window, faced all the flowers at 1 Pepys. Sam told him what he had found out. He said, "MyHotel."

"What about your hotel?"

"That's where Gideon is hiding out. It's called MyHotel."

"You sure?"

"Zankhana assures me. Zankhana is a smart girl. She contacted the driver of the black cab Gideon hired at Oxford Circus. Bribed the driver. Found out Gideon was dropped near the British Museum. She had been monitoring that area."

"And that's the teenage, Goth alcoholic crack- and gun-selling freak from the train, right?"

"Of course. She said Gideon's on the move as we speak."

"Gideon solo?"

"He's traveling solo."

"Last night two women were with him."

"I know. Zankhana lost Gideon, but followed the women all day, unseen and unnoticed by either one. That's how we found Gideon at Banners."

The man with the broken nose remembered how he received that call while he was at the Jamaican play with Tebby. He'd told

Tebby there was a business emergency, told her that he would meet her for jazz as soon as the business was handled. Tebby didn't question him. Just kissed him and told him to be careful, that she would see him later. A woman who didn't question his every move. Most definitely a keeper.

He asked Sam, "Are the women still with Gideon?"

"They stayed at the hotel. The women are still at MyHotel."

"So they might be on his team."

"Have to be. They've been with him since he arrived. They might have information."

"All of them have been holed up in the same room?"

"Looks that way."

"Remarkable."

"Maybe he's paying for their time."

"You never know."

"Well, that's my guess."

"Damn shame."

"What you mean?"

"I like to keep it clean, but looks like there is going to be some collateral damage after all."

"Whatever it takes."

"Can't dump anymore in the Thames."

"Quaggy and Ravensbourne. Two rivers that feed into the Thames."

The man with the broken nose nodded. "Get me directions to his hotel."

"Will do."

"Will need backup. I can't just walk into the hotel. He knows what I look like. And for all I know the women he's with, they could be in the business, they could be assassins. They could be working with Gideon and that Queen Scamz bitch. So make this happen, Sam. Make it happen *now*."

"I'm on it."

"Don't fuck this up for me, Sam."

He hung up.

Two women. Two more deaths on the horizon. And two more rivers to feed.

He went back to his hotel room.

Tebby gave him an awkward smile.

He undressed, sat on the bed.

She asked, "How is your nose?"

"Better. Thanks."

So much politeness and distance between them already.

Like the early stages of divorce.

She made him sit up, keep his nose elevated.

She asked, "How long is the flight from here to Houston?"

He smiled.

She smiled too.

She asked, "Who will teach me to drive on the wrong side of the road?"

They laughed.

Tension gone.

All better.

She said, "It scares me, you know."

"Scares me too."

They kissed.

She said, "While you were gone, I called my best friend."

"Lorato. Your childhood friend."

"Yes. I called Lorato. To talk. She told me that life is short. That I needed to take risks. That I needed to find my own happiness. Because tomorrow was never promised."

Bruno wanted to asked how Lorato was doing, but he didn't. He'd get to know Lorato.

"Bruno, I find it hard to believe that you desire me in that way."

"I do. More than you realize. You're more than what's between your legs, Tebby."

They kissed again.

She said, "I want to make you happy, Bruno."

"I want to make you happy too, Tebby. That's all I want to do. Make you happy."

Then. Her mouth moved south. Tebby took his penis in her mouth.

It surprised him that she did that. Surprised the hell out of him.

Not all surprises were bad. Not at all.

She took a condom, put it inside her mouth, put her mouth over his penis, and with no hands, all mouth and tongue, rolled the latex on his penis.

He moaned, "Good Lord."

He thought about Jacksonville. They'd live in Houston awhile, then Jacksonville.

They'd get married in the spring.

Go snow-skiing in the winter.

Open a restaurant the next year.

He saw it all.

Saw every detail in his mind.

Tebby's mouth.

So hot.

So smooth.

So unexpected.

Tebby's oral loving curled his toes, left him dizzy and on fire.

She smiled, straddled him.

She whispered, "Maybe I should skip work."

"Maybe you should."

"I should skip work so I can fuck you proper. I'm about to fuck you so good."

"Sounds like you're dick-whipped."

"I am about to fuck you from here to Houston."

"So, you're coming?"

"I will be coming . . . coming . . . coming in more ways than one."

Tebby was talking gibberish, riding him with an intensity he'd never before felt.

He decided that he'd marry Tebby the same day his divorce was finalized.

He deserved to be happy.

He deserved Tebby.

Tebby would be his Mpule Kwelagobe.

Tebby would be his Miss Universe.

He imagined her. With him. Living life. Loving life without condition.

Her wicked moves moved him in wicked ways.

Took him places beyond those four walls.

His orgasm rose like the waves of a tsunami.

He was riding the waves of the good feeling.

Then he was overwhelmed, submerged in pleasure.

He was having an out-of-body experience.

It was a wonderful out-of-body moment. So vivid.

He wore dark sunglasses. A white T-shirt. Khaki shorts. Brown sandals.

The sun was warm on his skin. Blue skies, not a cloud in sight. The air so clear.

Tebby worked her magic. Worked him deeper into the pleasure zone. He felt so free.

He was leaving Katy, passing through Houston, Pasadena, and Webster, Tebby at his side, laughter and music between them as he drove I-45 toward Galveston in a convertible AMG.

Twenty minutes later he showered.

Dressed while Tebby closed her eyes and relaxed.

He ordered room service. Had a quick breakfast with Tebby. Kissed her good-bye. Told her he had to go to a meeting. Real estate. A meeting with an anxious investor that shouldn't take too long. Later they would get out again. Maybe the cinema. Or another play.

Umbrella in hand, dressed impeccably, he took a black cab toward Central London.

En route, he took the picture of the AMG out of his pocket. Stared at the car.

Imagined. Tebby up front. The kids in the backseat. Top down. On a road trip.

Not long after that he was in the Borough of Bloomsbury. The black cab dropped him off a block away, in front of the Sony store. He walked Tottenham Court to Bayley Street. Left what seemed like hundreds of electronic stores, an Odeon, and many restaurants behind him.

People passing, he paused outside Jack Horner, the restaurant next to MyHotel.

Desert Eagle adding five pounds to his frame, he crept down to MyHotel, went inside.

Sushi bar to the left. Restaurant to the right.

He pretended he was going inside the restaurant, and when the workers at the front desk were occupied with other travelers, he slipped head down, through a door and took to the stairs.

He took easy steps until he made it to the third floor.

Then he slipped out into the empty hallway. In search of two women. Women he had to torture and question. Women who he wouldn't be able to leave alive after he was done.

He heard them inside the room. Talking. Laughing.

They would see his face. Regrettably he would have to feed two more bodies to the freezing waters. This time he'd leave them in the Quaggy and Ravensbourne.

He raised his hand to knock on the door.

Sometimes death entered the easy way.

Twenty-seven

thieves' highway

Skies darker than my soul. Rain pouring down like thoughts.

Arizona said, "Gideon?"

"I'm in the lobby."

"He found you last night."

"And brandished his Desert Eagle. Showed me a book. *Big Bad Wolf.* Walked away."

"Let me arrange passage, get you out of England. To Germany or Italy."

"That won't matter. He knows too much. They know too much. I'm not running."

"I respect that."

"Let me come up. Need to sit and think. What's your room number?"

"You're early. Still in bed. Not dressed. Need to shower. Give me thirty minutes."

"Too much popping." Thelma's claws were deep inside me, her fingers dragging across my psyche, leaving my mind in shreds. I said, "Let me get out of this open lobby and come up."

"After I shower and get dressed. You're safe down there."

"Safe? Did you hear what I said? The fool brandished a Desert Eagle, made a threat."

"Did you hear what I said? After I shower and get dressed."

She was all attitude. My life was on the line and she was giving me grief.

I was across from Hyde Park, standing on the marbled floors of the Corus Park Hotel, a short distance from Knightsbridge, Oxford Street, and the bright lights of Theatreland.

I looked around, spied the entrances and exits. "Okay. Thirty minutes. What room?"

She told me her room number.

She said, "Relax. Big Brother is watching. I got your back."

"What you mean?"

"Jeans. Backpack on your left shoulder. Coat. I see you."

I looked around. "Where are you?"

"Don't worry about where I am. Meet me in half an hour."

She hung up.

I looked at my watch, started a countdown.

I needed to know if she had any new information. The information she had already given me, the details of a job he did back in the States down in Jacksonville, that wouldn't do me any good this morning. I needed to find him. Then find who he was working for, if I could.

Arizona said that she thought the contract came from Big Bad's brother.

That made sense.

More sense than anything right now.

I just found it hard for him to be laid up in ICU issuing a hit, not this fast.

Either way I had to find two people. The man who took the contract. Had to find him before he found me again. Then I had to find the man who paid for the contract.

I rubbed my eyes.

Margaret. That name wouldn't leave my head.

I tried to remember that far back in my life.

I couldn't.

Didn't remember much before I fired that .22 into the middle of Midnight.

Remembered almost everything that had happened since.

My morning had disturbed me. Thelma haunted me. She crawled over my skin.

Thelma. My mother. Not my mother.

Sven. My brother. Not my brother.

All she had was five thousand pounds to take care of a kid the rest of his life. Five thousand British pounds, the equivalent of ten thousand American dollars, she was leaving that chump change to take care of a child the rest of his life. Cost that much to take care of a kid for half a year. The kid would be abused and living on the streets by Christmas. Or would get shipped from foster home to foster home.

I wanted justice.

The justice I had given to others, I wanted to find that justice for myself.

I kept my face down, moved away from all the people connecting to the Internet in the lounge and BT Openzone area, found a chair, put my back to the wall, kept my hand hidden inside my backpack, my gun inside my hand, my eyes hunting for anybody who might be in search of a violent morning.

Prostitute from Opelika, Alabama. Killed. Left rotting in a Dumpster.

Buried wherever the State of Alabama buried her dead whores.

Pandemonium arrived.

Just like that the lobby was crowded with loud Germans, middle-aged and old, but the younger ones were creating the havoc. A group of French tourists had arrived too. Russians were also in line. The Germans were in a group, yelling back and forth across the lobby, insulting the French. A bus filled with Americans showed up and added to the early-morning chaos.

The French started taunting the Americans, screeching out some *Vive la France* anthem.

The Americans sang their national anthem. The Germans and Russians yelled theirs.

Twenty minutes of that screaming and singing was enough to make me want to throw stones at them all. That twenty minutes dragged by like a week in a deafening insane asylum.

I headed for the lift. Pushed the button. Looked up, saw that the lift was delayed, sitting on the eighth floor. The others were going up. That was the only one coming down. The lift on eight began its descent. At a snail's pace. It came down to the lobby without stopping.

The lift opened and a man wearing a tailor-made suit faced me.

He was Latin, tall, wavy hair slicked to the back. Dry umbrella at his side.

His forehead was dank. Tie loosened.

As we passed, I smelled hints of perfume mixed with the sweat on his skin.

On the lift, I pushed the button for the sixth floor.

Left rotting in a Dumpster. In Alabama. I told myself that that was another lie.

On the sixth floor I exited the lift, took to the halls, checked my shadow, found the stairs, walked up two flights. Then I stalled. Listened. Nobody was coming up the stairs behind me.

When I was sure no one was following, I searched the narrow corridor for her room.

Her room was back in the corner, no way to approach without being seen.

I tapped on the door. Heard music coming from inside. Jazz. Wes Montgomery. I looked down. Outside the door was an empty bottle of wine, two glasses, one of those glasses having lipstick on the rim. And food, two plates of pasta. Food from the night before.

She called out, "You forget something?"

Something inside me crashed.

Arizona opened the door. Surprised to see me. Her hair pulled back from her face.

She was dressed in a sheer housecoat. Nothing else. Her nipples were swollen beyond belief. Her skin was dank and glowing. Every movement filled with postorgasmic energy.

Her face was closed, unsmiling.

Arizona said, "Thirty minutes hasn't gone by."

"Early is on time."

She covered herself up. "Come on in."

Arizona's sweetness wafted toward me. I inhaled her perfume. I smelled her primal scents. And I smelled a man's cologne. I smelled the barbaric aroma he had left behind.

A quick glance toward the bathroom showed me the toilet seat was still up.

I stepped over a dark dress, high heels, thong, bra. Her clothes were scattered on the floor, like she had undressed in lust and haste. I drifted toward the garbage near the bed. Saw discarded condom wrappers. Her perfume. His cologne. The aroma from their sex swimming in the damp air. Tried to hold my breath. But breathing was a habit that was hard to break.

My eyes avoided the disheveled bed. I told myself that I had bigger problems.

Her suite looked like a scaled-down version of *24*'s Counter Terrorist Unit. Three laptops were up and running. All had wireless cards giving her Internet access.

Jazz flowed from one. "Stompin' at the Savoy" ended and "Stranger in Paradise" began.

She moved away from me like what I saw was no big deal.

I did the same. Reminded myself to stay focused on my mission.

I said, "You find his connection over here or what?"

"My connection in Jacksonville didn't have anything new. It dead-ended there."

"Okay. Now what?"

"Was filtering it though my U.S. connections, but the time change, you know."

"Evil never sleeps. You just have to find the right evil and get your information."

"Your guns came from my contact. And a lot of these guys know each other. They go to the same well to buy the clean firearms they sell to people like you. They only work on referral."

The clothes scattered on the floor. The tossed room. The aroma of pleasure.

And the heat. Body heat. It radiated like a furnace. No more than fifteen minutes old.

I moved to the computers. Tried to focus.

I said, "Get me in contact with Pit Bull."

"You want to get in contact with Big Bad's brother?"

"And when you get that motherfucker on the line—"

"Slow it down, Gideon. Slow the shit down."

Thoughts were coming down like an avalanche. Burying me in their wake.

I took a breath. Walked the small room to shake it off.

On one laptop she had tapped into all the CCTV cameras throughout Central London. She went to that one, eyes trained on the screen, monitoring Covent Garden, Seven Dials, Shaftesbury Avenue, Battersea Park, Trafalgar Square, Knightsbridge, a few other areas.

I asked, "What's up with all this?"

"I've been searching the areas you said you saw your stalker. Covent Garden. Knightsbridge. Lancaster Gate. Looking for him on old footage and at the same time monitoring the outside of the hotel, making sure he doesn't sneak up on you right now."

That wasn't what I was asking.

Despite what she said, the room itself was evidence that she had been too busy talking care of her own needs to sit up in front of a computer monitoring anything.

I motioned at another screen. "That's MyHotel. That's the hall in front of my room."

"I tapped into their system. Did that after we were attacked in Chinatown."

"You've been watching me come and go?"

"Like I said, just watching your back. Watching my own back as well."

She'd seen me and my female companions coming and going.

I took another deep breath. "Unfuckingbelievable."

"Get over it."

"You have a camera in my room?"

"You wish."

She'd had me under surveillance. But she had all this security for her own benefit. Her sister had her terrified. She'd never admit that. But it was obvious. Arizona had been rattled.

And, one by one, she was killing off everyone she was afraid of.

Gun in hand, at the window, I looked through the cold winds and downpour. My eyes toward Queensgate. Same area I had chased the man with the broken nose through.

Sweet music continued to flow out of one of her laptops.

My mind was still on whores and Dumpsters.

I opened and closed my hands. Felt the pain from last night's club fight.

Hoped that pain wouldn't affect my trigger finger. Or my aim.

Stupid. Everything that had happened last night had been stupid. Everything.

I downed another BC Powder.

"Gideon. Need to show you something."

Arizona slid a stack of papers toward me, pages downloaded from the *Los Angeles Times* Web site. The top page was an article about eighty people being sold the same Social Security number. The page after that had to do with millions of dollars being scammed in the UK.

I asked, "Some of your scheming?"

She did a double take on what I was reading, then took a few of the sheets back, stuffed them in her backpack. "Yeah. But didn't mean to give you those pages. Look at the others."

I went to the next page. A tragedy about a Los Angeles family with roots in Kingston.

Standing between husband and daughter, her hair straight, I recognized her.

In color, Mrs. Jones's image was smiling up at me.

Twenty-eight

the asphalt jungle

Mrs. Jones's tragedy had been ripped from the front page of the L.A. Times.

Arizona said, "I pulled it off the Internet."

I did my best to sit on my new anger. "How did you know her full name?"

"You said she was on the plane in the seat next to you."

"Bullshit."

"That's all I needed. Former flight attendant. Used my connections. Got her name from reservations. Got her passport info. Can tell you the charge card she used to buy her ticket. She's done a hella lot of shopping since she arrived. You know me. Was in charge of computer operations for Scamz. Did what I do. Got her name. Google. Wikipedia. Classmates.com. Checked to see if she was legit. Would hate for her to be in on bringing you down."

"Why?"

"A strange woman fucks you as soon as she steps off a plane, that makes her a suspect."

Arizona was right. I hated to admit it, but she was right.

Underneath the newspaper article was family information. There was a copy of Mrs. Jones's professional résumé, her credit report, home address, the kind of car she drove, more.

Arizona said, "Had to see who she was. For you. For your safety."

"She's a square."

"Do you have any idea how many people think I'm a square? Think you're a square?"

My eyes went to the picture of Mrs. Jones with her husband and daughter.

They looked like a happy family. All-American in their own way. The article was more about Mrs. Jones's daughter than anything else.

Arizona said, "Looks like her kid took justice into her own hands."

The kid that had been drugged and raped was Mrs. Jones's teenage daughter.

Mrs. Jones's daughter had extracted her own revenge, left a few people in a bad way.

Arizona shifted. "After what she went through, the kid should be a local hero. Google the kid's name. Or go to MySpace. So many blogs have been dedicated to the Jones kid."

The article said Mrs. Jones's father had been incarcerated around the same time. Attempted murder. The woman who used to be Henrietta Kellogg had a much darker past.

Arizona said, "Her father died in prison."

"Somebody put a hit put on him?"

"Natural causes. Heart attack. But you never know."

Mrs. Jones. On the plane crying. Divorce and death, the two things that made people crack. So much had gone wrong in her world, getting divorced being the least of her problems.

The family photo had come from happier times. I assumed. Smiles meant nothing. Smiles hid the truth. Mrs. Jones used to be Henrietta, her family run out of Jamaica. Her husband robbed banks before they married. And her daughter had carried on the family drama.

Arizona said, "Her old man left her a ton of money."

I pushed the copies of Mrs. Jones's personal life back toward Arizona.

We stared at each other. A mild face-off.

I asked, "What does this have to do with my situation?"

"Nothing. Had to make sure she didn't have you in a trick bag."

She turned the mood music off. Picked up the remote. Aimed it at a small black television. Local news came on. The Brits were having a World Naked Bike Ride. An oil-dependency protest that was starting at Wellington Arch, Hyde Park Corner. A 10K route around the streets of London on bikes and skates. Naked. What the British cared about.

I said, "Can you find something where they don't have a bloody British accent?"

She changed to CNN.

Arizona said, "Put the gun away. Order me a traditional breakfast too."

"I'm not your Stepin Fetchit."

She went back to working on her laptop.

I picked up the phone, called the kitchen, did what Arizona asked me to do.

Long hair down, flesh exposed, she headed toward the shower.

I looked at the laptop that was monitoring MyHotel. She had turned that screen off.

Arizona had been watching me. Spying on me like she was George W. Bush.

Sergeant had said that Arizona was not to be trusted.

I asked, "Why did you shut down the screen at MyHotel?"

"Because you're here."

"Can I turn it back on?"

"Why do you need it on?"

I rubbed my temples. "Never mind."

I looked around, spied on her like she had spied on me.

Her room wasn't bad. But my hotel room was nicer. Nicer and had a better fragrance.

CNN. In between talk about the killings in the Middle East and the British wanting their troops out of Iraq, a report came up about U.S. news. The lead U.S. story was about rapper Sledge being killed in Trinidad, then a tie-in to rapper Big Bad Wolf's slaughter down in Florida.

From the bathroom door she called out, "Big Bad . . . it's been on all night and morning."

The news report was brief, no more than thirty seconds of airtime. The next report was on the WAG who had been found in the Thames River, London's top news.

I asked about what concerned me. "That WAG been on all morning too?"

"Nonstop. That's all they've been talking about."

CNN moved on. Mozambique was using rats to find land mines because of their acute sense of smell. Prince Charles's cellular phone calls being intercepted. Fuck Squidgygate. Fuck Camillagate. Fuck CNN. Fuck the rest of the goddamn world. I had my own fucking problems.

Arizona came out, soap on her skin, towel around her body, dug inside her luggage, took out Dermalogica products, took out hair products. Arizona glanced at me, paused with her eyes on mine, rose, went back to the shower without comment, the bathroom door left open, shower curtains not closed all the way, her golden skin damp and inches away from where I stood.

I wanted to be with Lola and Mrs. Jones, taking the TGV, the high-speed bullet train that zoomed through the Chunnel toward Parisian culture at close to two hundred miles per hour.

They were no longer a part of my world. Still I wondered what they would do in Paris. Wondered if they would take on another lover. Part of me was happy, another part jealous.

My eyes locked on the bed; covers were tossed, unmade in a violent way.

Arizona turned the shower off.

She came out, towel around her frame, crossed the room to her luggage.

I put my eyes on the television. Battled with the legion of demons inside my head.

Arizona dropped her towel, pulled on her thong, let her full breasts hang free.

I knew how those breasts felt in my hands. Knew how the nipples tasted.

She went to the computer, went back into the bathroom, went to the nightstand.

Her breasts bounced with her sweet sashay.

I bit my tongue so hard I tasted blood, swallowed that blood, refused to let her get to me.

She said, "Looked up the Desert Eagle. It says you can change barrels after each job."

"That gun fascinates you."

She floated by me, again, hit the light switch outside the door, clicked it down to make the light come on inside the bathroom, went to the miniature sink, came back brushing her hair.

She said, "Swapping barrels . . . is the same as getting rid of the old fingerprints and getting a brand-new gun. It's good to get a new barrel. Good to get rid of old fingerprints."

I asked Arizona, "Your new barrel, who was he?"

"Let's not go there, okay?"

She passed by me, both her stench and her sarcasm floating between us.

I had inhaled her arrogance one time too many.

I snapped, "Bitch."

She exploded, "Fuck you."

"Get dressed. Put some damn clothes on."

"Worry about the Jones lady. Worry about the other girl you took up to your room."

"He looked like Scamz. What, you still trying to resurrect your ghost?"

She didn't respond to that.

She pulled herself together.

I did the same.

Twenty-nine

his kind of woman

Arizona went to her suitcase, moved weapons to the side, took some clothes out.

She dressed while I stared at the computer.

She went to the bathroom, brushed her teeth.

Brushed his flavor from her mouth.

Then she came back, hair in a ponytail, wearing jeans, T-shirt, eyeglasses, feet bare. Arizona sashayed to her computer. She looked like a nerd. A sexy nerd, but still a nerd. My clothes were still damp enough to give me pneumonia. My mind fucked up enough to not care.

She asked, "We cool or what?"

"We're so cool we're frozen."

"Just want to make sure we're simpatico."

"Yeah. Simpatico." I cleared my throat. "I have other things going on."

"Relax. You're safe here. We'll find this guy."

The ache in my hand sang to me. I said, "Things more important than him on my mind."

"What?"

"Nothing I need to talk about right now."

"You okay?"

I wasn't okay. I would never be okay. Still I nodded.

Arizona asked, "Your flight . . . you said he was in first class?"

"Business." I told her his seat number. "Pulling up the airline info?"

"Hacking into reservations again. See if I can find a name, see how he paid for his ticket. International travel. Even if he paid cash, he'd still have to use a passport, even if was bogus."

Then came the knock at the door.

Arizona jumped.

I raised my gun.

She looked down at the computer, made it switch to the camera outside her door.

I thought her friend had come back, but it was room service.

I put my gun away, let room service inside.

Dressed in black and a red shirt, the waitress brought us proper English breakfasts: eggs, beans, toast, orange juice. I paid for the meals while Arizona kept working on her laptop.

The waitress left. Again we were alone in a hotel room.

Arizona typed and typed. She sipped her tea. Ate beans and toast. Put salt and pepper on her eggs. Sipped orange juice. Waited. Got a response. Then she typed some more, no doubt communicating with associates all across the globe, calling in favors with each keystroke.

She pretended nothing was wrong. I pretended too.

I went to my tea. To my beans and toast. Went back to my thoughts of Thelma.

Arizona said, "No matter what you think . . . I'm looking out for you."

"With a thousand cameras aimed at my hotel, monitoring my every move."

"I think my head is clearer than yours. That means I have to consider all possibilities. That means I have to trust no one until they are proven trustworthy, and even if they are proven trustworthy, to not trust them then. There is no such thing as absolute trust in this business."

I looked around her room. At her disheveled bed.

Arizona said, "I came here to be with you, you know."

"Too bad you didn't send a postcard to let me know where your head was at."

"Yeah. Too bad."

I nodded. "For the best."

"Yeah. For the best. Never should have crossed that line."

"Never should have."

This was what happened when an unstoppable force met an unmovable object.

We were Tracy and Hepburn. The stubborn against the stubborn.

Done eating, she fired up her Djarum.

As soon as I pushed my food to the side, Arizona slid another picture across the table.

Another photo of Sierra, her sister, same as the one she had given me before.

I wanted to ask how long Sierra had been working in Amsterdam. Years ago when I had gone to Amsterdam, I had spent both time and money, bought the affections of a whore who looked like Sierra. My longing for Arizona had been the root of that quest for pleasure. I stared in Sierra's eyes, wondered if she was the same whore I'd been with. Then I put the picture to the side. I should've asked Arizona how long her sister had been working in Amsterdam. I didn't want to know, not right now. Not when Arizona wanted her dead. Truth be told, I was afraid to know.

I said, "Like sex, killing somebody isn't something that can be undone."

Arizona lit another Djarum. Took two puffs. Put it out.

She asked, "What's it like to take somebody's life?"

I hesitated, rubbed hand over hand. "It bothers me. If you have to know, it bothers me."

"But you do it."

Again I hesitated, dealt with many thoughts. "Probably would've stopped years ago."

"Why didn't you?"

I winked at her. "Had a million reasons to keep doing it."

Arizona tapped the picture of her sister, did that to redirect my wavering focus.

She said, "Take care of this for me. Get to Amsterdam. Take

care of Sierra. She . . . this anger . . . hate makes me weak. I need to be strong. I need her gone so I can be stronger."

"You're not that cold-blooded. This is your little sister."

"Cain killed Abel. Don't forget that."

"And he regretted it."

"He regretted that he got caught."

"So you're Cain killing Abel because you are jealous of God's love."

"And who would God be in this little parable?"

"You stole his name. Put Queen in front of the moniker. Scamz was your king. The God you still worship. A man who looks just like him just left your room. You're sleeping with ghosts."

She frowned, ran her tongue over her lips.

Arizona got on her cellular. Emotions on high. She turned her body away, made a call.

My eyes returned to the picture of Mrs. Jones, her husband, their teenage daughter.

I didn't want to, but I read some more. I scanned words describing the agony that drove Mrs. Jones to London. Her daughter had been in shock and become a vigilante. Her husband's former lover had taken a DVD to the police. Despite the rape, the police came for the victim.

My hand throbbed. I saw Thelma on the ground, piss between her legs.

We did terrible things out of love. Almost as terrible as the things we did out of hate.

Arizona finished her call and closed her cellular phone.

I put the bad news down, papers flipped over, Mrs. Jones no longer staring at me.

My cellular vibrated once. Just once. A signal that a new text message had come.

I read the text message: FUNDS TRANSFERRED.

Animosity rose above my nose, covered my eyes, and blurred my vision.

Arizona's expression remained stern. "Guess we're back in bed together."

"Guess so."

"When this is done, I expect you to honor our contract in an expeditious manner."

"I'll handle your sister. I'll break her neck. I'll cut her throat. I will drown her. I'll take a chain saw to her while she screams and cut her up like I'm trying to become Butcher of the Year."

My coldhearted words made Arizona shiver. She talked shit. She stole from people. She hurt people. But she wasn't a killer. Didn't have what it took to put somebody down forever.

I said, "I'll kill your sister however you tell me to execute her. I'll disembowel her. I'll give you a permanent solution to your familial problem. I will be bloody professional."

She looked at me, eyes wide, shaken by my dark tone.

I whispered, "But only if you watch."

Arizona shivered again, then steeled herself and nodded.

Her eyes watered and she opened her mouth, but no words came out.

Her computer beeped.

That beep saved us from talking about Amsterdam. For now.

She closed her mouth, typed and typed, nodded, and typed, then looked at me.

Arizona was on her BlackBerry and one of the laptops sang. She put the BlackBerry down, and whatever was on the computer created a sweet smile in the corner of her lips.

I asked, "What did you find out?"

"I just found who sold a brand-new Israeli-made Desert Eagle wrapped in titanium."

"Find the gun and you find the man."

One small-time dealer had unloaded a Desert Eagle the same day I arrived at Gatwick. It was picked up a couple of hours after the WAG had been tossed into the Thames River.

Arizona said, "Transfer was made on the DLR somewhere before Canary Wharf."

She pulled up a map of the DLR system. Docklands Light Railway. I looked over the map of the aboveground train, which was as easy to read as a tube map.

I said, "That leg of the DLR runs from Bank to Lewisham. What else you find?"

"Got a name from my contact. Gun was delivered to Bruno Brubaker. Ring a bell?"

I shook my head.

She cross-referenced the name with my flight. Brubaker had been in business class.

She said, "Says Brubaker boarded in Atlanta."

"He could've arrived at Atlanta from anywhere."

"Or be anywhere at this moment."

I asked, "How do we find Bruno Brubaker now?"

"Same way the FBI tracks all Americans. Same way the government tracks our every move. Same way companies on the Internet track customers and their spending habits."

"Good old credit cards."

"See if he slipped, left an electronic trail. Those bread crumbs are food for Big Brother."

"Let me cross-reference Bruno Brubaker with the American Express he used to buy the ticket. If the Bruno name is a new alias, doubt if he would have dumped it this fast."

"I wouldn't use the same passport after I landed."

"Even if he dumped the name and started using a different passport, the credit card could still be hot. He wouldn't have to show his passport. The Brits never ask for ID with credit cards, so long as the signatures match. He could still be dropping bread crumbs."

"What about—"

"You're starting to stress me out. Can't think when I get stressed."

"Thought your friend handled your stress."

"Fuck you."

"Been there, done that. Trip wasn't worth the gas."

She took a deep breath. "I can't keep doing this with you, Gideon."

"I know. That was uncalled for. I apologize. Here on out, I'll be professional."

I gave her space. Like a restless dog, I walked around in circles.

The skies remained dark. The rain kept falling. The temperature dropped.

London became as cold as a whore's heart.

I drifted by the unmade bed, looked down again, saw the empty condom wrappers in her trash. Thought that if I frowned at those empty condom wrappers long enough, they would vanish.

I knew how Arizona tasted. Knew how she smelled. How she moved. Felt.

But I didn't know her.

I was dead tired. So tired I had to sit down in a small chair and close my eyes.

So exhausted that sleep crawled over me the moment I stopped moving.

Just like that I was a child in Montreal, at Parc Mont-Royal, playing with a ball.

The sun went away. Someone was standing behind me. A big man. Mr. Midnight. He moved to the left, the sun now in his face. His skin wasn't the color of midnight. He wasn't dark at all. His eyes were green. His flesh had been darkened by lies. Now I saw him clearly.

Blood dripped from the bullet hole in the middle of his head.

That terrified me. I turned around to run away. But what I saw stilled me.

Behind me was a Dumpster. Flies and trash spilling out its mouth. As I got closer, mixed in with the rubbish, I saw a naked woman's bloody leg hanging out of its opening.

Arizona screamed and yanked me from my nightmare.

She said, "Fucking firewalls. God, all these damn encryptions, they are making this hacking shit so damn hard."

"Can't get in?"

"Oh, I'm in. Took a while, but I'm inside American Express."

Sleep-deprived and amazed at what she knew how to do, I leaned toward her.

She said, "Let's see where Brubaker has been using that charge card."

Thirty

notorious

Big Brother. Big fucking Brother.

Just like that I saw where the man with the broken nose had been eating. Good old American Express showed us where he had rented a hotel room, Novotel Hotel at Tower Bridge. He'd been bold enough to rent a room a short walk from where a WAG had plummeted forty-three meters from that Victorian bridge into freezing waters. Based on the time of the charge, his room had been rented right after the WAG's body had been fished out of the Thames River. Hours later he paid for two new suits. Suits that had been charged to a tailor in South London.

His ticket to London had been booked same day, same American Express card, paid for at the counter, cost him more than six grand to sit in British Airway's version of business class.

He had stopped at a gift shop near the world-famous tea clipper *Cutty Sark*, then hiked up the hill and gone to the Royal Observatory Greenwich, the spot that originated Greenwich mean time. An hour after that he had stopped off at Canary Wharf, probably the best-looking and most high-tech tube station in London, and shopped at the mall. After that some charges were made in Camden Town, then he had eaten and hung out in the lounge at the Lush Bar.

Around the time I was visiting a pedophile in Wimbledon, he'd gone to some play called *Dutty Wine*. He'd caught a cab from Hackney to Crouch End.

Stalked me.

Threatened me.

Threatened the women I was with.

Then he'd gone back to a jazz club in Camden Town after he'd confronted me at Banners.

I'd killed a pedophile and gone to dinner and the man with the broken nose had threatened me and gone out for music and drinks. His tab being closed out at 2 A.M. While I was in the middle of a club fight, the man who had threatened my life was chilling out.

Arizona said, "He's been doing a lot of shopping too. Harry Potter books, movies. He probably has a kid. Or kids. The movie, looks like he was on a date. Could have a hottie here."

I flipped open my phone, called the Novotel, asked for Bruno Brubaker.

My heart sped up when they transferred the call.

No one answered the phone in his room.

That didn't mean he wasn't there.

By then Arizona had pulled Bruno Brubaker's passport photo up on the screen.

I nodded. "That's him. Without a broken nose. That's him."

She said, "What do you think?"

"Who are you sending his photo to?"

"Someone I work with."

"Who?"

"Don't worry about it. Just tell me what our plan of action should be at this point."

"I think I need to go down there, guns blazing. End this shit. Then get some sleep."

"Have to be smarter than that."

"Then get back to the States. Break into the hospital in Tampa. Handle Bull Dog."

"Pit Bull."

"Whatever that mutt calls himself. I'll put his ass to sleep."

"Don't go stupid on me."

I rubbed my burning eyes. "Better idea?"

"Give me a minute. One more contact has to get back to me."

I closed my eyes again.

Her BlackBerry sang again. What she had been waiting for had arrived.

Arizona said, "I just got a major hit from François Bertin. This might break the case."

"Who is he?"

"He supplied the Eagle. Actually sold it to a competitor, some Moroccan named Sam, did that transaction with a major markup. François is an asshole. Did some business with him once."

"Once."

"François uses kids to run his merchandise. Wasn't feeling that. Stopped using him."

"What, he has something that's going to help me out?"

"He knows we're looking for the gun. He uses kids to run his weapons, keeps himself clean. Says the man with the broken nose did a number on one of his friends down in Camden Town. Beat the guy down real bad over nothing. He's pissed. Now he has information to sell."

I nodded. Knew where this was going. "How much this information cost?"

"He wants two thousand."

"Dollars?"

"Quid."

"Tell him I said one thousand."

Arizona passed on the message.

I was anxious. I was scared. Like a soldier heading into war.

"He won't compromise."

I didn't have time to negotiate, so I nodded.

They exchanged information via BlackBerry.

She said, "He's not comfortable with this."

"With what?"

"He's not exchanging information before he's been paid."

"Tell him to meet me in Leicester Square. Tell him to come to

Häagen-Dazs Café. I can hole up at Burger King, sit on the second floor and watch him. When it's cool, I'll get to him."

She passed that information on. Then she shook her head. Leicester Square was out.

The man with the information always had the upper hand. We had to meet when and where he felt comfortable. Where he felt like he wasn't going to be trapped in a sting operation.

I asked, "How does he want to do the exchange?"

"Wants to meet in Southwark. Said he's coming up from Blackfriars and he'll wait for us on the Millennium Bridge. Said he'll wait thirty minutes, then he's on the tube, history."

I had to make a choice.

Arizona said, "Let me handle Novotel."

"How?"

"Don't need you going over there. He knows you. You know the man has an Eagle. And he's a pro. Last thing you want to do is risk having a possible shoot-out in the lobby."

"I could get a better advantage."

"But you don't know if the guy's there. He might be in the lobby. Then what?"

"So you think going to Novotel first would be a bad idea?"

"You going to Novotel without scouting the place is plain stupid."

"Is that right?"

"You're getting emotional. And this is personal. He made this personal so you'd fuck up. When it's personal, you don't think right. And you're not thinking right. That's a very bad idea. I wouldn't advise you showing your face there. Not until the situation has been assessed."

"Who are you sending messages to?"

"I'm multitasking."

"Who are you sending messages to?"

"Don't worry about what I'm doing. Stop transmitting and listen. Worry about what I'm telling you. The guy has been trailing you. Vanishing. Trailing you again. Vanishing. Popping up in your face at dinner. All I know is this: you don't know if the guy is working solo. No way he can be. And you're running around London on no sleep with a ton of stress weighing you down."

I nodded. "So I need to go meet a man on a bridge."

"Let's see what he has. Let's see how that changes the landscape of the situation."

"He could text you the info while we head to Novotel."

"He's all about money. Face-to-face. He wants to get paid. In cash. No wire transfer."

"Nothing traceable."

Some shit people want to be face-to-face to talk about. And get paid for. A two-minute conversation cost two thousand pounds. Four thousand in U.S. money. Just to get the information on a location to stalk. But this was about life and death. My life. His death.

He was selling his own client down the river, selling him the way Judas had sold Jesus.

Everyone sold everybody out at some point.

Throw enough green on the table and friend betrayed friend.

I said, "Tell your boy I'm on the way. And I'll wait ten minutes. No longer. If he's not there, I need to take my chances and stake out the hotel. Slide in, find a place to hide and hunt."

I grabbed my backpack. Made sure my gun was loaded and on pause.

I asked, "How long will it take to get to the Millennium Bridge on the tube?"

"I have a car on standby. Just have to get to the car park."

"Location of car park and car keys?"

"I'm going. And you know I'm going. So don't act like I'm not."

"I don't need you."

"I'm going."

"You got me the info. I can take it from here."

"Look. François Bertin is not going to chat with you. Not without me. He's my contact."

"You said you stopped using him."

"I did."

"Something go wrong? Another old lover?"

She made a frustrated sound.

I took a breath. "Shit."

"And I didn't ask you if you needed me."

I didn't want to argue with her.

She packed up one of the laptops, turned the other two off. She told me the only way the other systems would come online was by using her thumbprint. If someone tried to compromise either system, data would be destroyed. Data that was backed up elsewhere. Then she opened a case. Inside was a set of knives. The kind she loved to throw at people when she was pissed.

She also picked up a small gun, loaded that into the small of her back.

She said, "No, François and I aren't lovers. All business. The way things should be."

She pulled her hair back, put on glasses, became a college girl once again.

She went to the room safe, punched in the combination, took out a stack of bills.

She counted off two thousand pounds, tossed it to me.

She said, "I'll deduct this from what I'll owe you for handling my Amsterdam problem."

"Killing your sister."

"My Amsterdam problem."

"Hard for you to say that, huh? That you just paid me to kill your sister."

"I paid you to kill the bitch who had a beat-and-rape contract out on me."

Again I thought about Amsterdam. About the whore I'd gone to see. The woman who looked like Arizona. Again I glanced at Sierra's picture. Again I wondered.

I said, "Let's go."

We took the stairs down, did that with both style and paranoia.

I walked down a floor, waited. She passed me, went down a floor, waited.

We did that until we hit the bottom floor, one level below the main level.

Rain was still falling hard. Temperature was still dropping.

She said, "You know the rules, right?"

She was nervous, talking about if things went south, if the police showed up.

I nodded. I knew the rules in this game.

I said, "You don't have to go with me."

"Look. I referred you to Sledgehammer. I have to fix it."

"You didn't force me to take the job."

"I did. In a million different ways."

That silenced me.

She repeated, "Just remember the rules."

We left it at that.

We caught a hackney to Mastercar Car Park. There was nowhere to park near the hotel, the closest car park being a half mile away at Queensway. She had changed cars, the Mini Cooper she had yesterday gone, now her ride so small it looked like a one-seater. A Tango. One of those electric cars that was about three feet wide. She hopped in and took off fast. The car was small but moved with the speed of a 'Vette, was as nimble as a motorcycle.

We remained shoulder to shoulder as she drove.

Not like Bogart and Bacall.

No longer like Tracy and Hepburn.

We rolled out like Bonnie and Clyde.

Thirty-one

farewell, my lovely

The rain slowed down, but didn't stop.

Few were out walking postal code SE1. Those who were out had rain and winter coats on, some had on galoshes, all had umbrellas up high.

Globe Theatre. Tate Modern. St. Paul's Cathedral. All looked abandoned. This was the business side of town. Nothing was open but pubs and tubes.

Sharing an umbrella, backpacks on, we headed toward the designated meeting spot.

We saw her contact coming from Queen Victoria Street, taking the walkway between the international headquarters for the Salvation Army and the City of London School.

He came out on Millennium Bridge, a contemporary pedestrian bridge that was about twelve feet wide and made of some sort of aluminum, a finish that was slippery when wet. He was alone, carrying a copy of *The Voice*, black iPod on his hip.

It was a four-minute walk across the bridge.

He stopped two minutes into his walk.

We headed toward him.

Right before we got to him, he turned around and we followed him closer to the side by the school, staying at least twenty yards behind him until we made it close to the end nearest St. Paul's Cathedral. I looked at the humongous historic building, thought about how Lola would've loved seeing the landmark where Princess Diana and Prince Charles were married, then looked back at the Tate Modern. Imagined Mrs. Jones being excited about Kandinsky.

Bad time to think about them, but I couldn't help it. I missed them. Like I missed family, I missed them. It was more than sex. For a moment, in my mind, I was with them, here on this bridge in the rain. We'd go inside. We'd have to. Mrs. Jones would have to see Kandinsky.

Mrs. Jones would ask, *"Have you ever sat in a chair and marveled at a piece of art?"*

I'd shake my head. *"No."*

"Let's."

Imagined Lola wandering away, iPod on, moving from room to room, not really impressed by the paintings. Then imagined us leaving and having dinner at an Italian restaurant in Covent Garden, laughing and walking, stopping in almost every shop between Charing Cross and Leicester Square, then having drinks on that strip of serious partyers in the heart of the theater area, where a thousand people congregated to eat and watch street performers.

Maybe we'd go see *The Lion King*. Lola would want to see a musical. Maybe *Wicked*.

But Mrs. Jones would want to see something dramatic. Like *Embers* with Jeremy Irons.

That square life was over.

Lola. Mrs. Jones. Had to keep reminding myself that square life was behind me.

And Arizona was in front of me.

We stopped walking, cold wind in my face, few people passing, her contact looking nervous. He was gangly, emaciated, sallow. He needed his drugs. He needed his drugs bad.

He said, "Me money."

Arizona said, "Drop some knowledge first, François Bertin."

"Me money."

"Don't bullshit with me."

The gaunt man shook his head. "Sod off. Me bloody money or I walk."

"Problem, François?"

"You shorted me on the last deal."

"I shorted you?"

"You heard me. So I want me money up front this time."

"I didn't short you."

"The people who came to me on your referral, they robbed me."

Arizona. "But I've never robbed you, have I?"

"I told you what they did. You bloody left me hanging. So me money up front. All of it. I have to make sure you don't do that again."

Tired of this shit, I stepped up. "Do you know who I am?"

"Sod off. Does it look like I give a bloody wank about this bloke? About any bloke?"

With force and darkness, I said my street name. "Gideon."

That jarred him. He repeated, "Gideon. No way."

Arizona nodded. "Way."

"You didn't tell me that bloody psychotic wanker was your client."

"You didn't need to know."

"Gideon?" His attitude adjusted. "Shit. You're the grim reaper . . . you're bloody death."

I stepped closer to his rancid breath. "So don't sod with me, you wanker."

He held his hand out, fingernails long, like Howard Hughes in his final days.

This time his voice trembled. "Please? Me money. I really, really need me money."

I dropped two thousand pounds in his palm.

Without counting the cash, he ran his finger over his dark hair, then took off running.

Without thought, I chased the drug addict through the rain.

I slipped on the bridge, almost went down, that shiny finish not giving me a lot of traction.

Arizona was behind me, her trainers sliding as well.

It looked like he was running toward the cathedral, but he made a hard left at the end of the bridge, before he made it to the international headquarters for the Salvation Army, ran down the concrete stairs to St. Paul's Walk, the paved route that ran parallel to the Thames.

He was racing by that side of the City of London School toward Blackfriars.

I made it to the bottom of the concrete stairs, Arizona right behind me, and raced after him. Seagulls took flight. No more than fifty yards later I stopped chasing him.

Not because I couldn't catch him.

He wanted me to chase him. He was leading us into the mouth of danger.

He ran by a group of men. He stopped right on the other side of those men. Right after a freestanding pay toilet. As if that were his landmark. Those men started coming toward me.

I turned around. Didn't see Arizona. Started running. Heard them running behind me.

In front of me, more men had come from under the bridge where they had been waiting.

I stopped running, stuck my hand in my backpack, put my hand on my weapon.

Arizona had vanished. She had set me up. The bitch had sold me out.

Then I looked up the stairway.

Arizona was struggling with two men, one with a gun pointed at her head. A third thug was on the ground, doubled over, one of Arizona's blades deep in his rib cage.

They hit her with a swift fist and she spun around, went down fast.

She rolled down the steps hard.

Two more men were rushing up behind me.

They came at us from both ends of the bridge and the stairway all at once.

Two from each direction, pulling out Glocks from underneath their coats and hoodies.

My life had become the prelude to a showdown in a bloody Peckinpah film.

My hand went inside my backpack, pulled out my nine-millimeter.

But it was too late.

They had a gun pointed at her head.

Once again my heart beat so damn fast it scared me.

I couldn't think.

Teeth gritted, finger on trigger, gun trained at the motherfucker threatening Arizona, I made a decision. And that decision was to save her life. To offer mine for hers.

As if I were in a position to bargain.

My baggage wasn't Mrs. Jones. Wasn't Lola. Arizona was my baggage.

She'd been my baggage for more years than I could remember.

Without saying a word I offered myself. I dropped my nine, let it clank on the concrete. Kicked it away. Dropped my backpack in surrender. Raised my hands to the dark clouds.

They came for me, dressed in Lonsdale hoodies, a family of handguns leading the way.

One of them stayed with Arizona. Kept that gun trained on her brain. Rain fell on her as she struggled to get up. They knocked her back down. Her eyes came to me.

I shook my head. Told her not to do anything stupid.

I told Arizona that it was okay. Even though I knew it wasn't. I told her not to fight. But telling her not to fight was like telling a fish not to swim. They knocked her down again.

Arizona got up, leaned against the three-foot-high concrete wall.

On the other side of that wall was the Thames. She saw there was no way out.

She sat on her haunches, cursed, battle glowing in her eyes as she held her injured face.

Rain dripped into my eyes, over my mouth, as men in trench coats surrounded me.

I blinked cold water away from my clouded vision, looked beyond them.

Arizona was smart, but she was out of her league.

They had come for me. They had trapped me.

Like I had gone after many.

My eyes drifted away for a moment, went beyond everyone to the museum.

For a moment I wondered what Kandinsky's work looked like.

Wondered what it was like to sit in a chair and stare at his art.

Wondered if I would see something so beautiful it would warm my soul to tears.

The business end of a Glock touched my side.

A couple of men with guns aimed at your head, it rearranged your way of thinking.

It made you remember some things while you forgot about others.

I forgot about Kandinsky.

In the shadows, underneath an umbrella, the man with the broken nose stood waiting.

He came toward us. Pristine black suit. White shirt. Like an undertaker.

All those thoughts about Lola and Mrs. Jones at the Tate went away for good.

That would never happen.

I looked toward Arizona.

She was a con artist. Not a killer. But she was a fighter. Raised in the streets.

She used to be Scamz's right-hand woman. He had trained her well.

Another blade was inside her coat. I saw her as she eased it out, gritting her teeth.

With force and rage she swiped below the calf of the leg of the man holding her.

That swipe severed his tendons. Sent him screaming to the ground.

Another came after her, only to meet her blade; she threw it hard, hit his neck.

He fell holding his neck, going into shock, trying not to bleed out.

That disrupted the soldiers. That put some fear in their hearts. Stole their focus.

I tackled one of the men near me. Did that to draw attention away from Arizona.

I got in a few good punches. Took one down, staggered another.

Arizona was slicing and dicing whoever was close to her, cutting her way toward me.

Until the man in the black suit grabbed her. Punched her. Dazed her.

He lifted her up over his head.

And threw her over the rail.

I screamed.

The motherfucker threw her into the muddy Thames.

Threw her into the frozen river.

Then he took out his gun. Fired six or seven rounds where she had splashed.

I yelled, fought my best fight, the odds against me.

I was ready to kill. Ready to die.

A blow took me down. Knocked the wind out of my body. Then more blows kept me down. I should've shot them all. Wished I had charged at them, lethal weapon blazing.

Too late. Too fucking late.

Arizona.

Had to get to my feet.

Had to jump into the Thames. Had to save Arizona before she drowned.

They stopped beating me. Left me in pain. Made it to one knee.

They laughed. He laughed.

His expensive shoes tapped as he stopped in front of me.

I frowned up at the motherfucker who had thrown Arizona into the Thames.

Glowered at his expensive suit.

Scowled at the bandages on his face. Bandages that covered his broken nose.

I growled, got my strength to go after him. But I had to get to Arizona.

I stood up swinging, hit nothing but rain and damp air.

They let me stagger by them.

I made it to the rail.

Screamed down at the muddy water.

Couldn't tell if blood was mixed in the filth.

The man in the expensive suit, that broken-nose bastard, stood behind me.

I didn't see him raise his Desert Eagle.

Didn't see the blow before it struck the back of my head.

Just found myself collapsing into a never-ending blackness.

Thirty-two

aces and eights

"How many?"

Inside that blackness I was dead and they were loading my wooden coffin on a train, that train whistle blowing as Johnny Cash stood to the side and sang a woeful song about the 309.

"How many, Gideon?"

A voice floated through that final darkness.

"How many have you killed? How many?"

I coughed, blood running from my mouth.

I didn't give in to the pain. Refused to give up. I was the son of a mercenary. The son of a man who killed bulls with his bare hands. My mother was a whore. My mother was a fighter.

"That's it. Open your eyes. If you can."

Pain struggled with agony, their song a nasty melody exiting my lungs on a rugged groan.

I struggled, out of control and angry. "Arizona. Where the fuck is . . . she?"

"The mean-spirited girl you were with? No need to worry about her anymore. No need to worry about any woman. The rivers are rising with the blood of many women this morning."

Felt like I was bleeding from eyes, nose, and mouth. Felt like every orifice was bleeding.

I groaned. "Son . . . of . . . a . . . bitch . . . I'm . . . going to . . . kill you."

He laughed. "Oh, I doubt if you live long enough to do that."

My head was covered. My hands were bound. So were my ankles. I was on a hard, filthy floor. The sound of buses and street traffic were outside the window. I was still in the city. Where screaming meant nothing. Probably not too far from where he had captured me.

I had a hard time breathing. Kept coughing. The pain rising like a river during a storm.

He said, "Gideon. Questions. If you don't mind."

I coughed. Sweated. Listened. Tried to determine who else was in the room.

Somebody else was moving. Someone else was breathing hard.

Footsteps came across the room.

Felt him squatting near me.

He said, "If you promise to behave, I'll take this off for a few moments."

I didn't move.

His hand pulled the material from over my head, tugged the material over my eyes.

Someone was moving a lot, breathing damn hard.

Sweat had my face as wet as a man after being baptized.

I looked up at the face of the man with the broken nose.

Eyes black. Nose in bandages. He smiled.

He moved away from me. That was when I saw the other man sitting there.

Three feet away, sitting in a wooden chair, was François Bertin. The man who had double-crossed Arizona. His face was beaten, his hands behind his back. Tied.

A plastic bag was over his head.

He was suffocating. Kicking, unable to move, suffocating, struggling for air.

He kicked hard, kicked like he was trying to buck Death off him.

He kicked again, and again, each kick less than the one before.

Then he stopped kicking.

Piss drained from between the man's legs. Soon his bowels would do the same.

The man with the broken nose looked at me. His grin was pathological.

I looked at the dead gunrunner. He'd been double-crossed as well.

He said, "I hate loose ends. And my supplier hates competition. Two birds, one stone."

I coughed up a lot of fear, tried to spit it out, my mouth tasting like blood.

He went to the window, his glasses on, staring at a computer printout.

He asked, "What do you think about a brand-new CLK63 AMG Cabriolet? AMG. V-8 engine. Client is offering me that to finish you off. Would you take it if you were me?"

I stared at the dead man.

"Gideon? Would you take it?"

I coughed.

"Did you do the Memphis contract? The police officer who was left dead in the trunk of his car. Now, that was wicked. Bold and wicked. The hatchet job in Tunica, was that you?"

Again, I coughed.

"The job in the Boulder City desert, did you do that one too?"

The only way I knew I was alive was because of the blood bubbles and the pain.

"De Kalb County, was that your work as well?"

"What is this, a job interview?"

He kicked me in my gut. I dealt with that new pain.

He said, "Of course you didn't do those jobs. I did. I fucking did. I'm better than you. I'm smarter than you. How do I know? Look at where you are now. Look at where I am. I'm the smart one in this room. I could've killed you a hundred times by now. I am smarter, dammit."

Both eyes felt swollen, had to be blackened.

"Still, your work fascinates me. I must confess. Your work fascinates me."

I coughed, struggled.

He asked, "How many contracts have you taken, Gideon?"

I groaned. He'd asked me that over and over. He was as fascinated as a tourist.

He said, "I turned down the one in Tampa. Bet you didn't know that. You did a god-awful job on that one. You were fucking brilliant, I must confess. I'm one of your biggest fans."

I coughed. "Don't know . . . what you're . . . talking about."

"You actually demolished them with sledgehammers. One-man job. Amazing. Did you know that you're a legend because of that? People are terrified of you. Simply terrified."

Again pain rose as grunts vacated my sweating body.

"But I'm not."

I coughed.

He asked, "Now the big question is this . . . two women? You have tell me how."

I coughed again.

"How do you manage to pick up two stunning women? On the same flight. Saw you and one woman, in the rear of the plane. You were smooth. I've never been a ladies' man. Always have had problems with the tender sex. I watched you at Banners. Honestly, I was going to take you out there. Do like the black guy did at the McDonald's in Brixton. You hear about that one? He walked into a crowded Mickie D's and killed a few people. Then walked back out. Awesome. Was going to shoot you, then walk out the front door as everyone dove to the floor in panic. But . . . it seemed wrong. The way you were with the women. The one with the big hair, I liked her. Really did. Saw her on the plane. Before you. That should've been me with her. You were cool. Like watching James Bond. No, not even James Bond has that much savoir faire."

Underneath the pain, what I felt was the sensation I'd had before. Years ago. In Montreal. When Thelma had abandoned me to go service one of her customers. My body owned that same sensation of dread, that angst of being alone, of being small in a large world, my well-being and fate controlled by someone else, only this was magnified by pain and suffering. In the blink of an eye, I'd moved from being the powerful one to being powerless.

I was alone.

In the room with a messenger. Three feet away from a fresh dead man.

He said, "The AMG is worth one hundred thousand. Someone

wants you dead in the worst way. To give up a one-hundred-thousand-dollar car. You know, you will make me famous? After word gets out that I took care of Gideon, my stock will rise, and inside these wretched gates from which we work, I'll become more famous. People in the business will talk about me, brag about how I killed the great Gideon, the man who killed an army by himself."

His tone was business, made it sound like my death would be a corporate takeover.

Sweat dripped in my eye.

He came over, wiped the sweat away with a paper towel.

Then he walked away, went back to the window.

He said, "The book I showed you. *Big Bad Wolf*. That was only to play with your head."

The dead man's bowels began to stink up the room.

He said, "It was a red herring. Found that out. Thought you should know. That was a little something to throw you. In case this didn't work out. Then you'd go after the wrong people."

The man with the broken nose walked around, pondering.

"Revenge. Best served cold. Better served frozen. Like a Popsicle."

He looked at me.

He asked, "From a professional perspective, what do you think I should do at this juncture? You could give me your name. And walk away. I could become Gideon."

I struggled.

He said, "Yeah. I could become Gideon. Pick up where you left off."

He chuckled.

"Can't let you live now. No way. Nope. Queen Scamz. Just fed her to the Thames."

He took the plastic bag off the dead man's head and came toward me.

He said, "Suffocation is clean. Not too noisy. No blood everywhere. No DNA left behind. Suffocation is clean and simple. Cheap plastic bag does the trick. Amazing, huh?"

He squatted in front of me.

He said, "The other women you were with at Banners. The two

women from the plane. I found them. MyHotel. Bloomsbury. Real nice spot you had. Went by there looking for you. Paid your lady friends a visit. Beautiful women. At least they *were*. But don't worry. They will be found. One will be fished out of the Ravensbourne. The other the Quaggy. I've fed enough pretty women to the Thames. What do you think? Relax. You'll be with them in a few minutes."

I kicked, strained, tried to break free.

"Thought you'd feel that way." He smiled. "AMG. I'll take the AMG as payment."

I struggled in vain as he eased the plastic bag over my head.

Thirty-three

kiss of death

.

The great Gideon was dying.

The man with the broken nose stood to the side, watched Gideon suffocating.

Trains rumbled as the moon gradually moved between the sun and Gideon's life.

Gideon was fighting his final eclipse, eyes wide, holding his breath like he was the magician David Blaine. One minute. Two minutes. He watched Gideon in amusement. Gideon held his breath almost three minutes before he gasped like his lungs were burning for oxygen.

He had been beaten. And still he held his breath for three minutes.

Now he was running out of air. Wouldn't come close to breaking the world record.

His breathing became rugged. Rugged meant desperate. Desperation led to expiration.

The bag inflating and deflating with each breath.

Then came the kicking. The useless struggle.

Just like the dead man across the room had done a few minutes ago.

They always kicked. They always tried to kick Death away from them.

The plastic rose and fell against Gideon's face.

The man with the broken nose tap-danced, did the dance of life, and Gideon did the dance of death. The man with the broken nose only did that a few seconds, then he adjusted his suit, checked his watch, and went to the window. He felt the sun shining through all the gloom.

The avenue that led to London Bridge was lined with shops, red buses going by, offices-for-let signs posted in every other window. He was in one of the vacant offices. One of Sam's safe houses. He took a breath and looked out on all the shops lining Borough High Street. Rymans was directly across. London Bridge and the tube to his left. Elephant and Castle in the direction of his right. One dead and one dying man behind him.

He was thinking about Tebby. He'd get her back to America.

Sam. He wondered about Sam. Part of him believed that the money was in place, had always been in place, and Sam was engaged in duplicity, trying to get him to do the job, then had come back at him with a reduced price, trying to nickel-and-dime him, get himself a larger cut.

He looked back at Gideon.

Still kicking. Like that suffocating woman in that movie, *The Life of David Gale*.

Mr. Hot Shit was suffocating just like that woman in the movie suffocated.

About time.

He looked at the photo of the AMG.

He could see his soon-to-be-ex-wife's face. As he drove through Katy. Top down. Tebby at his side. Maybe his soon-to-be-ex-wife would see him with Tebby, see him happy, see him laughing, then stroke out and die. Or have a heart attack while she fucked her Frenchman.

Didn't matter. He had Tebby now.

With the Gideon contract done, he could work less, charge more, do less than ten jobs a year, ideally no more than five, spend more time at home, deal with the divorce and the kids.

The world was still cold. Still raining.

And he felt so peaceful.

The kind of weather that made a man want to call in sick and fuck all day.

Tebby was still in his room.

He had talked her out of going to work. She was going to run his package to the post office, get breakfast, then come back to the hotel, undress, and wait for him. She was going to watch television, sit up in the soft bed and eat room service, be his queen until he returned.

Yeah. This weather was made for the simple pleasures.

He told himself that Tebby was a good woman. In a country where a third of the women were heavy drinkers with bad livers and teeth that looked like the roads in Detroit, he'd walked into a Starbucks and met a damn good woman. Smart. Sexy. A hardworking woman.

He took out his cellular, took a photo of the dying man. Sent it to Sam.

Gideon was still kicking. Only not as hard. Not nearly as hard.

A roach that refused to die.

It reminded him of a Hitchcock movie. With Paul Newman. Newman and some woman were trying to kill a man. And the man just wouldn't die. The murder scene was one of unbelievable savagery. Left most people shaken. He thought it was brilliant, the funniest shit he'd ever seen.

He mumbled, "*Torn Curtain.* The name of the movie was *Torn Curtain.* I'll take guns for two hundred, Alex. What's that? The Daily Double. An audio Daily Double? I'd like to risk it all. What does a Desert Eagle sound like when it's blowing a man's brains out?"

Gideon was taking too long to die. He had shit to do, places to go, people to see.

He took out his Desert Eagle.

"It sounds like this, Alex. In the form of a question? I'm sorry. Fuck a question, Alex."

He aimed at Gideon's head.

His cellular rang. The hotline.

He looked at the caller ID. It was from Novotel.

Impossible.

He answered, "Talk to me."

The voice sounded stressed. "Bruno. Bruno. Oh, God. Bruno."

"Who is this?"

"Tebby. It's Tebby. It's me, Tebby."

He looked at his phone again. Double-checked. It was his hotline.

"Tebby . . . how did you get this number?"

"These people . . . this man . . . I left for the post office . . . came back . . . this man was here . . ."

"Who?"

"Oh, God. Bruno, oh, God."

Somebody took the phone.

A voice whispered, "Skeeter. Melanie."

His children's names. A subtle threat that rang so loud.

His heart stopped beating. Just like that everything had changed.

The man had his attention. "Who in the fuck is this?"

"Put Gideon on the line."

Desert Eagle in hand, he gritted his teeth.

The voice said, "Skeeter. Melanie."

He shuddered. "Who the fuck is this?"

"What matters is I know who you are."

"Who the fuck is this?"

Gideon wasn't kicking anymore.

"Put Gideon on the phone. Show me he is alive. Or it will get nasty."

The plastic bag over Gideon's face was no longer rising and falling.

The man with the broken nose dropped the cellular, put his Eagle back in its nest, and hurried, ripped the plastic away from Gideon's face. Gideon wasn't moving. He had killed him.

Tebby. The AMG. A better life. A wonderful wife.

All of that was supposed to be his.

He tilted Gideon's head back and listened for breathing.

No breathing.

Gideon was a hollow shell.

Used to killing and not giving life, he struggled to remember what to do, pinched Gideon's nose and covered Gideon's mouth with his, started blowing until he saw Gideon's chest rise. Two breaths. One second. Two breaths. The blood that Gideon had been coughing up, he tasted it inside his own mouth. Again he put his mouth on Gideon's mouth. Gideon's dead-man drool invading his mouth, more blood being exchanged. Like they were brothers. Or lovers.

Nothing.

No breathing.

No coughing.

He shuddered. "Chest compressions. Chest compressions."

He pressed down on Gideon's chest.

Nothing.

The son of a bitch was dead.

The son of a bitch wouldn't come back to life.

He refused to give up, pressed Gideon's chest, his own blood pressure rising, time no longer in his favor, and counted to thirty, pumped faster than once a second, was pumping at least one hundred times a minute. Just like he had learned in CPR. Classes he'd taken in case his kids ever had an emergency. He had wanted to be prepared. For anything.

He was doing this for the people he loved.

For Skeeter.

For Melanie.

For Tebby.

They knew his children's names. He didn't know what else they knew.

And they had Tebby.

Somehow they had found their way into the darkness where his fears resided.

Then.

Gideon coughed.

Gideon fucking coughed.

The man with the broken nose spat on the floor, ran his hands over his head.

Sweating.

They had him sweating.

Then Gideon was choking.

Choking on his own blood and saliva.

Almost dying again.

He let Gideon suffer.

Almost die again.

Then he turned Gideon on his side.

Watching his beautiful work come undone one stubborn breath at a time.

He slapped Gideon's face over and over.

He sat back and watched Gideon come back to life.

From the dead.

Breathing.

Coughing.

Opening his eyes wide.

Coughing.

The man with the broken nose fumbled, grabbed his cellular. The hotline.

"Here's Gideon, you son of a bitch."

He put the phone by Gideon's ear. Gideon coughed. Cursed. Let out painful sounds. Struggled to speak. Managed a few phrases, enough to let his associates know he was back among the living. Still Gideon sounded loopy. Was disoriented. Like a newborn.

Of course he was disoriented.

A minute ago he was dead.

Dead.

He'd only been reborn for a minute.

And the man with broken nose told himself he'd kill Gideon again.

They had brought his children into this. They had threatened his children.

Tebby.

He heard her in the background. She was okay. She was being terrorized.

They had found his hotel room.

Somebody had slipped.

Sam had dragged him along on this transaction.

Sam had slipped.

This could've been over days ago. Now everything had turned bad.

Fucking Sam.

He took the phone from Gideon's ear, put it up to his. "Where we going with this?"

"Excuse me?"

"What the fuck do you want?"

"At the moment it is quite simple. We trade hostages."

"Sure. Where do we do this?"

"London Eye. Come over the bridge from Waterloo. Be there in thirty minutes."

"I look forward to meeting you."

"Likewise."

The voice hung up the phone.

The man with the broken nose spat on Gideon. He wanted to kick him. He wanted to kick him and jump up and down on his guts. He had killed him. He had resurrected him.

Had to put his mouth on another man and give him life.

The man with the broken nose called Sam. Went off. Screamed, kept asking what had happened.

Sam said, "I have no idea what is going on."

"Get the Brixton Boys back up here. Now. London Eye. Get them there in ten minutes."

"What the fuck happened, Bruno?"

"You fucked up, Sam. *Now fix it.*"

He hung up.

His other phone rang.

He looked at the caller ID.

It was Novotel.

On his personal line. The number reserved for his real life, for friends and family.

His hands went clammy. Heart rate went off the meter.

He answered. Held the phone to his ear for a moment before he asked, "Who is this?"

The voice said, "Now that we've given you time to try and double-cross us by calling your mates, we have to inform you there has been a change of plans. Your mates are not invited."

He rubbed his broken nose, gritted his teeth.

"Give the other mobile to Gideon."

He swallowed. "Just tell me where and I'll bring him."

"This is not a negotiation."

"You touch the girl and I kill Gideon."

"I repeat, this is not a negotiation."

"I could kill him right now."

"No problem by me. Let me know so I can get on with my day."

"I will. Then I will come looking for you."

"As if you have any idea who I am."

He gritted his teeth.

"Feeling a bit out of control, are you?" The voice. "Quit stalling, wanker. Hand Gideon the bloody mobile. We will tell him where to meet. You come. Gideon stays on the mobile, we chat as you travel. Anything goes wrong—call drops, anything—negotiations are over."

"Sure you want to play it this way?"

"Skeeter. Melanie. Say the word and it gets nasty."

"Sure. Whatever you say."

"Then we agree it's a push."

"Yeah. It's a push."

"Now be a gentleman and hand the mobile to Gideon."

He untied Gideon. Took his time about doing it. Then handed him the phone.

Gideon looked at the dead man in the room, rubbed his wrists before putting the phone to his ear, groaning like his every movement came with severe pain, every movement was a struggle.

Gideon found his voice, asked, "Who is this?

He watched Gideon. Saw that the recently brought-back-to-life Gideon looked confused. Like his world was moving in slow motion. Sepia-colored. Gideon looked back at him with anger.

Again Gideon addressed the caller, asked, "Who?"

He watched Gideon's confusion turn into something else. What he saw he could only describe as disbelief. As if Gideon thought he were being tricked. Then Gideon nodded as if he understood. He panted. "He threw Arizona into the Thames. Shot her. Between Millennium Bridge and Blackfriars, St. Paul's Cathedral side, closer to end of School of London, by the toilets. Said he killed two of my friends, threw them in other rivers. Two women I know. I just met."

Gideon took a breath and looked like his pain deepened.

Desert Eagle in hand, the man with the broken nose said, "They're all dead."

Gideon glowered at him like he wanted to rip his lungs out.

The man with the broken nose almost smiled, the Eagle aimed at Gideon's heart.

Next time there would be no raising of the dead.

They had called him on his personal number. They had threatened him.

Had called his friends-and-family number and threatened him.

He felt violated.

Yes, this was personal.

No, this was beyond personal.

He would kill Gideon.

Again and again, he would kill Gideon.

Would kill Gideon and anyone who spoke his name, would slaughter all of his friends.

For free.

As they walked, he stayed right behind Gideon, his hand on his gun, that Desert Eagle hidden inside a folded newspaper, Cagney and Bogart style, his mind on his kids.

With a Southern smile, he told Gideon, "You know this is just business, right?"

Gideon didn't answer.

Thirty-four

friends and enemies

Safe zone.

Where enemies could stand side by side without things getting out of hand.

The heart of ceremonial London.

Statues of Churchill, Smuts, Palmerston, Disraeli, Peel, and Abraham Lincoln.

Houses of Parliament Clock Tower. Houses of Parliament. Westminster Abbey.

Gideon stopped at the corner of Parliament Square and Bridge Road, near the entrance to Parliament. That entrance heavily guarded. Near Victoria Station and Trafalgar Square.

The rain had stopped. Streets were wet. Skies still gray.

The man with the broken nose kept the gun hidden inside the newspaper as Gideon took instructions.

The man with the broken nose looked around, tried to see if anyone in the crowd was holding a cellular phone, communicating with Gideon. Thousands of people were on cellular phones. Half of them using discrete earpieces. No way to tell. He needed an out, had to plan an escape route. If things went bad, real bad, became gunshot-loud and bloody, he had to see what his options were. The tube was directly behind them, but that station was a no-no. They would have that station locked down before he made it to any of the trains. It would be a footrace.

He looked toward the stores Boots and Tesco, knew the road on the other side of those stores headed back toward the Eye and Waterloo. He cursed. The area as busy as Las Vegas on New Year's Eve. He had a gun ready to explode and people were bumping into him.

Gideon was holding the phone. Saying nothing. Looking across the street.

The man with the broken nose tried to see what Gideon was looking at. Hundreds of tourists were across the street at the park, the grassy area the roundabout circled, taking pictures in front of Churchill's statue. A group of men was over there. He wondered.

Gideon looked at him, said, "You said AMG. One-hundred-thousand-dollar car."

Newspaper in hand, the man with the broken nose remained poker-faced.

Gideon asked, "Who? The AMG. Who's the owner?"

The man with the broken nose stared Gideon down.

He saw pain in Gideon's eyes.

A lifetime of pain.

He saw a stupid, arrogant man who owned no fear.

But most of all, he witnessed the look of death in Gideon's eyes.

He saw what people feared.

He adjusted the Eagle in the newspaper and wished he had left Gideon dead.

Then Gideon looked back toward the tube, took a few steps in that direction. He followed. He searched for the voice that had been on the phone. He wanted to see who was stupid enough to threaten his children. Thousands of people were walking the street, half of that foot crowd stalling in front of Parliament, some trying to get the Parliament Clock Tower in the background of their photographs. Some were on the Westminster Bridge getting the London Eye in their shots. Some were walking beyond the Westminster tube toward Victoria Station, others toward the Aquarium and Thames Path. A flock of tourists were trying to get the heavily armed guards in their shots. Guards were plenty. Assault guns in every hand.

The area was controlled pandemonium. Controlled pandemonium.

The same way he felt inside.

Skeeter. Melanie. Tebby.

Those three kept that pandemonium in check. Those three kept the Eagle in its nest.

Even if he pulled out his Desert Eagle, he was outnumbered and outgunned.

Then Gideon looked across the street at the statue of Winston Churchill.

Gideon walked by Parliament, made a right and crossed, blended in with the crowd passing by St. Margaret's Church, paused in front of Westminster Abbey. He walked into the courtyard, weaved through the tourists who were going in and out of church doors, then paused, turned back around, exited the courtyard, made a left, and crossed the street, now on the side of the roundabout opposite Parliament, now walking Little George Street. Gideon paused again, this time in front of the statue of Abraham Lincoln. Gideon was in pain. And he looked confused.

The man with the broken nose asked, "What in the hell are we doing?"

The mobile still up to his ear, Gideon didn't answer him.

Then Gideon started back walking, limping actually, did that like he was following instructions, went to the end of the block, looked around, stopped at the statue of George Canning. Then Gideon took the phone from his face. He looked at the number. And he pressed the send button.

"Hello? . . . A friend of your daddy. He can't get to the phone right now."

The man with the broken nose realized that Gideon had intercepted one of his calls, panicked, broke character, tried to snatch the phone from Gideon, but couldn't, not with the gun hidden in the newspaper, not without a battle, not without exposing the gun on a crowded street, not without placing his kids at risk. There was nothing he could do. Gideon moved the phone away, scowled at him. Losing it. He was about to lose it and take the Eagle out of its nest.

His voice losing control, he snapped, "Keep my kids out of this."

"Scared they might end up in the Thames?"

"Don't fuck with me."

"Would you like your little girl to take a swim in the river?"

That image was too strong.

It angered him and weakened him all at once.

Gideon, back on the phone, said, "Your daddy will call you back, Melanie. . . . Sure, I'll remind him about the Harry Potter books. I sure will, young lady. Okay. Bye-bye."

Gideon pushed the send button, switched back to the other call.

Gideon said, "Yo. It was his kids. He's huffing and puffing over here. In case I don't make it through this, do what you said you'd do. Remember what he did to Arizona."

There was a pause, long enough for someone to get pencil and paper.

Gideon said, "Seven one eight four four six eight . . ."

It took the man with the broken nose a moment to realize the number. His home phone number. Numbers were programmed in, not memorized like they used to be in the old days, even home phone numbers.

He caught on too late and snapped, "Son of a bitch. What is your fucking problem?"

He eased the newspaper away. Revealed part of the Eagle.

Gideon said, "If the call ends, or you hear a bang, kill them all. Shoot 'em. Drown 'em."

The man with the broken nose paused, struggled with himself as people walked on by.

He scowled as he eased the Eagle back in its nest.

Gideon asked, "So, from a professional perspective, what do you think I should do at this juncture? Since you're giving me nothing, maybe I'll go to Texas. Katy, Texas. Visit Skeeter and Melanie. Tell them I'm a friend of their daddy. I could kill your children. They will be found. One will be fished out of the Ravensbourne. The other the Quaggy. Kill your entire family."

"I'd come after you."

"I'd meet you halfway."

He smiled at Gideon. Smoothed out his suit coat with his free hand. And smiled.

He told Gideon, "All things being equal, the simplest solution tends to be the best one. You go back to your friends. I get the girl. I consider the contract unenforceable. We move on."

"Who are you working for?"

"It's a blind contract."

"But you know they're willing to trade an expensive ride to take me out."

"Contract is blind."

"And you claim *The Big Bad Wolf* was a red herring."

"All I know is that an AMG was put on the table."

"Sorry you won't get to drive it. Now. Give me a contact name. Number."

"It gets dropped off at my room. I don't see anybody or talk to anybody."

"Sam. Who was the Sam guy you called?"

He paused. His lies coming to an abrupt end.

Excited utterance and that victorious feeling had made him tell Gideon about the AMG.

Gideon was supposed to suffocate and take that knowledge to his grave with him.

He had panicked and called Sam. Couldn't remember what he had said.

The man with the broken nose said, "No need for us to take this beyond the people involved."

"The women I was with last night."

"Sorry about that."

"You're shitting me."

"Bloomsbury. MyHotel. Third floor. Sorry, Gideon. Not one to bullshit."

Gideon swallowed. Looked like he was about to explode. "Give me something."

"Contract came out of the north. That's all I know. Never talked to the issuer."

"Who?"

"Just heard it was some politician."

"Kiss my ass. Sounded like you worked for Sam. You're giving me bullshit now. Either Sam put the hit out on me or Sam is the middleman. Either way, you need to give up Sam."

"I'm just saying, remain professional."

"Throwing a woman into the Thames was professional?"

"That girl cut up a few of the Brixton Boys, she was one of us. My kids aren't."

"You think I give a fuck about the Brixton Boys or your goddamn kids?"

"She had a blade so sharp that she damn near took one of the guy's legs off."

Gideon growled. "I'll take a knife just like that to your goddamn kids."

"I'll fucking kill you."

"Give up Sam."

"Or what?"

"Or my associates will leave Melanie and Skeeter in six rivers."

"Don't say my kids' names."

"You'll have a good time finding Melanie and Skeeter. What the fish don't eat."

He was about to lose it. "Don't you *ever* . . . don't you *ever* fucking say their names."

"Keep that black suit on. It'll look good at Melanie and Skeeter's funerals."

The man with the broken nose moved the newspaper again. "What, you think I won't drop you right now?"

"Drop me, motherfucker. Drop me. Drop me and buy two kid-sized coffins."

"You think I won't?"

"I'm supposed to be afraid of you? I beat an army of thugs with my bare hands. You needed eight armed men to get me. You ran from me like you were a fucking cartoon character. I'm supposed to be afraid of your bitch ass? You're a fucking joke. Drop the gun, we can take it over there to the park. Just me and you. Hand-to-hand. Man-to-man. Punk-ass bitch."

Gideon's anger was almost out of control.

The man with the broken nose was tempted. So very tempted.

In his mind Gideon's death warrant had been signed in a gallon of blood.

He smiled at Gideon. "That girl I threw in the Thames, you had a thing for her, didn't you? Which one of the other two did you like the best? The one I left in the Quaggy or the one I dumped in the Ravensbourne? Three women. And all three of them dead. Talk about bad luck."

He saw those simple words paused Gideon. Gave him grief. Stole his momentum.

Now Gideon's breathing had become emotional, choppy, he was about to lose it.

The man with the broken nose smiled. "And the two women from the plane, I mean, how attached to them could you be? You just met them. So not like there is a lot of love lost there."

Now Gideon was almost out of control. Looked like he had been gutted.

The man with the broken nose chuckled at the manic desperation in Gideon's eyes.

"Drop the gun. Me and you. Now."

"Sorry, Gideon, but I don't have time for hand-to-hand. Bullet to your head, yes. Hand-to-hand, afraid not. So you decide how you want this to end. For now. Go ahead. You decide."

"No, you decide."

Gideon started waking again, back toward the Westminster tube, now moving fast enough to weave and put a few anxious people between them, moved like he knew he was about to get gunned down, took to Bridge Road until he made it back to the Westminster tube.

The man with the broken nose asked, "How many times are we walking around the block?"

"Until I get tired of walking around the block."

"I'm not going to keep going in circles."

"Leave if you want to."

"I'd better see my girl soon."

"You think you're still calling the shots, don't you?"

"Tell your friends that. The girl better not have been touched in any kind of way."

"Shut up."

They were held up for a moment. A crowd came up out of the tube, never ending and never stopping, like a stampede of wild horses dressed in business suits and high heels. Gideon crossed and went to the other entrance to the Westminster Station, the one by Boots and Tesco, facing the Clock Tower.

He paused.

Then he handed the man with the broken nose the mobile phone.

The voice said, "Hello, mate. Are you okay?"

"Let's stop walking in goddamn circles and get this over with."

"Had to make sure you were not being followed by any of your bloody blokes."

"Let me talk to the girl."

"Sure. Tebby from Botswana, a gent from Texas would like to have a word with you."

Tebby came on. Her breathing frantic. "Bruno?"

He looked around, hoping to see her. "Where are you?"

"I don't know, I don't know, I don't know."

"Moving or parked?"

"We are moving. Moving fast. I'm blindfolded. They threat—"

"Did they hurt you?"

"My mouth is bleeding. He hit me over and over."

"Did they do . . . anything else to you?"

"They took my purse. My work identification. My passport. Took all of my information. Threatened my children. They threatened my children, Bruno. They threatened to kill my boys."

"Shit. Tebby. Just relax. "

"Bruno, what did you do to these people? What did you do?"

"I'll get you out of this."

"They are saying horrible things about you. What do they want from you?"

"It's . . . blackmail. But don't worry. I'll get you safe."

"I'm scared. So scared."

"I'll save you from these bad men. They are evil people."

Tebby's cries were cut short.

The voice came back on the line. "Mind handing the phone to Gideon?"

He had the Eagle, and the Eagle was ready to fly. But they had him by the balls.

He handed the phone to Gideon. Gideon crossed at the light, headed back toward Parliament. The man with the broken nose understood why they had come to this well-populated area. For two reasons. The dark skin of the Brixton Boys would stand out in this white European crowd.

Gideon crossed the street, went back toward Parliament, stopped in front of the armed guards. Hundreds of tourists. And thousands of children were there now. A field trip. All talking, chatting, and pointing at the sites, moving like rats and roaches, all with backpacks and cameras.

Police protection. Tourist central. Cameras were flashing everywhere.

His image being stolen accidentally by hundreds of digital cameras.

Not good. Not good at all. No way to stop the tourists from taking photos.

And CCTV was pointing down on them. Gideon had stopped underneath a camera.

Those heavily armed guards stationed a few feet away were the second reason.

Here he stood with a huge gun hidden underneath a folded *New Nation* newspaper.

In this age of terrorism, only a suicidal fool would start a gunfight in front of Parliament.

He had been a fool, just hadn't decided if he was a suicidal fool yet.

Skeeter. Melanie. They had his house number. And they had kidnapped Tebby.

He was bargaining for Tebby's freedom. He wasn't done trying to protect his kids either.

He reached inside his coat pocket. Took out the picture of the AMG.

That picture in one hand, the other hand close to the Desert Eagle. He stood there trying to decide. When they parted, it would be more out of control than it was now. His kids were an ocean away.

No way he could protect them, not immediately. As far as he knew, Gideon's friends were already sending a hit squad to Katy. Never trust a criminal. Never trust a killer. The idea of having to call his soon-to-be-ex and telling her to run out of the house and hide the children from an angry man who had slaughtered more than a few men in an alley down in Tampa, a man who had killed time and time again . . . a man like himself.

Gideon said, "Nottingham Country. Kelliwood. Exit is off I-10 at Fry Road."

That was the name of the community he lived in. His street. His exit.

Gideon said, "Last chance, Bruno. Last fucking chance. When we part ways, you know it's going to be too late. So if you give a shit about Skeeter and Melanie . . . last chance."

They had his information. Like they had reverse-engineered his mobile number in a matter of seconds. Skeeter. Melanie. His heart boomed inside his chest. Felt like cotton was in his throat. This was beyond a push. His kids were a noose around his neck and Gideon was threatening to kick the chair. He had to buy time. Buy time now, get Gideon later, serve his revenge cold.

Extending the photo like it was a plea bargain, he said, "Gideon."

Gideon looked at him, droves of children and tourists passing between their hostility. The man with the broken nose handed the photo of the AMG to Gideon. He no longer cared.

He said, "Partial plates in the photo. Trace that, you'll know who bought the contract."

"Who? Give me a name. Who?"

"All I know is that Sam told me. I don't believe the politician thing. They lie to me. Don't matter. I just did what I was paid to do. It's all business, you know that. That's the car that was offered to seal this deal. My guess is they were having money problems. And the car offer was a last-minute thing. Not sure. Trace the car and I'll guess you'll know more than I know."

"They offered you a car to kill me."

"Just think, if the money had been there . . . we wouldn't be having this discussion."

Gideon stuffed the photo inside his pocket. Now that photo was Gideon's property.

Gideon said, "Sam. Since he hired you, I'll let all of this be on his head."

The man with the broken nose gave Gideon a location in Hackney to find Sam.

Sirens were blaring in the distance. Police cars and motorcycles came from all over.

All were heading in the direction of the London Eye.

Gideon said, "The Brixton Boys. They're all dead."

"Ambushed."

Gideon nodded.

A coldness rested between them.

He asked Gideon, "Our business done? No more threats on my children."

"The women I was with. The women from the plane."

"Dead. Sorry."

"What the fuck did they do to you?"

"All business. With that said, once again, is our business done here?"

Gideon gritted his teeth and nodded. "For now. Our business is done for now."

A car slowed in front of them. Mini Cooper. Tebby was in the passenger seat.

He wanted to go to Tebby. The driver of the car raised and lowered a gun.

Gideon told him, "Don't move, Bruno. Stay your ass right here."

Things had been turned around and flipped upside down. Now he was the one in point-blank range. One shot and the car would be gone in seconds. They had walked the block. Were in a crowd. Any of these tourists could be on Gideon's team. He did what Gideon said.

Gideon hung up the cellular phone, tossed it to him.

He caught the phone and asked, "My other phone? Mind handing that one over as well?"

Gideon tossed him the second phone.

He smiled at Gideon, his expression looking friendly to every eye in the area.

Gideon returned the same smile, his eyes antagonistic and cold-blooded.

Gideon said, "All things being equal, the simplest solution tends to be the best one. I'm getting in that car. You get the girl. Consider the contract on me unenforceable. You move on."

The man with the broken nose nodded. Had to. He was 450 meters from Scotland Yard.

Then Gideon moved through the crowd, limped toward the waiting car.

Tebby got out. No purse. Just had on jeans, trainers, and a coat. Also shades. Huge sunglasses. She kept her head down, never made eye contact with Gideon.

It was easy to tell she had been instructed to not make eye contact with anyone.

Gideon got inside the Mini Cooper. It was decorated like St. George's Cross. There were hundreds with that design in London. Before Gideon closed the door, the unseen driver pulled away, took off fast, blended with the madness and vicious traffic in the roundabout, vanished toward Victoria Station.

He'd find Gideon again. Next time he'd put death on him like a tattoo.

The man with the broken nose moved tourists and children out of the way, went to Tebby.

He saw why she hadn't moved too far.

Underneath the sunglasses, her eyes had been taped shut.

Even when he told her it was him, that she was safe, she shook and refused to raise her head. They had terrified her. They had frightened her good. This wasn't part of Tebby's world.

He took her arm, led her away, took her to the side.

He took the sunglasses off. The tape came away easily.

Tebby opened her eyes, squinted like she was trying to determine where she was.

He said something to her.

She looked confused, totally disoriented, like a POW who had been released.

She couldn't hear him. Her ears had been plugged. Black earplugs.

He took the foam earplugs out of her ears, dropped them on the ground.

She held him like he had saved her. Like she was relieved he was okay.

She wept. She wept hard.

Tebby swallowed a hundred times, struggled to breathe, finally managed to say, "They threatened to kill me. They threatened to kill my children. They said they would kill my boys."

She was talking fast, at first he thought it was gibberish, then he realized she was so distressed she was speaking in her native tongue, Setswana, as if her English skills had abandoned her under trauma. She leaned against him, body almost going limp, and she cried.

She pulled it together. "I didn't cry in front of them. I didn't let them see me cry."

He put his hand on Tebby's chin, raised her eyes to his.

Her lips were swollen, the bottom lip split. She had been hit hard. To show they were serious. He held her up, helped her walk through the crowd. Wanted to get her away from the armed guards that were stationed behind them, letting dignitaries through the gate.

He said, "Let me get a black cab."

"No. No cab. He told me no cab. He told me to walk for twenty minutes. Not nineteen. Twenty. To not get in a car or on a bus or in a taxi, he said they were watching. And not to talk to anyone. He threatened to do bad things to my family. You have to walk with me. You have to walk with me, Bruno. If I stop walking before then . . . they have all of my information. You have to walk too. They told me that if I do not walk with you . . . no taxi. We have to walk. And walk fast."

"Tebby, they're gone."

Tebby said, "Start walking, Bruno. We have to start walking, Bruno. We have to."

Then they were moving fast. Like they were on the run.

Tebby asked, "What was it all about? Why did they do that? Are they terrorists?"

"Real estate. The real estate people. What did they tell you it was about?"

"I don't understand, Bruno. Real estate. Help me understand."

"They are angry because of valuable real estate I have acquired for a U.S. Realtor."

Tears in her eyes, Tebby was practically running, too horrified to listen.

She said, "They kept my identification. They have my children's information in Botswana. They have my address here. They know where I work. They know everything about me."

He said, "It's over, Tebby. It's over. Just take a breath. I've got you."

"Don't stop walking. Bruno. I'm walking for my children, for my family's safety."

Again she started talking fast, rambling in Setswana, her bald head stress-sweating.

He took her hand and headed up Bridge Street and hurried across the Thames, then turned right at a main road on the other side of Parliament, headed away from the London Eye.

Parliament was behind them, London Eye and Thames to their right as they headed toward Embankment. Tebby was still terrified. Trembling. Crying. Talking nonstop.

Tebby said, "They threatened my family. I need your phone. I have to call them now."

"They said no calls, Tebby."

She was frantic, wouldn't slow down, wouldn't shut up. "Give me your phone."

She was getting loud. No way to calm her down.

He kept the newspaper and the gun under his arm, handed Tebby his cellular. Then he ran his free hand over his head. He was anxious, needed to call home too. Had to call his kids as soon as he could and make sure they were okay, that he hadn't been double-crossed.

Tebby struggled to get his cellular to work, again talking in her native tongue.

He adjusted the Eagle, the gun feeling so damn big, took his phone back from her.

It wasn't working. He jabbed the buttons. His mobile wouldn't power up.

He flipped the phone over. Took him a few seconds to realize what was wrong.

He removed the back off the phone.

It was gone.

The SIM card.

It was gone.

Gideon had swiped the SIM card out of his mobile.

Telephone numbers, text messages, pictures, all of his personal information, stolen.

He didn't have to look in the other phone to know that SIM card had been swiped too.

Thirty-five

without a kiss good-bye

Gun tucked underneath his arm, shielded by a newspaper, he kept up with Tebby.

Tebby didn't slow down, was practically running until they were near Southwark Bridge.

She was still speaking in her native tongue. Still touching her bruised face.

He saw a City Volkswagen, Postbank, Five Kings House, lights from a Domino's Pizza a block up Queen Street, traffic on a high street that led into what looked like the financial district.

They had stopped between Millennium Bridge and London Bridge, surrounded by modern businesses and old churches, St. James Garlickhythe and St. Michael Paternoster Royal being less than a minute away, both living in the shadows of St. Paul's Cathedral.

Church bells rang as if someone above was sending out an alarm.

Tebby still had his hand in a death grip, was moving like she was trying to outrun the fear of God. Sweat dripped from her bald head now. Everything was fucked up.

His day was supposed to be simple.

Kill Gideon. Get paid. Make love to Tebby again. Make plans to get Tebby to America. Take her to see *Porgy and Bess* at the Savoy. Grab a bite to eat. Then out for jazz in Camden Town. Then back to No-votel. And make love to Tebby again. Same thing when they woke up.

Everything had been fucked up.

Mansion House tube was a block up, a short block to the left, three minutes away.

He headed *away* from Mansion House, took toward Southwark Bridge.

Tebby said, "That's the wrong direction."

"Come with me. Stay close."

Scaffolding ran the entire block, renovation being done on Five Kings House by Stonecrest Limited. That was a good spot to stop running, to try to think of what to do next. He wanted to get Tebby away from the traffic, the scaffolding shielding them from being seen by the four lanes of bidirectional traffic heading toward either Southwark Street or Upper Thames.

"Not that way, Bruno. The tubes are this way. Bank is up there. Monument is there. Cannon tube is there. We have to go toward Queen Victoria Street, not back that way."

"Hold on."

"Why are you going that way? Bruno? Why? Are they still after you?"

"Stay close to me."

He had to see. And he could see from the top of the bridge.

Tourist ships and other boats were moving up and down the Thames.

His attention and anger went toward Millennium Bridge. There was a lot of activity on its far side. Where he had captured Gideon. Where he had thrown Queen Scamz into the icy river. He saw police lights. Like the authorities were recovering a body from the Thames.

Teeth gritted, he nodded.

Queen Scamz would be on a cold slab in a London morgue by sunrise.

Her body cut to pieces and autopsied by the noon hour.

He hoped Gideon suffered throughout eternity.

He left Upper Thames Road, headed uphill toward Mansion House tube.

Tebby said, "I need you to go with me."

"Go with you? Where?"

"The Liverpool tube station. The police station is across the street."

"Sorry, Tebby." He shook his head. "We can't go to the police."

"Are you mad? My family is in jeopardy. I'm going to tell them what happened."

"Calm down, Tebby."

"Don't you dare tell me to calm down."

"Yelling and talking in African gibberish will not help."

"Excuse me?"

"You know what I mean."

"They beat me, kidnapped me, threatened my children. They have my information."

"Same for me. And I think they're more concerned with me than you right now."

The look of disappointment in her eyes. Unending disappointment. Same look his soon-to-be-ex-wife had given him countless times. That expression like a knife penetrating his heart.

He said, "Sorry for what I said. Just upset. And scared."

He hugged her. She held on to him.

Then things went from bad to worse.

When Tebby held on to him, he felt the depth of her fear. She held him in a bear hug.

And when she let his body go, she held his arms, the newspaper under his arm shifted.

The Desert Eagle slid south. He tried to grab his five-pound weapon, but it was too late.

Pulled by gravity, the Eagle slipped out of its nest and fell to the ground.

The gun hit the wet concrete hard.

Tebby's eyes went to the gun. To its titanium finish. To its hugeness.

Then her wide eyes came back to him, her head shaking ever so slightly.

She swayed like she was discombobulated.

Her mouth was wide-open. A thousand questions in her non-blinking eyes.

And the look that said she was more terrified now. Scared shit-less.

She stammered, "I didn't want to believe them."

"What did they tell you?"

"That you killed people. That you came to London to kill people. That the man that was with you, the one who got in the car when they set me free, that you were going to kill him."

He ignored the rain, picked up the Eagle. Tucked it back inside the newspaper.

"That's absurd."

"Why do you have a gun, Bruno?"

"I have this for our protection, Tebby. That's all."

"They told me you killed people." She paused. "The woman who was killed . . . when I met you at Starbucks . . . that woman had just been killed. Right by where you were. They said you killed some man in America at some Jacksonville place. They said that man broke your nose. They said all sorts of things. All sort of evil things. I don't want to believe them."

"Are you crazy? They kidnapped and beat you. Who are you going to believe?"

The rain fell harder and faster than the lies he told.

He said, "Just say nothing. Let me handle this, Tebby. I can get you to America. I can help you with your dreams. I can get you a nice place to live. And that restaurant you want, we can open it in downtown Houston. Call it Tebby's. Or whatever you want to call it."

She looked at the gun, at the dark and unforgiving look in his eyes.

Then she stood there, questioning, defiant, angry, terrified.

Like a warrior with a Molotov cocktail of emotions about to be thrown his way.

Talking in that African gibberish, each word at the speed of light.

She took off running.

He sprinted to catch up, asked, "Where are you going?"

She kept going.

He said, "Don't you want to go back to America?"

She snapped, *"Fuck America."*

He grabbed her arm, yanked her back to him.

He shook his head. "Sorry, Tebby. But I can't let you go talking to the police."

She said rugged things to him in her native tongue, then opened her mouth to scream.

He covered her mouth with his hand.

Underneath the scaffolding, as cars went by, they were unseen.

She head-butted him hard. With her bald head she hit him dead-square in his nose.

Assaulted the fracture. Rebroke what was already broken.

Before he could recover, she took her fist and hit him again. And again. And again.

Each blow coming faster and harder than its predecessor, each blow to his face.

Stunned him. Watered his eyes. Staggered him.

Pissed him off.

His hands became fists.

He swung hard, threw a devastating hook, hit Tebby in the face.

He punched her harder than he had punched the WAG.

That stunned Tebby. Wobbled her. Reminded him of the dazed horse that the cowboy, played by Alex Karras, had punched in *Blazing Saddles*. That nose-shattering blow silenced her cry.

Their relationship was at a point of no return.

That saddened him.

But he didn't hesitate.

He hit her again and she collapsed. He let the gun fall, caught her before she hit the ground. Swooped her up. Held six feet of beauty in his arms. He would take no chances.

He put her in a headlock.

A quick twist and there was a soft pop.

Her neck was broken.

Tebby was gone.

"Damn, babe." He felt the blood running from his nose, down over his suit. "Why did you make me have to go and do that?"

He sat on the concrete, under the scaffolding, cars passing, rubbing Tebby's head.

"Can't let you come between me and my kids, Tebby. Can't let you do that."

He sighed, a deep and woeful sigh that made him shudder with regret.

Rain falling on the streets, the winds blowing, he kissed the back of her sweaty head.

Felt sad. Felt very sad.

He could've loved Tebby. In some ways he already did. Probably always would.

Wished he had met her kids. Wished she had met his.

Skeeter would've loved her to death. Skeeter loved everybody.

Skeeter was different like that. Skeeter didn't have it in him to hate anybody.

Too bad Tebby didn't make it back to Houston. Back to Katy, Texas.

He wished the people in Katy had seen them living and loving and laughing together.

He would've taken her to Diedrich's coffee shop out on Westheimer Road.

He had desired Tebby more than anything.

But he loved his freedom more.

For a while cars went by. So many cars went by.

Then there was no traffic.

He lifted Tebby. Now dead weight. He dragged her to the rusted yellow and green bridge. Grunted as he pulled her up by her armpits, leaned her body against the railing.

Then, with urgency, he grabbed her legs and flipped her over the edge.

He raced toward Queen Victoria Street, Tebby's body splashing in the muddy Thames.

If only she had tried to understand.

It was just business that had gone bad.

He wanted to go straight to an airport.

But he couldn't.

He had left his extra barrels in the hotel room. Those barrels had his fingerprints all over them. The room had his fingerprints all over. And he had changed his bandages before he had left. That meant DNA was left behind as well. He had to rush, clean the room, and vanish.

He had to get a phone. Get a calling card and slide into a red phone booth somewhere.

He had to contact Sam.

He had to get out of London.

Had to get to Gatwick or Heathrow, maybe Stansted, and get out of London tonight.

He had to get back home to Katy.

Thirty-six

some like it violent

I snapped, "Where do I find the motherfucker who paid for my death?"

"*Please . . . Gideon . . . no . . .*"

I slammed Sam's head into the wall for the fifth time. Maybe it was the sixth. The skinny man's face-piercings didn't take to kindly to his being roughed around like that. He was middle-aged and stubborn. Blood from where his lip piercing had split vanished into his dark clothes. Same for where the eyebrow piercing had left an open wound.

He fell to the wooden floor again.

I'd become darker than Batman and Daredevil combined, had gone on a rampage.

First stop after the hostage exchange in Parliament Square. The Borough of Hackney.

This address came from information extracted from one of the SIM cards.

Sam.

I'd found Sam.

And this Sam guy was at one of his safe houses.

He moaned and groaned like he was singing a John Lee Hooker song.

I limped to his kitchen table, frowned down at papers scattered on the smeared glass.

On his table were flyers that had been put up at every business in the town. One was a reward for a Vietnamese man who had been stabbed to death on Mare Road. Another was for a young Polish girl who had vanished at Leytonstone, her body found out in Cockfosters.

Had to be Sam's work. His contracts. Small-time contracts. These flyers, his trophies.

A local newspaper was in the pile as well.

The front page of the *Hackney Gazette* said a new survey had named Hackney as the worst place to live in the UK. The *Hackney Gazette* was screaming that enough was enough.

They were tired of the middle-class snobs at Channel 4.

I agreed. I felt like the Borough of Hackney. I was tired. So damn pissed off.

I said, "Think about Hackney's reputation, Sam. From what I can see it looks pretty nice. Better than College Park in Atlanta. Better than Flint, Michigan. East St. Louis. South Central. So, my gunrunning and murder-brokering friend, help the borough lose its bum rap."

He said, "I can't give up . . . my contract."

"No problem."

I went to the kitchen table, picked up a metal chair.

I hurtled the chair at the living room window. The old crank-out window shattered.

Glass and a metal chair hurtled fifteen floors to the grounds of Trelawney Estate.

Apartment buildings that resembled East Coast public housing were sprawled out for miles.

This building was made of worn bricks and single-pane, crank-out windows.

I stepped to the window and looked out at the lively borough.

I said, "Long way down."

With the smutty windows gone, everything was much clearer. Tesco grocery store and car park were across the street. The Hackney Empire was now a clear view. *Dutty Wine! The Real Ghetto Story* was playing at the theater. *Da Kink in My Hair* was on the way.

The air became clearer. The scent of KFC mixing with the aroma of fish and chips, kebabs, burgers, and Vietnamese cuisine flooded the small apartment.

I turned to Sam. He sat on the floor bleeding.

I said, "Can you fly, Sam?"

"Please. Be reasonable."

"I think you can fly, but you don't know you can fly. Let's see if you can fly. You don't have to fly far. I think you can fly from here to the plaza down Morning Lane. See if you can fly past the Globe and Dilara's Café, see if you can land in front of The Yuppie's Barbers. The people standing out in front of the launderette and Pizza Go-Go, I bet they will all applaud."

"Come on, man. Don't do this."

"If you're really good, I mean really, *really* good, impress me and fly down to that Las Vegas Tattoo place. Or to that USA nails place down near Ellingfort Road. That's about a mile. I think you can fly a mile, Sam. Unless of course, you can't fly. And you drop straight to the concrete. Why did you have to live on a high floor, Sam? Anyway. Let's experiment."

He was breathing so hard he had elephant-size nostrils.

I grabbed him by his shirt.

He cried, "Wait . . . wait . . . no . . . no . . . please."

I took him to the window.

He said, "I'll tell you what you want to know."

He told me who had paid for the contract.

Ten minutes after that, I had an address.

The sponsor of my death was across the Atlantic. Right outside Windsor, Canada.

And the address was familiar.

It took me a minute to remember who the sponsor was.

But as soon as I remembered, I knew what this was all about.

I asked, "Did you get the picture Bruno sent?"

"With you looking dead?"

I swallowed rugged emotions. "You send it to the sponsor?"

"Yes."

"Were you paid?"

"The payment was with the car. The AMG. Arrangements are being made."

"Cash-flow problem."

"Sponsor wanted to use the car. Only have to pay the deductible when the AMG was reported stolen. And it was reported stolen a few weeks ago. So, in the end, the contract would only cost the client a few dollars. No money moved. The hit untraceable."

"Brilliant."

"Yes. Brilliant."

I went to the window.

Wondered how many men would love to have my head on a stick.

I said, "Don't tell the client anything different."

"I won't."

"And if you hear of any contracts, anybody else coming after me, you call me."

"How do I reach you?"

I picked up his cellular phone, dropped it in my pocket.

I said, "You have the number. Keep it topped up."

Then came the hard part.

I said, "Bruno said he killed two more women. Friends of mine."

"He told me he was going to your hotel. He went after your companions to get to you."

I paused. Swallowed. "Where are the bodies?"

"I have no idea. My only concern is the contract."

"He said they were in the Ravensbourne and the Quaggy."

"Black women."

"Yeah. Black American woman."

"You'll have to read *New Nation* and *The Voice* over the next couple of days."

"You're kidding, right?"

"If you want to hear about a black person dying, yes. A black noncelebrity, yes. And only if you're lucky. They find bodies in the Thames every other week, so it's not news anymore."

I didn't know what to do.

I couldn't go to the place Arizona had died. Too many police were in that area now.

And I didn't know where or how to look for Mrs. Jones or Lola Mack.

I looked at Sam, venom in my eyes.

Sam trembled.

I scowled at him and looked at the hole in the window.

I wanted to throw him out.

I should've thrown him out, should've tossed him to the birds and watched him fall.

But I didn't.

I growled, "Find the bodies. I don't care if you have to drag the rivers yourself, I don't care if you have to swim from end to end, *find them.*"

He nodded.

I stared at him long and hard, anger and grief in my eyes. Fear and terror was the mask he wore.

I left.

Ten minutes later I was at Dalston Lane and Amhurst Road.

I had left Sam to his own healing and limped by Marcon Court, stopped on the strip in front of Beverly Hills Video Library, Luks Supermarket, and Golden Blade Ladies Hair Salon.

Tubes didn't run this far, neither did the black cabs. None of the amenities of the West End existed in this part of London. As far as I knew, it was a surface-train and bus world.

A Mini Cooper whipped up the road, stopped between Bureau De Change and Anochikrom Palace Restaurant. Same car that had picked me up in front of the Houses of Parliament. The plates told me that it was the same car Arizona had been driving when she met me down on Baker Street. Same patriotic Mini Cooper she had picked me up in last night at Wimbledon.

I crossed the street and opened the car door, but didn't get inside. He had a computer hooked up, the power connected to the cigarette lighter. He moved the computer to the backseat and I slipped my injuries inside the car, sat on the warm seat where the computer had been.

For a moment all I could think was the same thought, that this was the same Mini Cooper Arizona had picked me up in last night at Wimbledon; the license plates verified that.

She wasn't driving this time.

She was dead.

The driver was the suave man who had left Arizona's room this morning.

The Latin man she had made love to last night.

I had been saved by her lover.

Her final lover.

Now I knew whose car she had borrowed.

She had sent him messages this morning. While I was in the room, this was who she was sending text messages to, this was who she had sent the passport photo of Bruno Brubaker to, this was who had gone to Novotel and looked for Bruno. He had been her unseen helper. He had kidnapped Tebby while we were out on Millennium Bridge. He had gone to Bruno's room.

No one was there at first.

Then Tebby got off the elevator.

And went to the room in question.

He had come up behind Tebby as she went back inside the hotel room.

Tebby had gone back to the room because she had forgotten to pick up a package. A package that she was supposed to take to the post office. *To Skeeter and Melanie. From Dad.*

A package that had the hit man's home address and his children's names written across the front.

A package decorated with smiley faces.

Arizona's companion had been behind Tebby as she opened the door to the hotel room.

She had never seen him.

Until it was too late.

I asked him, "Any word?"

He knew I was talking about Arizona. Mrs. Jones and Lola weren't his concerns.

He said, "The area is still hot."

"Brixton Boys?"

He nodded. "That was a bloody mess."

"All dead?"

"All who returned."

He drove like a whip. His left shoulder touching my right shoulder.

He told me, "The other SIM card you gave me."

"What about it? Damaged?"

"Not at all. I extracted all of the stored information. That phone is registered to Edward Johnson. The pictures confirm he is Bruno. I have a package. He's married. Two kids. One is mentally challenged. Wife works at the University of Houston. I have information on his siblings."

"Where is Bruno Brubaker slash Edward Johnson now?"

"A smart man would've changed IDs at this point."

"An angry man would go on a hunt."

"That would be unwise at this juncture."

"He could still be here."

"That is possible."

"The girl who was in his room, any idea who she was?"

"Tebby talked, said she met Bruno at Starbucks. Called her job while I had her in my company. It checked out. Bank worker. She was a wreck. An innocent girl who met a man at Starbucks, fell for him hard and fast. A romantic. Too bad for her. She'll never forget today."

"You were wicked."

"Thank you."

We stopped the conversation there.

He was smooth. He was good. In his twenties. His tongue made of silver.

I said, "You remind me of this guy I used to know back in the States."

In that British accent he asked, "Who might that be, mate?"

"Guy Arizona used to work for. Scamz."

"He was my father."

Then I understood.

Bigger things had transpired.

Things so big that it made that revelation insignificant.

I said, "You're a Brit."

"Brit to the bone."

I nodded.

I said, "Arizona paid me for a contract. She wanted me to go visit Sierra."

He nodded. "Her final wish."

He took out a pack of cigarettes. Djarums. He lit one. Cloves scented the air.

I let my window down.

He asked, "Where to, mate?"

"Tottenham Court Road and Bayley Street."

Mrs. Jones's Tumi suitcases and Lola's luggage were in the hotel room.

But they weren't.

Maid service had been there so the room was clean.

I checked the front desk. There were no messages. No one had seen them leave.

But they were gone.

As if they never were.

I called the hotel in Paris. They weren't there.

They had vanished and left everything behind.

I turned on the television, looked at the local news.

Nothing.

I picked up a *London Lite*, *The Sun*, *New Nation*, and *The Voice*. Found articles on Posh, on four-hundred-pound fees being imposed on SUV drivers, articles that said there was a surge in domestic violence during England's World Cup, with alcohol being a factor.

Nothing on Lola. Nothing on Mrs. Jones. Nothing on Arizona.

Bodies could take forever to be found.

If they were found at all.

Thirty-seven

the getaway

Rain fell on the man with the broken nose as if all the gods were weeping.

Maybe the abrupt death of an African queen had upset the balance of the universe.

The man with the broken nose wondered all of that as he hurried.

St. Olave's Church came up in a blur. As did Trinity Square. The apartment where the Reverend P. T. B. "Tubby" Clayton had lived was disregarded. No attention paid to Pitcher and Piano, Isis Bar and Lounge, he never focused on people going in and out of Fenchurch Station.

The black garbage bags lining the sidewalks in front of Cheshire Cheese and Ladbrokes were as important as the castles and churches that had become his background.

No thoughts of the goddamn IRS.

Or of his soon-to-be-ex-wife and their pending divorce.

He didn't think of his children.

Melanie wasn't on his mind.

Didn't imagine Skeeter.

All he could think about was getting the hell out of London.

He hurried by men dressed in dark colors.

Women dressed in dark colors.

Like a convention for morticians.

Like a funeral procession.

With umbrellas held high.

Faces unseen.

He was trying to see through the next thirty minutes.

All he needed was thirty minutes.

Enough time to wipe down the hotel room.

Get his hardware.

Change his bandages.

Put on a fresh suit.

Trash everything else.

Dispose of the Desert Eagle.

The Eagle was still in his hand, hidden inside a newspaper.

He wished he had dropped it with Tebby.

He wasn't thinking. No. He was thinking. He didn't know where Gideon was.

Didn't know if the man's word was bond.

His mind remained on the same channel.

Tuned to self-preservation.

Survival.

His nose ached. Maybe it was bleeding again. He was having a hard time breathing.

Tebby had hit him harder than he had realized.

His adrenaline was high. Masking the pain.

But his nose ached its way through the adrenaline.

Made it hard for him to breathe.

He felt as if someone had tied his hands and was holding a plastic bag over his head.

Despite the rain, despite the strong barley aroma coming from the pubs, despite the aroma of food coming from restaurants tucked in that narrow area, he smelled the flowers.

A sea of people was moving back and forth, from building to train and tube stations, black umbrellas up high, and even though he couldn't see them yet, he smelled each petal.

His nose broken, all he could smell was flowers.

He smelled all the flowers before he made the right that led to the front of Novotel. A strip that—at that moment—had no foot traffic. Just darkness and shadows being broken by streetlights.

He was alone.

He was safe.

Twenty minutes from now he'd be gone from this world, as if he never existed.

He turned the corner and what he saw caused him to pause.

Cars were parked on both sides of the street, barely enough room for a small car to pass that way from Savage Gardens. And the rain had washed flowers out into the damp avenue.

Hundreds of damp flowers had become thousands.

It had become overwhelming.

Novotel took up the entire block, damp British flags and hotel flags hanging out front.

But there were so many flowers Novotel had ceased to exist.

The aroma of flowers had the area between Fenchurch and Tower Hill stations reeking like a memorial park. More larger-than-life-size pictures of the dead WAG had been left in front of 1 Pepys, two hundred images of a dead woman facing Novotel, every image stationed right beneath his hotel room. He wouldn't wake here and smell the flowers. No more scent of death.

But there was another stench.

It slipped past the stink from all the flowers.

This stink like that of the muddy Thames itself.

He looked around.

Saw nothing.

Nobody.

Only shadows.

Then.

The demon rose up from between two parked cars.

Came up so fast he couldn't see.

The demon so dark it looked like it had spawned from the darkness.

He dropped the newspaper and tried to pull the Eagle away from its nest.

Too late.

The demon was quick.

The first knife went deep in his belly.

Came out.

Went deep again.

He dropped his Eagle.

Grabbed his pain.

Staggered backward.

Cringed as he looked at the demon.

The demon covered in blackness.

Blackness was all over.

Gritty. Grimy. Like the homeless.

Wet and black.

Like the evil creature that crawled out of the well in *The Ring*. Walking crooked, its foot dragging, like a monster that had risen up from the bottom of the ocean.

Not the ocean.

The Thames.

The demon's face was painted with the darkest fury.

The dead WAG had come back to life.

For retribution.

Tebby had come back.

With a vengeance.

The demon's arm went back, came forward, sent the same bloody knife flying through the rain. That knife hit him in the neck, blade first. Only the devil could throw a blade like that.

He was open.

Wide-open.

Blood was leaving him like water flowing through a burst dam.

Now he was discombobulated.

Blood was draining out of him.

He couldn't stop the blood from flowing.

Like the Thames.

He staggered backward. Fell on a bed of flowers. Those flowers cushioning his fall. Those flowers jumping up in the air. Landing on him. Covering his wounds.

The stench of fresh flowers.

Funeral flowers rested all over his body.

He couldn't breathe through his nose.

Now blood was coming out of his mouth.

He looked up at the picture over his head.

It was the image of the WAG. Her fans had put a huge picture of her up on the walls.

She had been beautiful.

So very beautiful.

The streetlights reflected on her image, put a halo over her head.

So damned beautiful.

The world always mourned the death of the beautiful.

Tebby.

He wondered if London would mourn beautiful Tebby. Or if her complexion would limit her *mournability*. He wondered if reporters from BBC and ITV would gather and make her news.

If strangers would come from all over and leave flowers for that beautiful child of Africa.

Mother of two.

Who wanted her own restaurant.

The American dream.

The demon's steps were rugged.

Like the demon was in pain.

The creature came and stood over him.

Hair long. Matted. Wild. Dripping black water that came from the pits of hell.

He expected to see the vindictive eyes of the dead WAG looking down on him.

It wasn't the WAG.

Wasn't Tebby.

Not with hair that long.

Her eyes.

He recognized her eyes.

So much hate and anger in her eyes.

So much vengeance.

She put her hand on the knife in his neck.

Twisted her blade.

Pulled it out of his fresh wound.

The other knife, the one resting deep inside his gut.

She twisted that blade as well.

She stared at him as his insides loosened and spilled.

Angry.

So damn angry.

It was her.

The other bitch he had killed.

She had risen from the dead.

The muddy Thames dripping from her hair.

The murk of the Thames slithering from her clothes.

Traces of the centuries of death the Thames had owned oozing from her skin.

So filthy she looked like gloom with the evilest eyes he'd ever seen.

She put the Eagle inside his bloody hand, then leaned into him.

Stabbed him again.

Then she wiped her bloody knives on his flowered suit, walked down the narrow street.

Became a shadow limping toward Savage Gardens.

He thought he heard her turn and go toward St. Olave's Church.

Flowers covered him.

No one would notice him for a while.

The WAG smiled down on him. She looked ethereal. As if she were in heaven laughing.

He closed his eyes. For the last time.

He thought about Melanie and Skeeter.

Mostly about Skeeter. His son. His buddy.

"Hey, Dad."

He coughed up blood, mumbled, "Hey, Skeet."

"Mom's gone, Dad. She took Melanie. It's just us now."

"That's good, Skeet."

"Want some cereal?"

"Not right now, Skeet. Not right now."

He wondered who was going to take care of his son now.

He hoped that poetry-speaking Frenchman did right by him.

He hoped his soon-to-be-widowed wife made it work.

He knew she would.

In retrospect, she wasn't so bad after all. They had just met at a bad time.

Melanie would be okay.

But Skeeter. Always called him Skeeter. Rarely called him by his true name, Fyodor. And Fyodor was special. Named after Fyodor Dostoyevsky. The best writer to ever live.

He summoned strength. But couldn't raise the Eagle. Couldn't put the barrel under his chin. He had lost too much blood. Everything that was cold turned warm. Like Tebby's kisses.

Death wasn't like they said it was.

There were no long-gone relatives waiting for him.

He didn't see his first wife, did not see his true love.

No angels. No devils.

Only darkness.

Only.

Death.

Thirty-eight

after dark, my sweet

Anger and despair drove me.

Anger and despair was all I owned right now.

I headed to Waterloo Station.

My work wasn't done.

Two hours later I was riding the Eurostar toward Bruxelles-Midi.

Paranoia on high, I kept checking to see if I was being followed.

I wanted to be followed.

I wanted to find somebody following me.

I marched the length of the train hunting for anyone who was stalking me.

Eurostar had screening, metal detectors, so I was safe from big guns.

For now.

Soon beautiful homes appeared with horses out in the icy pastures. The area on the other side of the Channel owned peace, even if it was assumed. Miles per hour had given way to kilometers per hour back in London. Now the British pound would be replaced by the euro.

Lola Mack would've loved this ride. She would've had her iPod on, Prince blasting.

Mrs. Jones would've sat across from me, sipping wine and reading an erotic novel.

Just like when we were on the plane.

The landscape became rural for hours before I saw buildings that had dome-type roofs, cartoonish architecture that reminded me of the buildings in Russia. Then the train whizzed by Antwerpen Dam and sped by cities filled with worn-out structures like the ghettos in New York and Philadelphia, those worn-out buildings being the best those areas had to offer.

Quaggy. Ravensbourne.

Those rivers stayed in my head.

Shetland ponies were on the farm in front of me, dressed in coats to keep warm. Churches and silos. Cows and trailer homes were out there too.

I changed trains at Bruxelles-Midi.

I followed the crowd down the stairs into the main terminal, checked the screen for departures to Amsterdam CS, saw the train was boarding, then waited at the bottom of the escalator that led to platform eighteen. I waited for someone to show up looking for me.

I waited until it was close to time for the train to leave.

Once the train was out of the station, I walked from car to car, end to end.

After I was sure he wasn't on this train, I sat facing the rear of the train.

The information I got from Sam, I looked that over.

Revenge was best served cold. His client had held a grudge for years.

And now they wanted to trade my life for a fucking car.

Anger manifested.

I passed signs for Haarlem.

That's where the boys who had been sent to rape and hurt Arizona had come from.

I opened and closed my aching hand.

I reached in my pocket for another BC Powder. I had run out.

It was just me and pain from here on out.

Then me and my anger had arrived at Amsterdam Centraal.

Last time I came here to kill. But I didn't achieve my goal.

This time I would.

The package told me where Sierra worked. And what time she clocked in.

It was showtime.

I frowned down at the photo of Arizona's sister.

I'd give her my anger.

I'd give her my pain.

I'd honor that contract and give her all that was bottled up inside me.

death never ends

Thirty-nine

killing Sierra

Red-light district.

From North Carolina to Montreal I'd been in more red-light districts than I could remember. This one had to be the most famous of them all.

Faded red velvet curtains opened and closed at the start and finish of each performance.

A Scottish man walked up and down the aisle, first taking orders, then delivering drinks.

Center stage was a circular bed that rotated to give a 360-degree angle of all the positions that were being utilized as various sex acts were performed.

It was a small cabaret-style theater that had bad lighting, a packed house with no more than ninety-nine old seats, a row of six on each side of the aisle. At least sixty of those narrow seats inside the narrow building were filled with middle-aged Asian men who looked like they should be at a board meeting at Sony; the front three rows were filled with eager, white college girls, all with American accents. More than fifty places like this were within a mile.

First a woman came onstage, stripped, and performed a vaginal muscle demonstration, then a male stripper came out dressed in cowboy leather. Tall and black as the night, looked like he should've been in the Village People. He took two of the college girls onstage and persuaded them to overcome their shyness and help him get naked.

A lesbian number came next, all fingers, then they ended their act with position sixty-nine.

Another girl came onstage, showed the room she knew how to make love to a banana.

A girl came onstage with her and helped her make the banana vanish.

Every act exited to tame applause.

Watching sex acts was nothing new to this crowd.

A godlike voice announced that it was time for the grand finale. What everyone had paid forty euros to see. The headliners at the live sex show were about to take center stage.

Techno music played. Lights flashed. Asian men leaned forward in muted anticipation.

Sierra appeared at one side of the stage.

Her skin was browner, hair shorter, her body was fuller, but she looked like Arizona.

I sat up straight.

A naked man appeared at the other end.

His skin was light. His hair short and wavy. A black Dutch I'd bet.

Sierra got on her knees.

He walked his limp penis toward her mouth.

The crowd sipped beers and hard liquor in silence.

This was where life had taken Sierra. From living like a baller on Hollywood's Sunset Strip to working the red-lit windows and live sex shows in Amsterdam.

This was where our lives crossed, where our damaged souls converged.

This was where it would end.

She moved her mouth away from her partner.

He was ready.

She lay on her back, legs open, bed rotating at a casual pace.

He mounted her.

Maybe five minutes went by with that red, orgy-size bed rotating nonstop. Lights flashing as he humped to the techno beat. With Sierra staring at the ceiling devoid of emotion.

They ended their act performing doggie-style.

The curtain closed and a few people put down their beers to offer applause.

Lights came on and everyone was asked to leave. Time for the next crowd.

I waited outside. Copper wire was in my pocket. Wire was better than rope.

Not much time went by before Sierra came out.

Jeans. Long coat.

Walking with the man who had been her partner onstage.

I could put him in the dirt before he realized what was going on.

But I only wanted her. There would be no collateral damage, not tonight.

Near the old church, she tiptoed and kissed him on his cheek.

He went in one direction, back over the canals.

She headed toward Damrak, the *rue* that led to the Sex Museum.

Too many people were between us, so I stayed back, kept her in sight.

Following her was another déjà vu.

Memories from window 693 came alive inside my mind.

Sierra stopped at a coffee shop and bought some Purple Haze.

I sat across from her as she smoked a joint.

Then she bundled up and took back to the streets.

I followed her, walked through the chill, stayed a few feet behind her.

The boulevard was crowded. Half a million people were out, most on bicycles. The greenhouse effect that had London's temperature going haywire would never happen here.

She went inside a packed McDonald's and bought a fish sandwich and fries, drank water.

She looked so regular.

I sat two tables over, eating a chicken sandwich.

I tried not to stare.

But I stared.

She could double for Arizona.

I followed her out of the red-light district, past people pulling luggage on wheels, past shop after shop, past a million coffeehouses, through a million cannabis clouds, followed her across the canals to Prinsengracht. Her flat was facing a canal near the Anne Frank House.

I stood outside.

I didn't know if Arizona wanted Sierra in the ground because of Scamz.

Didn't know if it was because of the FEMA scam.

Or because her sister had sent men to beat and rape her.

My guess was that it wasn't about any one thing.

My guess was that as long as Sierra was alive, Arizona never would've felt safe.

Sometimes people wanted other people dead simply because they didn't like them.

Because their existence interfered with peace of mind.

That was justification enough.

My job wasn't to ask questions.

Like the mailman, I just delivered.

Sierra went inside, didn't lock her door. This country was trusting, nothing like America. She left the curtains to the windows wide-open. Most if not all of the people here did the same. And most left their doors unlocked while they were home. No house alarms. A dead bolt at best.

Bicycle racks were all up and down the road, thousands of bicycles, some old, and I could tell they had been abandoned for seasons. I moved on the other side of the rack that was in front of her building, moved over and stood next to a tree, hung out in the shadows.

I watched her fire up another joint, move to her small refrigerator, take out a beer.

She ran her hand over her long hair, made a face like she'd had a long day.

Her living area, kitchen, and dining area were all crammed together. She could get up off her small sofa and be on the other side of her room and in her kitchen within four steps. Two more steps would take her to a twin-size bed that was pushed up against a wall.

She turned on her CD player. Classical music played at a gentle level. Mozart.

Still smoking her Purple Haze, she went into the bathroom.

It was time to finish this task. I headed for her doorway.

My cellular rang.

I checked the caller ID. Didn't recognize the number.

I answered anyway.

I said, "Talk."

First a lot of coughing, then a strained, coarse voice said, "Gideon?"

"Who is this?"

"You're alive."

"Who the fuck is this?"

"Chapel Hill did happen. So did New York."

I paused, my heartbeat galloping. "Arizona."

"It's me. It's me."

"Shit . . . what the fuck . . . Arizona? Is this really you? Are you okay?"

"I'm alive. Get over it. Calm down."

"Shit."

"Gideon . . . I thought he had killed you. Just got word that you were okay."

I was so fucking glad to hear her voice. My heart jumped.

Hearing her voice derailed me. Stole my focus.

My feet made me pace. I took a deep breath, let out so much damn relief.

I got my thoughts together, stammered, kept asking, "Where are you? Are you okay?"

"Northwest London. Between Willesden Junction and High Street Harlesden."

She told me she was beyond the congestion charge, hiding out in the London Borough of Brent, an area populated with immigrants from the Caribbean, India, and Africa.

I asked, "What's that noise in the background?"

"Lady out by the Jubilee Clock on a megaphone preaching the word to the Africans and Jamaicans. Loud. Kind of like Crenshaw Boulevard meets Pico Boulevard with a Harlem twist."

I took a breath, kept asking the same question over and over. "You okay? Shit. Fuck. I mean, I saw you get thrown off the Millennium Bridge, saw him shooting at you."

"I'm doing okay. Considering I swallowed half the Thames. Banged up a bit when I was thrown over. Lots of bacteria in that water. On antibiotics. Under a doctor's care right now."

"Are you in a hospital? What's going on? How bad is—"

"Relax. It's all under control."

"Are you at a hospital?"

"Doc I know came down from Harrow Road. Drinking river water is bad for your health."

"You get wounded?"

"Nothing that won't heal. Twisted my ankle. On bed rest. Antibiotics. I'm going to go to Brighton for a few days. Better doctor down there. Get out of the area. Recuperate in peace."

"He shot at you."

"And he missed."

She held the phone for a moment. Sounded like she was getting emotional, but there was something else mixed in. Some other emotion I didn't understand.

She said, "Shit. Thought you were dead, you know?"

"I'm not."

That settled between us.

I asked, "What happened? I came back for you . . . they . . . they . . . I tried to get to you."

"We were outnumbered. There were too many of them."

"I swear I did my best to get to you."

"I know, I know. Shit was my bad. Sorry my contact sold me out like that."

"He's dead. Your contact is dead."

"François?"

"Dead."

"You sure?"

"Bruno Brubaker . . . he killed François right in front of me. Suffocated him."

"Bruno. The man who threw me off the bridge."

"He killed me too."

"Killed you? What do you mean."

I paused, that feeling of suffocating still with me.

I said, "I'll find him. I'll finish this business between us."

"He won't be a problem for anyone anymore. It's taken care of."

"He's dead?"

"Bruno is no longer a problem. This is your confirmation."

"What happened? Give me the how and who and where."

"I happened. With my blade. In front of his hotel."

Then I understood the strangeness in her tone. It was the disturbing timbre a person had when they had just killed someone. After that first kill, Arizona had a new hardness in her voice.

She said, "I gutted that bastard. I gutted him good. The son of a bitch is dead."

I worried who she might become now.

Wondered if that was her one kill.

Or if more would follow.

Still, I wanted to know how she survived. But she was Queen Scamz. The main thing was that she had survived. Didn't sound like she wanted to talk about that ordeal, not at the moment, so I didn't push. She'd called so she could hear my voice, know that I was okay.

Arizona said, "Just got word. Pit Bull died."

"When?"

"This morning. He never came out of his coma."

"You said he was awake."

"Got bad intel before. He's dead. Wasn't him. The hit didn't come out of his camp."

I nodded. I already knew that, but it was nice to have that information confirmed.

She said, "Sledge is dead."

"So Big Bad didn't kill Sledge."

"He did. My guess is that they had hits out on each other at the same time. Big Bad knew Sledge was going to be in Trinidad. And Sledge knew Big Bad was going to be in Tampa."

Bruno had said the James Patterson book he had given me was misdirection.

He wanted to lead me down the wrong path.

I didn't tell her I knew who had me in their crosshairs.

I'd handle it on my own.

Crisp air blowing across my face, bright lights from live sex shows and strip clubs in the distance, the scent of Purple Haze in the breeze, hundreds of people passing me and heading toward those red lights in search of sex and alcohol, I leaned against a tree. Leaned and took a few hard breaths, tried to not feel overwhelmed. Arizona was okay, but I was still overwhelmed.

I said, "Bruno killed the two women I was with."

"I heard. Sorry."

"Your friend told you."

"Yeah. I talked with him. He told me you were okay. He forced information out of the African girl. He told me about the exchange at Parliament. I had no idea so much was going on."

"Is your friend . . . is he with you?"

"No."

"Tell him . . . tell him I said thanks. Tell him I owe him one."

"Sure."

"He was good. At what he did, he was good. Remained calm all the way."

"Trained by the best."

We paused.

Scamz's son.

I shook my head. Let her have her ghosts. Worried about my own.

Arizona asked me where I was.

I didn't answer right away. I just watched Sierra.

Arizona repeated, "Where are you?"

"Amsterdam. Been here over an hour. Came to do your job."

Arizona paused. "Is it done? Is Sierra . . . is it done?"

Her voice owned some tremble. Some anger. And something else.

"I'm at her front door. I see her. She's alone. It can be done in five minutes."

Sierra had taken off her clothes, had a robe on, her hair up.

I said, "Arizona? You still there? Hello?"

Sierra was about to shower away the residue from her working day.

Arizona said, "Wait. I want to . . . wait. Let me . . . let me think."

A moment passed. People went by me on bicycles, on foot, shoes clicking across cobblestone, lights on in a lot of the terraces, this being the normal side of town.

Arizona said, "Gideon?"

"I'm here."

She whispered, "Like sex, once it's done . . . it's done. No taking it back."

"Yeah."

"I don't need to make any more mistakes. Not right now."

"So what are you saying?"

"I killed two men tonight. One of the Brixton Boys died from his injuries."

"We were at war. You did what you had to do."

"But the last one . . . when I killed Bruno . . . even though he deserved it . . . it was horrible."

"Death isn't pretty. No matter how you dress it up, it's not pretty."

She told me how ice replaced her warm blood and she shivered like never before.

She said, "My teeth clattered and all went numb. Couldn't feel my feet. The world became a merry-go-round. Then a blazing fire invaded my belly, my throat. I threw up."

More silence while I watched her little sister.

Again Arizona paused before she answered me. She said, "I want to modify my order."

I didn't question her. Didn't ask what changed her mind.

But death had its way of changing us all.

Arizona said, "This is what I want you to do. Same fee. Do this without asking questions."

She talked for almost ten minutes. I listened without asking a question. When she was done with her message, when she had told me what she wanted me to do, we hung up.

I could've crept in the front door, been hiding when Sierra came out of the shower.

I knew over twenty ways to kill a man.

Cold air moved over me as I waited for Sierra to finish her shower.

Waited for her to get dressed.

Waited for her to fire up the second half of her Purple Haze.

She took out a small keyboard.

Then she played along with the classical music. She was decent.

I waited for a song to end.

Then I knocked.

She came to the door, opened it without hesitation. Her modest space held the scent of cleansers and marijuana. As if marijuana-scented paint had just been put on the walls.

She stood there, hair wet, smoke from her weed rising from her fingers.

Classical music playing behind her.

She was a beautiful girl. More beautiful than Arizona.

She looked at me, said nothing.

Her eyes told me she was high. And she was high most of the time.

She made an expression that told me she recognized my face, but didn't know who I was. Maybe she thought I was somebody who had visited her before or seen her shows.

Maybe she thought I was a customer.

But I think she was just high on the Haze.

I said, "Arizona sent me."

Only then did her expression change. Her breathing went staccato.

The men she had sent after her sister had been crippled. She knew that Sergeant, her friend in whatever scam they were involved in, was dead. She knew I had helped do it all.

Still I told her, "I killed Sergeant. The men you sent to hurt your sister, I was there. I helped take care of them. What I gave them was a fate worse than death. Ask them."

I believe that Sergeant was more than her friend. He had been her customer as well.

His picture was on her table.

In full military gear.

Like she admired him.

Or loved him.

Maybe she was the one he had wanted to retire to an island with and make babies.

Anger and fear. I'd seen that expression so many times over the last few days.

Every one wore that expression in a different way.

Sierra backed away from me. I had expected her to drop the Haze. She didn't. She put her burning joint in a small glass ashtray. She did that without taking her eyes away from me.

I said, "I need you to listen to me."

When she stopped moving, I didn't go near her.

I said, "Arizona paid me a lot of money to come here and take care of this problem. A lot more money than you paid those Dutch boys to ride to London and do harm to your big sister."

She didn't scream. Didn't say a word. Not a sound.

I said, "Arizona told me to tell you she loved you. And she wants this fighting to end. She doesn't want to be hurt. And she doesn't want to kill you. But I know she will. You are her baby sister. Her only sister. She sent me to kill you. I need you to understand that. I could've killed you when you left the stage. But Arizona changed her mind. She just did. She wanted me to tell you that she changed her mind. She didn't want the taste of your death in her mouth. So you have to decide where this goes from here. And she told me to tell you one more thing."

Sierra trembled and pulled at her hair, watched me without saying a word.

I didn't know if she understood me. Or if fear had numbed all of her senses.

I said, "Scamz is dead. She told me to tell you to let him stay dead. That both of you need to move on. It doesn't matter who was wrong. Scamz is dead. Time to let go."

Sierra cried. I mentioned Scamz. And just like that she cried.

Arizona had been crying when we were on the phone. Not hard, just soft tears.

While Arizona gave me those hard words to give her little sister, she had cried.

I said, "The money from the FEMA scam . . . she's going to pay you your part. Even though you didn't earn it, even though you double-crossed her along with Sergeant, even though you tried to have her beaten and raped on the streets of London, she's paying you."

This sibling rivalry had been going on for years. Had escalated and become deadly.

And had lasted years beyond the death of the man who had changed them both.

I said, "Sergeant is dead because of this. I know because I killed him. He was my friend and I killed him. I killed him because he wanted to do harm to Arizona. I care about your sister."

My own emotions were starting to ride.

I took a rugged breath. "So let's let today be a good day. For both of you."

I moved past her, picked up a scrap of paper, wrote down a number.

I said, "If you ever want to talk, this is where you can reach her. This number should be good for at least a day. She didn't tell me to give you this number. This is my doing. No traces. Or I will come back. Call her. Talk to her."

Sierra nodded.

I said, "Arizona said she used to come here. Stand in the shadows, watch you. It broke her heart to see what you were doing. She just told me that. She said she brought you in on the FEMA scam so you could make enough money to get away from this lifestyle, but you double-crossed her. I don't know what you did, but she says you and Sergeant fell in bed together and double-crossed her in the end. All I know is, she's your sister. I'm sure she's not the best role model in the world, but there has to be some way you two can exist without killing each other."

She took the mobile number from me.

I said, "Don't send anybody to hurt her anymore. Please. She'll ask me to come back. To find you. And if I do, the next time we meet, it won't end like this. And I will find you."

Quivering and crying, Sierra went directly to her phone.

She thought my intention was for her to call Arizona at this very moment.

I didn't stop Sierra from making that call. Maybe sooner was better than later. The forgiving mood Arizona was in now, it might change, and it could change back in the other direction.

So maybe now was better.

I left, went out the door and took to the cobblestone roads and canals.

Whatever was to be said between them, I'd let that be between them.

I had completed my order.

This job was done.

Seeing Sierra up close I knew it wasn't her.

Years ago I had come here looking for revenge, and while I was here, I'd seen a working girl who looked like Arizona, a girl who resembled Sierra. I had bedded that woman, had gone inside her canalside brothel and pretended she was the woman I desired. I had stepped into window 693 and asked that woman if I could call her Arizona while I made love to her.

For a while I thought that woman was Sierra.

Sierra wasn't the girl from window 693. Wasn't the girl I'd used as my own ghost.

It might've been a small thing, but I found my own relief in that.

I passed by window 120. The window where the woman I thought was my mother . . . Thelma . . . used to work . . . taking her customers and their fantasies to those come-stained sheets. I remembered that day. Remembered that shameful day. Then I moved on.

I had to get back to London.

Had to find their bodies. Had to find a way to search the Quaggy and Ravensbourne.

Sadness overwhelmed me.

I leaned against a wall for a while, my world a daze, leaned there wishing I could go back to when we were on the plane, wished I hadn't brought them into my corrupt world.

Now it was too late.

I headed back toward the canals and coffee shops. Only took a few short minutes for me to move from being a shadow to being lit up by the red lights. As I walked, I glanced up at all the girls in all the windows, modeling in lingerie, beckoning men to come spend some time.

If Arizona had called five minutes later, Sierra would've been dead.

Would've been seen not as a person, but as just another dead whore.

Like my mother. Like Margaret.

Troubled.

I was still troubled.

Brisk air blew down the avenues, chilled the already cold city.

Red lights and working women in every window. Cannabis-scented air.

A few minutes later, as I was passing by the Bull Dog Hostel, my mobile phone buzzed.

I looked down at the message: FUNDS TRANSFERRED.

I'd seen that message so many times over the last few years.

Then my phone vibrated again. Another message.

BE WELL GIDEON. TALK SOON. LOVE YOU. YOU WERE MY FIRST CHOICE.

I didn't know what to make of that. I really didn't.

What Arizona had said before: *Like sex, once it's done . . . it's done.*

Maybe she was talking about me.

Maybe she was talking about the night she spent with her ghost.

I didn't know.

I let that go the best I could. Had to get focused. The man I knew as Bruno was dead.

But the person who hired him was very much alive.

So my conflict wasn't over.

As long as the person who bought the contract thought I was dead, I had time to rest. I had time to heal. I had time to regroup. I had to plan and figure out how to handle this situation.

Provided Sam hadn't already sold me out.

I closed my jacket, limped through a swarm of hedonists, ended up mixed in a pleasure-seeking mob. Beer and piss stench rising up from the rugged concrete, I went deeper into the din, blended with the rest of the tourists. So many underage women smiled at me, pedophiles preferred. Smile after smile after smile. Business disguised as seduction.

I stopped and looked at the old church that stood tall and cast shadows on all the whores.

I wondered how many Hail Marys they would have to give for absolution.

I was heading through a different section of the red-light district when somebody called my name. They called out that they saw Gideon. And that chilled me. I'd dropped my guard.

My own fear came back. The fear of being tied with a plastic bag over my head.

Just like that I knew Sam had sold me out.

I turned around and once again I faced the Big Bad Wolf.

This time the Big Bad Wolf was running right at me.

Forty

Rembrandtplein 8, Amsterdam

The Big Bad Wolf was running right at me, arms flailing.

Yelling my name.

Breasts bouncing.

Frantic.

Hands waving.

Lola Mack.

It was Lola Mack. She was sprinting toward me. She was screaming.

Wearing an oversize R.I.P. BIG BAD WOLF sweatshirt.

Lola threw her arms around me, and before I could say anything, she was kissing me.

She held me so tight I had to get her arms loosed so I could breathe.

The injuries from being beaten came alive when she held me like that.

I asked, "What are you doing here?"

"You're mad at me, aren't you? I knew you were mad at me. Because I acted out at the club. I'm sorry. For real, I'll never do anything like that again. I was upset. Mrs. Jones told me you were gone and you had left and didn't say good-bye, and I said I didn't want to go to Paris, not with you mad at me, so I told Mrs. Jones we had to come here and I've been walking around looking for you for hours and I just don't want you to be mad at me. Don't be mad at me, please? I mean, you left money for me to go home like you were telling me to get the fuck out of London."

"Lola."

"I know. I'm rambling. But don't be mad at me. Okay?"

"Where is Mrs. Jones?"

"Back at the hotel. Oh, God, the hotels here are crappy. I mean crappy. And expensive. We're right behind you, by the Flower Market, crashing in the middle of the city at Rembrandt Plaza. Atlanta Hotel. Two-star joint. Man, they are giving the ATL a bad name. Crappy. I think the room at MyHotel has me spoiled. This is definite a fall down the ladder. But it's right by all the museums, galleries, theaters, cinemas, shops, restaurants, canals, bars, discos, nightclubs, and casinos. And if you don't want to buy any weed, you can open the window and get a contact high. Anyway. I've been all over Amsterdam. I walked by all that stuff looking for you."

I held her face, looked in her eyes. "You're okay?"

"I'm okay now. I've been looking all over Amsterdam for you."

"Nothing bad happened to you or Mrs. Jones?"

"Well, we had a club fight. You were there. I got too freaky, I think. Hold up. Is this some *Kyle XY* amnesia stuff? Are you and Mrs. Jones trying to punk me or something?"

"You sure you're okay?"

"I'm tired as hell and my feet hurt from all the walking. Been walking for hours. I was just about to give up and see if I could find some vodka and Prozac. I'm so happy I found you."

"Stop jumping up and down."

"I'm excited. Okay, let me jump two more times. Okay, okay. I'm done."

"Mrs. Jones is okay?"

"She's cool. The first room we had, would you believe the toilet was in the hallway? Like we were in a slop house in Mississippi. Then we upgraded and got a triple room. Private toilet and shower. Small, but at least we ain't sharing a toilet with some damn strangers who don't understand what the hell we're saying. I don't need no international germs crawling on my—"

"Lola."

"I'm sorry. I'm so excited to see you. Don't be mad at me for talking Mrs. Jones into coming here so I could look for you, okay? It was my idea. She had nothing to do with it."

I held her at arm's length. That sweatshirt. Stared at the image of a man I had killed.

Lola said, "They have Tupac, Biggie, Sledge, Big Bad, they have all the dead rappers in the alley down by the McDonald's and KFC. And the Internet cafés are a rip-off. One tried to charge me ten bucks for an hour. Elvis Presley and Marilyn Monroe, they had statues of them out front. And Levi's cost two hundred bucks here. Did you know that? If I had known that, I could've grabbed some Levi's at Marshalls for ten bucks a pair and made a killing over here."

"Lola."

"Okay. I know. I'm all over the place. I kinda-sorta had a beer and smoked some hash."

"Let's lose this sweatshirt."

"So I'm sort of in a weird place right now. Are you here or am I that high? I am loaded."

I smiled and I kissed her. She was real. She was alive.

Lola said, "Now that's what I'm talking about."

We walked by women in windows. By men shopping for sex. By the coffeehouses.

She said, "Let's go get Mrs. Jones."

"After we get you a new sweatshirt."

The walk was different now. Once again, for a while, I'd become a square.

Lola asked, "Where do you live? Can I see you after we go back home?"

The truth rose from within.

I told Lola that I had a small house in Stone Mountain, Georgia, right on Savannah Terrace, right across a two-lane road and a gravel parking lot away from Crazy Ron's barbecue and Lickety Split gas station. And I had a condo in the city where it never stops raining, Seattle, had a spot right above the market with a view of Elliott Bay; Macy's, Nordstrom, Déjà Vu, and at least a hundred Starbucks were right outside my door.

Lola said, "I love Seattle. Went there once. Drove up from L.A."

"I have property . . . a house . . . in California too."

"You live in L.A. too? Where? Orange County?"

"South of Palmdale. Nice house on a hill. Right below the California Aqueduct."

"Man, if you're in Palmdale, with L.A. traffic, you might as well be in another country. Traffic going up that way makes you wish Cali had a tube system and a congestion fee."

She was surprised that I had a house in the peaceful desert, the land of tumbleweeds and rattlesnakes. I told her that I owned a boat in Seattle, two horses in Palmdale.

Lola said, "You have three cribs?"

"Yeah. I do. Three."

"Gideon, you got it going on."

Lola was impressed by what Arizona had shrugged away.

The package that had been put together on me, I saw it in my mind.

I had three places that were known to a ruthless and vindictive enemy.

Right now it felt like I needed a fourth fortress of solitude.

Lola said, "Let me get you to Mrs. Jones. She's going to be excited too."

"You think?"

"Don't tell her I told you, but she cried. This time she was crying about you. She cried from Waterloo to Amsterdam. She had it bad. She thought you were gone for good. Like you were going to be dead or something and nobody would tell us. Then she had me upset."

I held Lola's hand as we walked by strangers in need of what I had.

Lola said, "Sure you're not mad at me?"

"I'm sure."

"I missed you, Gideon. I really did. I've been going crazy all day. You have no idea."

That got another smile out of me.

Mrs. Jones smiled.

She didn't jump up and down, just let out a long sigh of relief and put her arms around me, whispered that she had been worried, whispered she was glad that Lola had found me. She did all that in her cool and sophisticated way, the controlled way she behaved before she had a few drinks in her system, that lawyeristic way of keeping her emotions in check.

They had traveled light. Just jeans, trainers, and sweatshirts. Were backpacking it.

No wonder I couldn't tell they had taken anything out of their luggage.

She hugged me as tight as Lola had a while ago.

She touched my face. "You look a little banged up."

I put my hand in her wild hair. Put my breath on her neck. "It was a rough meeting."

"It ended in your favor?"

"So far."

"So it's not over."

"Not yet."

We all went down to the Bull Dog. Enjoyed beer and cannabis.

Then went back to the room.

The room had two twin-size beds.

We pushed the beds together.

A little before nine in the morning, sleep-deprived and with what Lola called a bona fide love hangover, I had gotten them up and we headed for the train station. We rode the train with the fewest stops to Bruxelles-Midi, then changed to the Eurostar, rode the second leg of the trip first-class back to Waterloo. Not long after that we were getting off the tube at Tottenham Court.

Room service.

Hot showers.

I slept the rest of the day. It was cold out and the girls kept me warm.

Then I had to get out. We rode the tube to Peckham Rye, an area that reminded me of Compton, Detroit, South Memphis, and the west side of Chicago. In between the mom-and-pop stores and swap meets and flea markets were butchers with freshly killed pork and chickens hanging in the windows, that fly-drawing scent blending with the raw-fish stench as we passed.

Sam met me down there. In an area that had been characterized by gang-related shootings, muggings, and burglaries, but also had a high population of artists and professionals.

Sam walked up to me and handed me a jump drive shaped like an ink pen.

He said, "Wotcha, mate."

"This is my package?"

He nodded.

Everything I needed to get to the person who had a contract on me was on that disc.

Alarm codes. Escape routes. Cell phone numbers. New identification. Much more.

I said, "And they still think I'm dead."

"No worries. They think you're dead."

Sam was in my camp now.

When Sam walked away, I saw Mrs. Jones looking at me.

We were across from Rye Lane Chapel, inside a swap-meet area, Lola flipping though bootleg DVDs. Lola was always in her own world. But her ears were always to the ground.

I faced Mrs. Jones. Faced Henrietta Kellogg. Saw much concern in her face.

Mrs. Jones asked, "Everything okay?"

"Time to leave the UK."

"I know. I just hate for this to end."

"Everything has to end at some point."

She smiled. "I know."

I flew to Windsor, Canada.

I'd been dead long enough for my enemy to relax and get sloppy.

At the border, I answered a lot of bullshit questions, went through the kind of search that had been going on post-9/11, passed, paid the toll, and drove my rental across the Ambassador Bridge into Motown. It was time I returned to Detroit and visited a dead man's wife.

Forty-one

the man in the basement

Never trust a preacher's wife.

Especially when she has paid a hit man to kill the preacher she married.

I still heard her husband's voice in my head: *"What's your goddamn name?"*

Still heard the reverend whispering at me from his shallow grave.

This had been his home. His castle. But now it was as if he never existed.

Not as many pictures of the widow's philandering husband were up inside their home. She'd kept just enough to make herself look like the grieving widow. But for the most part, the images of her cheating husband had been replaced with golden-framed photos of her family, of her children, who had grown taller. Preteen kids who still attended Christian schools in the area.

"Greater Life Academy. A Christian school. Children must attend schools that are not afraid to acknowledge Jesus and give praise to the Lord. Do you believe in the Lord?"

I had returned to Michigan. To the Bloomfield Villas Subdivision.

The $2 million, four-sided brick home.

The codes I'd gotten from Sam worked. This time I didn't have to cut wires. And Sam had arranged for keys to be waiting at my hotel. I'd deactivated the alarm, changed it from its AWAY setting to NIGHT DELAY setting. The alarm would still start chirping when the door opened, but the motion detectors were deactivated, so I was free to roam around.

There was new furniture throughout. She hadn't kept much from the marriage.

Just the house.

I went inside the basement. Most of it was the same. Made of marble and golden fixtures. Pool table. Video games. The full gym had been turned into a personal beauty salon. What used to be the kids' playroom was now a computer room. The wine room hadn't changed.

I'd almost died in this basement.

I'd almost died a lot of places.

I stared at the images of the huge man who wore the preacher's collar. He still looked like the main character from the *The Green Mile* dressed in a three-thousand-dollar suit and gaiters.

The man who had done the .38-in-the-Bible trick had almost killed me.

I looked at his obituary like it was a book I had written myself.

If he had had his way, that obituary would've been mine.

Then I read the newspaper clippings. Clippings that were in her scrapbook.

Articles about cash-strapped Detroit and how the mayor's residence, the Manoogian Mansion down on the Detroit River, was costing the taxpayers more than a quarter million a year, money spent on everything from holiday decorations to upkeep to take-out food.

The reverend's wife said, if elected, she would relieve the city of that burden. She would live in her own home and turn the mansion that was built back in 1928 over to the city. She said it wasn't right for the leader to live in a mansion with a cabana and a pool while homeless died out on the frozen streets. When elected, she would move into the city on her own dime.

She said that the Manoogian Mansion was a symbol.

But Detroit, itself, was a much larger symbol. She said she loved Detroit and she wanted to move it away from being the second most dangerous city in America, second only to St. Louis.

The paper had a picture of her standing in front of the mansion.

A symbol that had been defiled by wild parties that had a stripper fighting security on the front lawn. The stripper was found in an alley with a bullet in her head about six months later.

I wondered who got that contract.

The reverend's wife had come up. She was more than a preacher's widow.

She had political power.

"What political organization are you representing?"

She wanted to overturn the state's ban on embryonic stem-cell research. She was big on the environment, had done years of charity work, was still a spiritual leader at her church.

Another issue was highlighted in other new articles. Highlighted and a smiley face drawn over the top. The sitting mayor had been accused of having extramarital affairs. *Metro Times* was all over that one. That would guarantee the female vote.

Her being reasonably attractive without being intimidating would reel the men in.

And the auto industry was hurting bad. Layoffs at Ford. GM was asking people to take early retirement. The Big Three were getting killed by the Japanese carmakers. The entire region was depressed economically. Article said the unemployment rate in Motown was the worst in the country.

She'd found her platforms. Her ticket to running the cash-strapped city.

People might not understand politics and stem-cell research, but they understood money.

Murder.

And sex.

She had paid to have her husband killed and that made this road possible.

She had a good chance of becoming to Detroit what Shirley Franklin was to Atlanta.

After she had hired me for the contract on her husband, after I had killed the reverend downstairs in the basement, I had collected my money and left, never looked back at Detroit.

The preacher's wife had capitalized on her husband's death.

Not only did she inherit a fortune.

She made sure the sitting mayor was suspected. She'd also done a damn good job convincing . . . maybe just reminding . . . people that Detroit had been falling apart during his term.

The DVR was still in the same location. I stole the hard drive.

Then I took my shoes off, went upstairs toward the bedrooms.

Only one picture of her dead husband was upstairs. In the hallway outside her children's bedroom, at the opposite side of the four-bedroom house, away from her eyes.

"What if Jesus didn't have a name? What if Satan didn't have a name? Good or evil, everyone must have a name. We name what we praise, we name what we fear."

I headed toward her sleeping quarters, walked those gold-trimmed stairs with copper wire in my hand. I also had a newspaper article. Something from the Internet. A horrific story about a man who had died in Brazil. Strangled with copper wire. His body was burned beyond recognition.

Copper wire in hand, I looked at the clock.

I went to her computer. Popped in the jump drive I had in my pocket.

I downloaded the information I had on her.

All of her personal information.

Information on her children.

Information on her family.

She'd be home soon.

The woman who lived in a huge home paid for by tithes would be home soon.

She was home an hour later.

Her kids weren't with her. They were with her parents.

As soon as she grabbed her mail, she poured herself a glass of wine, then headed up the stairs, went straight to her bedroom, her cellular phone up to her ear, talking to a reporter, telling how

Lincoln Navigators would no longer be bought with city money once she was elected, over two hundred thousand dollars would never be charged to a city credit card on her watch, and she would never threaten to cancel the International Freedom Festival if the city council vetoed her budget. She said she welcomed all criticism and didn't think of the media as a lynch mob, that the media was supposed to hold up the truths, all truths.

She told them she had nothing to hide.

She vowed to not lose in her own district, to ensure there would be no missing ballots turning up in the trunks of election officials' cars, that the voice of the people would not be tampered with this time as it was before.

Then she hung up.

A big smile on her face.

A mayoral smile.

Then her house phone rang. Not the number most people had access to. The number that only a few had. Her family. Her lover who lived in Troy. The same lover she was seeing before her husband was killed during a home invasion while she was away preaching the gospel.

She answered, "Hello."

I said, "The reverend was fucking the babysitter. Clichéd, but true."

She paused. "Who do you want to speak with?"

"You."

"I'm sorry. Who's calling?"

"The babysitter was a live-in. That black bitch was living under your roof. You have them on tape having sex. Did you tell the media any of that? Or did you keep your husband saintly?"

There was a pause.

She asked, "Who is this?"

My voice was distorted. I was using a filter. "A dead man. This is a dead man."

"Who is this? How did you get this number?"

"It's me. The man you hired to kill your husband. The man you hired someone to kill."

Silence.

Her tone owned anger. "I don't know what you're talking about. Is this blackmail?"

Silence.

I said, "Go to your computer."

She hurried, went inside the office next to her bedroom. I told her to tap any key and the screen would come alive.

She moaned, "Oh my God."

"That's the man you sent after me. His autopsy photos."

"You. It's you." Her anger flipped and became terror. "What do you want?"

"Go to the next page. Scroll down."

She saw things that made her talk to God in a desperate way.

I said, "That's a crime scene from Tampa."

She talked faster, kept saying this couldn't be happening.

I said, "Keep scrolling. See the picture of the knife?"

"Yes."

"That's called an MXZ Saw. Have you heard of an MXZ Saw?"

Her breathing caught in her throat. That meant she saw images from a child abuser who had met his end down in Mexico.

"Wonderful blade. Can saw through a tree, bricks, pipes, ceramics. And bones."

She moaned.

Then I said, "Bones. An MXZ Saw can cut through bones."

Silence couldn't drown out her muffled fear.

I said, "Keep scrolling."

All of her personal information was below that. Information Sam had given me.

I said, "Now, go back to your bedroom. Look on your dresser. What's missing?"

"No. The pictures of my children."

"Now. Look under your big, fluffy pillows. The ones nearest the bathroom."

She did.

The copper wire and the newspaper article were there.

I said, "I could be behind you right now. That could happen to you tonight."

It took her a moment. She sat on her bed, stammered. "Where are you?"

"I'm in your basement."

"In my basement? You're not in my basement."

"I love what you've done with the place. You've upgraded just about everything."

Once again she sobbed smooth and easy, made anguish sound beautiful.

I asked, "Why did you send someone after me?"

"You stole from me. You stole sixty thousand dollars of my money. You threatened me."

"The penalty. This grudge was about the penalty?"

"*You* fucked up and blamed me. The gun in the Bible? He *never* should've made it to the damn Bible. That was *your* fault, not mine. Do not blame your *incompetence* on me."

I gritted my teeth. "Incompetence."

"I didn't mean that."

"Are you trying to hurt my feelings? Do you want me to come upstairs?"

"I swear. I didn't mean that."

"One thing I've learned. Motivation is never as it seems. Maybe he was fucking the babysitter. Maybe he wasn't. Right now it looks like your husband was a powerful man and you were tired of living in his shadow. He died and you received the sympathy of Detroit. Your camp leaked information just shy of accusing the sitting mayor of killing your husband. Just enough to get it into the public's head. Now you're about to live your dream. You have a good chance of becoming the Shirley Franklin of the Midwest. You're almost as good as Maxine Waters. Almost. And I don't think you wanted any loose strings. If your husband's murder was questioned, and I was gone, even if they found my body and tied me to the murder, no way to tie it to you."

Silence.

I said, "Do we have an understanding?"

"Yes. Yes, we have an understanding."

"It's up to you if this will be our last conversation. Forget you ever heard about me. If you ever see me, I will be the last face you see and I will witness your last breath. Now, do this."

She made sounds, said more things to her God and savior.

I said, "Stand up."

"Okay."

"Go to your dresser. Second drawer from the top. Where you keep your lingerie."

She did.

When she opened the drawer, she would see an envelope was on top of her sexy thong.

Inside was sixty thousand dollars.

I said, "Think of it as a sixty-thousand-dollar refund. Sixty thousand reasons for me to not have to come back to Detroit. Think what you want. Just don't make me use the copper wire."

She was too messed up to talk.

I said, "Are we done?"

"We're done."

"Two more things."

"Yes?"

"I downloaded information from your computer. And I noticed you have it synced with your BlackBerry. So I now have all of that information as well. Since you have information on me, now I have information on you. Friends. Family. Are we clear on this thing?"

"We're clear." She swallowed. "You said there were two things. What else?"

"The AMG is in Canada. You've hidden that Benz across the border in Canada."

"Oh, God."

"Make sure the GPS gets turned back on. Make sure that Benz gets found within the next twenty-four hours. Make sure your luxury car getting found in Windsor makes the *Metro Times*. I know the insurance has already paid you off, but make sure it's in the local papers."

She took a hard breath. "Okay. It will be found."

"And, oh. Have to tell you. If you win, I think you're going to make a great mayor."

"Thank you."

"I think you care more about Detroit than that other guy. Or your dead husband."

She was crying.

I said, "I'm joking. I like the other guy better. I'm partial to wild parties and strippers."

She didn't take to my joke.

Then I was serious.

I said, "The wrong you're doing . . . stop doing evil while you can. Stop because one day somebody will come for you. One day what you do to other people, that will be done to you."

She cried harder. Sounded like she was on the verge of a total breakdown.

She asked, "Are you inside my basement?"

I didn't answer.

She stammered, *"Are you in my basement?"*

"Come down and see."

I hung up.

I wasn't in her basement.

I'd left her home thirty minutes before she showed up. I'd taken her DVR and gone to my rental, parked across the street, and waited. That left me in range of the wireless cameras I had put in her hallways and bedroom. I saw her pull up into her driveway before I drove away. By the time I called her private house phone, I was parked on Squirrel Road outside Oakland University, watching her every move. The pictures of her kids, I tore those up and dumped them in the trash.

I took the SIM card out of the mobile I was using. Destroyed that SIM card.

Did the same with the DVR. Then I popped in a different SIM card.

I had more business to take care of.

This one bigger than all the rest.

I drove I-75 south to 375 and exited at Jefferson Avenue. That put me in front of the General Motors Renaissance Center, their world headquarters. I checked my rearview. Couldn't get a cup of coffee without watching my back. From there I took the Detroit-Windsor Tunnel to the Windsor Airport. I avoided the Ambassador Bridge. Lots of trucks. Long delays. Windsor had a small airport. That was good. Fewer people. Easier to see if I was being followed.

Nothing behind me but high unemployment and the wind.

I abandoned the rental car I was driving at the airport, headed toward the terminal.

My mobile rang.

It was Sam. He was the only person who had this number.

He asked, "What the fuck did you do to her?"

"Sometimes it's not what you do, it's what you don't do."

The mailman had been killed in London. And I'd shut down the post office in Motown.

Sam said, "Is our bill settled?"

"We're done, Sam."

"Will you kill me?"

"I need you, Sam. You're valuable."

"Thanks. I look forward to more business with you."

"Explain to me what happened. You double-crossed François."

"As he double-crossed Queen Scamz."

"Explain that to me. How did that go down?"

"François contacted me after Queen Scamz called him regarding the Desert Eagle. I put him in contact with Bruno Brubaker. And for a fee François led Bruno to you. I only put Bruno in contact with François. Once I established that connection, I wasn't involved in the rest."

"When François contacted you, you called and warned Bruno."

"Yes. When I reached him on his mobile, he was at your hotel room."

"Your call stopped him from going inside my hotel room."

"I can only assume."

"If you had called five minutes later and . . ."

"He was going to torture and kill the women. Five minutes later, all of that would have been done. It would've been a bloody mess. Yes, my call diverted him to your meeting."

I said, "Like a deus ex machina."

"I wouldn't go so far as to say that. Sheer luck. More coincidence than anything."

"I thank you for that coincidence."

"Bruno left your hotel straightaway. Didn't visit your friends. Rushed to ambush you."

"He ran out of the hotel and came to ambush me along with the Brixton Boys."

"He asked for backup. My apologies. But he threatened me. Not a nice man. If you asked me, I'd say he'd lost the plot."

"No problem. Understood."

"Just business."

"How much did you pay François for the information?"

"Three thousand pounds. But his and my relationship was different. He was my competitor. You and I, we can have a beautiful relationship. A very profitable one."

"Sounds good to me."

"I'll call you with the first opportunity on all major contracts as they come in."

"My fee has doubled."

"Lovely."

"Don't cross me, Sam. I need you. Later on down the line. I'll need intel."

"I look forward to doing business with you. Until then, take care."

"Speak soon."

"Cheers."

"Cheers."

Thirty minutes later a gruesome picture showed up on my mobile.

It was Sam's image. His throat cut wide-open. I nodded. I made a call and transferred the money for that job. A job I had ordered. I left no stone unturned. Left no trails behind.

Rotten business I was in. Rotten to the core.

I took the SIM chip out of the mobile. Destroyed the chip.

Once again a new chip was inserted.

Two hours later I was on a flight back to Europe.

My unfinished business was still unfinished.

Forty-two

wounds unhealed

Daytime on Berwick Street was filled with life.

Vendor after vendor lined the ten-foot-wide street to sell their wares. Fruits. Vegetables. Socks. Underwear. Purses. CD players. iPod accessories. Nuts and dried fruit. Suitcases. Wallets. Facing the direction of Oxford Street, leaving all the triple-X houses and pole-dancing clubs behind me, the strip almost looked normal. Almost. Red lights were still on in the windows. International men were still shopping, buying fruits, and vanishing inside stairways that were barely as wide as my body, those ceilings no more than a foot over my head.

The red lights were faint in the daytime. Hardly noticeable. But they were on.

Red lights never went off on Berwick Street.

And the pimps.

They were out leaning against walls. Upstairs, many of the women were part of the slave trade, brought here and lied to, beaten into prostitution. I smelled them all. Next to the drug dealers.

As women in business suits rode by on scooters, this route their shortcut.

I looked at Thelma's ragged door, that handwritten sign ready to fall to the ground.

I crossed the street.

I stalled before I went inside. I had been wrong. The hallway was barely as wide as my body. But the ceiling not more than six inches above my head, not a foot like I had thought. Maybe I was cowering when I came here before. This time I was standing tall.

Or maybe dying had made me taller.

As soon as I started walking up the stairs, Thelma appeared.

She stopped where she was, once again terrified of me.

But she didn't run.

She said, "You came back."

"I came back."

"I knew you would."

"We have some business to take care of."

She lowered her head, walked inside her apartment, leaving the door open.

I followed.

She stood across the room from me.

I reached in my backpack.

She trembled.

I took out a sheet of paper, extended it to her.

I told her, "This is the address of a three-bedroom house."

"Why are you giving me this address?"

"The house is in Atlanta. It's on half an acre of land."

She took the paper. "I don't understand."

"Actually it's in Stone Mountain. And it's furnished."

"Back in the States. I'm confused."

"The house isn't large, but it's better than this. And it's paid for."

She looked at me. She was trying to comprehend what made no sense to her.

I said, "You can have the house. If you want it. You can leave here. You can go back to America. You can have a home. With a yard. And a car. I can get you a car. A modest car to get around town in. But you have to stop being a whore. You have to be a better mother. You can't be a whore. If you don't stop being a whore . . . you have to stop being a whore . . . or . . . or . . ."

"Or you will kill me."

"No. I won't kill you. I'd never been able to. No matter how many times I told myself I wanted to kill you . . . I love you too much to kill you. I don't like you, not at all, but I do love you. I don't have a choice. You're the only mother I know. If I give that up . . . I can't. But if you are going to keep being a whore, the boy, Sven, he has to come with me. He can't stay here with you. He can't live like this. He can't live like this. I can't allow that to happen again. Not on my watch."

She cried.

I held on to all I felt inside me.

There were footsteps in the narrow hallway.

They ran up the stairs fast, feet rushing up chipped concrete.

The frail door flew open and we both jumped.

It was the dark-skinned boy who had walked in on my former rage.

And Sven.

Sven was in front of me.

They saw Sven's mother crying.

The dark-skinned boy saw me and shouted at Sven, pointed at me.

The dark-skinned boy told Sven that I was the evil man who attacked his mother.

The boy with Sven, he had been through a storm.

It showed in his face. Horrific events that had been indelibly ingrained in his mind.

Punctuated with screams.

He looked horrified, like a boy about to be mauled by a bear.

Fear bloomed in Sven's eyes as well.

Eyes wide, Sven ran past his mother, he moved quicker than anyone I'd ever seen.

He was in the tiny bedroom going under the mattress.

I stood up.

Sven rushed out with a gun in his hand.

His expression was fierce and his hand was steady.

He held a black .22, the business end of that gun aimed at my heart.

The dark-skinned boy was screaming for him to kill the monster.

The woman I'd known as my mother was crying and shouting.

I was speechless, living the wrong side of a déjà vu.

Sven and I were eye to eye.

Palms raised, I stepped toward him.

He looked at me the same way I had looked at Mr. Midnight.

Sven scowled like he was the judge, jury, and executioner.

Without hesitation, Sven pulled the trigger.

Forty-three

the long good-bye

The gun clicked.

Sven rushed and pulled the trigger again.

Again the gun clicked.

It wasn't loaded.

His mother rushed to him, got between us, pulled the gun from his hand.

My heart was about to explode.

She opened the gun.

I had expected to see empty chambers.

But bullets fell into her trembling hand.

Only two chambers had been empty.

Only two.

I had been one trigger-pull away from dying again.

She yelled at Sven. Was about to raise her hand to him.

I told her, "Don't punish him."

She looked at me.

I said, "For that, don't punish him. He did what he was supposed to do."

She said things in a language I didn't understand.

Sven said, "But, Mum . . ."

"I will tell you when to come back."

"Do I still have to go away? I don't want to go away."

"I will tell you later."

Sven looked at his suitcase. His few belongings were still there, crowding the small room, as was the envelope with his thin trust fund, and the boy frowned at me. As did his friend.

I didn't look at Sven. My eyes were on the other boy.

The dark-skinned boy left first, left running. Sven hurried out behind him.

Thelma took the gun back into the other room. The room where she worked.

I asked, "Has he . . . shot anyone before?"

"No."

I felt relief.

When I came here, I was doing this for Margaret.

But Margaret was dead.

She had been murdered and left inside a Dumpster in Alabama.

There was nothing I could do for the dead.

Nothing.

But I realized I had to do this for Sven.

So he wouldn't end up being the kind of man I'd become.

I just hoped it wasn't too late to turn him around.

Thelma came back.

I asked, "Will you get your son out of here?"

She held the address to her chest.

I took that body language, the tears in her weary eyes, as her answer.

I handed her another card.

My hand was shaking. Not much. But enough for me to know I was unraveled.

Death had visited.

Dying had been horrible.

But Sven had shaken me more than Death.

I said, "There is a number on there. Call it. Leave a message. Leave a number. Say what you need. And you'll get what you need or a response in less than twenty-four hours."

She nodded.

I wiped my eyes.

She said, "A house? You are letting us stay at your house?"

"It will belong to you. Will be transferred into your name as soon as you get settled."

"I don't understand. You're angry with me. And still . . . you're giving me a house?"

"A home. I'm giving you a home. I'm helping you get a better life."

"For me and Sven?"

I nodded.

She asked, "Where will you be?"

"I won't be there. I won't bother you."

I almost choked up.

She asked, "Will you stop doing what you do as well?"

I rubbed hand over hand.

I didn't answer her.

And then I stood up.

I said, "Margaret."

She looked at me and nodded.

I said, "She was your best friend."

"My only friend."

I sat on my emotions for a moment.

I asked, "Are any of Margaret's people still alive?"

"As I told you before, I don't know. She never talked about her people."

"Can I have the newspaper articles on Margaret?"

"I kept them for you. I kept you for her. And I kept them for you."

I nodded.

She gathered what she had. Put it all inside a worn notebook, one that had football stickers all over, a notebook that had belonged to Sven, and handed it to me.

For a moment we stood there.

Neither of us talking.

She asked, "Can I hug you?"

I nodded.

She came to me and put her arms around me.

It had been a decade since we had touched in kindness.

She said, "Be careful, Son."

I hugged her back.

Hugged her like I was seven years old.

We stood like that awhile.

Stood like that as feet raced back up the stairs.

As the door opened.

As Sven watched.

He was worried about his mother.

No words could make him stay away as long as the bad man was here.

Sven looked at me. I put my hand on the top of his head.

I said, "Footballer?"

He knocked my hand from his head and ran to his mother.

He didn't like me.

Not at all.

He loved his mother.

She was all he cared about.

I said, "Give me the gun."

Thelma nodded, went back to her room, handed the weapon and bullets to me.

She asked, "What happened?"

"What do you mean?"

"You seem different."

I didn't answer her, just put it all in my pocket.

Then I handed her an envelope. Money for plane tickets. Enough to get them started in the U.S. She cried. She cried hard. Happy tears. Sven didn't understand what was going on.

She said, "Good-bye, Gideon."

"Jean-Claude. Call me Jean-Claude."

"I always liked that name."

"Me too."

"We had fun in Montreal."

"For a while. Loved the park. Maybe one day I'll walk Sainte-Catherine again."

"*Dimanche. Lundi. Mardi.*"

I whispered, "*Mercredi. Jeudi. Vendredi. Samedi.*"

She smiled.

"Good-bye, Jean-Claude."

"Good-bye, Catherine."

My eyes were on Sven.

I waved good-bye to him. He raised his hand and did the same.

He said something to his mother.

She said, "He wants to know if you play football."

I almost smiled. "I'm not as good as he is. He's much better."

"He could teach you to be better."

I smiled. "Tell him I would like that."

No long good-byes.

Then I took to the stairs, took to Berwick Street once again.

I bought an *Evening Standard* newspaper and stuffed the handgun inside.

That newspaper was left in a Dumpster in Chinatown, left buried beneath tons of food.

The stench of Chinese food still bothered me.

At Shaftesbury Avenue, I struggled by all the foot traffic in Theatreland and took to the first available black cab I saw, rode that diesel guzzler to Paddington Station, let the red lights of Soho and the bright lights from Oxford Circus and Piccadilly Circus warm my back.

A load lifted, I hopped on an express train, headed to London Heathrow Airport.

Inside Heathrow I opened a FedEx envelope.

I pulled out plane tickets and another package.

Rubbed my weary eyes.

I was as exhausted as I was when I was a child.

But I had to keep moving.

Two hours later I was on a flight to Central America.

I studied the package like I studied all packages that had come my way.

Studied it and memorized it all.

Stared at the pictures that had come with the package.

Forty-four

running from shadows

Central America.

As the plane landed, I reread the package I'd been given.

Once again, bogus passport in hand, no weapons on me, I breezed through customs.

The person I was looking for was hiding out at Chiriquí Pacific Coast, West Panama.

I checked the package again. Had to get to the Las Olas Beach Resort; they had a suite at a five-star hotel that was hard to get to, an hour by air from Panama City, an hour and a half from the Costa Rican border. Fifteen miles of immaculate beaches with magnificent ocean views.

This was where rich people came to be pampered and tucked away from the rest of the world. This was where people went when they didn't want to be found by their own shadows.

Nothing bad was supposed to happen at a place like this.

But death was everywhere.

And as long as there were people like me, nowhere was safe.

I dropped my carry-on luggage off in the lobby of the resort and took to the beach. I had changed clothes at the airport, dumped the jeans I had on, changed into shorts and sandals.

It was hot. Too hot for clothes. So most of the people were damn near naked.

Sunglasses on, looking into the tanned faces of Spanish-speaking strangers, I crept across the sand, slipped out toward the clear waters.

So much wealth was at this resort.

I thought a heard a gunshot and jumped.

It wasn't a gun.

Just some newlyweds popping open a bottle of champagne.

I'd heard that pop and in my mind I saw Sven pointing that gun at me.

Saw that .22. Heard that click. Heard the second click.

I'd been one click away from Midnight.

Other memories remained, but the dead didn't plague my mind, not like Sven.

The scent of Chinese food didn't bother me.

Not like looking in Sven's eyes. It had been like looking in my own eyes.

I'd killed my father.

I'd saved Sven's mother.

Guess that meant I had saved Sven before he was born.

Right now there were a lot of things I didn't want to think about.

I'd lived under the glow of the red lights most of my life. As a boy I'd been homeless and hungry, sleeping on the streets and dining on stale bread, cold meat, and wilted vegetables.

I'd been running since I was a little boy.

And all of that running had brought me here.

The sun high over my head, I looked at the picture that had come with the package.

It took a while, but I found her. She was off to the side, alone. That was good.

I crept toward the unsuspecting woman, my breathing slow and even.

I knew twenty-two ways to kill a man.

She was so vulnerable right now. On the beach, in a beach chair, alone, hair pulled back in braids, dressed in a red bikini, margarita in her right hand, iPod on.

First I eased up behind her.

Stood there for a minute undetected.

Then I crept around and stood in front of her.

Her eyes were closed.

I waited.

Twenty-two ways. I knew twenty-two ways.

A minute later her eyes opened.

She jumped when she saw me. Then she pulled her earphones out of her ears.

"Shit. You found me."

"I found you."

"Thought I had escaped."

"You can't escape me."

I motioned at the empty beach chair next to her.

I asked, "This seat taken?"

"I was waiting on a friend. My friend is mean. My friend is fierce."

"Well, maybe I could sit here until your friend shows up."

She looked up at me, evaluated me, then said, "I guess. Have a seat."

"Your friend has a name?"

"Harvey."

"He wouldn't happen to be a six-foot-tall rabbit?"

"So, you've met."

"He sat next to me on a flight from Atlanta to London."

I kissed her, then sat in the empty seat next to her.

She smiled. I loved the way Mrs. Jones smiled.

I knew twenty-two ways to kill a man.

Maybe I needed to learn twice as many ways to love a woman.

She reached over to a small table at her side, picked up her margarita.

I said, "Nice spot you picked out."

"You get the brochure? You read it over?"

"Was just looking it over. All-inclusive. Great package deal they gave you."

"My treat this time."

"You're spoiling me over here."

She smiled. "How was your last business trip?"

"My return to London was successful."

She left it at that. "You worry me, you know."

"I know. I'm chilling right now."

"More work from the Hanso Foundation?"

"Not working. Might be retired."

"Might be?"

I nodded.

I was keeping my eyes on Detroit. If that was really over, only time would tell.

Mrs. Jones said, "Boys who molested my daughter, heard they came to a tragic end."

"Really?"

"They found both of them dead. One was murdered in Brazil, the other in Tijuana."

I shrugged. "What goes around."

"Yes, indeed."

"How does your daughter feel about that?"

"Happy. Very happy."

People were snorkeling. Women in bikinis all over. Men in shorts and Speedos.

I asked, "How are things going with your divorce?"

"It's done."

"Over?"

"Single woman again."

"You okay?"

"Why do you think I'm drinking and partying in Panama? I'm celebrating."

"No more tears."

"Never been better."

"Now what?"

"Thinking about letting a flat in London."

"Serious?"

"I can stay six months without having a visa. But I want to work on getting my visa. Need a new location for a while, new memories. Time for chapter two of my life."

"London. Wow."

"If I let a flat, come back to London when you can. Come stay with me awhile."

"Might do that."

"My daughter might come visit me. When she is free, I want her out of America."

"You're talking to her?"

"We're trying. In London we'll be away from all of her bad memories too."

"That's good. That's really good."

"It's hard, but we're trying."

Several people were parasailing high in the sky. Birds with colorful wings.

I motioned at the parasailing crew, asked, "You want to touch the sky?"

"After another drink, maybe. Afraid of heights. Have to get my courage up."

"Snorkel?"

"I could snorkel all day."

Someone snuck up behind me. Before I could turn around, wet hands covered my eyes. Smooth hands. Small hands. Sweet smell on wet skin.

"Guess who."

"Lola Mack."

She moved her hands. "You're no fun."

We laughed.

Lola was two shades darker. She gave me a kiss. And a hug. A long kiss.

Mrs. Jones asked Lola, "How was the spa?"

"Great." Lola's long hair was braided too, colorful beads on the end of each braid. She made the woman in the movie *10* look like a 3.5. "You have to go check out the spa."

"Do they massage better than you?"

"Of course not."

"Then what's the point?"

Lola wore a two-piece. The bottom a thong. The top just as dangerous. She put a towel on the sand, lay on her back, unsnapped her bra, let the twins get some equatorial sun. Mrs. Jones put down another colorful towel, lay next to Lola, undid her bra strap, did the same thing.

I asked, "Is topless legal?"

Lola shrugged. "We'll find out."

I pulled my tank top off. They made room for me between them.

I closed my eyes. Inhaled the soothing scents of the beach. Let the sun warm my skin.

I whispered, "*Mercredi. Jeudi. Vendredi. Samedi.*"

Then I smiled.

For the first time in a long time I didn't hear any ghosts whispering from a shallow grave.

We all relaxed in the sun, lived in peace for a while.

I said, "Mrs. Jones?"

"Yes?"

"You're awfully quiet."

"Was thinking."

"About?"

"Upside-down orgasms."

I yawned. "You are incorrigible."

"You asked."

"Sure did." I yawned. "You're awfully quiet, Lola. What's on your mind?"

Lola said, "Key lime pie."

I repeated, "Incorrigible."

They laughed.

We slathered suntan lotion on each other and tanned, let time drift by.

A while later we gathered our things and headed toward the lobby.

I asked, "Where should we go next?"

Miss Jones hummed. "Always wanted to go to Rome."

Lola spoke up. "Let's got to Riviera Maya."

I shrugged. "Maybe Curaçao."

Mrs. Jones said, "That would be nice too."

Lola said, "Let's swim awhile."

We did a few laps, played games in the water, ended up at the pool bar drinking.

Then we headed to our presidential-size suite and climbed into a huge tub together.

With the water soapy and warm, Coltrane playing, we gave each other massages.

Touching led to other things.

Wild things we hadn't tried before.

We popped in DVDs, watched *Intimacy*, *9 Songs*, and *Devil in the Flesh*, let those films play in the background and lived in much deserved pleasure until there was a new sun.

We'd exist like that for a while.

For as long as it was good.

As long as this lasted.

While we took in the gourmet restaurant, grill, wet bar, and swimming pools, in between diving and snorkeling, rafting and tubing and sports fishing, while we spent time on an ecological tour at Metropolitan Park, we talked about heading to South America. Maybe flying back to Europe. Taking in New Delhi, Bangalore, Shanghai, and Hong Kong.

I wanted to keep traveling with them. But right now it was time for me to rest.

I had no idea what would become of me.

But that was okay.

I was chilling in a place that was peaceful. And away from everything that was going on in the world. With two exotic women. For now I could have the best life that money could buy.

Maybe I'd grow a beard. Let my hair go long. Work out twice a day, run five miles every morning and swim naked in one of God's beautiful bodies of water every evening. Read the Bible from cover to cover. Repent. Find Jesus, get to know the Lord like I hope Mama knew Him.

Maybe.

The folder I had with information on Margaret, I had put that away. For now. Maybe I'd get in touch with Arizona, have her work her magic on the bits and pieces of information I had.

Maybe I'd go to Opelika, Alabama, myself, find my mother, give her a proper burial.

Wasn't sure.

I opened a BC Powder, got ready to swallow the grainy powder, but tossed it.

I wouldn't mask my pains anymore.

I'd deal with them head-on.

Right now I was living in the moment and having fun with the squares.

Was letting my life become normal.

As normal as it could for a man like me.

Acknowledgments

Before we get started . . .

If you're holding *Sleeping with Strangers*, its sequel, *Waking with Enemies* drops four months later and the story picks up where *SWS* leaves off and moves on, full speed ahead.

Sleeping with Strangers came out in April 2007.

Waking with Enemies will hit the bookstores in August 2007.

If you're holding *Waking with Enemies*, make sure you read *Sleeping with Strangers* first.

Well, this is the back of the book, so I guess it's kinda late to say that, huh?

Duh.

Oh well.

☺

I started playing *What if?* and working on *Sleeping with Strangers* and *Waking with Enemies* back in March 2006, tried to come up with a story line. Initially I wanted to create a dark narrative, maybe come up with an antihero who had his or her adventure play out while driving across the States, some sort of West-Coast-to-East-Coast voyage, his or her motivation (or motivations) yet to be determined, but I didn't come up with a decent way to keep that interesting for me.

No story came to mind. Not at that moment.

The well was dry.

Then I changed gears, decided to try and find a way to include most of the cities I hit on tour, London included, in one story. That meant I had to write and tour all at once. Had to take notes while people were keeping me busy. Trust me, that wasn't easy. Any writer will tell you, writing on tour, being creative while dealing with jet lag, no real sleep, and trying to be productive while sitting at the airport—it just ain't happening. But I gave it a shot. A lot of spots I went to on tour I was barely there a day, some places only a few hours, and didn't see much outside of an airport, one or two bookstores, and a hotel that I couldn't tell you how to get to if my life depended on it. All I knew was that I needed a good character. An antihero who traveled a lot.

And I wanted it to be noir. And sexy. And a challenge. Didn't want to recycle plots.

Enter Gideon.

I was in my office writing one day and when I turned around, there he was.

Gun in one hand and a knife in the other, the guy scared me at first. Could tell he was troubled. Thought he had come for me. But he said he just wanted to be in the book. Said he had a lot of personal shit he needed to work through and maybe being in a book would help.

I said cool. Told him he had a part. He left. Then I upgraded my security system.

If you believe that I have a freeway I want to sell you out in Los Angeles.

Gideon started off being a serial killer. I played the *What If?* game and wrote scenes with him, well, at work. Tijuana. Jacksonville. Detroit. Brazil. Some, if not all, of those original scenes made the final cut. Somewhere along the way, my man Gideon evolved into being a contract killer. When I'd flown to the UK (much love to Bill, Claire, and the rest of the staff at Turnaround Publishing) to promote *Genevieve*, I had moved on, started writing the scenes that included the supporting cast. Eventually the man with the broken nose showed up and asked me if I needed somebody like him to be in this one. I tried to say no but he pulled the Eagle out of its nest and that convinced me. Truth be told, I liked the crazy bastard. Great character. Every novel needs a supporting cast, and since this tale involved killers and grifters, for the most part, it gave me a chance to reach back into the Dickey Universe, tap on a few doors, and ask Arizona, one of my favorite characters, if she wanted to be in this one. She asked me if she would get a hot sex scene. I said no. She slammed the door in my face. I knocked again. She wouldn't answer. Then I yelled that I would put her in a damn steamy scene. She said she wanted *two*. Damn women. Anyway, I told her I would promise her one, and I'd do my best on a second one. Then she demanded to be more than a grifter, wanted to carry weapons and kick some ass. I told her that grifters didn't carry. She didn't give a shit. I think she had seen one too many Angelina Jolie movies. Anyway, my agent called her fictional agent and we got it worked out. She lit up her Djarum, grabbed her boots, and came along for the ride. Despite being so demanding, she's good people. If you like those kind of people. The queen of the grifters. I have no idea why I like her, but I do. She's evolved since she first drove on the pages of *Thieves' Paradise*, become a little more intense since *Drive Me Crazy*, now she's operating on an international level.

Anyway, once my plane landed in London, so did the rest of the story.

I have to thank my UK peeps for helping a brother out while he was over there locked up in hotels and flats, writing from sunup to sundown, taking a nap, then back in front of the laptop until sunup again. My UK peeps were great, showed me around London on buses and tubes, drove me around in clown cars that had steering wheels on the wrong side of the dashboard.

They were there for me whether it was sweltering, raining, or bloody cold.

Kayode Disu, thanks for collecting me at Gatwick, making sure I was okay, getting me to Paris and back in a day, and getting me and my luggage back to Gatwick every time I came over.

My homie Monique Pendleton out at www.myspace.com/soulful_women, I think you've read every version of Gideon, saw changes in plots and subplots, well over a thousand pages, that's my estimate, and I thank you for that. And thanks for making sure the book kept that Brit flavor.

Inca Nixon, my girl Sam from the Islands, Tosh from wherever, thanks for coming down from horse-and-grass to hang out and show me around. See y'all at TGIF in Piccadilly soon!

To my military peeps stationed at Lakenheath and Mildenhall, be safe and see you soon.

Neo Gwafila-Bulayani, thanks for Botswana and looking over the details of Tebby.

My boys at Progressive Entertainment (www.myspace.com/UKFridays), thanks for the birthday celebration. I'll see you guys at the Motion Bar soon. Save me a spot!

To my UK publisher, Bill, Claire, and the entire staff at Turnaround, thanks for everything. The events were fantastic and I look forward to returning in February 2008.

If you peeps find me a place to live, I'll become a UK citizen and rent an accent so fast . . . you have no idea. We just have to come up with something better than beans and toast.

☺

Everything I got right, I thank my friends.

Until I can find a scapegoat, I'll take the blame for all I got wrong.

Time to thank the rest of my crew. The ones on this side of the pond.

John Paine, thanks for the input and the notes. Writing is all about rewriting.

DeMarMc, thanks for reading this one over and over and over and . . .

Lon in IAH, once again, thanks for the information early on. It made a big difference.

Christine Pattyn, thanks for Motown! Hope to make it to your club one day!

Lolita Files! You're the best! Thanks for being you!

Hazel Verzola in Montreal, thanks for the Tagalog!

Thanks to my agent, Sara Camilli. How many books before I get to book number 100?

To my wonderful editor, Julie Doughty, much love. You rock!

Brian Tart, thanks for believing in this double-sized project. I hope it has wings and flies.

To Lisa Johnson, Beth Parker, and all the people in publicity, thanks for everything.

A big thanks to the BFF club at Oakland University back in cold-ass Michigan: Tamara Kukuk, Shalonda Dennis, Brittani Hobbs, and Crystal Allen.

And a special thanks to you. You, the person holding this book. You didn't think I'd skip you, did you?

O faithful reader, thanks for coming back.

And if you're a new reader, thanks for coming on board.

I hope you enjoy this journey across the pond.

And if you're across the pond, I hope you find this tale enjoyable.

In case I forgot anyone, which wasn't intentional, here's your chance to shine.

I wanna thank _____ for _____ because without your help I'd be _____ at a _____ with _____ and wishing I was _____ in _____. You're the best of the best!

Make sure you check out www.ericjeromedickey.com.
Or stop by www.myspace.com/ericjeromedickey.

Holla!

EJD

About the Author

Originally from Memphis, Tennessee, Eric Jerome Dickey is the author of fifteen novels, including the bestsellers *Chasing Destiny*, *Genevieve*, *Drive Me Crazy*, *Naughty or Nice*, *The Other Woman*, and *Thieves' Paradise*. His most recent novel is *Sleeping with Strangers*. Dickey writes full-time and in 2006 developed a six-issue miniseries of comic books for Marvel Enterprises featuring Storm (X-Men) and the Black Panther. He lives on the road and rests in Southern California.